THE YEAR
THE LIGHTS
CAME ON

**Center Point
Large Print**

**This Large Print Book carries the
Seal of Approval of N.A.V.H.**

TERRY KAY

THE YEAR THE LIGHTS CAME ON

CENTER POINT PUBLISHING
THORNDIKE, MAINE

This Center Point Large Print edition
is published in the year 2003 by arrangement with
Harvey Klinger, Inc.

The text of this Large Print edition is unabridged. In other
aspects, this book may vary from the original edition. Printed in
Thailand. Set in 16-point Times New Roman type by
Bill Coskrey and Gary Socquet.

ISBN 1-58547-286-7

Library of Congress Cataloging-in-Publication Data.

Kay, Terry.
    The year the lights came on / Terry Kay.--Center Point large print ed.
        p. cm.
    ISBN 1-58547-286-7 (lib. bdg. : alk. paper)
    1. Boys--Fiction. 2. Georgia--Fiction. 3. Rural families--Fiction. 4. Rural
electrification--Fiction. 5. Large type books. I. Title.

PS3561.A885 Y44 2003
813'.54--dc21

                                                                    2002033368

I have written this book to celebrate the memory of my parents—Toombs Hodges, Sr., and Viola Winn Kay. I draw still from their strength, from the invisible giving of their love and warmth.

AUTHOR'S NOTE

The REA (Rural Electrification Administration) does not make or transmit electricity. It is a government agency that provides financing programs and develops standards for cooperatives providing electricity to millions of Americans.

But to those who remember the adventure of electricity in rural America, it was, and is, the REA. The REA is synonymous with all that is real about electricity—lines, poles, transformers, meters, lights, etc. Few people ever think of the REA as a federal lending institution. For this reason, and because the setting of this book is 1947, I have used "REA" as an expression, as a forceful and meaningful inclusion of the American speech habit.

This book is fiction—if incident is the standard of fiction. Few things occurred as I have written them. But if mood is a consideration, then this book is, I hope, the biography of millions. It has been the mood that has most interested me, and I have earnestly attempted to remain faithful to those sensations of awe and innocence that visited our imaginations—the year the lights came on.

1

This was the Big Gully Oath:

"I swear that for the rest of my whole life I won't never tell what goes on in the Big Gully, and I swear I will always take up for everybody here, no matter what. Cross my heart and hope to die."

Solemnly repeated, the Big Gully Oath was a stirring commitment and was very often concluded in a cry of allegiance that boys of good friendship are certain to make when spirit is unbridled.

"Ain't nothin' never comin' between none of us!" That is the way it was said, fiercely, proudly, in a sentence perfectly cadenced for a single breath, stabbed with the finality of an exclamation point.

Freeman Boyd started the Big Gully Oath. Freeman had been deeply affected by a comic book about a group of boys (appropriately ragged) who made a unique vow of comradeship and citizenship: they would, together, smite all thieves, murderers, con men, and other vile underworld figures who infested their community. To remain anonymous and perform with desirable flair, the boys slipped into costumes that quaintly resembled the tailoring of Superman's garments, and immediately they were splendid warriors.

Inspired by his comic book, Freeman organized the Big Gully Crime-Busters. He ordered us into capes and masks of brightly patterned flour sacks, and he appointed us code names. Oddly, the code names were Indian names—Tall Bull, Swift Water, Red Sun, First

Star, Standing Fox. I was Little Bird. I wanted to be Little Beaver, but Freeman insisted we were not playing games. Fighting crime was serious business.

The Big Gully Crime-Busters lasted one afternoon, lasted until Wesley, my brother, said, "Freeman, what kinda crime we supposed to be fightin', anyhow?"

It was a sobering question. None of us could remember when there had been a crime in Emery. Old Man Joe Eberhart had once been arrested for stealing cows, but Old Man Joe Eberhart had been dead for three years.

"You can't never tell," Freeman advised us. "There could be a bunch of crimes any day. We got to be on the ready."

"Well, I ain't wearin' no flour sack waitin' on 'em," declared Otis Finlay. "What if some crook found us out, anyhow? We'd be cut up like a stuck hog!"

And that is when Freeman first delivered the Big Gully Oath. "To keep everything secret," he said. "We all got to remember the Big Gully Oath."

It would become, in time, part of our language.

The Big Gully was a ripped-open place, a deep, wide erosion with high walls and scoop-outs that we called caves. It had a flooring of white sand, sifted by rain from fields planted perilously close to its edge. On moon nights, the white sand was like a still stream frozen against shores of red clay.

None of us knew who had discovered the Big Gully, or who had capitalized it, big B, big G. It was always there, and we had always regarded it as a place of mystic character. The Big Gully accommodated our pretending, became what we wished. It was the West. It was the unknown mountain range surrounding Tarzan's jungles. It was the last stronghold of the Japs. It was another planet, uncharted, uninviting. In the Big Gully, there were cowboys and Indians, lions, soldiers, and curious little men who had lately zipped down from the clouds, chased by Flash Gordon.

There was another thing about the Big Gully: it was where we deliberated our lives, pondered our Now and Then in high, boyish voices with southern sounds— words with missing g-endings, vowels pressed until o's rolled out like hoops pushed by children.

In those early philosophic exchanges—emphasized by many yeahs and much spitting—we began to develop serious perspectives of our purpose, our destiny. We inevitably concluded that there were those whose status and fortunes were grander than ours.

"It beats all," Freeman would declare. "I can whip Dupree Hixon's butt any day of the week and five times before breakfast on Sunday, and he struts around like he was kin to Franklin D. Roosevelt, or somethin'!"

"Yeah."

"Yeah."

Spit.

Spit.

"It's just like my daddy says, boys, it's where you are when you're born in this world," Freeman would add. "That's it, I reckon."

"Yeah."

"Yeah."

Spit.

Spit.

Most of the people we knew had been born in Emery Community of Eden County, but to us Emery was a community divided. A gray concrete line split Emery and became, in an abstract manner, a Maginot Line—walling in one society and walling out another.

The gray concrete line was Highway 17, fusing Elberton, to the south, with Royston, to the north. Emery was leeched to Highway 17, one of those hundreds of small southern communities that rushed into existence with the railroads and, later, the highways. All the communities were like Emery, all nudged close to the railroad or highway, just out of striking distance. All were official places because of the United States Post Office Department, but none were cities. There were no city elections, no policemen, no firemen, no city limit signs.

Emery had two general stores. One was very small and belonged to Ferris Allgood, who didn't care if anyone traded with him. Ferris was lazy and his wife worked at the sewing plant in Royston, and that was enough, ". . . if you ain't greedy," as Ferris reasoned. The other general store belonged to A. G. Hixon, Dupree's father. It was a huge, two-room building with sidings of patterned tin, and it was located across the railroad from A. G. Hixon's warehouse and A. G. Hixon's cotton gin.

There was also Emery Junior High School and Emery Methodist Church.

And an old depot (musty, wonderful).

And Highway 17.

We did not live on Highway 17.

Dupree Hixon lived on Highway 17. Dupree and his buddies. The Highway 17 Gang.

We—Our Side—lived south of Banner's Crossing, which was a dirt road. The sorriest dirt road in Eden County.

It was not a very great distinction to adults—this thing of place—but it was important to us and it was often discussed at the Big Gully during Deliberation of Life sessions.

"Fact is, they's more snotty people around than ever was," Freeman would announce. "Especially on Highway 17. My daddy swears he never saw the likes of such snotty people. Like Dupree. Dupree ain't worth a damn, he ain't!"

"Yeah."

"Yeah."

Spit.

Spit.

We did not like Dupree Hixon.

But we were not prejudiced in our opinion; no one else really liked Dupree, not even his buddies.

The thing wrong with Dupree was his attitude. His attitude was so offensive it was visible. It was in his sneer, in the evil narrowing of his bird eyes, in his high upper lip, in his flat ears, in his fleshless jowls, in his knobby shoulders, in his wormy stomach, in his hairless legs, in his too-long feet.

Dupree was an only child and when he became old

enough to count change, his father had positioned him behind the candy counter in his general store ("Ain't he cute! Daddy's little helper!" people used to croon), and there, behind the candy counter, Dupree learned to behave in an arrogant and lordly manner.

If you cared to cater to Dupree's demands (and they were mostly nasty and harmful), you might expect special favors—free jawbreakers, or Bazooka bubble gum, or, occasionally, a whole candy bar. That is how Dupree became the leader of the Highway 17 Gang. At Emery Junior High School, Dupree was always rationing out penny Kits, bribing attention. Penny Kits were great persuaders. It was almost impossible to refuse penny Kits.

Once, Freeman and R. J. Waller and Otis Finlay told Sonny Haynes and Wayne Heath that they had observed Dupree dipping Bazooka bubble gum in a small pail of mysterious liquid, and then rewrapping it.

"If it's what I guess, it's that stuff farmers use for makin' pig oysters dry up," whispered Freeman.

"What's pig oysters?" asked Wayne, paling.

"Shoot, Wayne, don't you know nothin'? Pig oysters is balls, nuts." Freeman laughed. "I guarantee it works. Them ol' pigs start to squirmin' and then itchin' and then they go crazy a day or two, and them things just dry up and fall off."

Sonny and Wayne spent the rest of the day quivering and clawing at their pants, their lips dry and cracked, their faces splotched with anxiety.

Later, when they confronted Dupree with the fear that they were forever ruined, Dupree found Freeman and began to rage. "I'm warnin' you, butt-hole! You quit sayin' them things about me, and I mean it! You ain't nothin' but a Boyd, nohow, and everybody knows what a Boyd is. No better'n hogs, that's what. That's where you oughta be, boy, over there in that old swamp, wallowin' with them hogs! Cause you ain't nothin', boy! Ain't none of y'all nothin'! Maybe someday, boy. Maybe someday, but that's a long time comin'."

Freeman hit Dupree very hard. Freeman did not like people shouting at him.

On Sunday following, we pledged on the Big Gully Oath to be alert for future trouble.

And Otis cried, "Ain't nothin' never comin' between none of us!"

"Yeah!"

"Yeah!"

We were bold and we were loud. But we could not shout away the echo of Dupree's anger: "Maybe someday, boy! Maybe someday, but that's a long time comin'!"

2

Maybe someday, boy.

We often heard those words—heard them in voices, heard them in contemptuous stares, heard them in silky, knowing smiles.

Someday was Time.

To Dupree Hixon and his friends—those who accepted his favors and tagged obediently after him—

Time was their advantage. In their thinking, they had attained Time; to them, Time was position.

To us, Time was bodyless, formless. Time begged to be dimensional, to be real, to be touchable, to be placeable.

When you are very small and people sentence you to Someday, you understand how Time begs to be placeable.

Though we did not know it, Time began to have meaning for us in 1945.

In 1945, the hell ended.

The fighters stopped fighting, convinced by the finality of two puffy clouds polluted with itchy little particles of death. Two puffy clouds billowing up and lapping their shadows over Japanese cities called Hiroshima and Nagasaki, and the people caught in the umbrellas of those clouds watched horrified and defeated as skin and flesh and bone melted in the most peculiar pain anyone had ever known. Right or wrong, that was that. Period. Argue it forever. Give Truman hell, or praise him. It happened.

(It is a personal aside to that first atomic day, the day of Hiroshima, but I remember that Wesley and Freeman and R. J. Waller and I had been playing War in the Big Gully. We had killed many Japs and were no longer frightened of the bullets that splattered about us like great raindrops. We had become accustomed to Imaginary Death with Imaginary Men falling back through their lives, their voices weakening to primeval crying, and then vanishing into the remembered wombs of their mothers. But the dying, even of Imaginary Men, had given us a stern resolve: the war must be ended. Freeman suggested bombs, and we gathered an arsenal of dirt clods and bombed to smithereens every supply road and suspicious straw hut in the Big Gully. And then it became late in the day and we heard the yodeling call to supper. In Play War, there was always sundown, always the lure of home being only a racer's sprint through the woods, and we would put away our machine guns and pistols of mountain laurel and chinaberry sticks, and we would rise up from our wounds and bid those we had fought a peaceful rest. Then we would One-Two-Three-Go into our racer's sprint. At sundown, War was just a game. And so it was on that first atomic day, when our dirt clods killed Hiroshima.)

Those who lived in Royston emerged cautiously from a bomb shelter of fear and trembling after World War II. There was a feeble effort at a street celebration, but no parades, no jubilant shouting, "We've won! We've won!"

No confetti.

No foaming bottles of champagne.

The people of Royston looked about, took their dreaded census, and mourned those who had been spent in death at such places as Corregidor, Manila, Bataan, Iwo Jima, Belgium, the Hürtgen Forest, Morocco—faraway places, places with names as foreign as the realization that a son or a husband had been murdered in what mankind regarded as a curious dignity.

For a sliver of time (it passed so quickly into ether), the people of Royston lingered in cemeteries with rakes and shovels and hedge clippers, and tended the graves of their dead, their long dead. It would be months, perhaps years, before the United States government returned the bodies of the soldiers, but there was a need to be in cemeteries, a need to become acquainted with the mood of that postdated anguish; a need to trace, in the mind's tracing, the exact spot for that exacting rectangle. And there were the thoughts, always the thoughts.

Oh, Heavenly Father, What To Do?

How Can I . . . We . . . ?

This, You See, Was the Last Known Photograph of Him—See, by His Gun.

He Never Saw the Baby—Never . . .

Remember, Sweet Jesus—Sweet, Sweet Jesus—Is Thy Comforter and Thy Strength. Forever and Ever.

Amen. Amen. Amen.

In that lingering, in that sliver of time, The American Rehabilitation began. Reforms and pledges and G. I. Bills and no more collecting scrap iron, boys! No more rationing, Mother! Keep your eye peeled, Bargain Hunter, because—Lordamercy!—there's lots of bargains going up for the War Surplus Auction Block! And it was Over, Over, Over! Too bad FDR had not seen it through. Never mind, they'd not forget him. There's that four-column newspaper photo of FDR at his best, a stylish tilt to his cigarette holder, a sharp, affable gleam in his eye, and if you are Democrat and American you'd better, by God, have it thumbtacked

16

to the wall!

In that beginning, that sliver of time, all of this happened in the American Rehabilitation, and the people of Royston did not realize it had happened. Everything was spinning too fast. It was the tag end of 1945 and the world was on an endless drunk, whirling to a carnival barker's call—sassy and tempting. The people of Royston, like people in thousands of other places, were still anemic and pale from the Great Depression, and now this, World War II, and all these men, these men gone to God or Forever or Worms or Wherever.

That was the puzzle. The bewilderment. The lamentations of ministers could say God and Sweet Jesus and Ashes to Ashes, Dust to Dust, and Blessed Are They Who Suffer, but there was no one to answer— really answer—why these men were gone.

There was only one mercy: it was over. The Great Depression. World War Number Two. It was over.

A moment to rest, please. A moment to linger. Let the American Rehabilitation go forth with all good speed. One moment longer, please.

A sliver of time to take it all in.

After their moment, the people of Royston began again. It was a silent, numb beginning. Farmers from the tiny communities that surrounded Royston and were, by Rural Route, U.S. Postal Service, part of Royston, met on Saturdays in a ritual that was ancient and honorable. They came from Emery, from Vanna, from Harrison, Eagle Grove, Goldmine, Redwine, Sandy Cross, Airline, Canon, and other dirt-road directions, and they stood in twos and threes, like stark landscape paintings. They stood in front of Bowman's Drug Store, or Silverman's Clothing, or Foster's Hardware, and they talked in whispers about their sick, used-up land. They were all solace-seekers, a convention of solace-seekers, and they lingered, lingered, lingered, waiting for something—perhaps miracles. It was as though they believed someone (a Moses) would arrive to lead them away to some place better, some hauntingly beautiful place where the land was rich and they could plant crops in spring without being always a year behind in payment to the Boss, or the bank.

But Moses never appeared.

Just before sundown, each Saturday, on some cue instinctive to them, the farmers would drift off and climb upon their mule-drawn wagons that had been parked in a lot below the depot, and they would say their low, resigned goodbyes to one another. Their children would take their faces away from the windows of Harden's 5 & 10 and join their fathers. Always at sundown, you could see rings on Harden's 5 & 10 windows, where shallow-faced children had pressed their noses and breathed moist circles as they stood motionlessly and made up games with the dolls and balls and bats and gloves and toy cars teasing them from brightly painted counters.

In 1946, Time began to be identified with newness.

The economy bristled and people began to be healed of the disease of uncertainty.

You could hear it in voices, see it in faces, sense it in the energy of games and laughter, anger and restlessness. There was a mood, a fever, to 1946. Men who had returned from the war assumed positions of responsibility and admiration. They made inspiring first-person speeches about liberty and what it meant, and how the bullies of the world had better mind their manners. Occasionally, they even told light, breezy stories about the war, laughing heartily at themselves as though humor freed them from the inescapable seriousness of what they had seen and known.

The cotton mill placed an advertisement in *The Royston Record*, seeking employees. A sewing plant was officially opened by His Honor, the mayor. Farmers began to listen to what County Agents had to say about subsoiling, land-testing, seed-treating, or about planting kudzu and lespedeza to stop topsoil from washing away in the ugly scars of erosion. The sound of John Deere tractors stuttered even at night. There was a rousing demonstration against some northern union which tried to infiltrate the labor market, and a group of noble people, born of the heritage of independence, staged a funeral and buried the union in rites that were both circus and frightening. Everyone seemed aware of being embraced by a new history of the world, and everyone knew it would be a history never forgotten.

The awful years were tender, healing scars by late summer of 1946. The World Series became a festive event again, and Roystonians began telling outrageous lies about Ty Cobb, who was a native and a legend. If you were born in a twenty-mile radius of Royston, you were reared believing, without compromise, in God, Santa Claus, and Ty Cobb. Older citizens who had known Cobb as a boy, loved to trap strangers with the trivia question, "What was Cobb's lifetime batting average?" It was .367, the best of them all, and that, by shot, was more than most north Georgia towns could talk about.

And, then, there was 1947.

Time became placeable in 1947.

The ump-pah-pah was everywhere, a rhythm like a Vachel Lindsay poem, with reader and chorus, cymbal and trumpet. It was a year for putting pennies in loafers, for "Just a sec," and mustard seed necklaces, for giddiness and once-a-month socials at Wind's Mill. It was the year the Home Demonstration Club was organized, and the Eden County Fairgrounds Committee advertised an all-out, better-than-ever Fall Fair, with rides and thrills and games of chance and (Freeman told us) a freak show with the most astonishing membership of any freak show in the world.

Ump-pah-pah.

Ump-pah-pah.

1947.

Wesley's year.

I think of it as Wesley's year because Wesley was the real and touchable and placeable something of 1947.

Wesley was eighteen months older than me. Lynn, our sister (people often called her Lynn-Wynn, fusing her name with a hyphen), was eighteen months older than Wesley. In the spring of 1947, Lynn was in the ninth grade, Wesley was in the eighth grade, and I was in the seventh grade. Nine, eight, seven. Seven, eight, nine. A, B, C. Mother used to call us her triplets, her Stair-Step Triplets. It was Mother's way of confessing her failure in selective family planning. That failure was humorously extended because she had had ample practice: before her Stair-Step Triplets, she had given birth to eight other children. I am told Mother vowed I would be the last; eleven children represented a superlative effort. Six years after I was born, Garry arrived, and he was not adopted as we often told him he was.

By adhering to the most elastic of mathematical permissions, we learned to round off numbers and concluded that an average of two years separated the first eleven children. We had to omit Garry from this formula; to include him would have forced us into fractions. And two years was a neat, certain figure, accountable and rhythmic. I preferred to think I was accountable, not accidental.

The reason it was necessary to understand and accept the reference to age separation, was that there were inevitable occasions when someone, somewhere, would exercise their right as an Official and request Facts of the Family. It happened each year at the beginning of the school term: we had to introduce ourselves to classmates we had known all our lives, and we were expected to know the names, ages, and whereabouts of our brothers and sisters. To me, this was an ordeal considerably more agonizing than the multiplication table, but I had learned a dependable system: my answer was a monotone reading of names, slyly clicked off on behind-the-back fingers; I had ten older brothers and sisters and ten fingers (God is marvelous in the way He complements things). Each brother and sister was a finger, a special finger.

I would say, "My name is Colin Wynn. I have a little brother, named Garry. He lives at home and gets what he wants."

Then I would continue: "I have a lot of older brothers and sisters. Some of them live at home; some do not. Their names are . . ."

And I would begin with Wesley. Wesley was the little finger of my left hand. Lynn was my ring finger. And I would work my way around the left hand—"Louise, who is the oldest one living at home . . . Hodges . . . Susan (who was the thumb of my left hand) . . . Frances (little finger, right hand) . . . Ruth . . . Thomas, who was killed when I was little . . . Amy . . . And, Emma, who is my oldest sister." Emma was the thumb of my right hand. According to our equation, Emma was twenty years older than me.

Each year, I offered the same recitation. Each year, the teacher oohed over the unusual size of my family. Each year, my classmates giggled.

Because we were the Stair-Step Triplets, Wesley and Lynn and I were extremely close. We even behaved as triplets at times. But Lynn, being a girl, was not entirely reliable as a playmate, especially when we were very small. She was inclined to play Doll and House and Princess—fantasies that were as confining as they were senseless. Wesley and I were far more serious. We performed games requiring strength and cunning, daring and justice. He was Batman; I was Robin. He was Red Ryder; I was Little Beaver. He was the Green Hornet; I was Kato. He was Captain Marvel; I was Captain Marvel, Jr. Occasionally, Lynn would agree to masquerade as Mary Marvel. Usually, though, it was Wesley and me.

We were close, the three of us. But Wesley and me . . . Wesley and me—it was special, that closeness.

And it was beautiful.

He was my brother, and I was prejudiced, but in those years when it was easy to trust unreservedly in the magic of people, I regarded Wesley as the most gifted person I knew, or would ever know. He was an Always There person. Once—I was eleven, I think—I was certain I saw a cosmic blessing descend on Wesley. He had walked out of the sunlight into the shade, and the sun twisted and bent to follow him. Wesley had presence, and that presence filled the emptiness of many moments and many lives. In his sometimes-sad face, people recognized the simplicity of a powerful confidence (faith?) that could not be tempted, or distorted. I once heard my mother say, "I just gave him birth; Wesley got what he is from somewhere else."

I believe that. Wesley was born with a divine appointment to be special.

But in 1947, when Time became placeable for us, Wesley was thirteen years old. He had not reached the considerable influence of his manhood. He was merely a leader of boys—me and Freeman and R. J. and Otis and Jack Crider and Paul Tully and a few others who were reared south of Banner's Crossing, in the community of Emery, in the county of Eden, in the state of Georgia. Emery was south of Royston and Royston was northeast of Atlanta by one hundred miles, and east of Athens by thirty miles.

Emery was a pencil speck on the state map, a quarter-inch distance from the Savannah River and, across the river, South Carolina.

Wesley did not look like a leader, even of boys. He was skinny. A map of freckles spread like the Hawaiian Islands across his nose. You could slip a dime between his two front teeth. He looked very much like Butch Jenkins, the actor. Girls used to giggle and call him Butchy-Boy, and Wesley would blush and I would get angry and Freeman would cuss until Wesley stopped us with a firm "That's enough!"

Wesley could lift a hundred pounds of dead weight. In softball, he played shortstop and it was like watching Marty Marion's ballet motion when he siphoned off a skimming grounder, pivoted on his left foot and whipped it to first base.

In basketball, he had a magician's hands. In pasture football, he had more moves than Don Hutson. (In pasture football, you *had* to have more moves than Don Hutson to dodge cow splatterings.)

Wesley was a better shot than Sergeant York. One afternoon I saw him bring down a crow from two hundred yards with a Remington short-range .22 bullet. We were walking through the pasture and Wesley saw a lookout crow perched on the top limb of a majestic water oak. He stopped, and in a graceful, unbroken motion, he dropped to one knee, lifted the rifle and fired. The crow rose up, the oil of its purple-ebony wings glistening in the sun; the crow rose off its perch, fluttered one heroic, desperate, clawing fight with escape, then tumbled through the tree. It was an unbelievable shot. Wesley's face trembled and he slumped to both knees. He was very quiet, as though he had witnessed something I could not see. I do not think he ever again fired the gun at any living thing.

3

Spring. 1947. Wesley's year.

"Boys," said Wade Simmons, "this is going to be a team that is organized. A-to-Z organized. Now, I mean there won't be any favorites one way or the other. Softball is a sport and a game and we're going to keep that in mind. We're going to practice, and practice hard. We're going to learn to hit and run and throw. We're going to learn to slide. We're going to learn fundamentals. That's F-U-N-D-A-M-E-N-T-A-L-S. And that means how-to. We're going to learn the lesson of playing together, as a whole, one team for one purpose. Organization, boys, that's the key. Organization. Now, when we don't have games, we'll be practicing and playing choose-up with the old game balls and keep the new ones for when we do have games. Understand?"

No one answered, or moved.

"O.K. We've got our first game against Bowersville

in two weeks, I think it is. That'll be up there. Then we'll be playing two games here before we go off again. Understand?"

"Yessir," Dupree said in his big-shot, know-it-all, behind-the-candy-counter voice. "Yessir, got it."

Mr. Simmons continued. "All right, now keep one thing in mind. Keep the trademarks up. Every broken bat means money out of PTA."

"Trademarks up, yessir," echoed Dupree, acting like Babe Ruth.

Freeman spat on Dupree's shoe. "Dupree broke three bats last year, Mr. Simmons," Freeman volunteered.

"Didn't!" shouted Dupree.

"Did!"

"Didn't!"

"Did! Ain't that right, Wesley?!"

Mr. Simmons interrupted. "Makes no difference, boys. We have to remember to keep the trademarks up. This year's another year, Freeman. Teamwork, that's what counts."

"Yessir."

"All right, boys, now go on and choose up and get in a practice game and let's see if you remember what you learned last year."

Wade Simmons was principal of Emery Junior High School.

He was also a man of wisdom.

He used the word organized because it was a teacher's obligation to suggest orderly conduct, but Mr. Simmons knew there was nothing organized about us. We knew rules, yes. Sometimes we even employed them. But we were not organized. We knew too well the difference between Victim and Victor. Losers were Victims. Winners were Victors. Being a Victor often required the First Law of Primitive Boldness, which scientists of social behavior have defined as survival. If you exercised the First Law of Primitive Boldness and won, the losers referred to the practice as cheating. None of us considered it a compliment to be accused of cheating, and many of our choose-up games were terminated behind the lunchroom after school. On those occasions when we did obey Mr. Simmons' doctrine of Orderly Conduct, it was out of respect for his patience and the PTA budget.

Wade Simmons had a talent for keeping his duty as principal and teacher in perspective, and for presiding in a dignified manner over the good and bad of Emery Junior High School—a school that belonged to the quaint system of housing elementary and junior high students in one building, grade one through grade nine. He and his wife, Margret (a woman I loved and the first person to distill words into an intoxicating liquid for me), had lived and taught in Emery for three years. They were the most influential people any of us had ever known, and they worked with uncompromising devotion to improve the ambition as well as the deportment and academic standing of their students.

Teaching was more than a profession to them; it was an obsession. It meant developing civic awareness as well as instilling the What and How and Why of formal knowledge. Teaching meant demonstrating the practice of decency and good manners, and we spent hours rehearsing how to walk quietly, or the procedure of closing doors with a butler's reserve, or how to correct our slouching posture. Sometimes, Wade and Margret Simmons surrendered to despair. Sometimes, you could read in their faces the torture of inevitable failure with such people as Freeman, who could not tolerate the indignity of a book balanced on his head.

It was not an easy determination, but the Simmonses' method refused to accept the theory that education was qualified only by the A-B-C-D-F barometer of a Six-Weeks Report Card. There were other experiences, wondrous experiences that spilled out of books, overran the pages, and flooded the mind with a narcotic vapor. But those experiences could not be imposed. Wade and Margret Simmons knew that. Persuasion was their technique. Persuasion for discipline and order, and out of discipline and order, we were to discover freedom.

Persuasion was one reason Mr. Simmons exhorted the gospel of organization in sport. He organized a basketball team to complement our softball team. He taught us the Side-Straddle Hop and Toe-Heel-Toe-Kick. He lectured on fundamentals. He even had the mothers of the Home Demonstration Club tailor red-and-white basketball uniforms for us, and he solicited money from the PTA to purchase caps for softball.

But realizing sport was competitive, and recognizing our flair for the First Law of Primitive Boldness, Mr. Simmons organized a Boy Scout Troop. We were the Lone Eagles. The fierce, proud face of an Indian brave

(Freeman said it was a copy of the Indian on the hood of the Pontiac car) was our emblem and the sweet night music of the whippoorwill was our secret call. We were positively splendid Boy Scouts, strict in our allegiance to the Boy Scout commandments—until the night, camping on Broad River, when Freeman tied Dupree's foot to a tent peg and then released a king snake inside the tent.

Even the girls were affected by the persuasion technique. After Mr. Simmons organized the Boy Scouts, Mrs. Simmons organized the Get Together Club. I do not think they had an emblem or a secret call. They held hands at the beginning and end of each meeting and sang: "The mo-o-ore we get toge-e-ether, toge-e-e-ether, toge-e-e-ether . . ." But all they did was cook and sew and make crepe-paper flowers. And giggle. In fact, it was the behavior of the Get Together Club that made me first realize how young girls budding with the mysteries of becoming young women giggle and squirm with uncommon energy.

"Choose up! Choose up! I'm the captain! I'm the captain!" Dupree chortled in his singsong appointment. "My team's up! My team's up!"

Dupree's candy-followers circled him. They were saying, "Attay, babe! Attay, boy!"

"All right," agreed Mr. Simmons. "Makes no difference, anyway. Everybody gets a chance to bat. By the way, Dupree, who's your visitor? Maybe he'd like to play."

A stocky, brooding boy with a frozen, mean face

stood silently beside Dupree.

"Oh, this is Mason, Mr. Simmons," explained Dupree. "He's my cousin from Anderson, South Carolina, and he's over here to visit today, so his mama made him come to school with me."

"Well, that's fine," Mr. Simmons said pleasantly. "Let him play on your team."

"Naw," Mason answered abruptly.

"He don't want to play softball," Dupree added. "He ain't much for playing with kids."

"Well, that's all right," Mr. Simmons replied. "Whatever he wants."

Mason turned defiantly and pushed his way through a gathering of younger boys. He marched to the shade of lugustrum and stood, alone and sullen.

"Just take it easy, Mason!" Dupree called, swinging three bats. "This ain't gonna take long. They'll be givin' up in a few minutes!"

Dupree laughed and his teammates laughed.

"Attay, babe, Dupree!" yelled Wayne Heath.

"You tell 'em, Dupree!" yelled Sonny Haynes.

And from the pitcher's mound, Freeman said, coolly, "You better just hold on, boy. You ain't gonna get a foul tip." Dupree struck out.

Wayne struck out.

Sonny grounded to Wesley, who threw to R. J. at first, catching Sonny by five steps.

"Hey, Mason!" Freeman called as he strutted from the mound. "You just take it easy. This ain't gonna take long." And it didn't.

Our Side defeated the Highway 17 Gang, 12-0, in

three innings of lunch-recess softball.

After the game, Dupree slammed a Louisville Slugger against the iron piping of the batter's cage, splintering it from the handle to the fat part. Freeman retrieved the bat and delivered it with appropriate ceremony to Mr. Simmons.

Dupree pledged to meet Freeman later.

"Better bring Mason," advised Freeman.

"I will, buddy," Dupree retorted. "I ain't puttin' up with you much longer."

After school we strolled confidently below the lunchroom to witness the scheduled bout. We were amazed at the punishment Dupree could endure.

Dupree and the Highway 17 Gang were waiting.

"You ready, candyface?" Freeman asked, smiling.

"*I'm* ready," answered Mason, Dupree's cousin.

Freeman was surprised. "Well, I'll be damned," he said.

"You know what you lettin' yourself in for?"

"Better'n you," Mason replied icily.

We circled them in two half-moons, the Highway 17 Gang and Our Side. Dupree was cracking his knuckles and giggling.

Freeman rushed Mason, and Mason stepped neatly to one side. He caught Freeman by the shoulder and turned him. Then Mason assumed a boxer's stance.

"Get him!" shouted Dupree.

Mason hit Freeman with three quick left jabs, faked a right, faked a left, and then exploded a right cross on Freeman's nose. Freeman fell backward, dazed.

The Highway 17 Gang laughed and cheered. They

began dancing around Freeman and chanted, "Freee-e-man got his butt beat! Freee-e-man got his butt beat! Freee-e-man got his butt beat!"

Wesley stepped between Mason and Freeman.

"I don't know nothin' about you," Wesley said to Mason, "but you have just made a mistake."

"He's my cousin, Wesley Wynn, and he's a Golden Gloves champion!" Dupree hissed. "And he'll whip your butt, too, buddy!"

Wesley did not move. He kept staring at Mason.

"Dupree knows that Freeman's got a temper," Wesley said, his voice low and soft. "Now, I can keep him off you, if you tell him you're sorry."

Mason's eyes widened in disbelief. "Kiss my tail, hick!" he snapped.

Wesley smiled and stepped aside. "Freeman," he said.

Freeman rose slowly. Blood seeped over his top lip. The crowd became silent.

"C'mon," teased Mason, motioning Freeman toward him.

"Get him!" Dupree urged. "Get him, Mason!"

Freeman stepped in, ducked a jab, reached through Mason's defense and slapped him on the face with an open hand. Mason rolled to his right, stunned. Freeman lunged forward and landed five bruising blows so fast it sounded like an automatic rifle. Mason crumpled to the ground.

No one moved. Mason swayed on his knees, looked at Freeman through two glass eyes, then fell playfully on his side.

"Dupree," Wesley said quietly, "you ought to know better."

4

The Great Depression and World War Number Two had been our only experience with the Larger World, and we had inherited—through some curious process of osmosis—a possessed sense of belonging. Belonging was our constant defense, our way of warding off the suspected Great End. The Larger World had issued messages that we lived in a temporary time, that we, ourselves, were temporary. (The atomic bomb was one thing; now, in 1947, there was rumor about a bomb of such unpredictable destruction that certain international scientists were afraid it would create a molecular reaction and Earth would disintegrate in a series of explosions, like a string of Chinese firecrackers.)

Because of the Larger World, and what it said to us in the voices of the Radio Evening News Network and eight-point type of *The Anderson Independent*, we had been mightily influenced and had adopted the habit of clustering, as though clustering was an affirmation of our existence: if we saw one another, spoke with one another, then it must be true—we had survived.

In clustering, we became isolationists; in isolation, we assumed identities; in identity, we were assigned value; in value, we learned of imperatives; and, in imperatives, we realized perspective.

To the members of Our Side, perspective was conditioned by boundaries. Boundaries gave us reach, held us, dared us; boundaries tutored us in the deeper significance of belonging.

Wesley and I lived by the boundaries of Black Pool Swamp, circling us in a horseshoe from the south and east and west. To the north we were somehow contained by Banner's Crossing and Rakestraw Bridge Road.

There was a sense of being centrifugally leashed to the center of our north and south, east and west boundaries; the center was Home and Home would spin us out, but only to the invisible, protective edges of where we wandered, and then Home would draw us back again.

We could not mark those boundaries by stake and flag. They were not taught by a line drawn in shoe-edge, or plotted on some map from the Official Office of Official Boundaries. Our boundaries were established by instinct. We knew. We simply knew. We could chase after laughter and echoes of laughter until we were exhausted with exhilaration, and we could wander farther and farther away, safe, protected, until that one step—that one step too far, too threatening— and then we would retreat. No one told us to return. We knew. We simply knew. We knew when we had ventured too far, as though our sense of equilibrium had been savagely attacked.

But the Highway 17 Gang did not understand about boundaries. Highway 17 was alive with people moving, going great distances, and once having passed, whizzing in their automobiles, they were not likely to return that way again. The Highway 17 Gang watched those passing people and believed directions—north and south, east and west—were gray concrete roads drawn in heavy lines on service station maps.

The Highway 17 Gang did not have boundaries. They had yards. Somehow, they believed they were blessed.

To Dupree and his friends, we were mutants, outsiders, and when we argued or fought, it was to defend against the hurt of our treatment. We won our battles, those private, quick, angry battles, but we could not assuage the ache. We wanted to know why—*really* why—we were mutations. *Why* plagued us. *Why* gnawed at us, made us wonder about our traditions of Christian forgiveness. *Why* made us doubt our birthrights as premium Southerners, whose bloodlines had been purified in the mating beds of humble but bold English and Irish emigrants, with an occasional Indian partner to make the claim of being American a genetic fact as well as an assumption. *Why* was a forever question. *Why* was an initiation chant we learned as first graders, when we were tiny and frightened and willingly asked anyone who would listen, "Why?"

We were told excuses, not answers.

And as we grew older and perhaps more vulnerable, the Highway 17 Gang continued its assault. They laughed at the way we dressed. They giggled when one of us committed an embarrassing error in school. They made obscene little tooting sounds and pointed accusing fingers at the smaller children of Our Side.

They called us white trash, or turds, or hicks.

And no one could tell us why—*really* why.

Until spring, 1947, when Time became placeable for us. Until Wesley's year.

Two weeks after our first day of softball practice, as competition festered for positions on the team, Jack Crider slapped a double past Wayne Heath in a choose-up game. Jack belonged to Our Side; Wayne was a member in good standing of the Highway 17 Gang. As Jack stood on second, clownishly accepting our cheers, Wayne retrieved the ball, rushed to second, pushed Jack off base and tagged him out.

Jack did not appreciate the tactic. He determined that Wayne should be retired from softball and proceeded to administer the service. Dupree rushed to Wayne's aid and Freeman sprinted after Dupree to even the conflict.

Jack was dismissed from the softball team for two weeks. Freeman was sternly lectured. Wayne was sent home to get a shirt with buttons. And Dupree's eye was dressed in an ice pack.

It was an ancient argument, and it had occurred too often.

At recess the following day, Wesley led Our Side below the school lunchroom and canning plant, into a small stand of new ground pines and oaks. Freeman kept his rabbit tobacco buried there in a Prince Albert tobacco tin and at recess he loved to get in a couple

36

of quick puffs.

"It ain't right," complained Jack. "Shoot, Wesley, I didn't do nothin' to Wayne. I was just standing there on second and he come and knocked me off and tagged me out. It just don't seem right."

A chorus of yeahs endorsed Jack's anxiety. Wesley nodded his head and picked up a pine needle and began to braid the three slender shoots. Freeman rolled a cigarette out of a torn front page from a *Grit* newspaper.

"Somethin' ought to be done," Freeman declared, tipping a kitchen match to his cigarette. "Ain't that right, Wes?"

Wesley stared at the braided pine needle. He ran his fingers over the sharp intertwining. He said, "Well, I guess I might know somethin' about what's wrong."

"What, Wesley?" I asked.

Wesley dropped the braided pine needle and picked up another. He began to twirl it. He was being deliberate. "I got a notion why everybody living on Highway 17 thinks we're different," he said simply.

"Damn, Wesley, they got a paved highway. Makes 'em think they're big butts," replied Freeman, puffing frantically to keep his rabbit tobacco burning.

R. J. spat through the slit in his top teeth. "Yeah, they think dirt roads is for hogs, or somethin'."

"Maybe. I think it's more'n that," countered Wesley.

Freeman blew a smoke ring that grew into a perfectly round cloud and stood swirling six inches in front of his face. He then blew three smaller smoke rings through the center of the big one. He thought

Wesley was playing. "Well, we're waitin', Wes."

"Yeah," I added.

"It sounds crazy . . ."

"C'mon, Wes," Freeman urged.

"Freeman, if you laugh you're gonna have to fight me right here, and I mean it."

"I ain't gonna laugh, Wesley. Shoot, not me! Cross my heart. What is it?"

Wesley tied his pine needle into a knot. He folded his arms around his knees and laced his fingers together. He looked intently at each face surrounding him.

"It's because they got electricity and we ain't," he announced somberly.

Freeman started to smile, then remembered Wesley's warning. He could easily have defeated Wesley in a fight, but it would have been embarrassing. He sat back against a tree and a jigsaw puzzle with missing pieces crawled into his frowning face. "What?" he asked.

"It's because they got electricity and we ain't," Wesley repeated. "Electricity, that's what it is."

"How you figurin' that, Wesley?" asked Paul.

"Simple. It's the one thing we don't have, but they do. Paved roads are paved roads. Anybody can ride on a paved road. Electricity is somethin' else. You got electricity and you got somethin'."

"Yeah!" Freeman exclaimed quickly. "Yeah, Wes! It don't make sense, but, by God, I'll bet that's it."

Paul whistled softly in disbelief. We sat stunned, looking at one another.

"By granny!" R. J. muttered, and spat through his

teeth again.

Freeman began laughing easily. "Wes, old boy, I'm a sonofabitch if you ain't right! You know that! I never thought about it before. Electricity! I'm a sonofabitch! Been hangin' there all the time, big as day, and we ain't seen it for lookin'."

"Freeman, how come you got to cuss so much?" asked Wesley. Wesley was always tempering Freeman's language.

"Sorry, Wes, but damned if you ain't right, more I think about it. Boys, Wes is right on it. That's got to be it!"

R. J. tried to spit through his teeth again, but couldn't. He was dry. "By granny!" he said again.

"How come you never said anything, Wes?" asked Freeman. "You knew, why ain't you said somethin'?"

"Because there wasn't nothing we could do about it—until now."

"Now? Why now?" I wanted to know.

"Well—" Wesley hesitated. "You got to promise me you'll keep it quiet. All of you."

We nodded eagerly. "I'll shuck corn for a whole year if I say anything," I promised. I was the youngest of the group. Sometimes I said things that didn't make sense.

"I'll bust their butts, they say anything, Wesley," Freeman volunteered. "On the Big Gully Oath, boys. Cross your hearts and hope to die."

We crossed and hoped.

"Well," Wesley began, satisfied with our pledge, "I heard this man talkin' to Daddy last month, and he was saying that the REA was comin' through for sure this summer, and by fall we'd all have electricity."

Otis moved closer to Wesley. "What's the REA, Wes?"

"It means the Rural Electrification Association, or Authority, or somethin' like that. Daddy said Franklin D. Roosevelt got it started because he got mad about electric charges at Warm Springs, where he used to go for them hot water treatments for polio."

"Yeah, I heard about that place," Otis said, whispering the words as though Warm Springs were a leper colony.

Freeman pushed his cigarette into the ground, burrowing it under some pine needles with his thumb. He began to giggle happily. "Boys, we have got that bunch of snot-asses on the line," he declared.

"I mean it," Wesley warned. "Don't nobody say nothing about this until the time is right."

"They promise," Freeman said. "Electricity! I'll be damned."

For the rest of the day, Emery Junior High School was a whisper, and there was a rippling laughter that never quite surfaced, was never quite heard. The only suggestion that something remarkable had taken place was the again-and-again winking and exaggerated crossing of hearts.

I was very proud of Wesley. He was my brother. MY brother. And that made me special. I strutted beside him and accepted, with him, the knowing exchanges of Otis and Paul and R. J. and Jack and

Freeman, the privileged.

It was a serene feeling, being with Wesley, but something battered my mind, some ethereal thing imprisoned somewhere in my memory.

I asked Wesley about it.

"How am I supposed to know what's going on in somebody else's head?" Wesley responded.

"I don't know—I thought . . ."

"What is it you don't understand?"

"Well, I never heard Daddy talking about the REA, but I've heard of it before. I know I have. I can't remember why."

For a moment, Wesley did not answer. Then he said, "It took me some time to figure that out. Maybe we ain't old enough to remember much about it, but the REA used to be talked about around home. Thomas was working as a lineman for the REA when he was killed."

The apparition of Thomas rushed into an eerie, distorted vision—a baby's vision. I was high in the air, dizzy, flying, falling, falling, falling into Thomas' face.

"Oh," I said.

"Yeah," replied Wesley. "That was a long time ago."

Thomas would have understood our joy. He would have celebrated our giddiness.

Thomas would have told us marvelous stories about electricity. He would have made it real for us—real with places and dates and names and wildly funny happenings.

Thomas. My older sisters loved to talk of him.

He had a smile and a laugh and eyes with This Morning's Sun burning blue. He knew how to say hello and make the exuberance of that hello surround you and follow you everywhere you traveled that day. He had a dancer's step and there was a dancer's tune playing forever in some mysterious, secret place in his mind. He was a man-child, or a child-man, and he had a way of making that magical confusion seem distinctly his, and his alone. He was restless and a wanderer, quick for joy and quick for pain.

Thomas was First Son, the family's Other Man, and he had a fierce temper against threat to his brothers and sisters. Once, when some unknowing fool of a Saturday drunk made a too-teasing suggestion to one of my sisters, Thomas jerked the fellow up by his shirt, hoisted him overhead, and tossed him against a kerosene drum in a service station. He was only fourteen, but Olympian in strength and courage. Even my father knew that. There was a time when my father decided to be humorous and he hid in the old Civil War cemetery with a cotton sheet draped over his head, and waited to leap out when his children passed. Everyone ran. Everyone except Thomas. Thomas scooped up a rock, hurled it at my father, and shouted, "C'mon, dammit!"

But Thomas had always been an apparition to me. A blur.

There was a face I thought was his. It was the same face that was in the photo album my mother kept safe in a cedar chest. It was below me, looking up. Somehow, in slow motion, I have always been falling

42

into his face, feeling the powerful jolt of fingers sinking into my armpits and the swishing sensation of being dropped and pitched, soundless and weightless, into the air. And there was another baby's vision: lying peacefully still and reaching for a face—the same face that memory tells me is Thomas and the same face that is in the photo album—and not being able to touch it until he bends in obedience to my reach, and my fingers slide over the ticklish softness of his eyebrows. There was never any sound to any of this. I do not remember the laughing and whistling and singing my sisters tell of. I know they have not lied to me; I simply did not hear it. (The smile of that photo-album face was too explosive not to be noisy and wonderfully musical.)

J. P. Wynn drove down from Royston with the message of Thomas' death. J. P. Wynn was a distant cousin and he operated a small grocery, where we had an account that was more an understanding than a legal contract. He did not always charge for jawbreakers.

My sisters agree that Mother recognized Cousin J. P. Wynn's car as it topped the hill near the old Civil War cemetery, recognized its age and color and keep.

Mother said, very suddenly, "Oh, no! Thomas is dead!"

That premonition fascinated me. Mother knew. She knew. It was raining that day. Perhaps something in the rain drove its sound waves into her mind in that moment, and Mother knew the incomprehensible truth. She knew.

Thomas had been hitchhiking and a man in a pickup truck offered a lift and there was a crash and Thomas was flung from the cab of the truck and his head struck viciously and he rolled into a ditch and died hours later in a small country hospital, with my oldest sister, Emma, sitting alone beside his bed.

When they tell of Thomas' death, my sisters remember the painful irony: only a few weeks earlier, one of Thomas' dearest friends had been killed in an automobile wreck and Thomas had vowed he would never again drive.

He kept his vow.

He did not drive.

He hitchhiked.

On the day he was killed, Thomas was hitchhiking to another assignment with the REA.

I have watched their faces when my sisters talked of Thomas. The faces of women have a quaint way of expanding when they are in memory. (It is a butterfly of the eyes, spreading wide, powdery, transparent wings.) My sisters' faces have always betrayed them, betrayed their longing for another time in another place.

Thomas would have understood our joy.

He would have known what we knew, what we thought of, whispered about: the Highway 17 Gang had the Georgia Power Company, and it made everything about them different from us. Their houses had indoor bathrooms (Sonny used to go home at recess to pee). Their mothers had electric washing machines for washing clothes, and electric irons for pressing creases in trousers. Their food came steaming from electric stoves—with four eyes and top-and-bottom coil oven. Electric refrigerators kept their milk from spoiling and made ice that snapped out of trays in tea-size cubes. Electric water pumps sucked water out of the ground and sent it spurting through iron arteries, ready at the touch.

Our Side had draw-bucket wells and iceboxes in smokehouses and wood-burning stoves and big iron wash pots and outdoor toilets.

Because of electricity, our habits were not the habits of the Highway 17 Gang. The way we bathed, cooked, dressed, looked—even the way we voided ourselves—was different.

At least, with our knowledge of the REA, we had solved one mystery: we knew why all the Boy Scout and Emery Methodist Church parties were held at one of the houses on Highway 17. We could not expect one of THEM to use the facility of OUR outdoor toilets, but it was a carnival experience for one of us to pee into a white enamel-steel bowl and flush it to a swirling doom somewhere below the ground.

Thomas would have understood our joy.

Thomas would have celebrated our giddiness.

5

We were drunk with our knowledge of the REA. The Select Seven. Smirking, preening, laughing demonically.

The Highway 17 Gang thought we were batty.

We didn't care.

We knew about the REA—knew, fully, the impact of electricity—and that was *our* advantage. We were smug, but we deserved that delicious satisfaction. To our delight, we realized an additional benefit in our behavior: it confused the Highway 17 Gang. They could not understand our suddenly patronizing attitude, and we extended our dramatics to repulsive extremes.

One day, Freeman even opened the lunchroom door for Dupree, bowing graciously as Dupree passed, amazed, and tripped over the top step.

Wesley warned us often about secrecy. He knew we would be regarded as idiots if—in the loose tongue of anger—we began babbling about electricity. To be dynamic, the telling would require a dynamic moment, and we had vowed on the Big Gully Oath to permit Wesley that decision.

"I mean it, now," Wesley said. "We waited all our lives for this, and there ain't no need to throw it away just because somebody gets mad."

Freeman assured him none of us would violate our oath, or the consequences would be terrible.

"That goes for you, too, Colin. I don't care if you are Wesley's brother," Freeman emphasized.

"A team of wild mules couldn't drag nothin' out of me," I promised Freeman. "Shoot, there ain't nothin' that could make me talk a word."

"You better be right," cautioned Freeman. "You ain't

big enough to make a good grease spot, but I'd give it a try."

I believed Freeman. Besides, Wesley was my brother. No one could make me betray a promise to Wesley.

Megan Priest could not be considered a No One.

Megan Priest was a girl who belonged, by geography, to the Highway 17 Gang.

And Megan Priest was my girl.

At least, I suspected she was my girl. I did not know for certain how those experiences developed. Megan was kind and gentle and there was a warmth about her that only I seemed to feel. She smiled each time I looked at her and her smile would lodge in my breathing and suffocate me for an eye-blink of time. When we played softball, I could sense her eyes following me and if I stole a glance to the place where I thought she would be, she was always there, watching. (Once in a softball game, I was knocked senseless by a foul tip and when I later regained consciousness, I knew I was on a table with an ice pack on my face, and I knew, even with my eyes closed, that Megan was also there. I moved the ice pack and opened my eyes and saw her. She smiled faintly and I pretended great pain. She oohed quietly. In the thrill of her ooh, I rolled off the table and almost killed myself.)

Megan had been in my mind for a year. I did not care if she belonged to one society and I belonged to another; it was unspoken, but Megan was special to me and I longed for the abstract language of her presence—even if I could never, ever, for all eternity and the rest of my life, permit anyone to know of my feeling for her.

I did not know Megan was in the room that day, two weeks into our celebration of the REA. It was lunchtime and everyone was recessed to the invitation of a blazing outside. Because the little kids were using the softball field, I had sneaked back into Mrs. Simmons' room to complete a drawing I had promised. Mrs. Simmons believed I had artistic ability and she carefully, quietly, begged me to practice, baiting her encouragement with delicate overpraise. The thought of scorn for drawing bees and horses and dogs at recess haunted me and I perfected excuses for returning early to my desk. Everyone—including Wesley—believed the lies about studying for spelling. The only person who must have known the truth was Megan. She said, from across the room that day, "What're you drawing?"

Her voice frightened and excited me and the two emotions collided and fell in a clumsy heap in my stomach. I flipped the paper and covered it with a book.

"Drawin'? Who's drawin'? I ain't drawin' nothing!" I snapped.

"Yes, you are. You're always drawing."

"Where'd you hear that?"

"Oh, I've seen some. I know. Mrs. Simmons showed me some."

"You better not tell!"

"What'll you do? What'll you do if I tell?"

"Well—you'd better not. That's all."

Megan crossed the room hesitantly, stopped and moved toward the blackboard and silently read a poster about tooth decay. The Prichard twins, Ed and Ted, had drawn the poster. The Prichard twins had six teeth between them.

"Want a Three Musketeers?" Megan mumbled.

"Huh?"

"A Three Musketeers. I got one and I don't want it. It'll just melt." She turned to face me, holding the candy. It was a beautiful sight, Megan holding a 3 Musketeers.

"Naw . . ."

"I saw you out there lookin' at the candy. You got a nickel?"

It was a painful question. Megan knew I didn't have a nickel.

"I don't want no candy," I said resentfully.

"I'm just gonna throw it away . . ."

"That's crazy. If you gonna throw it away, I'll eat it."

"I told you I don't want it."

"Well, give it here, but don't tell nobody you gave it to me."

"I won't," she said quickly. "Nobody's business."

Megan eased away from the blackboard, cautiously looking toward the door and planning what she would do if someone walked in. She pretended to control the unquestionable treason of approaching me, but her hand was quivering and I knew her boldness had weakened.

"Aw, just throw it," I said.

She stopped abruptly and looked straight into my eyes. "No! No. It—might get mashed up." Her eyes were pale green, her hair as blond as a full moon.

"Well, it won't make no difference," I replied. "Gets mashed up when you eat it."

"It was my nickel," she declared. Then she moved five steps and placed the 3 Musketeers in my hand. Her fingernail brushed the length of my thumb and I dropped the candy. She stood frozen, staring at me.

"Uh—I'm sorry," I muttered, scooping the candy off the floor.

Megan was rigid, not breathing.

"Is it—squashed?" she asked.

"Uh—naw."

"Good!"

She turned on her heel and swiftly crossed the room. Her body sagged and she breathed deeply.

"You—you want a bite?" I offered.

"No," she said softly. "You—eat—it."

I ate the 3 Musketeers. It had been touched by Megan's hands and it was delicious. I folded the wrapper and slipped it into my spelling book. Megan crossed to her desk three rows and four seats over from mine. She began to scribble in her Blue Horse tablet.

"You ever say 'thank you' for anything?" she asked as I swallowed the last bite.

"Uh—I'm sorry. Thanks."

Her back was turned to me. "I bought that with my lunch money," she blurted.

I didn't know what she meant. "Why? Thought you

said you didn't want it."

"I didn't."

"Why didn't you eat lunch?"

"I wanted the candy. I still got a dime."

"That don't make sense. You didn't eat lunch and you wanted candy and then you didn't want to eat it. That don't make sense."

She turned in her desk. She looked furious and suddenly dominating.

"You don't understand the first thing about people, do you?" she said curtly. Her voice dismissed me, and it made me angry.

"I don't understand crazy people. That's for sure. That's for damn sure!"

"You hang around Freeman Boyd too much. You're as nasty-mouthed as he is," she snapped.

"Freeman's my friend."

"Wesley wouldn't cuss."

"I ain't Wesley."

"No, you're not! That's the truth!"

"I can't help it."

"You could try."

"I didn't ask you to come in here with that da—uh, candy! I didn't ask you."

"I wish I hadn't."

"You don't have to get snooty about it."

She whirled in her desk, ripped the page from her Blue Horse tablet, and wadded it. I slipped out of my seat and started toward the door.

"Where're you goin'?" Megan asked, pleading.

"Out."

"Why?"

"Because you ain't no different'n Dupree. I thought you was. Well, you'll see. All of you . . ."

"See what?"

I had said too much and I knew it. "Nothin'."

"What?" Megan was questioning, apologizing, asking my anger to be calm.

"Just—nothin'."

"Something's going on, Colin. I can feel it."

She had never before said my name. Not directly. Not when the two of us were alone—but we had never been alone before. The sound of my name was a two-syllable song when Megan said it, a velvet reprise of a mysterious musical nerve, and it made my knees tremble. I returned to my desk as violins wept in reverence over the immortality of a note.

"I can't say nothin'," I told her. "Not now."

She did not face me, but I could sense her awful deliberation of what to say, and how to say it, without offending me.

"You didn't have to say I was like Dupree," she finally whispered.

She was right. She wasn't like Dupree. No one was like Dupree. Especially Megan.

"My favorite candy's a Three Musketeers," I said, because I didn't know what else to say.

"I know it." Her voice was moist, quaking.

"How'd you know that?"

"That's all you ever buy when—when you get a nickel." There was sadness in her words. I felt like an orphan in rags.

"Heck, I got lots of nickels," I lied bravely. "I got two or three dollars' worth at home, tied up in the toe of a sock. I'm savin' for this air rifle . . ."

Megan did not answer. She put her head in her hands and gulped air. She then became very still and placed her hands on her Blue Horse tablet.

"Yeah. There's this air rifle at Harden's Five and Ten," I bragged. "I'll get it. By summer, too."

Megan did not answer.

"Anyway, Three Musketeers is my favorite candy."

Megan did not answer.

"I'll draw you a picture and pay you back," I suggested.

"I—I'd like that," she whispered.

"You like dogs?"

She nodded. "I've got a cocker spaniel."

"Me, too," I said. "Well, I used to have one. Ol' Red. But he died. One time I knocked Paul Tully's bottom tooth out because he called Ol' Red a son of a bitch, and you know what he . . ."

Oh, my God! I said son of a bitch! I couldn't believe it. Everything was going beautifully.

"I'm sorry—I—I . . ." I stuttered.

"That's all right."

"It just came out."

"I know."

"He did, though."

"What?"

"Called Ol' Red a—a S.O.B."

"Oh."

The bell rang and I jumped two feet. Dear God in

Heaven, I thought. They'll be coming in and catch me. Catch me talking with her, someone from the Highway 17 Gang. Megan turned for one last penetrating look, an I'm Glad We Had This Time Together look. Pale green eyes, hair as blond as a full moon.

Wayne and Dupree were first through the door, laughing, shoving, playing. They saw Megan and me and stopped abruptly. We were both buried in spelling books. Paul and Otis and Freeman and R. J. followed Wayne and Dupree. Then half the population of Georgia slipped noiselessly into the classroom. I wanted to melt into butter, to disappear into another time and place like some victim of Mandrake the Magician's powers.

Otis walked past me and paused just behind my desk.

"What you been doin'?" he pried, whispering.

"Studying this spelling."

"What's she doin' in here?"

"Otis, you tryin' to start something?" I hissed.

"Don't look right."

"I can't help it. She come in right before the bell." I said in an even, mean voice. Damn Otis Finlay, anyway. I could whip him and I knew it.

"Shut up," Freeman ordered Otis, and Otis obeyed.

I did not move my eyes from my desk for two hours. I missed eight of ten spelling words.

No one said anything about discovering Megan and me together in a classroom, but I knew what they were thinking. Aha! was penciled and exclamation-pointed on every face in school. Wesley smiled and gave me an easy, playful shot in the ribs and said, "Aw, forget it. Ain't your fault she come in there."

Wesley was the only person who believed me, but Wesley was enough. No one would dare question me if Wesley had faith in my innocence. I felt relieved, but I also felt guilty. I wanted to tell Wesley, but I couldn't. I couldn't. On the school bus, riding home, I began to imagine I was Judas and that afternoon I stole away into the dark tomb of Black Pool Swamp and hid, and drew a picture of a dog for Megan.

I had almost talked of the REA to Megan. Our Side had changed and she knew it. Everyone knew it. The pressure was building.

On Saturday, a man in a jeep drove into our yard and asked for my father. We were working in the field beside the pine stand, breaking cotton land with a two-horse turner, and when Lynn called, my father left Wesley and me to watch the mules. From where we were resting, in the edge of the pines, we could see the man and my father walking through the woods. Occasionally the man would stop and gesture toward Emery or Goldmine and I knew from the mime of his arm-waving that he was from the REA.

I asked Wesley, "That the same man who talked to Daddy before?"

"Yeah, I guess."

"What're they talkin' about?"

"I don't know. I ain't there."

"What'd you *think* they're talkin' about?" I could be tormenting at times.

"How you think I know? Where the lines are going. I don't know."

Of course, I thought. There would have to be lines and electric light poles and transformers and fuse boxes and meters. I closed my eyes and heard the deep bass of men at work, saw the statuelike lean of their bodies tilting backward as they worked against safety belts high up on black, creosoted pine poles. I saw their hard hats and equipment holsters and spike boots.

I saw Thomas. Smiling, swinging a rope across his shoulder, jabbing a spike into a pole, and climbing. Thomas. Soundless Thomas.

I opened my eyes and looked for Wesley. He was sitting against a pine. His eyes were half closed and he was holding a braided pine needle, slowly twirling it in his fingers. Sometimes I confused Wesley and Thomas. They were part of my mood and belonging, yet they seemed removed—Thomas by death and Wesley by ordination. It was bewildering. I was inseparably fused with two people, yet they were somehow removed from my offer—my longing—to know them wholly.

"I saw that man pointin' over to where Freeman lives, Wesley," I said. "You think Freeman and them will get electricity?"

Wesley opened his eyes and looked in the direction of Freeman's home across the swamp. "I doubt it," he answered. "They live too far off the line."

Freeman lived with his parents in a shotgun house that was wrapped like gauze in tarpaper. The house had been built for a WPA crew during the thirties.

After the crew left, finished with its work of draining Black Pool Swamp, Odell Boyd moved his wife and young son into the house and, in the following years, he had piddled with improvements and failed to improve anything. Odell Boyd worked the sawmills and made whiskey by moonlight, and he had taught Freeman the honorable art of cussing. Freeman was an able student. I have never been privileged to know anyone who could cuss with Freeman's authority.

"It just don't seem right," I protested. "Freeman and them ought to get electricity like everybody else."

"Yeah," agreed Wesley. "Maybe they'll move up to where the Grooms used to live."

"I wish they would."

We did not question our father about the man, or the REA. We had been taught to honor the adult privilege of silence. Be patient, we were told; be patient and you'll know soon enough. I think I understood even then that patience was the gift of the Southerner. If anything made a Southerner different, it was patience, and an instinct for the Right Time. That was what Wesley had said to us: "Be patient, and the time for springing the REA will come; don't worry, it'll happen."

Days eased into a bubble of other days. We were patient. We waited. But we also lived with the fear that someone from the Highway 17 Gang would begin to smart-mouth about the REA. And that would settle it. Too late. Our play for the Right Time would have been lost. We complained to Wesley, but Wesley pleaded with us to wait, to be patient—*more* patient. I thought he was probably testing us, teaching us one of the values of life that was natural with him. He was always doing that. Wesley was born to teach.

But still we waited.

Our celebration turned to sulking, our joy peaked and paled into fatigue. Our nerves were frayed (Freeman said we had Hot Nerves and the only way to cure Hot Nerves was a rousing fine conflict). But nothing was as bothersome as the new energy of the Highway 17 Gang in tormenting us. It was more than any of us could tolerate and it became difficult for Wesley to control our tempers.

"Dammit," Freeman declared one afternoon. "I ain't gonna take much more of all that smart-aleck talk I been gettin', Wes. I ain't now, and you better know it."

"Freeman, it ain't gonna hurt you to wait, is it?" replied Wesley.

"It ain't gonna hurt me? Lordamercy, Wesley! It's killin' me! You ain't got feelings, you know that? That's your trouble, boy."

"The time will come, Freeman. I promise it."

The time came two days later, on a Friday. It came on a day that screamed from the splendor of its blueness, burning with a fever of early summer oozing from the spring ground, and suffocating us with the smell of crushed grass.

On that day, Wesley ended our waiting.
On that day, Wesley caused a riot.

It happened at midmorning recess. Shirley Weems was a thin, pale girl who was Wesley's age but two years behind him in her class in school. One of my older sisters, Amy, who had studied nursing, said Shirley and her brothers and sisters were suffering from a lack of vitamins, or something. They were undernourished and their bodies could not react as quickly as they should. "Never, never, never, never make fun of them," Amy had warned us. "They're the poorest people in Emery." And they were. Poverty had left the Weems family totally, completely defeated. Shirley wore washed-out gingham dresses, colorless and dead. Scabs were always on her arms and mouth. Once, the county nurse had found lice in her hair and Shirley was herded out from the rest of us standing at attention in the auditorium, and her head was powdered until it turned white. She stood very still in one corner of the auditorium and tears rolled off her empty face. Dupree had started giggling and pointing and Freeman gave him a bullet shot in the kidneys. Dupree complained loudly, accusing Freeman of ". . . picking" on him. Wesley quickly embraced the argument, saying it was Shirley, not Dupree, who was being "picked on." Mrs. Simmons agreed with Wesley; she led Shirley out of the auditorium, away from the careless indignity of being an example to those who did not exercise proper hygiene. After that, Wesley was teased miserably by the Highway 17 Gang about being Shirley's boyfriend, but it never bothered him. He never replied to any of the taunting, and occasionally he would sneak something out of the lunchroom and give it to Lynn to give to Shirley.

The Weems children did not eat in the lunchroom.

The Weems children did not eat lunch.

And on this screaming, burning, spring-summer day, Shirley Weems was standing alone at recess when Dupree and Sonny and five or six others began to circle her and sing:

> "Shirley, Shirley, I been thinkin',
> What would keep your feet from stinkin' . . .
> A barrel of water and a cake of soap,
> Put 'em in and let 'em soak . . ."

Walter Weems, who was eight and a first-grader for the second year, rushed up to Dupree and kicked him. "Quit it!" he yelled, his voice a shrill bird's cry. "Leave Sister alone! Leave her alone!"

Dupree whirled and slapped Walter viciously across the face. Walter fell and rolled over the hard clay of the outside basketball court.

"DAMN YOU, DUPREE HIXON!"

It was Wesley, from in front of the canning plant. His voice was guttural, an animal's voice, an explosion of agony. Freeman knew what would happen; if Wesley resorted to foul language, it always ended in a fight. Freeman reached for him, but Wesley ripped away and bolted the distance separating him and Dupree. Sonny stepped in front of Dupree, cutting off Wesley's rush.

"What'd you think you're gonna do, hick?" snapped Sonny.

Wesley cried from deep in his chest, caught the larger Sonny by his shirt, and lifted him off the ground. He threw Sonny to one side and hit Dupree three times before Dupree could lift his arms. Wayne Heath circled quickly behind Wesley and kicked him in the lower back and Wesley fell forward as someone else hit him on the ear.

I tackled Wayne and turned him, grabbed his hair, and bit into his shoulder. Wayne jerked and fell, tossing his head wildly. I was on him like a tick. He bucked and rolled, and I bit deeper.

"Bite a plug out," Freeman yelled gleefully, as he threw bodies aside and pulled Wesley away from the pounding. I could tell by his voice that Freeman was proud of my fighting style.

"Let me alone," Wesley commanded and Freeman dropped him.

"Wes," Freeman shouted. "Hey, boy! I'm a sonofa-bitch if we ain't got one helluva fight on our hands!" He hit Ted Prichard and Ted fell in a lump. "Where's that damned R. J.?"

Wayne clubbed at me with his fist and I wrapped my legs around him and started squeezing. His eyes crossed and he began to slobber. I heard someone yell, "Colin! Sonny's got a rock!" I looked up and saw Sonny standing above me, saw the hammer swing of his arm, and I felt something cracking against the back of my neck. I released Wayne. The sky turned black, then scarlet, then silver. I could feel blood running down my neck. I could hear Freeman directing R. J. and Otis and Paul, like a general: "Hit 'em, dammit. Hit 'em!" And then I heard Wesley's pained cry: "You bastard! That's my little brother, you bastard!"

The sky turned black again and I saw someone running inside the corridor of a long, blinding-white building. The muscles of my legs tried to lift me, but couldn't. I fell forward on my hands and the running figure in the corridor of the long, blinding-white building flashed into focus: it was I, and I wondered where I was and why I was there. The blackness rolled into my head like a tornado. There was a thunderous, deafening sound, then no sound, then a frightening, loud, sustained whistle. I could feel the blood circling around my shoulder, and then the familiar touch of a familiar someone, and I knew Lynn was on her knees, cradling me, rocking me in her arms, and crying. "He's gonna die. He's gonna die," she sobbed, swabbing at the stream of blood with her dress.

"Shuttup, Lynn!" I whispered through dry lips. "I ain't dyin' . . ."

The terrible blackness returned and, for the first time in my life, the thought of dying *was* real—clouds enveloping me, lifting me effortlessly. Yes, I thought, that's what *The Anderson Independent* meant when it printed that Death Takes So-and-So.

"He's gonna die," Lynn repeated. I believed her. Lynn was amazingly perceptive.

"I'll be damned. He better get up and do some fightin'," Freeman ordered, dropping Seymour Hillary with a knee to the stomach. Freeman did not know I had been hit with a rock, and for some ridiculous reason I wanted to laugh. I loved Freeman Boyd. He was incredible.

"He's been busted with a rock, Freeman," Lynn screamed angrily.

Freeman turned quickly toward me. "Well, I'll be damned!" he said, and turned back to the fight.

I rolled on my shoulder in Lynn's arms and looked through a blood-blur screen. It seemed every boy in school was fighting, grade one to grade nine. Otis was pounding on Edward Roach; Freeman was rearranging Dupree's facial features; R. J. and Jack had five younger kids backed up; Alvin Bond, the tallest boy in school, was slapping at anyone in reach; and Wesley was straddling Sonny on the ground. He had Sonny's arms pinned and was spitting in his face.

I had never seen such a fight. It was fantastic. Beautiful. Kicking and swinging and pinching and tackling. A haze of red dust was ankle-deep, rising like early morning fog over a river of years of antagonism and frustration. The fight we'd waited for, prayed over, talked about, was finally taking place and I could not join the battle.

Suddenly, teachers appeared. They were everywhere, pulling, pushing, threatening, demanding—until the Highway 17 Gang and Our Side was separated and glaring, group to group, from across ten feet of clay basketball court that somehow perfectly symbolized the difference we had known: they were in the free-throw lane and we were out of bounds.

Wade Simmons was away for the day, attending a meeting in Athens, and the only male teacher present was Dewitt Hollister. He was a cranky old man who thrilled at the thought of administering punishment. It was a sickness with him. He had a ready temper and because he dealt with children he had no fear of challenge. Now, in the aftermath of a riot, his face was blotched in anger and he waved his thin leather belt around like Al "Lash" LaRue in a saloon.

"Now, who started this?" Hollister demanded.

"Wesley Wynn," shouted Dupree. "Wesley Wynn started it, by granny!"

Freeman took one step toward Dupree and Hollister lashed him with his belt. Freeman growled and turned to face the second blow. He was in a nasty, fighting mood.

Wesley pulled away from Old Lady Blackwall's hammerlock. He caught Freeman by the arm and jerked him away from Hollister. Both groups froze. Hollister raised his belt. Wesley did not move. Hollister dropped his arm. Hitting Freeman or me or anyone else was one thing; hitting Wesley was another matter. Wesley defied such punishment.

"This fight started," Wesley said in a measured, perfectly calm voice, "because Dupree and them was makin' fun of Shirley Weems. I know that's wrong and you know it's wrong. But Shirley's put up with that since she's been in school and she'd of taken it again today. We would've watched it happen again . . ." Wesley looked at Shirley and apologized with his eyes. She dropped her head and stood perfectly still.

"Ain't so," Dupree interrupted. "That's his girl."

"Dupree, you keep quiet," Mrs. Simmons ordered, and even Hollister recognized her presence.

"Well, like I said, it would've been just like before," continued Wesley, "but that little brother of her's, well, he ain't learned what it's like to be pushed around all the time, and when Dupree slapped him to the ground for tryin' to help out his sister, well, Mr. Hollister—" Wesley turned to include the other teachers "—and the rest of you grownups, that's when we don't take it no longer."

Hollister studied Wesley from squinted eyes. He looked for help from Mrs. Simmons, but she offered none. No one moved or made a sound.

"You got to be punished, Wesley," Hollister finally said, raising his arm.

Wesley locked his hands behind his back and lifted his face to Hollister. It was a martyr's pose; Wesley looked like Daniel surrendering to the Lion's Den.

"Well, sir, you can punish me if you want to, but I have told you the truth and you know it," Wesley replied calmly. "You know I don't lie—never."

I had never known Wesley to be so direct. I could feel a quiver of pride flutter through Lynn's body as she stroked my head.

Hollister was struck by the lightning of Wesley's words. He was speechless, paralyzed from his jowls to his lips. The red left his face and a pale, drained-out expression of defeat crawled around the tight circle of his thin mouth. He had, at last, been challenged, and by a child, and he had lost.

Mrs. Simmons moved to Wesley. She placed both hands on his shoulders and spoke quietly. "Mr. Hollister's not saying you've lied, Wesley. He's just trying to find out what happened."

"Yes'm. I know that."

Hollister was confused. His voice pleaded with Wesley. "But—but, why, Wesley? Why didn't you just come and tell me or one of the other teachers about Dupree?"

"Because this is between us and them. Because you would've let it go. Because you would've got mad at me for tattling."

"No—no, Wesley. I—would have . . ."

"No, sir. There's two sides in this school, and any side gets stepped on, it's us."

"Wesley, that's not true. There's no difference."

"Yes, sir. There is a difference."

"What difference, Wesley?" Hollister was begging. "What're you talking about?"

Wesley stepped back and turned around. He looked at me and I knew it was the Right Time for telling. He looked at Freeman and Freeman smiled; Freeman also knew. He turned back to Hollister.

"Well, Mr. Hollister, you may not believe it," Wesley said, "but the difference is electricity."

Hollister looked toward Mrs. Simmons and opened his mouth to speak, but he was suddenly dumb. He gestured with his belt and hands, asking for help.

"Electricity? I don't understand," Mrs. Simmons said quietly. "What do you mean about electricity, Wesley?" She had an angel's way of settling confusion.

"They got electricity and we ain't," Wesley told her. "That makes them think we ain't worth much. But that's changin'."

Dupree spat and wiped his mouth with his shirt sleeve. "What're you talkin' about, hick?"

Hollister turned on his heel. "Shut up, Dupree Hixon."

"We're getting electricity, too," Wesley continued. "The REA is comin' through this year."

"That's right," Freeman added triumphantly.

Dupree laughed. "Electricity ain't got nothin' to do with it, boy. You ain't never gonna get cow turds outta your toes!"

"Dupree Hixon, you're going to pay for that foul-mouthed remark, young man," Hollister snapped.

"Mr. Hollister," Wesley interrupted, "can I say something to Dupree?"

Hollister looked angrily at Wesley. "What?"

Wesley walked easily, confidently, across the divide separating the Highway 17 Gang and Our Side, walked straight to Dupree.

"Dupree," Wesley began, "it's a thing called psychology. Truth is, there ain't one dab of real difference between us. It's what you think, and what I think, that makes us different. All our lives, we been without some of them things you think were God-given to you and your kind. You been acting like we had some kind of disease because we ain't got all them things. But the REA will fix that. The REA will make things a little more equal, and you'll see what I'm talkin' about."

None of us knew what Wesley meant by psychology,

but he knew. And I suppose Hollister knew. The fight that had begun with the fury of a hurricane was over. Hollister looped his thin leather belt back through his pants and walked away. Mrs. Simmons helped Lynn and Wesley and Freeman carry me to the lunchroom to have my neck bathed and bandaged. It was not a deep cut, but Mrs. Simmons washed off the dirt from my face and rubbed my back and whispered that she was relieved I was not seriously injured.

As I sat on a table and looked through a lunchroom window, I saw Wesley talking with Shirley and her little brother, who had buried his face in Shirley's gingham dress. After a moment, Wesley squatted and turned Walter to him and Walter whipped his arms around Wesley's neck. It was the first time I realized Wesley's embrace, and in that moment I saw him suddenly go limp, as though something had gone out of him, something the rest of us did not have.

Years later, after Wesley had been ordained a minister of the Methodist Church, he would return to Emery to perform burial rites for Walter Weems, because Walter Weems would grow up to face unbearable abuse, and one day, while plowing corn for Howard Wages, he would take a plow line and hang himself in an abandoned house.

6

On Saturday morning, Wade Simmons drove over to meet with our father, and the two walked away through the apple orchard to talk privately.

"I'll bet he's tellin' Daddy he's gonna kick us out of school," I said.

"He ain't kickin' us out of school," counseled Wesley. "He's just talking. Maybe he wanted to make sure you didn't get hurt bad. It ain't nothing. Just talk. Teachers love to talk. Anyway, Daddy's chairman of the board of education. They have to talk about problems with Daddy."

Wesley tried to sound confident and authoritative. He didn't. Wade Simmons was not Dewitt Hollister.

"I wonder what would've happened if Mr. Simmons had been there," I said. "What'd you think, Wes?"

"I don't know."

"I'm glad he was gone."

"Yeah. Me, too," agreed Wesley.

We waited anxiously, hidden, until Mr. Simmons and our father returned from the apple orchard and Mr. Simmons drove away in his Hudson.

"C'mon," Wesley said. "We might as well get it over with." We walked in full view of our father, but he did not say anything. He ignored us.

We walked away, then retraced our steps, moving closer to him. Being ignored was not a happy omen; usually, that meant pressure was building.

"Uh—anything you want us to be doin'?" asked Wesley.

Our father knew how to handle us. He hammered off a heel bolt on an upside-down plow and inspected the dull gopher. Then he said solemnly, "Catch the mules and hitch up the mowing machine. That high grass in the flat needs cuttin'."

"Yessir," Wesley replied. "Yessir. We'll—we'll get to that right now."

We left quickly to find the mules.

"Wonder why he didn't say nothin'?" I whispered.

"He will," Wesley predicted. "Don't worry. He will."

That night, after we had eaten, he spoke—our father spoke.

"Wesley, was all that fighting worth the trouble it caused?" he asked.

"Uh—yessir," answered Wesley. "I think it was."

"Mr. Simmons is lettin' you off this time. Said he'd expel you if anything else like this happens. He means it."

"Yessir."

"I don't like you boys fighting, but if there's a right cause for it, I don't want you turning tail and running."

"Yessir," said Wesley.

"Yessir," I echoed.

"All right," our father continued, satisfied that he had extracted a moral and presented it as irrefutable truth, "now I told Mr. Simmons that the two of you would help him at the school tomorrow, doing some cleaning. I expect you to be there and work and not say anything else about this fight. You understand me?"

Wesley answered, "Yessir, we understand. We'll be there." Then he asked, "Daddy, we were right, weren't we? Electricity makes a difference, don't it?"

The question lingered. "I guess, son. I guess," our

father finally answered, staring into the kerosene lamp on his rolltop desk.

My father had always been a giant to me. I had marveled at his stories. My father knew—actually knew—men who had fought in the Civil War. He had sold Bibles in Kentucky, had worked in Florida as a carpenter, and had once supervised the farming operation at Madison A & M. Now he was a farmer and a nurseryman, and a man all other men respected. He had an obsession for seeing things grow and he was a genius with trees. My father could take one tree—any tree—and explain the most perplexing and incomprehensible mysteries. A tree was a cycle of life, reproducing itself again and again, remaining part of itself, and, yet, becoming part of everything around it. A tree purified the air, pulverized the soil, trapped water, deposited quilts of leaves to decay. A tree bloomed green, flowered, faded, colored in a final ceremony of splendor, and then bloomed green again. A tree could do more rooted to one spot than most men rushing about the globe, high-stepping in the name of Ambition. To my father, the most astonishing fact about a tree was that it grew out, not up. He used that fact to confirm the shortcomings of man, and to teach us the difference between taking what we could get and reaching for those things that exhilarated us. Expanding, my father declared, was greater than conquering. "Put a nail in a tree trunk and it won't move a hair in a hundred years," he said. "A tree grows out, not up; a man grows up, not out." How did that happen—that about the tree? The Almighty, my father said. He was stubborn in his use of that description of deity. Other men pondered over Scriptures and discovered answers in arm-long words. My father took his budding knife and slit the bark of young tree stalks and, gently, he slipped delicate baby buds into the wounds—buds shaped like tiny sailing ships—and then he watched his trees become an appointed fruit: Yellow Delicious, Red Delicious, Stuart, Orient, Bartlett. That act was his scripture and easier read than the Bible. It was my suspicion that my father could not understand why a man needed to seek Great Answers if he had ever budded a tree and watched it live.

Because my father had known many experiences and because he was quick to feel what others could not feel, Wesley and I escaped the wrath of the angry parent lashing out. There was something about the fight, about Wesley's deliberation, that agreed with my father's observations of man's shortcomings. It was not that we had fought and won—not that at all; we had fought for a reason, and that reason was more in the name of reaching out (for something romantic?) than in striking back.

My father also understood the immense release of that fight. Wesley had confused Dewitt Hollister with a declamation on the REA, and Dewitt Hollister forgot about the issue of Shirley Weems. But to us, the fight *was* about Shirley Weems and Walter Weems. Hitting Dupree and Sonny and Wayne and the others was pleasurable because we were stealing from God's thunder and fighting in the name of vengeance. But it was our privilege—even more than God's. It was our privilege because we had endured, and because the fight was a sign of the Right Time. It couldn't have been righter; our nerves were frayed and knotted from such long waiting, and Mr. Simmons was away from school. (Perhaps God did have something to do with it.)

It was not easy confronting Wade Simmons on Sunday afternoon. He was not a man to dodge responsibility and the fight was his responsibility; it could not be dismissed until we had learned The Lesson of it. That conviction was Mr. Simmons' most distinctive characteristic, and the reason he was a brilliant teacher: he knew the difference between a lesson and The Lesson.

"Hello, boys," Mr. Simmons said, smiling. "I appreciate you coming over and helping, it being Sunday."

"Yessir," I mumbled.

"We're glad to help," Wesley added.

"Well, c'mon. A couple of the others are already doing some picking up in the auditorium," replied Mr. Simmons.

Freeman and Otis were moving chairs and sweeping. They smiled awkwardly and muttered hellos.

"Won't take long, boys, now with all of us working," Mr. Simmons assured us. "Not long at all. I really appreciate this, and I mean it."

We knew immediately what had happened, and later it would be confirmed by the whispered comments of the Highway 17 Gang: we were being punished, but not openly, not as public nuisances, not in ridicule, not as examples to deter the temper of others. We were being punished quietly, on a Sunday afternoon. If anyone saw us and wondered, Mr. Simmons would praise us for our unselfish willingness to volunteer a Sunday afternoon in spring.

As we learned, there had been a compromise. The parents of the Highway 17 Gang were indignant over the fight—Wesley had started it and Our Side had won it, and we were guilty. Their sensibilities had been offended and they demanded retribution in discipline. Mr. Simmons had pleaded our case, had responded with the story of Shirley Weems' being subjected to a degrading insult, but the parents of the Highway 17 Gang dismissed that argument. "Kids will be kids," they said. "Our boys didn't mean anything by that."

But Mr. Simmons would not accept dictated terms of punishment. He would not discipline the entire school, he warned. He would discipline certain participants; symbolically, the few would represent the whole. And he imposed one other condition: no one would ask who had been selected for punishment.

And, so, on Sunday afternoon at Emery Junior High School, Wesley and Freeman and Otis and I swept floors and washed blackboards and emptied pencil sharpeners and dusted erasers and scraped away year-old dirt-dauber lodges and obeyed all the other suggestions of Mr. Simmons. We did this agreeably, if not eagerly. We did it because we understood Mr. Simmons was trying to tell us that he believed in us, that he endorsed our awareness of a social Maginot Line splitting Emery. We did it also because being treated with dignity and as very important people was a most novel method of discipline.

In midafternoon, Margret Simmons arrived, driving the Hudson. Mr. Simmons interrupted our window washing and led us to the lunchroom, where Mrs. Simmons was spooning generous portions of home-cranked ice cream into soup bowls.

"This is peach ice cream, boys," Mr. Simmons announced, reaching for the dasher. "Now, you may not like it, but I do, and if my wife's doing the turning, then it'll be peach. And that's something you boys will do well to remember: when you're looking for a wife, find a woman willing to crank the ice cream freezer."

We laughed fully. It was the first time we had ever heard Mr. Simmons attempt humor.

Mrs. Simmons spoke warmly to each of us. She offered oatmeal cookies. She praised us for working on Sunday. She playfully massaged my neck.

I loved Margret Simmons.

We enjoyed the ice cream, the ease, the calmness, the informality of being with our teachers. Wade Simmons was relaxed and—and *unorganized*. His voice was different—lighter, quicker, less official. And she—she was girlish, free with laughter, slyly playing sly games with her husband, telling him in her own language that she was proud of what he was doing.

The mood was party, and even the question Wesley asked did not change that mood.

Wesley said, "Mr. Simmons, did you have electricity when you was little?"

Mr. Simmons laughed. "No, Wesley, I didn't. And on

that farm where I grew up, it's still not there."

"You mean, you didn't have electricity, either?" responded Otis, surprised.

"Not at all, Otis. Not at all," Mr. Simmons replied. "You know what I remember about electricity? What I remember most about it? You know what it was?"

We did not know.

"Well, it was reading a story. A story about a chicken in Kentucky. It was, I think, nineteen-thirty-eight or 'thirty-nine. Anyway, this chicken was raised in a hen house that had electric lights, and one day the chicken up and produced an egg shaped exactly like an electric bulb."

Freeman was amazed. "I don't believe it," he exclaimed. "Is that right, Mr. Simmons? A light bulb?"

"That's right, Freeman. That chicken was known as the Inspired Kentucky Pullet. Newspapers all over the world carried stories of that egg. It was even displayed in the World's Fair in New York. That chicken had sermons preached about it. Yessir, there were some preachers who said it was a sign from God that electricity was hatching and, someday, electricity would be everywhere."

We were sincerely moved by the story of the Inspired Kentucky Pullet. Otis was very nearly converted, for he confessed openly that it must have been God's work and he would give anything to see a picture of that egg.

"I'll try to find one for you," promised Mr. Simmons. "Once, in college, I wrote a paper on the effects of electricity on farm families, and it seems to me I have a clipping of that egg."

"I'd be grateful, Mr. Simmons," Otis said. "I surely would."

"Well, I guess I know how you boys feel about electricity," Mr. Simmons continued easily. "Growing up the way I did, the way you boys are growing up, I used to wonder why we were always being put down, too. You know, it just goes to show you that people are curious. People are always and forever looking down on other people for the strangest reasons—like not liking somebody because somebody else said he came from a bad family, or not wanting to eat certain kinds of good, nutritional food because somebody else said it tasted awful, or not wanting to see other people do good because their nose is too long, or their eyes are brown, or their skin is black or red or yellow . . ."

And we sat, listening and nodding agreement.

Later it occurred to us that Wade Simmons had performed his noblest teaching on that Sunday afternoon. We had accepted The Lesson, and we did not realize it.

For several days, we were gentlemen beyond our training and inclination. Whenever we became tense, we instinctively moved into the physical presence of Wade Simmons, as though Wade Simmons were an incantation to deafen the hissing slurs we were receiving from the Highway 17 Gang.

But on Friday afternoon of the following week, the unsteady peace ended.

Delano Ford, prissy Delano Ford, called Betty Tully a ". . . heifer."

77

Betty was not lean, but she did not waddle when she walked.

Betty was Paul's sister.

Paul proceeded to inflict minor damage across prissy Delano Ford's skull, and the rest of the Highway 17 Gang rushed to the scene like sharks after blood.

Freeman and Wesley and Otis and Jack and I formed a circle around the two combatants.

Dupree was astonished. He said to Freeman, "You mean you ain't doin' the fightin' for Paul?"

Freeman shook his head. His face was contorted in anguish. He looked like someone struggling with a terrible temptation.

"I don't believe it," exclaimed Dupree.

"Aw, shuttup, Dupree!" whined Freeman. "It—it just don't seem right to pick on Delano."

"Why?" asked Sonny.

"Well, you know. He's got FDR's name," Freeman declared defensively. "Anyhow, he ain't big as a gnat."

"I don't believe it!" Dupree repeated. "I just don't believe it!"

Freeman wrestled with the fury rising in him. "Dammit, Dupree! You don't like Delano yourself. So what's it to you?"

"I just don't believe it," Dupree mumbled.

7

"Well, you know what they say: You can lead a mule to water, but you can't make him drink none."

"Mules ain't hims or hers, R. J. Mules are its."

"Well, that's what they say."

"Yeah . . ."

"Yeah. The tiger don't change spots."

"Leopard, Otis. Tigers has got stripes."

"Yeah . . ."

"You can't teach a old dog new tricks."

"Yeah . . ."

"You'd think somethin' would've changed."

"Ain't, though."

"It's easier to drive a camel through the eye of a needle than—than, uh, somethin'."

"That don't make sense, Freeman."

"I forget how it goes. Old Preacher Bytheway's always sayin' it."

"Who?"

"Preacher Bartholomew Bytheway."

"That's the craziest name I ever heard."

"Preaches a tent meeting. Speaking-In-Tongues Traveling Tent Tabernacle. He's crazy as his name. You oughta hear that fool."

"It's easier to drive a camel through the eye of a needle than for a rich man to enter the kingdom of heaven."

"Yeah, Wesley, that's it! By God, you got it!"

"No need to take God's name in vain, Freeman."

"Sorry, Wes. Wes, what's the matter with them, anyways?"

"Nobody takes easy to change, Freeman."

It was Sunday. Freeman and R. J. and Jack and Otis and Paul had appeared out of Black Pool Swamp after lunch and asked Wesley and me if we wanted to hit softball. We had played, but without enthusiasm, and finally we quit and stretched out on a quilt of pine needles and rested. The Highway 17 Gang was on everyone's mind. They had become vicious in their determination to put us in our place after our bold assertion of equality. It was a response none of us had expected, and it was annoying.

"I'll tell you one thing," Paul boasted, "I'm ready to do it all over again. Maybe it'll take another lickin'."

"Aw, Paul, that's crazy," Wesley replied. "We had our say, and it got to 'em. They're the ones who're aggravated."

"Well, poot on 'em! I tell you somethin' else—it's them that's got to change, not us," argued Paul.

"That's right," I added.

"Another thing, we catch anybody from us makin' up to them, we got to beat somebody's tail." Paul was ranting.

"That's the truth," Freeman said. "And, Wesley, you may be thinkin' we ought to be forgiving and all that, but it ain't gonna happen. What goes for us, goes for you, too."

Wesley didn't move. He looked asleep. "Freeman, I ain't arguin' that," he said defensively.

"Well, let's vow."

"Don't need to," Wesley replied. "We know what we got to do."

"Wes," R. J. warned, "we ought to vow."

Wesley turned on his side, picked up a pine needle and began to braid it. That was always a signal he was thinking.

"I'll tell you what," Wesley finally said. "Let's have a hearin' if anybody gets to bein' buddy-buddy with them. Best that way. Some of the little kids just don't know no better."

"All right," R. J. quickly agreed. "I reckon that'll do it." R. J. liked the idea of a kangaroo court. That made it dramatic.

"Everybody agree?" asked R. J.

Everyone nodded.

"No playing around with them," I emphasized. "No—uh . . ."

"What's the matter, Colin?" Freeman asked.

"Uh—nothin'. Nothin'. I'm agreeing, that's all."

Megan. That meant I would have to summon all my cunning, employ every instinct I had, not be caught with Megan. These were my friends and Wesley was my brother. But Megan—Megan belonged to another me. She gave me 3 Musketeers candy bars and I drew her pictures of dogs.

"You wait," Wesley said slowly. "You wait. Something's gonna break for us."

At the exact moment we were sealing our strategy in the High Council session of a Sunday afternoon, Alvin Bond was discovering The Secret. We did not know it, but Alvin Bond and The Secret would be Wesley's ". . . something . . ." that broke for us. It would happen the following day, on Monday, and it would work because Alvin would become the most unlikely hero in the history of Emery Junior High School.

Alvin Bond was an Our Sider, geographically and by heritage, but he never quite belonged to that inner circle of rule and example. Alvin was like a leftover thought in a conversation, something you meant to say but didn't and when you remembered it, the conversation was over. It was partly because he lived on the Harrison side of Highway 17 and the rest of us lived on the Goldmine side. And it was partly because he was sixteen years old and only a ninth grader. Alvin had failed the fourth, the sixth, and the eighth grades—not because he was dumb, but because his teachers did not understand his nature.

Alvin was shy, shy in a thin, emaciated way that described him emotionally as well as physically. He was at least five feet, ten inches tall and his arms were three inches longer than those of anyone in Emery. He weighed, probably, one hundred and twenty pounds, and the way he stood, shoulders pointed, hands folded in front, he looked like a praying mantis. During all his years at Emery, Alvin had stayed to himself. If he had any friends, none of us knew it, though everyone from Our Side had a kind feeling for him. Alvin was all right, as far as we knew.

We had even become accustomed to watching Alvin walk backward. Alvin walked backward all the time. Even when we lined up to march into the auditorium for Friday assembly, Alvin walked backward. And he never spoke. Never. There was a story that he had once talked during an arithmetic lesson in the seventh grade, asking Old Lady Blackwall if he could go pee. But that flood of rhetoric was followed by a two-year silence. Some of the Highway 17 Gang would occasionally kid Alvin about the cat's having his tongue and Alvin would stare them down with a contemptuous, never-blinking gaze. I once heard Dupree whisper, "Damn! That boy's the champion stare-downer of all time."

Staring people down used to be a test of character in Emery.

It was recess on Monday, and we were working out for a softball game against Airline. It was a day of high-pitched chatter, the ripe swat of a Louisville Slugger against a bruised Spalding practice ball, the "Attay, babe! Attay, babe!" compliments for a perfectly fielded grounder, and the grand posing of swinging three bats in the on-deck circle. We were not a great softball team, but when we worked out we looked able enough.

And during this workout, Alvin slipped up to Freeman in a kind of backward shuffle and said, "I can throw a curve."

Freeman almost fainted. The workout chatter died to a funeral quiet. Alvin Bond had spoken. After two years, from needing to pee in the seventh grade to a workout for a softball game with Airline, Alvin Bond had finally spoken.

"What'd you say, Alvin?" asked Freeman.

"Uh—I—I can, well, throw a curve."

"With a softball?"

"Uh—er—uh-huh." Alvin cleared his throat. He had overworked his voice. "Uh—with anythin'."

"Good God! He talks!" Dupree exclaimed. "Whatta say, boy?"

Freeman whirled toward Dupree. "Shuttup!" he snapped.

Alvin twisted his head, exercising the vocal cords in his neck. He was embarrassed. "I can throw a curve, that's all," he said timidly.

"If you can throw one, I damn well wanta see it," Freeman said, handing Alvin the ball.

Alvin held the ball in both hands, tucked his head and tried to drag a sound out of his throat.

"Go on, Alvin, ol' boy, you can do it," coaxed Freeman.

The team gathered around Freeman, who squatted behind home plate.

"Go on, Alvin."

"Yeah, boy, c'mon."

"Attay, babe, Alvin."

"C'mon, boy. You can do it."

The encouragement was coming from everyone, including members of the Highway 17 Gang. Dupree scowled, but he knew to keep quiet.

Alvin inched his way toward the pitching mound, twitching and trying to hide behind himself. At the mound, he hesitated and took five long steps backward, toward second base.

"Whatcha doin', Alvin?" yelled Freeman.

Alvin tried to explain with his hands, but he looked like a spastic in a semaphore contest. "Too close," he finally called. "Ain't baseball distance."

"You gonna throw from out there?"

Alvin nodded, his head bobbing awkwardly on the hinge of a foot-long neck. "Where you supposed to be, throwin' baseball-like," he answered.

"Damn walkin' expert, ain't he?" Dupree said.

"Shuttup, Dupree." It was Sonny, Dupree's buddy.

But Alvin had heard Dupree's sass. He dropped his head for a long moment and plowed at the ground with the toe of his shoe.

"You gonna plant cotton out there, boy?" razzed Dupree.

"Shuttup, Dupree," Sonny repeated.

"C'mon, Alvin! Anytime you ready, let rip!" Freeman called.

Alvin fidgeted with his fingers on the softball, turned his back to Freeman and went into his windup, a grotesquely funny contortion of arms and legs. He whipped suddenly around and the ball hummed like a faraway airplane. Three feet from a direct path to Freeman's glove, it snapped left and Freeman missed catching it by two feet. The ball hit Dupree in his crotch and Dupree hit the ground. If Dupree had not had his hands poked down inside his pants playing with himself, the ball would have castrated him.

"Damn!" Freeman muttered in disbelief. "Damn!"

Alvin had actually thrown a curve. None of us had ever before seen a curve, and Alvin, backward-walking, never-talking Alvin, had thrown a curve that deserved to be bronzed and kept forever.

We were humbled by what we had seen. Dupree wallowed in the dirt, gasping for air, but no one moved to help him, not even Sonny.

"I can't believe it," exclaimed Freeman, leading us to Alvin. "Hey, Alvin! How'd you do it?"

We were in a circle around Alvin. He pulled at his pants, kicked at a clod of dirt, and looked away toward the railroad track. Finally, he said, "The Secret. My daddy taught me The Secret."

"What's The Secret, Alvin?" asked Freeman eagerly.

"Uh—it's a—uh—secret."

"Well, hell." Freeman laughed. "I reckon it would be. When'd you learn it, Alvin?"

Alvin looked at Freeman, then looked away. "Yesterday."

"Can you throw a curve underhanded, Alvin?" asked Wesley.

"Uh—I guess."

"Sure would be good if you could pitch softball for us," Wesley suggested.

Freeman agreed. "That's the truth. What'd y'all think, boys?"

"Attay, babe, Alvin!"

"Attay, babe, boy!"

Alvin smiled and blushed. I had never seen Alvin smile. He even had skinny teeth.

It was symbolic, in a pleasing way, that Dupree had been cut down by Alvin Bond's curve. Alvin captured the fancy of every boy in school and his new leadership on the mound inspired a unity between Our Side and the Highway 17 Gang. It was a cautious, guarded unity and it did not spill over into our social behavior, but it was real enough when we performed battle with Airline and Goldmine and Harrison and the other junior high schools in our area. Alvin could throw a rising underhand curve, and he had amazing speed and control. As an added attraction, Alvin was persuaded to offer a demonstration of his ability with a baseball after each at-home softball game. He was so unbelievable with a baseball he became a community celebrity within two weeks and farmers would actually quit plowing to watch him pitch. William Pruitte, who had lost a leg in World War II and returned to Emery to become the only wooden-legged umpire of organized baseball in America, was so impressed by Alvin he began to make plans for Alvin to pitch for the Harrison Hornets, a Sunday afternoon team of men who were part of a five-county amateur league. William said Alvin was the greatest baseball pitcher he had ever seen in Georgia, and Alvin had never pitched a game.

"Don't matter," William declared. "You'll see."

Alvin's wondrous talent gave Our Side a hero, and an improved image. We quickly included him in every new ground decision. We encouraged him to talk, applauded his concentration in learning to walk sideways, and we never stopped talking about The Secret. To us, The Secret was as perplexing as the formula for Coca-Cola. And that is the way Alvin liked it. Nothing could pry The Secret from Alvin, not even a crowbar.

"No need to guess," Alvin advised us. "You could look at me throw a million times and you'd never see it."

Alvin was rapidly nudging his way into adulthood, yet he still honored Wesley's leadership. Alvin had been in the fight, swatting anyone who stumbled in his direction, and he had heard Wesley's challenge of Dewitt Hollister and the entire Highway 17 Gang, and he knew he would never do anything to match that courage. Besides, Alvin thought of the REA as a miracle and Wesley was someone who could peer in the haze of Time Unknown and describe sensations of things to come that made our nerves freeze with anticipation. Alvin used to say, again and again, "My mama's gonna love it when the REA comes."

In small, incomplete ways, Alvin's presence enabled us to intrude on the dominance of the Highway 17 Gang in Emery. We knew we were about to step into their world, yet we insisted on keeping our identity. There were days when Sonny, or Wayne, or Ted and Ed, or others, made guarded suggestions about joining us for weekend games, but Dupree would impose his influence and his straying troops would fall back into their places, whimpering for forgiveness.

The restrained stand-off between our two societies was orderly and almost lasted to the end of the school term.

Almost.

Two days before school ended in spring of 1947, Wesley's year, Our Side suffered an unspeakable horror: the relationship between Megan and me became an embarrassing public spectacle.

"Megan Priest! Bring that piece of paper to me, young lady!" It was Old Lady Blackwall. Her buzzard's eyes danced with glee, and her buzzard's voice squawked its claim on the small folded note in Megan's hand. Megan's body convulsed with the fear of having been discovered. She could not move.

"Megan Priest! Do you hear me, young lady? Bring that piece of paper to me. Now!"

I did not like the way Old Lady Blackwall yelled at Megan. If she made Megan cry, I silently vowed, I would put nails under her car tires.

"Megan!"

Megan slipped slowly, fearfully, out of her desk. Her hand clutched the note. She started toward Old Lady Blackwall, paused and turned quickly to look at me.

Dear God in Holy Heaven! It can't be! It can't be!

"So, what's this, Miss Megan?" Old Lady Blackwall said. "We don't have passing notes in this room, young lady. Let me have it."

"I—I wasn't—goin'—goin' to pass it . . ."

"Don't tell me what you were and weren't going to do, young lady. I know all about note-writers, I do! Let me have it!"

Megan surrendered the note and started easing back to her desk. The entire class listened and watched.

"Stay! Stay right where you are," Old Lady Blackwall ordered.

"Yes'm," Megan whispered.

Paul Tully giggled and I made a quick note to kick his tail after school, or knock out another tooth.

Old Lady Blackwall unfolded the note with sickening ceremony, mocking each crease Megan had pressed into the paper. She read to herself with a smiling, conquering expression, mouthing the words.

"Well, well, well," she finally said. "It seems we have a little romance going on right here in our room at Emery Junior High School."

O Holy Father, strike her dumb and I will go to revival every night this year!

". . . And you'd never guess between who . . ."

Maybe I should fake a heart attack, I thought. Roll over and fall out right here on the floor.

". . . Well, of course, you must expect little Megan here is one of the parties, unless, of course, she's passing along a note for one of her friends . . ."

Yes! Yes! Yes! O God, if you love me, please let that be it!

". . . Is that it, Megan?"

Megan shook her head and whispered, "No'm."

"Well, I suggest that the entire class should share in this rare experience. Why don't you return to your seat, Megan, and I'll share your, ah, lovely thoughts with the rest of the class."

Megan retreated to her seat. She was crushed, totally humiliated. She managed to peek at me as she turned to sit, and I knew what to expect.

Old Lady Blackwall took her position dead-center in front of the class. She cleared her throat, adjusted her glasses, and began to read in a voice of great pleasure.

" 'School will be out in two days and I know I shouldn't do this, but I just had to write you a letter to tell you I'll miss you this summer. Maybe I'll get a chance to see you when you come to the cotton gin with your daddy. I'll watch for your wagon . . .' "

Old Lady Blackwall looked up from the letter and

smiled. She wanted Megan to feel every knife blow of her insult; Old Lady Blackwall wanted bloodless blood, a soundless scream for mercy.

" 'I hope you didn't think I was pushing myself on you,' " Old Lady Blackwall continued, pronouncing each word with severe emphasis. " 'And I want you to know I've kept every picture you've drawn for me, and will always keep them for as long as I live. Maybe you'll draw some for me this summer and I can get them if I see you at the cotton gin.' "

I could feel a thousand eyes turn toward me. Megan stared at her desk and Old Lady Blackwall turned the dagger in my heart: "And it's signed, 'Love, Megan.' Now isn't that sweet? Pictures? Who do we know who draws pictures?" She looked straight at me. Dupree laughed aloud. Sonny and Wayne buried their faces in their arms and giggled. No one from Our Side stirred to stop their taunting.

"Colin . . ." The sound of my name from Old Lady Blackwall exploded in my temples and my bravery shattered like fine crystal being dropped. "Colin, could it be you that this letter is meant for?"

Ten thousand eyes hated me. A judge with a skull face laughed at me from a high, black podium. A gargoylish hunchback stood beside a hangman's noose and motioned for me with long, dirty fingers. Wesley stood before St. Peter and begged for my admittance into heaven. "He told the truth and they killed him just the same," Wesley was saying.

"Colin?"

"Me? No'm," I lied. "It ain't me. I can't draw a

straight line with a ruler."

"Well, now, that's odd," Old Lady Blackwall insisted. "Just last week, Mrs. Simmons was telling us how proud she was of your artistic ability. She even showed us some of the examples of your work and I agreed with her. You're quite talented, indeed. Especially drawing dogs."

A million mouths spit at me. Two giants held my hands as midgets drove needles under my fingernails. Tiny tongues of fire licked at my feet as old women in rags threw torches on the kerosene-soaked heart-of-pine kindling surrounding me. Wesley stood in a corner with his back to me.

"Ah—uh—them," I stuttered.

"Yes, Colin?" teased Old Lady Blackwall.

"Uh—I—I done them by—by tracin'. Yes'm, that's it. Tracin'. Just helping out Mrs. Simmons. She wanted some stuff for the kids."

"Tracing? Now, it didn't look like tracing to me. Megan, why don't you bring me your Blue Horse tablet and let me see what's in it? I'm sure there must be something in it that could help us solve this little mystery."

Old Lady Blackwall's investigation revealed drawings of three dogs and one Persian cat, unmistakably committed in my hand. She pinned the drawings to the bulletin board with great theatrics, slicing open the wounds both Megan and I had suffered by describing each drawing with deadly cynicism. There was nothing to do but die and take my chances. I held my breath, thinking I would faint. Splotches of purple danced and ping-ponged behind my eyes, but I could not pass out. Some mechanism in my body forced me to breathe.

The recess bell finally rang and the classroom erupted in giggles and snickering. Except for the members of Our Side; they were absolutely silent. The Highway 17 Gang danced happily out of the room, and Paul walked over to me.

"I reckon you better meet us down at the new ground," he said, his voice chilled with hate.

"Leave me alone!"

"You be there," warned Paul.

Old Lady Blackwall stopped the exchange.

"Paul, you and the others clear on out. I want to talk to Megan and Colin for a minute. Go on, now. Scat!"

Paul and the others from Our Side moved slowly outside, staring at me.

When they left, Old Lady Blackwall leaned against the front of her desk. She had a ruler in her hand and kept tapping it against a chair in front of her.

"Now, I want you both to know that I strongly disapprove of this kind of conduct," she preached. "You're far too young to be having sweethearts and I just will not have note-passing in my room. I'm tempted to let your parents know about this and let them take care of it, but I won't. Not if you promise to stop this silly behavior right now."

Megan did not answer. She looked angry. I wanted to kick Old Lady Blackwall.

"We ain't done nothin'," I protested. "Nothin'. It ain't against the law to draw pictures and give 'em away, and it ain't against the law to be friends."

"Now, you just hold it, young man!" Old Lady Blackwall was suddenly furious. "You hold it a minute, or I'll wear a hole in your pants, and I mean it! I'm tired of you and your brother sassing me. Talking to me like I don't know as much as you. Well, I'm a schoolteacher and I know more, and you'd better get used to that!"

Of course, I thought. Now I knew why Old Lady Blackwall decided to make an example of Megan and me. It wasn't because of Megan and it wasn't because of me; it was because of Wesley. Wesley was constantly correcting her mistakes as she attempted to teach us the conjugation of verbs or the capitals of the 48 states, or some other mystery. Wesley was a frustration to her, but she would never dare cross Wesley; such a match would have been embarrassing, and she knew it.

"Yes'm," I mumbled. "I'm sorry."

"Now, that's better! But I want a promise from both of you. Quit this silly carrying on. I know what it can lead to."

"Yes'm," I said.

"Megan?"

Megan tossed her head proudly, angrily. "Yes," she said sternly. "I promise."

"All right. Now you can be dismissed," Old Lady Blackwall said sweetly. Then she added, "If either of you ever have any problems, let me know and I'll be happy to talk to you. Go on, now, you're dismissed."

Dismissed?

Dismissed to what? Outside, Paul and Freeman and R. J. and Alvin and Otis and Jack waited to escort me to the new ground. They circled around me, like some prisoner being led before a firing squad. They said nothing, but occasionally Freeman would shove at me, his strong, bony fingers digging into my side. As we marched to the Condemned Man cadence, Dupree led the Highway 17 Gang in a victory dance around us.

"Hey, boy, can't you find no girls over there in the swamp good enough for you?"

"Why didn't you tell us you was a ar-tise, Colin? We'd of posed for you."

"You gonna let me have a autograph, boy?"

"Draw me a pig, sweetie!"

"You better watch it, boy, that girl belongs to ol' Dupree here and he's gonna whip your butt, boy!" teased Wayne.

The remark about Dupree and Megan was too much. I whirled and made a dash to break through the ring of my escort. Megan wouldn't give Dupree the time of day, and I was going to whip Wayne Heath's tail in front of God and recess for telling such a lie.

Freeman grabbed me by the shirt, picked me straight off the ground and handed me to Alvin and R. J. Sometimes I forgot that I was the youngest and smallest of Our Side.

"Let me go, Freeman!" I screamed.

"Shuttup!" Freeman commanded. He turned to face Dupree. "I don't know what you think's so funny, Dupree. At least Colin went for a girl at school when he started courtin'."

Dupree's face clouded in suspicion, and he shivered slightly under Freeman's steel gaze. "What're you talkin' about, butt-hole? That ain't just no girl he's messin' around with. That's my girl."

"She don't know it if she is," Freeman answered. "Besides, I hear you ain't got no idea about girls."

Freeman's words fell like stone on Dupree. The laughing stopped. The jeering stopped. The moving stopped.

"You better say what you mean, hick," cautioned Dupree.

"I don't have to say nothin'. Everybody in Emery knows what you did when you was spendin' the night on your granddaddy's farm last summer."

Dupree turned red. Sweat popped out on his forehead.

"Did?" Dupree shouted. "I didn't do nothin'. What you talking about, boy?"

"In the barn," Freeman answered. "One of your granddaddy's hands saw you, whether you think he did or not."

Dupree was outraged. Sonny and Wayne stepped away from him.

"What'd you do?" Sonny asked. A dozen answers must have flashed in his mind.

Dupree was foaming at the lips, a mad dog cornered.

"I didn't do nothin'!" groaned Dupree. "Nothin'! He's making it up! I'm tellin' you, he's making it up!"

"You must've done somethin'," Wayne said. "Everybody knows it."

"Everybody? Who, everybody?" raved Dupree.

"Ain't nobody ever heard anything, because he just made it up, butt-hole! Didn't nothin' happen on that farm when I was there last summer. Nothin'!"

"Don't sound right," Sonny replied.

"It ain't right," exploded Dupree. "Freeman's makin' it up."

"Well, boy, that's for me to know and for you to find out," answered Freeman in a man's deep voice. He turned easily and pushed us away toward the new ground. "Yessir, for me to know and you to find out," he repeated, laughing.

"I'll pay you back for that, Freeman Boyd," shouted Dupree. "I swear to God and Jesus, I'll pay you back, boy! You gonna hate this day before I'm through with you, boy!"

Wesley was hurt and displeased with my behavior, and I knew he was remembering the lie I had told him about being in the classroom with Megan. I wanted to explain about the lie. I wanted to tell him I had hidden away in Black Pool Swamp to find courage, but that was an ancient transgression. The discovery of my drawings in Megan's Blue Horse tablet was the issue. I had broken our code. Worse, I had broken our code because of a girl.

The punishment was proposed by Paul and it was severe: I was denied the privilege of running with Our Side for a month. No matter what happened, I could not belong. A beating would have been far kinder, far less painful. For the first time, I would be separated from Wesley, and for the first time I experienced the fumbling, remote feeling of insecurity.

I stayed to myself the rest of the day, voluntarily removed from Wesley and the others of Our Side. Freeman's cloudy accusation of Dupree's conduct was a higher grade of gossip than any awkward romance, and I was soon forgotten in the crossfire of charges and denials, speculation and certainties (it was shocking how many people remembered hearing "something" about Dupree).

I entertained my aloneness by thinking of my punishment as a sacrifice for Megan. In geography we had studied about monks in several Asian countries and how they could go forever being alone and purifying themselves with the harsh discipline of inner meditation. If they could do it, so could I. I was the descendant of a Cherokee Indian—even if the English and Irish and Scottish coagulation did dominate 95 percent of my heritage—and everyone knew Indians could sit for hours without moving or blinking.

I was thinking about this, and imagining Megan off in a whispery, other world, when Wesley interrupted.

"You better c'mon," he said. "The school bus is loading."

"I ain't ridin' the school bus," I answered defiantly.

"What're you gonna do?"

"I'm walkin' home, that's what."

"Daddy'll give you a whippin', too."

"What'd I care?"

"Ain't no need to be mad," Wesley said gently. "You knew the rules. You got to live by them, just like the rest of us."

I wanted to tell Wesley that it was his fault, that Old Lady Blackwall punished me because of him. But I couldn't. That would've been babyish. Besides, Indians knew how to take punishment and I was a descendant of a Cherokee.

"Don't care," I finally said. "I'm walkin' home just the same."

"All right. But there ain't nothin' I can do when Daddy whips you."

I waited below the canning plant for the school bus to leave, carrying its chattering, writhing, covey of birdlike passengers to be deposited at mailboxes, intersections, and turn-offs over thirty-three miles of unpaved, red, washboard country roads. Watching them leave numbed me. A cruel, sarcastic reality echoed in an obscene falsetto of the chattering and laughter trailing the bus: one of its covey was missing and no one cared.

I tucked the two books for study in the crook of my arm and began walking rapidly through Clarence Sosbee's cotton field, headed for Clarence Sosbee's woods, where the finest natural spring in Emery bubbled up at the roots of a stately beech tree. Sosbee's Spring had the sweetest water in the world and there were Negroes in Emery who swore the nectar of that water cured illnesses, and that it was somehow connected to the Jordan River through an underground channel. I had believed that story, or half-believed it, for years, and I could never pass Sosbee's Spring without cupping a swallow of water in my hands and drinking slowly, waiting the miracle of the Jordan River. There were times when my body would tremble as the water released its coolness, and for the briefest flickering of time, I would see wholly the vision of Shining Heaven and Shining Jesus wearing a crown of stars.

I needed the water and I needed its curative, mystic powers. I had betrayed Our Side, but it was I who felt betrayed. Long, snaking vines of emotion twisted and climbed the trunk of my neck, choked off reason and sapped whatever false energy my defiance had forced to surface. The water was cool, sweet with the sweetness of moss and earth and roots and millions of years of slow evolution. I listened for the muted, whistling sound of the spring water happily swirling down the throat of a slender gully, playing against the delicate reeds of swamp grass that folded its leaves into the water. Somehow, to me, that sound was in perfect concert with the lyrics of mockingbirds and sparrows and wrens that flitted through the small undergrowth of mountain laurel, and that sound enveloped anyone who stopped to listen, and wonder.

I was slumped against a pillow of leaves when Megan spoke.

"Are you mad at me?" she asked.

I rolled to one side and brushed the leaves off my shirt. Megan. Pale green eyes, hair as blond as a full moon.

"No," I said. "I'm not mad. How'd you know I was here?"

"I watched you. Why didn't you ride the bus?"

"I wanted to walk home," I answered. "Wesley was pretty upset about everything."

"Pleasing him means a lot to you."

"Naw," I lied. "Naw. I just didn't want to do no arguin' on the bus, that's all."

"Oh . . ."

Megan sat beside the beech tree that fed from Sosbee's Spring. She picked up a long stick and began to make cursive sweeps across the top of the water, skimming the surface like a nimble water spider racing its own reflection in the silver of sunshine that had shattered on impact. She looked very peaceful.

"It made me mad, what Mrs. Blackwall did," she said.

"Me, too."

"I meant what I said in that letter," she added boldly. "I will be missin' you this summer. Sometimes I wish school wouldn't take off for the summer."

"Yeah, well, me, too. Sometimes," I agreed. "Especially after workin' all day in the fields."

"I don't have to work in any fields."

"You're lucky and just don't know it," I said. "Gets hot."

"I watch the workers come in sometimes, down at Dupree's daddy's store," she sympathized. "They look all used up, or somethin'."

"You didn't have to mention Dupree," I replied cynically. "You ain't his girl, are you?"

Megan's face snapped up. She was angry. "No! Where'd you hear that?"

"What he said," I told her. "That's what he said, and

Sonny and Wayne said the same thing."

"Well, they're liars, that's what! I wouldn't snap a finger for Dupree Hixon."

Megan's denial of Dupree pleased me, made me alive and joyful.

"You mean that?" I asked.

"Of course I mean it. I don't know how you could even think such a thing." Her eyes sparkled with anger. She threw the stick to one side and stood.

"Well, you don't have to go gettin' mad at me," I said. "I ain't done nothing but tell you what they said, what they said was true."

"It ain't."

"All right. You say it ain't, it ain't."

"You don't know nothin', do you, Colin Wynn? If I got a boyfriend, it's you. I bought you enough Three Musketeers to prove that, I guess, and it was me who wrote that letter and got caught at it. Me!"

"Well, don't yell at me," I said, standing. "I didn't do nothin'."

"I got to go," Megan said quickly. "Mama'll be wonderin' where I am if I don't get home."

"Yeah, me, too."

Megan paused and turned to look at me. "Well, are you?" she asked.

"Am I what?"

"Are you my boyfriend or not? I don't want to go spendin' the whole summer not knowing."

"Uh—yeah—yeah. I reckon. Ah—what—what am I supposed to do?"

"Do? You don't have to do nothing. Goodbye." She

pivoted and walked briskly away. Then she stopped and again turned to me.

"Uh—goodbye," I replied feebly.

"I just wanted you to know something," she said. "You remember when I won that last spelling bee for being able to spell the word 'semicolon'? Well, I remembered how to spell it because I broke it down and sounded it out to say 'See-Me-Colin.' And that's all I want you to do. See me. Sometimes when I think you don't notice me, it hurts so much, it—it burns! And—and—goodbye!"

See-Me-Colin. See-Me-Colin. Megan wanted me— *me*—to notice her.

I ran the two miles home. Daddy whipped me for missing the school bus. I didn't care. It didn't hurt. I had been to the Jordan River and the Jordan River could cure pain even before it happened.

8

For three weeks I obeyed the probation that had been approved as punishment. School was closed and we worked the fields from early to late, from gray smoke of morning to gray smoke of night. It was hard work, hard and silent and tediously slow. But it gave dreamers a chance to dream, and in the repetitive swing of a hoe or the again-and-again curl of dirt sliding off the sweep of a plow, I began to realize wondrous changes were taking place in my life. I was older and I had wrestled with the sensitivity of caring for someone who did not belong to my north and south, east and west isolation. The REA was coming, and its thin wires would knit us into the fabric of the huge glittering costume, Earth. We watched the survey crews, with their tripods and funny little telescopes, and hand signals that said, "No, no! To the left! Too much! Ah, that's it! That's perfect!" At night, sitting in the orange-yellow light of a kerosene lamp, we would talk about electric stoves and electric refrigerators ("It'll be a Frigidaire," declared Mother) and running water and an indoor bathroom, and we imagined our home beaming and twinkling with light, a Christmas-tree home in dark nights.

Sundays were gloomy, painful days during the three weeks of probation. Wesley and Freeman and R. J. and Paul and Otis and Jack would ride with Dover or William Pruitte to Harrison to watch Alvin pitch baseball, and they would return home to tell splendid tales of Alvin's exploits. Their stories hurt more than not being with them.

Wesley must have sensed my longing. On the Sunday of the fourth week of probation, he said, "C'mon. You can go with us."

"Wait a minute, Wes," objected Paul. "He's got today left before he can tag along. That's what we said."

"Well, let's cut it short," Wesley replied. "Bein' out of school, and all that, Colin ain't been with nobody to play with."

"Well . . ." Paul stammered.

"Aw, hell, let him come along," agreed Freeman. "Alvin's goin' after his third no-hitter today."

"All right," Paul muttered, "but it ain't exactly right."

As the Harrison Hornets' only pitcher, Alvin had become a legend in less than a month. William's prediction had been conservative: Alvin was probably the greatest pitcher of baseballs in the entire world, not just the state of Georgia.

According to Freeman, Alvin's accomplishments in baseball were due only in part to The Secret. More important was the inspiration of an unusual bargain.

As Freeman interpreted it, Alvin's career in baseball almost ended before it started. Alvin had begun dating the daughter of a Holiness preacher, discovering a new meaning to the scriptural admonition that God ". . . moves in mysterious ways . . ." Alvin—said Freeman—did not know the difference between a holy twitch and a bump and grind. He was inclined to become disturbed with either intention, and the preacher's daughter was given to holy twitches.

William and Fred Thaxton, who managed the Harrison Hornets, became distraught over the thought of losing Alvin to all-day church services and they plotted to divert Alvin's attention.

And that is how Delores Fisk became involved.

Delores Fisk was a rare young woman whose passion was equaled only by her physical agility and sense of logic. But Delores was not a regular lady of questionable virtue. Leaping into bed at the snap of a finger did not appeal to her; she needed a cause. Fred explained the plight of the Harrison team and Delores agreed the cause was worthy. Helping a baseball team in distress was certainly as noble as the celebration of Confederate Memorial Day, she decided.

Delores ripped Alvin limb from limb. She bounced him off the walls of her house trailer. She corrected his sideways walk and made him strut, then she reduced him to a quivering lump of disjointed flesh and bone.

Fred later thanked her for her cooperation.

"Well, he ain't much to look at," Delores reportedly told Fred, "but he's somethin' when he gets it in gear."

"Yeah," Fred reportedly agreed. "You couldn't call him a ballplayer by lookin' at him, that's for sure. Alvin's so skinny you could x-ray him with a flash-light, but he's hell when he's throwin'."

And then Delores proudly announced her bargain: "I told him, for every no-hitter he could come back."

Fred was ecstatic. "Honey, you better put a pallet on the floor; Alvin'll be livin' here," he said. Reportedly. According to Freeman.

I suspected there was some truth in Freeman's tale. Alvin was a changed man, even in warm-ups. His fast-ball was a lethal weapon. His curve and screwball had three breaks—30 degrees, 60 degrees, and 90 degrees. His knuckleball looked drunk; it would run up to a hitter, stop, tap dance, take a bow, and flutter back to the catcher's mitt like a butterfly landing on a honey-suckle. He developed a pitch he called the Buckdance, one called the Gee-Haw, one called the Balloon, and one he reportedly (according to Freeman *and* Dover) named for Delores, called the Do-It-Again. And Alvin had control. I swear he could have thrown in the strike zone of a piss ant if the piss ant could have hoisted a bat. It was easier to hit a flying gnat in the tail with a Red Ryder BB gun than it was to hit Alvin.

But there was even more astonishing proof of Alvin Bond's greatness as a baseball pitcher. After his warmup, Alvin waited and chatted to Freeman and Wesley and me as Winslow Dees, his catcher, unlaced his catcher's mitt and put a thawed-out steak in the lining.

"What's he doin' that for, Alvin?" I asked.

"Shoot, that's right, ain't it? You ain't been around," replied Alvin. "Well, that's so ol' Winslow can catch my stingers without breakin' his hand."

I was stunned. "What?"

"Yeah," Freeman explained. "That meat takes the pounding. Shoot, it ain't as thick as a piece of paper when the game's over."

On that Sunday there was a scheduled double-header against Danielsville. Alvin won the first game, 5-0, on a two-hitter, and it was thrilling to watch his long body whipping off the mound in an awkward contradiction of arms and legs working independent of his body. Alvin's windup defied gravity and the laws of anatomy, but it worked for him and all of us knew that somewhere in that tangle of movement was The Secret.

But it was the second game that I remember.

In the second game, Alvin volunteered to pitch for both teams because the Danielsville pitcher had to leave early to lead singing in a revival.

In the second game, Alvin did something that should

have made the *Guinness Book of World Records*, or the *Book of Baseball Records*, or at least *The Royston Record*: he threw two no-hitters in the same game. He struck out 32 batsmen, walked only five and was tied with himself, 0-0, in the thirteenth inning when the game was called for frustration.

Alvin was philosophic about it. "If I could have hit against myself," he said, "I'd of struck out a bunch more men."

And Alvin left smiling, steering his daddy's Ford in the direction of Delores Fisk's house trailer.

On those Sundays when we watched baseball at Harrison we did not attend Methodist Youth Fellowship at Emery Methodist Church. It meant not seeing Megan and Megan had become hauntingly important. The REA and Alvin had made summer alive and adventuresome, fuller than any summer, and I could feel energy spilling out of me, expiring in the heat of work and the heat of play. Yet, I missed Megan.

But there was the upcoming week of Bible school and revival, when Methodist members of the Highway 17 Gang and Our Side would meet for a week of play and treats, subtly conditioned by spirited tales of the Old Testament and nightly invitations to submit our worthless souls to the altar of the hymn, "Revive Us Again." I would see Megan then. I was even half-considering two or three occasions of conversion, just to impress her.

Wesley and I had been talking about Bible school and revival as we worked. Wesley was wondering about the qualifications of the guest preacher; I was concerned with a rumor that we would not have a final-day party. We often talked about different things in the same conversation. Wesley forgave me for being secular, and I forgave him for being ecclesiastical. We were very close.

We did not see Freeman, as he emerged from the pine stand below us.

"Hoooooo, boys!" he yelled.

He was shirtless and barefoot. In summer, Freeman became a bronze boy god. His skin turned deep brown the first day he peeled his shirt and he swam so much that the muscles of his chest knotted into tight bands of rope. He was only a year older than Wesley, but at least two inches taller, and in summer, with his bronze body, his faded-blue eyes and auburn-blond hair, Freeman could have passed for a sixteen-year-old.

"Slavin' away, I see," Freeman called cheerfully as he walked up to where we were mopping cotton for early boll weevils.

"Yea," answered Wesley. "You ever done any work, Freeman?"

"Nothin' as crazy as slopping molasses and junk on cotton. There's better ways, boys. Better ways."

"Yeah, doin' nothing," I said.

"Nothin'? Who said anything about nothin'? I'm about to take me a full-time job, ol' buddy."

"Doin' what?" I asked.

Freeman laughed and plopped down on the ground between two rows of cotton. "Well, you ain't gonna believe it, boys, but I'm goin' to work next week for

Old Man Hixon."

"Hixon!" I exclaimed.

"Dupree's daddy?" asked Wesley. "You going to work for Dupree's daddy?"

"That's right, boys. That is absolutely, dead-on-it right."

"You know you ain't supposed to have anything to do with them," I protested. "Ain't that right, Wesley? What goes for me, goes for Freeman."

"Why, it ain't the same at all," Freeman argued. "I'm just gettin' me a job. Ol' Wesley's always after me for bein' lazy."

"It's the same," I snapped.

"Aw, c'mon, Colin, it ain't and you know it," Wesley replied. "How'd you get a job workin' for Mr. Hixon, Freeman?"

"Damndest thing you ever saw, Wes . . ."

"Watch your cussin', Freeman. I got sisters at the end of the row."

"Sorry, Wes. Anyway, Dover Heller's been workin' summers in the warehouse and cotton gin for Old Man Hixon for years, but he's caught on with the REA, bound and determined he's gonna be a lineman, or somethin'. So when Old Man Hixon asked him about work this summer, Dover turned him down, told him he ought to hire me. And, by God, that's just what he done."

"I bet Dupree's having a fit," I said.

"I don't care if he stands on his nutty head and rattles his brain," Freeman declared. "It don't make one whit to me. Ol' Dupree don't do nothin' but stand around that candy counter all day, playin' big shot. Anyhows, I'll be out in the warehouse. If I work it right, I won't even have to see him."

Wesley dabbed at the top of a cotton stalk with his mop. A black wad of calcium arsenic and blackstrap molasses rolled slowly to the edge of a leaf, pooled up, and thickened.

"Well, Freeman, I hope it works out," Wesley said. "I hope nothin' happens to get Dupree any madder'n he is at you."

"Hell, Wes, ol' Dupree stays mad at somebody all the time."

"Yeah, I reckon. Anyway, you better understand that his daddy expects you to be a hired hand, and he won't be puttin' up with any of your games, or cuttin' up. He'll fire you right on the spot, and you know it."

"Wesley, you worry too much, you know that? Anybody ever tell you that you're too plain serious about things? I know how to behave. You'd be shocked at how well I behave when I have a mind to."

"Freeman, I'd probably faint."

"Now, maybe you would, Wesley. Yessir, you just may."

Wesley picked up his bucket of molasses and dipped his mop into it. "Well, we gotta get to work, Freeman. Hope everythin' works out on the job."

"Tell you what, get me a bucket and I'll help you," Freeman volunteered.

"Naw. That's all right," Wesley answered. "Daddy'll think we takin' it easy if he sees you up here talkin' to us."

"Well, just thought I'd offer."

"We ain't got much more to do and we'll be finished," I said. "We quitting early so Mama can go have a meeting about revival."

"Revival," Freeman said suddenly. "Yeah. That's what I was gonna ask y'all about. You remember me tellin' you about ol' Preacher Bytheway? Well, he's havin' his Speaking-In-Tongues Traveling Tent Tabernacle revival next week over in Sosbee's pasture, down by the spring, and I thought maybe y'all would like to go over one night. It's a sight, boys! I'm guaranteeing you, it's somethin' not to be missed."

Wesley squinted at Freeman. Wesley did not like the way Freeman regarded a preacher's earnest attempt to spread the Lord's word. "Freeman," he said, "if you think it's a big circus, why do you go? Someday you're gonna need the help of the Almighty and you'll be sorry for everything you ever said about Preacher Bytheway."

Freeman grinned. He secretly enjoyed Wesley's sermonettes, because he knew Wesley cared.

"Yeah, Wes, you're right. Forgive me."

"It ain't me you need to be askin' forgiveness of, Freeman."

"You're right, Wes. Forgive me, Colin."

Wesley looked at Freeman and shook his head. "Someday, boy, you'll be regrettin' every little funny thing you ever tried to pull."

Freeman tried to supress a giggle. He wiped his hand over his face and the smile disappeared. Then he looked up with a serious, pleading expression. "Yea,

Wesley, I know. I know." The smile reappeared.

Freeman could not resist the temptation to tease and bewilder Wesley's simple confidence in spiritual matters. To Freeman, nothing was as joyful as being in Royston with Wesley and me on Saturday afternoons, and being confronted by a street preacher. The preacher would flail the air and gasp and quote something from the Bible, usually John 3:16, and he would pray and lay his hands on our heads and ask us if we had been saved. Freeman would tremble and quiver, and a whimper would rise out of his throat, and he would say, over and over, "Not till now, brother! Not till now! Oh! Oh! Oh! I feel it, brother! I feel it! The spirit's a-comin', brother! Lay on them hands, brother!" And the street preacher would get spastic and praise God from Horton's Drug Store to the Rialto Theater. Such behavior on Freeman's part would leave Wesley speechless and he would ignore Freeman for the rest of the day. I thought it was funny, because the same street preacher saved us an average of a dozen times each summer.

Freeman pestered Wesley until Wesley agreed to attend the Speaking-In-Tongues Traveling Tent Tabernacle one night during the following week.

"You won't regret it, Wesley, ol' boy, and I mean it," Freeman promised. "That ol' Preacher Bytheway's a quality preacher, even if he does look like a skinny boar hog when he's took up with the spirit."

"Freeman!"

"Well, Wesley, he does. Ask your mama or daddy. I bet they know of him."

Wesley did ask Mother if she had ever heard of Bartholomew Bytheway.

"Who, son?"

"Bytheway," Wesley answered. "By-the-way. That's his name, Freeman said."

"I believe I have heard of him. A traveling preacher . . ."

"Yes'm. That's what Freeman said, too."

"Well, I don't remember what it was I heard, but I'll ask around. Maybe he's that old man that's kin to Hilda Marsh's first cousin. Hilda was a Sutherland before she married. I'll ask, Wesley."

Mother believed even then that Wesley would someday stand behind a pulpit himself and she radiated with gladness whenever he asked questions about religion.

"Well, I'd appreciate whatever you can find out," Wesley answered. "Freeman wants us to go over to hear him at revival next week, and since it's the only time Freeman ever gets to a church, I thought we'd go."

"That's nice, Wesley. Are Freeman's mama and daddy going?" asked Mother.

"Freeman didn't say. Maybe his mama. His daddy won't, I guess."

"Well, there's people like that, Wesley," explained Mother.

"Yes'm."

Mother did ask about Rev. Bartholomew R. Bytheway and learned only that he was a fixture in certain small towns in Georgia and the Carolinas. Freeman, in a remarkably incoherent session of laughter and half-sentences, told the better story of the good reverend and his famous tent.

The tent had been purchased at auction in Greenville, South Carolina, when a traveling carnival called it quits one Saturday afternoon because the show's only trick horse choked on some oats and died. The Rev. Bytheway had been street-preaching in Greenville, practicing his call to evangelism. He needed experience, and he knew it. Until his calling, Bartholomew Bytheway had been a fertilizer salesman grasshopping up and down the Savannah River Valley for the Green Grow Fertilizer and Plant Food Company. But he had had his troubles. He didn't know 6-8-6 fertilizer from 6-10-10 fertilizer, and each year he lost more and more customers in the small towns along the rich bottomland of the Savannah River. It had been his failure as a fertilizer salesman and the gnawing aggravation of believing he was meant for better things that had driven Bartholomew Bytheway to street preaching—that and one night at a Holiness church, where he had gone to please a potential customer. On that night, with the spirit overflowing, Bartholomew Bytheway put down his fertilizer catalogue and picked up a Bible.

And so it happened that Rev. Bytheway purchased his tent and promptly dedicated it as the Speaking-In-Tongues Traveling Tent Tabernacle. Two months later, he bought a retired school bus with a dying Ford motor and a Blue Bird body. He had a sign painter scrape off the county school inscriptions and cover them with a picture of a man speaking fire. The fire rose out of the man's mouth and ballooned over his head. In the balloon, the words BE SAVED! had been printed in letters that looked like spears. Bartholomew Bytheway had then hired two guitar players from Gaffney to travel with him, and he had begun his ministry in the same small towns of the Savannah River Valley where he had tried to peddle fertilizer. Things had worked surprisingly well for Rev. Bytheway. People loved him. They loved his name, his anger, his shouting, his pleading, his threats. They loved the way he danced around and the way he slapped his hands in a tamborine rhythm. In short, they loved his showmanship, and to prove it they were willing to fling themselves before him and declare personal salvation.

We went to the Speaking-In-Tongues Traveling Tent Tabernacle revival on Tuesday evening. Freeman came up from Black Pool Swamp wearing an old pair of crumpled Sunday pants and a white shirt frayed around the collar. Wesley and I were sitting on the front porch with our mother, who had fussed and dusted us off for over an hour. Her face was literally blazing with pride. In the middle of the week, her two sons were going to a revival meeting with Freeman, that poor, misunderstood child who had nothing but a tubercular mother and a drunken father. In her way, Mother loved Freeman as much as she loved us.

"Hello, Freeman," Mother said. "My, but you're sure lookin' smart tonight!"

Freeman tucked his head. "Yes'm. Y'all ready?"

"They're ready, Freeman. Oh yes, they're ready. Freeman, it's real nice of you to invite the boys to go to your church. Some Sunday, you'll have to go with them to the Methodist preachin'."

"Yes'm."

"Now, you sure you don't want me to drive you over?"

Wesley was quick. "No, Mama. It ain't far. We'll walk."

Wesley knew that Freeman was too proud to accept a ride, even in a 1938 Ford.

"Yes'm. We'll walk. It ain't far through the swamp," Freeman assured her.

"But you might get all messy."

"No'm. I know the way."

Mother smiled and resigned herself to Freeman's determination. "Freeman, I do believe you know more about that old swamp than any man alive. I just can't believe you get around in it so easy in pitch dark."

"Yes'm."

Wesley stepped off the porch. "Well, Mama, we'll be in later."

"Be careful," Mother begged. She had never trusted the swamp.

But Mother was right about Freeman. He did know Black Pool Swamp. He knew Black Pool Swamp the way other people know their homes. Freeman had charted every rabbit path, every squirrel nest, and every foxhole in the swamp. He could walk through the mud and mire and never make a footprint. In Black

Pool Swamp, no man was Freeman's equal.

We crossed through the swamp, carefully following Freeman's exact steps. At the top of the hill overlooking Sosbee's Woods and Sosbee's Spring, we heard the faint singing of "The Old Rugged Cross."

". . . till my trophies at last I lay down . . ."

Their voices were muffled under the tent, and the wheezing of the tenors and altos pitched and bounced around the drooping canvas in a frenzy of discord wanting to escape.

". . . so I'll cherish the old rugged cro—osss . . ."

Freeman stopped and stood on a pine stump.

"You listen," he said happily. He smiled and spread his arms to hush us. "Hear ol' Preacher Bytheway singin' away?"

Preacher Bytheway's voice was clearly unusual. It came out of his nose and was compressed into a sound between the scratching of fingernails on a blackboard and the stripping of gears on Mother's old 1938 Ford.

". . . and exchange it some day for a crown . . ."

Freeman laughed aloud. "You ought to hear that fool doin' 'O For A Thousand Tongues to Sing.' Now that is class!"

We crossed into the pine-tree windbreak separating Sosbee's cotton field and Ben Looney's wheat field.

"C'mon, Methodists," Freeman said. "We are goin' to a circus!"

There were thirty-five or forty people sitting on wooden chairs that had been borrowed from the Emery Junior High School lunchroom. Fresh sawdust from Wray's Sawmill covered the ground and had been cooking all day under the heavy canvas. In the tent, it smelled like resin burning. People fanned themselves with fans that had a picture of Jesus knocking at a door without a handle on it. An advertisement for Higginbottom's Funeral Parlor was on the back of the fan, containing the message: Give Your Life to Jesus, Trust Your Remains to Us. Babies wiggled at their mother's feet, playing in the sawdust. Old men wearing bib overalls over starched, white shirts, sat rigidly still and mouthed the closing verse of "The Old Rugged Cross." Freeman and Wesley and I eased into three chairs in the last row, as the song ended.

"Glory! Oh, I say it again—glory! Glory! Glory! Glory! The Lord God Almighty and His holy house must be smilin' with pure pleasure sittin' out somewhere on a front porch of a cloud, rockin' and listenin' to such singing! Oh, I say it—help me, Jesus!—say it again! Glory! Glo-o-o-o-ry! Say it with me, good people! Say it so's the Lord God Almighty and His holy house can know we all feel the same wonderful way! Glo-o-o-o-o-o-ry!"

A half-dozen women answered.

Preacher Bytheway cupped his hand to his right ear and leaned forward, straining as though he had been struck deaf.

"What?! Now, the Lord God Almighty and His holy house couldn't hear that! Lordy, Lordy, Lordy! There's a reunion of angels and saints takin' place, havin' supper with the Almighty tonight, and they sure wanta hear that praise! Yessir! A big rush of wind come thunderin' by just as you let loose, and the Lord God

Almighty knows you was drowned out by it, so He wants it again! Glo-o-o-o-o-o-o-ry!!!"

The two guitar players lunged forward together and strummed hard and Preacher Bytheway stepped out toward the congregation.

"Say it, brothers and sisters!" he ordered. "Say it!"

His voice was begging. He closed his eyes and raised his head. The congregation looked up with him, all the way to the top of the tent where a swarm of gnats and moths were circling an electric light that had been strapped to the tent pole by tape. The electric lines running to the tent had been strung and connected to the school, which fed from Georgia Power Company.

"Say it! Glory! Glory! Glo-o-o-o-o-o-o-o-o-rrrrr-rry!"

He lifted his arms and locked his wrists together as if they were handcuffed. He sucked in his lips until they wrinkled in the gaps where he had missing teeth, and he began to nod his head up and down. His eyes and nose and lips drew together until they were a scab on his skinny face. His hair looked as though some maniac with scissors had whacked gaps out of it.

"GLO-O-O-O-O-O-RY!"

The congregation was overwhelmed by Preacher Bytheway's frenzy.

"Glory! Oh, glory, glory, glory!" The women's voices were shrill screams. The men rumbled in bass counterpoint.

"Wesley," I whispered, "he does look like a skinny boar hog, like Freeman said."

"Shuttup! It ain't how you look, it's what you say," Wesley shot back.

"He's right, Wes," Freeman said.

Wesley whirled to stare at Freeman. Freeman grinned and jumped up. "Glory!" he shouted. Wesley grabbed him by the shirt and jerked him down.

"Freeman, you doin' that to make me mad, and I know it! Now you shut up, or I'm leavin'!"

Freeman giggled into his hands and slipped down to the edge of the chair. "Glory, glory, glory," he said in a snickering, low, mocking voice.

Preacher Bytheway had reached the takeoff in his trip to the outer space of evangelism. The two guitar players from Gaffney began a soft chording of "What A Friend We Have In Jesus," and Preacher Bytheway picked up the bass dips with his arms, still locked at the wrists.

"Oh, the Lord does love joyful noises! Help me, Jesus! Make a joyful noise unto the Lord! Yes! Yes! And you can do it! You can! You can do miracles makin' joyful noises unto the Lord! Help me, Jesus! Give it over! Let it roll out of your souls! Say it to the Lord! And He will hear! He will hear! He will hear!"

Preacher Bytheway's voice began to singsong. He began to siphon off great gulps of air, nodding up and down, pumping with his locked wrists, twitching in the knees.

"He will hear! Go—go out and preach! Go OUT! OUT! Oh, oh, yes! Preach the gospel! Gos-pel! TO ALL MY PEOPLE! TO ALL MY PEOPLE! Help me, Jesus! ALL OVER THE WORLD! And tell them—tell them—tell them—OF MY WORDS!"

In the back of the tent we could see the congregation beginning to sway and rock, leaning into the beat. Someone started clapping in time. And another. And another. A baby crawled out into the aisle and started eating sawdust.

"Tonight! Tonight! I tell you! We are goin' to talk about—oh yes, talk about—God's holy word in treatin' all the creatures of the world with love and kindness! And how—help me, Jesus!—oh, how it is that hell's a-burnin' a thousand times hotter'n the sun to them that's mean and hateful and spiteful and—oh, help me, Jesus!—and stompin' on the weak and downtrodden! Oh, yes! Remember the Good Samaritan and how he stopped to help out the stranger! That's God's world a-workin' in God's word! Oh— oh, yes! It's there in the Bible! I say—help me, Jesus!—the Bible! It tells us about evil and good and how the two go 'round and 'round fightin', and how—oh, help me, Jesus!—how the Devil is sneakin' into every life he can find not tended by the good shepherd, Jesus . . ."

Wesley leaned forward in his chair. He could not believe Preacher Bytheway. He held his right hand over his heart.

"What's he sayin', Wesley?" I asked. "Is he all right?"

"He's being took. He's got the spirit," whispered Wesley.

I moved closer to Wesley. "I don't want it," I said.
"What?"

"Wesley, let's go home. That spirit may get down here."

"It ain't no spook, crazy! He's took with the Holy Spirit!"

"Oh," I said. Preacher Bytheway was retching on holy words stuck in his throat. "Wesley, anybody at the Methodist Church ever been took with the spirit?"

"Lots of 'em. Hush."

"I never seen any."

"There's different ways of being took."

Freeman leaned into Wesley. "That's preachin'! Now, Wes, ol' boy, you ever see such preachin'?"

Wesley shot Freeman a look that would have killed a snake. Freeman laughed and sat back in his chair and began clapping his hands out of rhythm.

Preacher Bytheway was again behind his pulpit, pounding on the Bible and declaring that an Atlantic Ocean of ice water wouldn't last a split second in hell, hell was so hot. He jerked in his shoulders, jabbed the index finger of his right hand in the air, and swatted at mosquitoes with his left. He broke in midsentence to talk about God's having a special love for animals and birds because He created them first and put them in the Garden of Eden and when it came time to flood the earth, he made ol' Noah gather up two of every kind and float them around until the rain stopped and the ark landed. The two guitar players broke out of a vamp and slipped into "Amazing Grace," and Preacher Bytheway started on a fox hunt of Scripture until he treed the passage about Jesus riding a donkey into Jerusalem, and that became his topic.

It was as though Preacher Bytheway had been jolted by a charge from an Atlas car battery. He broad-jumped from behind the pulpit in a convulsion. He landed flat with his back bent at an awkward angle, and he whipped forward bringing his right arm over his head, like Alvin letting fly a knuckleball. He then began to stutter step, dragging his left arm behind him. He snapped the fingers of his right hand and did his singsong about Jesus selecting a lowly animal—"Yes! Yes! A ass! It was a ass!"—and how that meant we all needed to humble ourselves.

"Amen! Amen! Amen, Preacher!"

A loud voice erupted from somewhere in the middle of the right side of the aisle. Rev. Bartholomew R. Bytheway stopped dead between twitches, startled by such quick response to his sermon.

"Yes, brother, that's what I say! Amen!" Preacher Bytheway echoed.

Suddenly, Laron Crook jumped straight out of his seat. "Oh, Preacher, I know what you mean! Oh, yes, I surely do!"

"Tell us, brother! Tell us all! Let it out! Praise God! Make a joyful noise unto the Lord! Is Jesus touchin' you?"

Laron was wringing his hands. His chin was revolving as if he had a chicken bone caught in his throat and he was trying to cough it up. "Jesus—oh, Preacher, Jesus is touchin' me! Helpin' me! Leadin' me!" Laron's chin was spinning. If Jesus had him, it was by the throat.

"PRAISE GOD! AND WHO IS THIS BROTHER?"

shouted Preacher Bytheway.

Laron Crook was nearly forty years old. He was six feet, five inches tall, and he had a sunken chest. He was slightly retarded—retarded in that gray land of sad confusion. As long as he had lived in Emery, no one could remember Laron ever saying over a dozen words a day. Next to Alvin, before his conversion by baseball and Delores, Laron was the quietest man in north Georgia. He and his daddy had a farm near the Bio community and they traded mules, and sometimes field-trained them to know gee from haw. Occasionally, Laron's daddy would get drunk and wander around Emery yelling, "Gee" or "Haw" and he would conduct a mule-training lesson under the tin roof of the cotton gin. Laron would bring a two-horse wagon and drive his daddy away, as his daddy yelled out at the snickering crowd of onlookers, "Gee. Haw. Kick 'em in the ass." It would take weeks before Laron could speak to anyone without blushing.

"Tell us what the Lord's doin' for you, brother! Tell us all!" begged Preacher Bytheway, motioning for Laron.

Laron began to weave out to the middle of the aisle. There were a few restrained amens and everyone was stretching to see Laron.

"Jesus knew what He was doin', Preacher! Oh, I feel it! Feel it!"

"It's tinglin', ain't it, brother?!" encouraged Preacher Bytheway. "The spirit's tinglin', ain't it?!"

The two guitar players from Gaffney upped the tempo and cheated into a mild boogie sound. The applause picked up and matched the rhythm of the guitars.

"If you love this good brother, say amen!" Preacher Bytheway shouted. "Do you hear me, people?! A-a-a-a-men!"

"A-a-a-a-MEN! Hallelujah!"

"God bless you, Laron . . ."

"I'm prayin' for you, Laron . . ."

"Amen, Laron . . ."

"I'm filled with you, Laron . . ."

Laron moved slowly toward the front of the tent. The back of his neck began jerking involuntarily and he held his elbows close to his sides and began to pump his shoulder blades up and down. His head was bobbing to the bass beat of the two guitars and the hand-clapping swelled in stereophonic wildness around him. His feet were tapping out a buckdance step.

"Good God!" Freeman exclaimed. "Look at ol' Laron, Wesley. You see that? I'll be damned. Look at that fool."

"What's he gonna do, Freeman?" asked Wesley, slipping back into his seat. Wesley and I had never seen such behavior in the name of God.

"Depends on how took he is," replied Freeman. "Maybe talk in tongues."

Laron Crook, nearly forty, six feet, five inches tall, was took. He was seized. Obsessed. Possessed. Surrendered into and commanded by. Laron was converted.

"Preacher—Preacher—PREACHER! Uh—Inee! Ddaa—pogg—UH—EEE! Ahhh! GUNNNNN—UHHHHH!

Gunnnnn—gunnnnn! AHHHHHHHHHH . . ."

Laron was talking in tongues. Preacher Bytheway was talking in tongues. The guitar players were playing in tongues, wild Latin-sounding dance music, and one of them was doing a click-click-click castanets sound with his lips.

Laron Crook's conversion made St. Paul's experience on the road to Damascus seem like a migraine headache in comparison.

Laron whipped up on his toes—I swear, his toes. He jabbed and hooked his arms like Joe Louis shadowboxing. He came crashing in on his heels on a downstroke by the two guitarists, held a quick freeze, and then broke into a couple of German goose steps.

"Show us the Lord, brother!" Preacher Bytheway urged, stepping out of Laron's way and waving him front and center.

"Amen, Laron. . . ."

"We're with you, Laron . . ."

"God bless you and your daddy, Laron. . . ."

Laron had circled to one side of the sawdust altar area. He began to jump and bicycle in midair. When he landed, he would skid into a split, claw at the air with his hands, and pull himself up. A couple of German goose steps and Laron would be leaping and bicycling in the air again. On his best jumps, he probably cleared four feet and he could pump three times with his legs before he hit ground.

Then Laron slowed the tempo. He began to stiffen and skip on his left foot. Suddenly, his body snapped and went rigid. He pulled his left arm close to him, cocked his elbow and folded his wrist under his chin. His right arm shot out, straight toward the ground, two inches below his knee. His right hand was hinged and opened, his fingers spread like web feet. His right foot was lifted ankle high and he hop-scotched in tiny, frantic steps across the sawdust.

Laron Crook looked like Red Grange stiff-arming a midget.

"God bless you, bro-THER!"

Rev. Bartholomew R. Bytheway anointed Laron Crook a preacher of the gospel of the Speaking-In-Tongues Traveling Tent Tabernacle, instructing him to continue the ministry of humanity that had moved him to the grandest, most spectacular display of being invested by God's mysterious spirit that anyone had ever demonstrated. It was a touching ceremony. Laron confessed to sins as fast as he could invent them. He told long, funny stories about how he had been taught to mistreat animals by being master over them, but how that had now stopped and how he believed the Lord God Almighty had called him to do something special with ". . . them poor creatures."

Everyone amened and hallelujahed and hugged Laron and wished him luck. Dover Heller promised he would quit kicking Bark in the head for chewing up rabbits. Laron said he'd work with Bark and try to train him with God's gentle help.

The Speaking-In-Tongues Traveling Tent Tabernacle left at the end of the week. It had been a triumph for

Rev. Bartholomew R. Bytheway. He had attracted his largest crowds, had delivered the Thursday noon prayer following the Obituary Column of the Air on the Edenville radio station, and he had ordained his first minister. The fact that Laron was Preacher Bytheway's convert became the most exciting news event in Emery in years. Laron spoke up, proudly and often. If he wasn't talking, he was meditating. He put himself on a strict disciplinary program—prayer at morning, prayer at noon, prayer at night, and no more R. C. Colas between meals. If he was in God's service, Laron wanted to be in shape.

During his first days of spiritual growth and adjustment, Laron's constant companion was Freeman, when Freeman wasn't working for A. G. Hixon in the warehouse and cotton gin. To Laron, Freeman was someone who had been misunderstood and poorly treated by life. It was a sympathy fired by the parallel of their childhoods, and oddly confirmed by their opposite personalities. If, in his new Born Again self, Laron could help out a fellow human being, it would be Freeman. Besides, no one in Emery knew animals as well as Freeman and Laron needed help in that commitment; Laron knew mules, but he had a way of repelling other creatures.

Freeman loved the attention. He amened at appropriate times. He allowed Laron to save his worthless soul at least twice a week. He had visions so fearful and vivid, Laron would hyperventilate with excitement as Freeman, wallowing on the ground, described scenes that made the Book of Revelations read like a

Flash Gordon comic book.

On days when his personal evangelism fell on deaf ears, Laron would persuade Freeman to meet him in the late afternoon and they would go into the pastures and woods to communicate with God's animals. These were special missions for Laron, and his zeal was inspiring. He was kicked by a goat in Horace Wilder's pasture, chased across a cornfield by Otis Harper's breed bull, bitten by Bark, pecked in the face by a nesting hen, and Freeman left him one night in the middle of Black Pool Swamp hooting away with a distressed owl. Laron had no idea it was Freeman hooting back.

But Laron considered all these trials a test of his faith and, like Job, he would endure. "God forgive this dumb beast for kickin' me," Laron would say. "He knows not what he's doin'."

The injury and humiliation suffered by Laron was God's way of preparing him for a revelation. "When it happens, it's gonna be mighty," he claimed. "It's gonna come like a hold-up man at night, when I ain't expectin' nothin'."

He was right.

Laron was at Hixon's General Store one Saturday afternoon, sitting under a water oak, recuperating from a severe clawing he had received while trying to separate two cats intent on mating. We had been listening to his wonderful interpretation of Old Testament stories for an hour when Freeman asked his question.

"Laron, tell me something," Freeman said innocently. "How come there's a heaven for folks, but there ain't no heaven for animals?"

"Who said there ain't?" Laron replied. "Of course there is. Why, heaven ain't much different'n earth. Except that it's freed of sin, and maybe a little cloudier. What makes you think God don't believe in havin' pets? Why, think about how nice it must be up there with birds tweetin' and chirpin' all the time. Must be awful pleasin' to God and Jesus, and the saints and holy angels, to hear them birds."

"I thought they only had gold harps in heaven," Freeman said.

Laron peeled back the bandage and looked at a deep red wound on his hand. "Oh sure, they got harps. Gold harps. But they's only for special occasions. Like Sundays, or Christmas, or Easter, or the Fourth of July. Rest of the time, heaven's filled with birds singin' and dogs barkin' and things like that."

Freeman measured his words, folded them around in his mouth and dropped them like diamonds of pure wonderment. "But, gosh, I thought the only way you could get to heaven was by bein' baptized," he said.

Laron's head snapped like a whip. His eyes dilated. His sunken chest began to heave. You could see his heart pumping in his jugular veins. "That's it! That's it, Freeman! Praise God! That's what the Lord has called me to do! I know it, Freeman! You are an instrument of the Lord God Almighty Jehovah!"

Freeman crossed his arms over his chest, as if hiding from the fearful face of God. "What, Laron?!"

"The Lord God Almighty Jehovah, He who said I AM THAT I AM, has done delivered me a message,

Freeman! Oh, yes! Not from no mountain, mind you, but from the mouth of a babe! I can hear it, Freeman! I can hear it!"

"Me, too, Laron! OH, YES! Go out yonder and baptize my creatures!"

"That's it, Freeman! Them's the Lord's words, right outa His mouth! Praise His holy tongue! Amen! A-a-a-MEN!"

For the next few days, Laron was lunatic in his determination to baptize every walking, flying, and crawling animal in Emery. He carried a Boy Scout canteen filled with water from Sosbee's Spring and if he couldn't lay his hands on a cow or a crow, he would flit water in their direction and declare the deed accomplished.

Laron was as crazy as Don Quixote, and, in his way, just as noble, but Wesley was greatly saddened by the spectacle of Laron chasing stray dogs and cats up and down the railroad track, and he blamed Freeman for encouraging such mad behavior.

"It ain't my fault," Freeman protested.

"Freeman, it is and you know it," Wesley preached. "Laron ain't got good sense, and all you're doin' is havin' a big laugh. What you don't understand is that Laron's all caught up in doin' what he thinks he ought to be doin'. It don't matter to him if everybody's laughing and making fun. He'd do anything anybody tells him, if it's said in the name of God. That's sad, boy, and you know it. Laron believes God's hidin' in that canteen of water and that He comes out like some magic monster every time he flings some water around. Freeman, that ain't God. That's people sayin' God's a white-bearded old man floating around in the air somewhere, and that He's goin' around keepin' count on who is baptized and who ain't."

"Wesley, you know what it says in the Bible," argued Freeman.

"I don't need to read the Bible to know that water ain't gettin' you to heaven, Freeman. It ain't the water."

"Wesley, I'm tellin' you, Laron heard a voice."

"Freeman, what Laron heard was what you wanted him to hear. You think God's talkin' out loud, like Sam Spade on the radio? You really think such things?"

"Now, Wesley, that's what ol' Preacher Bytheway said."

Wesley was quiet. He wanted to say the right thing and say it in a way that even Freeman could comprehend him.

"Freeman," Wesley finally said, "if a man's got to learn about the Almighty by bein' scared to death because somebody's screaming about hell boilin' over with fire, or bein' fooled about heaven bein' paved with California gold, then he ain't learned nothing. That's just a way of trying to pin down something that can't be pinned down. If you got to say what God is, or ain't, you're just talkin'. That's all. Just talkin'. Knowing the Almighty don't need that."

Freeman did not understand a word Wesley said. Neither did I.

9

Dover Heller was proud of his job with the REA. He had hired on as a member of the right-of-way crew, but his ambition was considerably greater: Dover wanted to be a lineman, climbing poles while others stood around on the ground and admired his steel nerves.

Dover was our favorite adult. He regarded life as a comic-book adventure and he treated us as equals. If something happened, Dover wanted to know about it, and we knew we could depend on him to listen attentively to our woes and keep confident our most anxious confusion.

Dover had a happy, expressive nature that was accented by one brown eye, one blue eye, and a quaint habit of stuffing cottonseed in his ears. He explained that working in the cotton gin had prompted his cottonseed habit; the noise level was deafening and Dover had sensitive ears. We thought it was a sensible explanation and, unlike adults, we did not perceive the humor of one brown eye and one blue eye.

We had become especially fond of Dover after he brazenly defended Our Side following the fight at Emery Junior High School. Dover declared it was time someone had the guts to square off with the ". . . high and mighty" of Emery and, further, he proudly sided with our argument. It was after his declaration that Dover applied for his job with the REA.

At the end of his first full week's work on the right-of-way crew, Dover was overwhelmed by the promise of the future. "It's like comin' to a fork in the road," he told us, "and you don't know which one to take. Well, you flip a nickel or a dime and go one way or the other, heads or tails, and then you find out it's where you should've been all the time! Yessir, boys, I'm right on it, right on the right road!"

To celebrate his enthusiasm, Dover took a Captain Marvel comic book to a sign painter in Royston and the sign painter painted a likeness of Captain Marvel's lightning bolt on each door of Dover's wine-colored Chevrolet pickup. Dover kept those lightning bolts waxed and gleaming. Someday, he told us, that would be his truck when he advanced from right-of-way crew to lineman. He wouldn't need a company truck, even if they offered it. He just needed enough money to keep his Captain Marvel Chevy rolling.

But Dover was on the right-of-way crew, and in late July the crew arrived in Emery, shouldering axes and slingblades and crosscut saws. They began in Sosbee's Woods, slicing in straight lines out of the lush, dark green of pine and oak and beech and blackgum and poplar, leaving a path—a pale underbelly—of scrub trees and grass.

The men were easy workers. They measured a day's work by the delicate, surgical neatness of their cut. It was just-so, an artistic tracing of the expedition of the surveyors, with their tripods and funny little telescopes and hand signals. At the end of a day's cut, the men would sit on the tailgates and sides of their trucks and inspect their work, and they would laugh happily and make book on how far they would slice the next day.

It would take them weeks to run the gash from Sosbee's Woods to the tie-up between Goldmine and Eagle Grove, but they knew they would complete their work before the heat of summer and autumn lost its energy. Dover told us the foreman of the crew had an eye for reading sap in trees and he could tell, almost to the day, when winter would come howling its way along the foothills of the Blue Ridge range. "We'll be done before then," Dover explained. "And then them linemen will come in and before you know what's happened, every house on the line is gonna have electricity."

Electricity. The word became a vocabulary of meanings. It had the same delicious aftertaste as of winning a close softball game, and telling over and over the indisputable, to-the-point motion that caught a hitter or runner leaning off the business of the game. We rolled the word around in our mouths—electricity. We separated its syllables with our tongues and pushed the word out in segments—E-LEC-TRI-CI-TY. It was a big word. It did not sound southern, the way we said it.

The right-of-way crew foreman must have known hundreds of waiting, watching children, and he understood the terrible curiosity in those mute onlookers. He did not object to our presence, and we followed the crew with great devotion when we were not working the fields. The way the foreman talked about electricity, it was a mystery as bewildering as the Soldier Ghost who sometimes slithered out of his unmarked grave in the old Civil War cemetery and wandered aimlessly, an oblong, grotesque fluorescence against

136

the spotty black velvet of night.

"You know what electricity is?" the foreman asked one afternoon.

"Yea. Makes lights," volunteered Paul.

The foreman laughed easily. "No, son, that ain't it. That's what it does, among other things. Truth is, don't nobody on God's green earth know what electricity really is. Know how to make it. Know how to use it. But ain't nobody figured what it is."

The foreman was wrong. I knew what electricity was. It was a million-trillion Z's snatched off an alphabet stack, Z-ing along so fast no one could see just one by itself. And when all those million-trillion Z's piled up in one place, they shocked you because of their sharp edges spinning crazily about. If you stood beside a transformer and listened, you could even hear the Z's—Zzzzzzzzzzzzz, Z's humming in a monotone pitch. If there was one thing I was certain of, it was the fact that a Z was the sharpest letter in the alphabet. Anyway, a Z looked more like a lightning bolt than any other letter.

One day, after the REA right-of-way crew had stopped work, Dover drove Wesley and Paul and Otis and me to visit Freeman at Hixon's Seed and Fertilizer Warehouse. Dover felt responsible for Freeman and he had heard a rumor that Dupree was ordering Freeman around like a servant. It was not the kind of treatment Freeman appreciated and, apparently, there had been a minor confrontation.

"Yeah, ol' Freeman ain't the kind to like that,"

fretted Dover. "And he's been doin' good, too. Old Man Hixon said so. Said Freeman was about as strong as any man he's got. I'm tellin' you, boys, it don't take but one snotty person to make a barrel of rotten apples."

Otis was confused by the rumor. "I didn't think Dupree had anything to do with the warehouse," he said. "That was why Freeman agreed to take the job, first off."

"Way it's supposed to be," agreed Dover. "But ol' Hixon keeps a lot of supplies stored in there. Coffee, flour, Royal Crowns, Dr. Peppers, that kind of stuff, and anytime Dupree wants somethin', he makes Freeman get it. Nobody else. Just Freeman."

"Freeman won't take that long," observed Wesley.

Freeman was leaning against the warehouse talking with Willie Lee Maxwell, who worked the sawmills with Freeman's daddy. Willie Lee was our friend and the strongest black man we knew. Once each year, during ginning season, Willie Lee would be persuaded by the whites of Emery to lift a bale of cotton. Willie Lee would strip to his waist and stand under the cotton scales on a plank platform and four or five men would slowly lower the giant bale, bundled in burlap cord. Willie Lee would quiver and bend under the crushing weight. His legs would fight in woozy, sliding steps for balance, and the muscles of his great arms would leap and tremble as he pulled the bale up on his neck. Suddenly, Willie Lee would draw in a quick, deep breath and his gleaming ebony body would begin to rise. Two steps and Willie Lee would stand straight and drop the cotton bale, bouncing and rolling, at his back. For a moment, as the whites cheered and applauded, Willie Lee would stand proud and triumphant, a black Samson freed of his blackness, his wide nostrils fanning as his lungs fought to clear the blood from his head, and his small, dark eyes flashing a wild, primitive brilliance. That was Willie Lee's moment, and in that moment Willie Lee was a superior, not an equal.

Willie Lee smiled and nodded his hello to our hellos. He started rolling a Prince Albert cigarette. Freeman told us he had had a second run-in with Dupree and was waiting to see if Dupree's daddy would fire him.

"What happened?" asked Dover.

"Aw, Dupree and Sonny was playing around in the store and Sonny kicked over a sack of flour," explained Freeman. "Anyway, I was carryin' in some tenpenny nails and Dupree told me to sweep the floor."

"Damn!" Paul whistled.

"Yeah, well, I told him I worked the warehouse and he could sweep it up," Freeman continued. "And you know what that fool did? He threw a broom at me."

"What'd you do?" asked Wesley, fearing the answer.

"Nothin', Wes. Nothin'. I just walked out. And Dupree come yellin', sayin' he was gonna get me fired."

"That's all?"

"Well, Wes, let's just say Dupree made the mistake of coming outside the store, where I was. It's a good thing Willie Lee come along and cooled me off, or I'd of kicked his butt."

"Didn't wanta see you get put off a job over nothin'," Willie Lee said. "Yessir, your daddy's proud of you havin' this job."

"Well, I reckon I won't have it long."

Dover laughed. "Sure you will, Freeman! Shoot, Old Man Hixon ain't too crazy about Dupree, hisself, and he ain't about to fire nobody who's doin' the job—especially if he ain't paying no more'n he's paying you."

"Yeah," Freeman said dryly.

"You just gotta stay clear of him," advised Dover. "Just don't pay him no mind. Shoot, carry all that ol' junk for him. Just keep on carryin' and smilin', carryin' and smilin'. All that smilin' will get to him, boy. I guarantee it."

Dover bought a bag of raw peanuts and Dr. Peppers for everyone. He loved Dr. Peppers and he tried to be faithful to the suggestion of having a Dr. Pepper at ten o'clock, two o'clock, and four o'clock each day.

We sat in the breezeway of the warehouse on Anderson 6-8-6 fertilizer sacks and discussed everything from Alvin's success in baseball to Dover's chances of becoming a lineman for the REA. We all agreed Dover deserved such an opportunity and Willie Lee declared he would put up a dollar bet that Dover would be wearing spike-boots before spring.

"Well, by granny, now that's sure good of you, Willie Lee," Dover said. "And I'm believin' you're right! I can feel it!"

"Willie Lee's going up in the world, too," Freeman announced. "Ain't that right, Willie Lee?"

"Naw. C'mon, Freeman."

"Well, hell, it's true!"

"Naw . . ."

"Whatcha doin', Willie Lee?" Paul asked.

"He's workin' weekends down in Elberton with that flying circus," Freeman answered for Willie Lee.

"Flying circus?" asked Otis.

"Yeah. You ain't heard about it? Man named Brady Dasher got this flying circus down in Elberton. Ol' Willie Lee's been helping him build this platform for a special trick."

"I ain't heard about it, either," Dover admitted. "What kind of platform you talkin' about?"

Freeman told us about the trick, interrupting himself constantly to ask Willie Lee, "Ain't that so?" and Willie Lee would smile his thick, wide smile and mumble his musical, "Uh-huh."

Brady Dasher and his brother Harold had decided to do something that had never been done and something so spectacular it would reduce brave men to blithering fools: they would land a Piper Cub on a platform that had been fitted on the top of a new 1947 Ford. It would be advertised as the World's Smallest Runway, and if it worked the Brady Dasher Flying Circus would make headlines from Europe to China.

Dover was impressed. "That so?" he said, whistling his amazement. "I ain't never seen a flying circus. Heard of 'em, but I never saw one."

"You reckon they gonna make it, Willie Lee?" asked Otis.

"Don't know," Willie Lee admitted. "They's crazy. I

just do the sawin' and hammerin', and Mr. Brady and Mr. Harold do the flyin' and drivin'. Find out on Saturday. They's got a show in Elberton to try it out."

"Damn! I'd like to see that, that's for sure," Dover exclaimed.

"Don't cost but a dollar a car," Willie Lee said. "And they's doin' more'n the platform landin'. Got a parachute jump, and they's this little ol' boy, Mr. Brady's boy, who flies all by hisself, while Mr. Brady's sittin' out there on somethin' they call the struts."

"A boy flyin'? Now that's something," Dover said, ticking his head in disbelief.

"It's the truth, Mr. Dover. He ain't but four. Mr. Brady says he's the littlest flyer in the world."

"Boy, I do wanta see that!" Paul said.

"Yeah, me, too," echoed Otis. "Why don't we all cram in the truck and go down there, Dover?"

"Suits me, boys. Get permission and, by granny, I'll take the whole bloomin' lot," Dover promised. "We'll make us a day of it. May even come back by Wind's Mill and roast us some hot dogs and marshmallows!" Dover shelled a raw peanut and looked up in the changing blue of the late afternoon sky, where invisible Piper Cubs twirled like hummingbirds in fancy acrobatics. "Yessir, we'll make us a day of it," he muttered.

Dover had carried us many places, but always with the objections of our parents, who thought of him as an honest, diligent man who was possibly a little crazy. They could not understand why Dover refused to ". . . grow up a little," as they phrased it. Dover had common sense, but he was also gullible when it came to any adventure of mystery or danger. My mother told us that Dover had once paid a man fifty dollars to teach him the art of reading palms, and everyone in Emery conceded that Dover had, at last, snapped and was a nominee for being committed. He was forgiven only when he became the most popular attraction ever presented at the Halloween Carnival.

The thought of an airplane propeller decapitating us while we were under the care of Dover Heller did not appeal to my mother. She was astonished that we even wanted to see such put-on entertainment.

"But, Mama," I promised, "we won't even get nowhere near that airplane. We'll just stay back and watch it from the top of Dover's truck. Besides, me and Wesley ain't been to Elberton for a year."

Mother finally surrendered to my pleading. I was far more accomplished than Wesley at winning approval; Wesley was too quick to appreciate parental logic, and therefore too quick to agree. In pure debate, Wesley was remarkable, but he lacked poetic expression when the argument required weeping and chest-thumping, and I always thought he deprived himself of one of life's most memorable experiences.

Early afternoon, on Saturday, Mother drove Wesley and me to Hixon's General Store and left us to wait for Dover. R. J. and Otis and Paul joined us, eager for the day. Because Wesley was going, they were permitted to go; Wesley had sense, even if Dover didn't.

"My mama said she wouldn't trust Dover far as she

could throw a mule," declared Paul, "but she guessed I'd be all right if I was with you, Wes. Shoot, Wes, if you was a horseshoe you couldn't bring a man any more luck!"

Otis wanted a Coca-Cola, but refused to go into Hixon's General Store alone.

"I might bust Dupree up," Otis said.

"Maybe he ain't in there," suggested Paul.

"Yeah, he's there. I seen him," replied Otis. "Standin' off in the shadows, hidin' his sneaky face. Thought I saw Sonny and Wayne, too."

"Yeah, ol' Wayne's in there!" Paul whispered, trying to act nonchalant.

"What's he doin'?" asked R. J., his back to the store.

"Probably lickin' on a Sugar Daddy, or kissin' ol' Dupree's tail," Paul answered.

"See anythin' else?"

"Naw—wait a minute! Yeah. Ol' Colin's gonna love this. That skinny little Megan's in there! Sure is!"

Megan. I had seen her at church, but I had not spoken to her since the day at Sosbee's Spring. I prayed she would stay in the store. I prayed Dover would drive up. I prayed for the face of Megan to stay buried in my memory.

"Colin? You hear me?" Paul repeated. "Megan's in there."

"So?"

"So, I thought you'd like to know, that's so."

"What'd I care?"

"I bet she's butterin' up to Dupree."

I could feel Megan's face begin to slip out of its

hiding. Pale green eyes, hair as blond as a full moon.

"Hey, look at ol' Colin. He's blushing." Otis snickered.

"Otis, you better watch it!"

"C'mon, Colin, what's the matter? Hey, boy, you gettin' red, you know it!"

"Otis, by granny . . ."

"Stop it," Wesley said firmly. "Ain't no need to go kiddin' him, Otis. It'll just make him mad, and he'll start fighting and I'll have to take him home."

"Aw, I was just kiddin'," Otis said. "She ain't in there."

"Well, kid about somethin' else."

Otis looked at R. J. and Paul for support. Both of them turned away and started kicking at the gravel beside the water oak.

"Hey, I didn't mean nothin'," apologized Otis.

"Well," I said, "me, neither. Let Dupree have her. Don't make no difference to me."

Someday, I thought, I am going to grow and I'll order a Charles Atlas muscle-building course and I'll kick Dupree Hixon from one end of Emery to the other. He would regret stealing my girl.

Dover and Freeman arrived in Dover's Captain Marvel Chevrolet pickup. They had packed an ice chest with hot dogs and Coca-Colas and potato chips, and Dover had made cabbage slaw that spilled when he tried to cram it into the chest, and the slaw and ice water slopped together in a sick, cold mayonnaise soup.

"Don't worry about nothin'," Dover said. "There's

enough left for everybody."

Dover made me sit in the cab with him. If anything happened to anyone, it wouldn't happen to the smallest and youngest of the group. I had become accustomed to such treatment, but it was always awkward and embarrassing, and Dover tried to compensate by telling dirty jokes as we bounced down Highway 17 toward Elberton.

"I ain't never been to that airport," Dover confided, "but I got the directions from Hugh Spencer. He run the bulldozer that scraped out the runway."

The directions Dover had scrawled on a piece of paper showed the airport was on the south rim of Elberton, off Highway 17, at the end of a road that had been gravel-topped to encourage the post-war airplane industry, an industry that was more a symbol of progress than a necessity. Every town with a county courthouse had an airport, and on Sundays small, colorful airplanes crisscrossed rural skies like odd, visiting birds.

The gravel-top road ended at the Elbert County Airport, twenty acres of level land with a makeshift hangar and a red-clay landing strip that had been peeled out of thin, gray topsoil. Four or five Piper Cubs lined the runway and were guy-wired to the ground by steel cords and pegs, with wooden stops shoved snug against the wheels. Brady Dasher's two stunt planes were parked in front of the hangar, and a body was half-buried in the engine of one of the planes, making a final check on the motor. There were forty or fifty cars already parked in a pasture behind

146

the hangar when Dover paid his dollar and eased his truck through the narrow opening of a plank-fence gate.

"Damn!" Dover exclaimed. "You can feel it, can't you? We are gonna see somethin' today, boy, and I will flat-out guarantee it. Wonder where ol' Willie Lee is?"

Willie Lee saw us and nodded. He was double-nailing the supports that held the World's Smallest Runway to the top of Brady Dasher's 1947 Ford.

"Nail it down good, Willie Lee," shouted Dover.

"It ain't gonna work, Willie Lee," predicted Freeman.

Willie Lee turned his back. We were his friends, but we were white, and he could not be certain our friendship would be understood by strangers.

"See you later, Willie Lee," I called, as Dover led us away to the hangar.

The crowd was festive, a circus crowd with circus fever. Some of the men were sneaking sips of beer and moonshine whiskey at the trunks of their cars, while their women grouped and pretended not to notice. Children played tag, weaving and ducking and laughing like frisky baby animals discovering the ticklish joy of running. Aubrey Hill, who had been a P-47 pilot in World War II, sat in a cane-bottom straight chair and answered questions about flying, and what the crowd could expect from Brady Dasher. Brady and he had become friends, Aubrey said, and they had spent hours plotting the risk of landing a Piper Cub on a platform latched to a car. Aubrey set the odds at 80-20 in favor of success.

"Things is about to get started! Boy, I can feel it already!" Dover exclaimed, leading us to a fence in front of the airplane.

Harold Dasher grabbed the propeller blade of the Piper Cub he had been attending and yanked, firing the motor. It sputtered and choked, belched smoke and died. Harold walked around to the side of the plane, conversed briefly with a short, balding mechanic who was sitting in the cockpit, and then he motioned for Brady and a radio announcer named Floyd Alewine to join him. The three huddled and talked in low, mumbled tones. Brady gestured toward the plane like a mad Gypsy, and you could tell he was questioning his brother's genius for coping with mechanical objects. Floyd nodded authoritatively and kept making negative motions with his hands. The conference caught the attention of everyone at the airport and the crowd quieted to a whisper. Finally, Brady kicked at the dirt and stalked away. Harold removed a screwdriver from his hip pocket and stuck his arm down into the motor of the ailing Piper Cub. Floyd walked over to a table in front of the crowd and picked up his loudspeaker microphone. He performed a squawking "Testing, testing, testing" routine. Then he cleared his throat.

"Ladies and gentlemen," Floyd began in his deep bass announcer's voice. "We've encountered something of a minor problem and we ask for your patience. There will be an air show, and we guarantee it. Even if it involves some risk and danger on the part of the members of the Dasher Brothers Flying Circus. It seems the engine of Brady's favorite Piper Cub has the summer droops, and just plain won't run like it's supposed to, but, ladies and gentlemen, Brady Dasher is bound and determined to fly that plane!"

Floyd paused and cupped his hand over the microphone. He motioned everyone's attention to Brady Dasher, who had walked out to the center of the red-clay runway and was standing with his back to the audience, hands on hips, head bowed, a red scarf drooped about his neck.

"As you can tell," Floyd continued in a voice that would tell secrets, "Brady's a determined man. Now, let's see how brother Harold is doing . . ." Floyd turned his head toward Harold and the Piper Cub. Every head in the audience swiveled with Floyd's. "How about it, Harold?" Floyd called inquisitively. "Is Old Faithful finished for the day, or can you get her going?!"

Harold gave a thumbs-up signal and caught the propeller of the Piper Cub.

"Well, we're about to see, folks," Floyd said, lowering his voice. "Harold says thumbs-up, everything is in order. Now, if he didn't get his spark plug wires crossed . . ."

Harold signaled to the mechanic sitting in the cockpit, then he yanked the blade. The engine hissed and the propeller rolled and stopped. Harold tried again. A loud pop exploded from somewhere in the motor and a circle of black smoke whirled upward, like a volcano erupting. The propeller twirled, slowed, kicked again, and, suddenly, the motor jumped with life.

"There it is, ladies and gentlemen! There it is!"

Floyd cried into his microphone. "How about that, Brady?"

Harold's success with the Piper Cub pleased Brady Dasher. The sound of the motor was a cue and Brady raised his arms above his head in a melodramatic salute to the air gods. He strolled across the runway, buttoning his blue gabardine dress suit and flipping his red scarf in the wind. With each step, Brady acknowledged the applauding crowd like a general reviewing his troops. He had the style and strut of a matinee idol, and by the time Brady reached his waiting plane there was no doubt that Charles Lindbergh didn't know enough about flying to qualify as Brady's copilot.

Floyd had begun a loud, excitable account of Brady's narrow escapes from death, as Brady taxied his plane out onto the runway. ". . . And five times, our pilot has crash-landed his plane without ever getting so much as a briar scratch! Yessir, ladies and gentlemen, this is one of the four or five greatest daredevil pilots ever to climb into a cockpit. And today . . ."

Floyd's narrative was interrupted by Harold, who tugged at Floyd's sleeve and whispered something into his ear. Floyd's body slumped, and Harold nodded gravely. The crowd leaned forward, trying to hear something that had already been said and lost in the sputtering roar of Brady's Piper Cub. Floyd dropped his microphone on the table and mechanical pain thundered through the loudspeakers. Harold grabbed Floyd's arm and cried something inaudible. Floyd ran his hand through his hair in a desperate attempt to stimulate his brain, and Harold seemed to panic. At that precise moment, Brady released his Piper Cub and it began to roll down the runway. Harold screamed, "No—no—oh, no!" He leaped away from the table and began to run and stumble toward the moving airplane. Fear seized the crowd of onlookers.

"Oh, my God!" a woman sighed.

The plane was gathering speed and Harold made a valiant lunge to grab a wheel, and everyone knew that Brady Dasher was riding a Death Plane. It had to be that. Harold's lunge missed by one hundred feet and only a man completely insane would make such a ridiculous effort.

Brady's Piper Cub lifted gracefully off the ground, began to rise, then dipped dangerously and did a half-roll to the left. Harold lay on the ground, his arms covering his head.

"Ladies and gentlemen! Ladies and gentlemen! Your attention, please," Floyd begged. "A terrible thing! A terrible thing! Harold Dasher has just discovered that he used the wrong drums in fueling Brady's plane. Brady Dasher is flying on kerosene instead of gasoline!"

The crowd oohed and stepped back in unison.

"Goda'mighty!" an old man mumbled.

"We have absolutely no idea what to expect," wailed Floyd. "Let's pray that the Almighty is flying with Brady."

"Ooooooooooooh!"

A woman covered her eyes with her hands and began to sway.

"Look! Look!" Floyd shouted over the loudspeaker.

The Piper Cub fought to climb. It sputtered, dropped, tilted, climbed again. A thin wisp of smoke trailed its blue ribbon from the engine.

"Oooooooooooooh!"

"Is it on fire? Harold? Harold? Is Brady's plane on fire?" Floyd's voice cracked, sputtered, dropped, tilted, and rose with Brady's plane. Harold did not answer. Harold had rolled into a ball in the red dirt.

The plane climbed laboriously, inching its way upward. A second ribbon of smoke unfurled from the engine. Then another.

"Ladies and gentlemen, I must ask you. Will this be Brady Dasher's last climb into the skies? Has the charmed life of the daredevil finally met its destiny? How will Brady Dasher ever escape? And you must remember, he does not have a parachute . . ."

"Don't worry about nothin', boys," Dover said. "Don't worry about nothin'. If he goes down, it's gonna be in some cow pasture, and you can bet on it. Shoot, them pilots know what to do."

I looked around. A woman had fainted and two men were fanning her with their straw hats. Groups of women were gathering children and retreating to the safety of their cars. Aubrey Hill was leaning back in his cane-bottom straight chair, arms folded across his lap, and laughing.

"Dover, why's Mr. Hill laughin'?" I asked.

"He ain't laughin'," Dover replied, as he strained to see Brady's plane.

"He is. He is so laughin'."

Dover looked quickly toward Aubrey Hill. "Well,

I'll be damned. He is. He sure is."

Dover caught me by the shoulders with both hands and guided me over to Aubrey Hill.

"What's goin' on, Aubrey?" asked Dover. "It ain't funny, is it?"

"'Course it's funny," Aubrey Hill answered. "Ol' Brady's got everybody scared to death and he ain't doin' nothin' but cuttin' up."

"Cuttin' up?"

"That's what I said, Dover. Cuttin' up. Havin' him a fine ol' time. Look at that!"

The Piper Cub nosed up, its tail section folding underneath its wings until it seemed to stall. Then it flopped over upside down and began plummeting toward the ground in a nose dive.

"Ooooooooooo-o-o-oh!"

Suddenly, the Piper Cub snapped and rolled upward, leaving a V-shaped smoke trail, thin as a scratch across the sky.

"Ladies and gentlemen! Ladies and gentlemen! Brady Dasher is in the fight of his life! Can he do it? Can he manage to control his crippled airplane and bring it down?" Floyd was standing on his table, directing the oohs and aahs of the crowd, coaxing them into trembling.

The plane was a dot in the sky, a fuzzy, smoking dot that turned lazily and began to glide back toward the airport. It gathered speed and the dull roar of the distant engine closed over the crowd. Brady Dasher was bringing his airplane in, but it was a runaway plane, a kamikaze plane, and it could not be stopped.

"Oh, my God," Floyd yelled into his microphone. "Ladies and gentlemen . . ."

Wesley was hypnotized by the diving airplane. He stood fearless. He seemed to belong to the airplane, and the airplane belonged to him, each an extension of the other and each secretly thrilled by the coolness of the space that separated them.

The sound reached us first, a booming, shrieking sound, echoing and re-echoing, crushing our nerves with its awesome weight, and then Brady's Piper Cub swept down over us, curled right and followed the runway, its right wing hanging ten feet above the ground. The plane swayed and righted itself, gained altitude, folded over into a gentle loop, and then the engine hissed and stopped. We could hear the wind lapping against the silent airplane as it came out of its loop at the end of the runway. Brady Dasher was gliding his Piper Cub to a landing, sliding in under the disappearing echoes of the sound explosion that left us frightened and defenseless. The wheels of his plane touched the red-clay runway and two funnels of dust were skimmed off the top of the ground, and the plane stopped dead center of the crowd.

"He did it! He did it! Ladies and gentlemen, Brady Dasher has cheated death again!" Floyd shouted, and the crowd went wild, shouting and whistling and applauding. Harold was in front of the fence, leading cheers and blowing kisses to heaven.

Brady Dasher escaped death three other times that day, and each challenge was more spectacular than the one preceding it. He climbed out on the struts of his plane and waved to the crowd as his four-year-old son performed graceful turns above the airfield. (Aubrey Hill later told us that Brady was actually flying the plane by manipulating wires attached to the elevators and rudder.) Brady's landing on the World's Smallest Runway was perfect, as his Piper Cub and the 1947 Ford, driven by Harold, hit exact speeds and Harold carried the plane to a gentle stop. A parachute jumper flirted with death by refusing to pull his ripcord when Floyd assured us that a split-second delay would be disastrous. Floyd Alewine was more dramatic than John Barrymore with his description of the parachute jumper, and he had people screaming, "Pull it! Pull it! Pull it!" before the parachute streamed open, saving the miserable fool who misjudged his closing distance to the ground.

"Yessir, boys, there ain't nothin' as good as a roasted hot dog," Dover declared, sloshing ketchup on the charred, lumpy hot dog bedded like a black stick in its bun. "One time I had me some French food in a New Orleans hotel and it was hog slop next to a good ol' hot dog." He gouged relish out of a jar with his fingers and sprinkled it across the ketchup.

Dover was not an authority on foods, but he knew how to appreciate the spirit of an occasion and the hot dog roast at Wind's Mill was a splendid way to close a day of marveling at airplanes performing reckless, childish games in the skies. The hot dog roast made a special day a lingering day, and we celebrated each thrill again and again, easing into absurd exaggerations by the mutual consent that seemed always to begin, "Yeah, that's right . . ." By the time we had finished two dozen hot dogs, four bags of potato chips, the leftovers of Dover's cabbage slaw, and two cartons of Coca-Colas, Paul and Otis had decided to join the Air Force and Dover was determined to take private flying lessons as soon as he made his promotion to lineman for the REA.

Night calmed our bragging and our exuberance, and night drove its soft darkness between us, separating our bodies and leaving warm, orange faces sitting in a circle around the fire. It was the feeling I liked most about roasting hot dogs at Wind's Mill. I knew the rhythm of language, the long, lazy lapses between Yeahs and the occasional quiet laugh, and I knew that Dover or Freeman would soon tell again the ghostly history of Wind's Mill, and their telling would be orchestrated by a gurgling swirl hole below the shoals in Beaverjam Creek, and by deep-voiced frogs, and by katydids and owls and whippoorwills.

Wind's Mill had been a gristmill even before the Civil War. Its great paddle wheel was pushed by water that had been diverted from Beaverjam Creek and forced into a narrow race made of oak planking. The wheel had rolled over and over for more than a hundred years before farmers stopped bringing their corn and grain to be mashed to pulp under the heavy stone. The water was no longer diverted and the race had filled with trash. The great paddle wheel was stilled. Some of the paddles were splintered and cracked, but Wind's Mill was a monument and the level, clean grounds with outcroppings of flat, gray surface granite had become a favorite picnic spot of everyone in five communities.

It was true, too, that Wind's Mill was more than a picnic spot. There were the stories, and as time changed whatever truth had existed, the stories became wonderfully romantic—grand speculations of legendary proportions.

Wesley and I well knew the stories. They were part of our heritage. Once, it had been Wynn's Mill. But the W-Y-N-N spelling had been mutated to W-I-N-D. It was even spelled W-I-N-D in church bulletins and in the social columns of local newspapers, where religious and civic activities were chronicled. The change of name—sounds alike, different spelling—was not deliberate; it was the impact of folklore.

During the Civil War, in that final, desperate gesture of defense against northern forces, one of the sons of the Wynn family became obsessed with the fear of dying in battle, so he made a hiding place behind the great paddle, beneath the flooring of the mill, and there he stayed as Confederate troops rode through and enlisted farmers to fight for the honor and heritage of the South. Fear and shame made a hermit of the deserter. No one really knew what had happened to him, but the stories had him dying in his hiding place, and his spirit condemned to that same prison. At night, the wind moaned through the paddles and there were those who swore it was the dead man's spirit begging to be released. That is when the name changed to Wind's Mill—because of the wind and the dead man's spirit. Skeptics would make pilgrimages to discount the dead man's pitiful cry for forgiveness. "It ain't nothin'," they would say, standing on the steel-beam bridge crossing Beaverjam Creek. "Nothin'." But you could tell by the tightness of their voices that none of them would spend the night alone at Wind's Mill.

It was Freeman who told the story of the dead man, with Dover gravely nodding his appreciation and saying quietly, "Uh-huh. That's right. That's what folks say."

Somewhere far off a dog bayed and Dover thought about Bark.

"We better be goin', boys," Dover said. "Ol' Bark ain't been fed."

"Yeah," agreed Freeman. "I got to work in the warehouse some tomorrow."

"On Sunday?" asked Wesley.

"On Sunday, Wes. You do what you're supposed to."

"Freeman, you are bound to get in trouble workin' on the Lord's day," Dover joked.

"I am bound to get myself fired if I don't, and Old Man Hixon didn't do no cartwheels because of my run-in with Dupree. He done warned me." Freeman laughed easily. "I reckon I lead the world in bein' warned by the Hixon family."

"You better watch it, that's all."

"I always do, Dover," answered Freeman. "I always do."

Before she married and moved from our house, my sister Susan would cover herself with a quilt in a corner of the middle room when it rained, or thundered, or when lightning staged its primitive dance across the skies. She would not move except to breathe. In our very, very young years, we thought Susan hid as a game and we delighted with wiggling in and out of that dark quilt cave as thunder lashed its terrible complaint outside. But as we grew older, we realized Susan was not playing games; she was afraid. The loud voice of thunder was the loud voice of demons and it was advisable to cover your face and close your eyes and not anger the demons—who were angry enough if you knew how to translate their popping, cruel language.

We missed Susan when she married. On days of storm, the middle room seemed lopsided, out of balance, and unnatural, without Susan.

It was lopsided, out-of-balance, and unnatural on the Sunday following our afternoon with the Dasher Brothers Flying Circus and the hot dog roast at Wind's Mill. It had begun to rain in early morning, the kind of rain which would fall through the day, into night and into sleep. High, black clouds boiled up and tortured Earth with lightning, spreading like witches' fingers, and Earth (or the demons) screamed and trembled with each painful jolt.

We crowded near the radio in early night and listened to Sunday gospel quartet singing. Mother lit the huge kerosene lamp we reserved for company and placed it on the rolltop desk. "Just for warmth," she said.

My mother had a gift for warmth. It was in the way she spoke, in the way she touched, the way she surprised us with gingerbread and hot chocolate; it was in the way she yearned to hurt when we hurt and rejoice when we rejoiced.

"Remember this rain," Mother told us. "Remember sitting here and remember how warm a kerosene lamp can be. Soon, it'll be different every time it rains. When we get the REA, we won't all be bunched up in a corner like this."

"Why, Mama?" asked Lynn.

"Because there'll be a drop-cord light and it'll make the whole room bright, instead of one little corner, and you'll all be playing instead of sittin'."

"If Susan was here, she wouldn't be playin'," I said.

"Well, maybe not Susan, but that's all right," answered Mother. "We're all afraid of something. It's just that Susan's afraid of thunder."

"Well, I'll be glad when we get some electricity," said Louise. "Maybe we can get us a radio that don't have static all the time."

It had stopped raining on Monday, but it was a gray morning and there was a fine, chilling mist, part fog. Wesley and I went to the corn crib after breakfast and began to shuck corn, stacking the ears in neat, yellow pyramids. It was hateful work, and frightening. My father always kept a king snake in the corn crib. King snakes love to feast on rats, but king snakes are not poisonous. It didn't matter. We knew that somewhere, warm and cozy under the heat of corn shucks, a king snake was curled, waiting. Garry absolutely refused to go near the corn crib, and, once, my sister Frances had accidentally sat on a king snake and she gave a horrible description of snake fangs sinking into flesh.

Corn shucking was a wet-day ceremony, the always-something-else job. But there was one consolation, one promise: if we worked long enough to achieve my father's predetermined goal of the number of bushels needed, we would be permitted to fish the swollen streams that fed into Beaverjam Creek. When it rained, catfish rallied by schools at the mouth of those streams, gobbling away at the fresh supply of land food washed into the inlets. We knew R. J. and Paul and Otis would be fishing one of the spots. We would find them, and if we were lucky we would find Willie Lee and his brother, who was named Baptist. They were the two funniest fishermen in Emery, and we loved to sit with them as they argued over the size of catfish nibbling the bait off hooks, or who had eaten the last can of sardines that Willie Lee's wife, Little Annie, had packed for them. We seldom saw Baptist, except while fishing. He was a nervous man. He believed in ghosts and good luck charms and he was an encyclopedia of dos and don'ts in man's efforts to solicit fortune from the spirit world. Baptist claimed to hold the world's record in the number of times he had seen the Soldier Ghost floating in the trees of the old

Civil War cemetery, but Willie Lee said Baptist was crazy and the only thing he had ever seen in the cemetery was the moon shining on the leaves of the guarding oaks.

Wesley and I were talking about Willie Lee and Baptist and predicting where they might be on Beaverjam Creek, when Mother appeared in the doorway of the corn crib. She had driven to Emery to buy groceries and had promised to tell Freeman we would be fishing. Sometimes Freeman could beg off work, if the invitation to do something was irresistible.

Mother's face was splotched with anger. "Boys," she said, trembling, "Freeman's just been arrested."

Wesley stood. "What?"

"Freeman," Mother repeated. "He's just been arrested."

I remembered what Dover had told Freeman, that someday he would get in trouble for working on Sunday.

"Why?" I asked. "What's Freeman done, Mama?"

"Mr. Hixon said he stole twenty dollars from the store. He called the Sheriff."

"Freeman wouldn't steal no twenty dollars," Wesley said. "Who said he stole it?"

"They did," Mother said, releasing her anger. "Mr. Hixon said it was Freeman. Said Dupree and that little Haynes boy saw him take it off a counter." Mother cared deeply for Freeman. He was her personal social concern, and she had spent hours prying into his personality and saying silent prayers for the welfare of his soul.

"Did you see him, Mama?" asked Wesley.

"Just for a minute. Mr. Hixon was holdin' him in the back of the store for Sheriff Brownlee to get over from Edenville."

"What'd Freeman say?"

"Not much, Wesley. He was ashamed to see me, I guess," Mother answered. "He did say he didn't do it. Said Dupree was telling a lie, and asked me if I'd tell his mama that."

Wesley sat on the floor of the corn crib and began to slowly strip the shuck away from an ear of corn. "I bet Freeman's tellin' the truth," he said, finally. "I bet Dupree had somethin' to do with it. He's been tryin' to find some way to get to Freeman all summer."

"What'll they do to Freeman, Wesley?" I asked.

"I don't know," he replied.

"They'll take him over to the jail," Mother said angrily. "He'll be locked up with drunks and crooks and God only knows what else."

"He ain't but fourteen years old," Wesley said, almost as an afterthought.

"That won't make no difference, boys. It's a stealing offense and that means jail, no matter what age he is." Mother was trying to contain her temper, but she could envision Freeman shoved behind bars with criminals who worked the road gangs in their striped convict uniforms.

"What're we gonna do, Mama?" I asked.

"I told your daddy. He was up at the house. He said he'd go over there and see what it was about. Said something might be worked out. Maybe he could post bail for Freeman, or something."

"Can we go with Daddy?" I pleaded. "Me'n Wesley?"

"No!" Mother answered sharply. "No. I'm sorry, boys, but it's something you ought not be around."

"Freeman's our friend, Mama!"

"She's right," Wesley decided. "It'd just make Freeman feel bad, and I reckon he feels bad enough already. If Daddy can do somethin', he will. If he can't, it's just gonna be Freeman's word against Mr. Hixon's."

"Couldn't we wait in the car?" I begged.

"No," Mother answered. "You can wait up at the house, but it's best that we handle this, and we need to be goin' on over. If Freeman's daddy gets there before the Sheriff, there may be some real trouble. Your daddy can stop all that."

We waited for more than an hour before we saw Mother's 1938 Ford appear, sliding cautiously along the slippery red road, and as she stopped beneath the pecan tree in the front yard, we saw she was alone.

"What happened?" I asked eagerly, as Mother opened the front door. "Where's Daddy?"

"He's with Sheriff Brownlee. Freeman escaped over on Rakestraw Bridge Road."

"He . . . ?" Wesley exclaimed.

"Escaped," Mother repeated. "We were followin' them over to Edenville to see about postin' a bond, and when Sheriff Brownlee slowed down to cross Rakestraw Bridge, Freeman jumped out and ran off in the swamp."

"He got away?" I asked, amazed at Freeman's boldness.

"I don't know," Mother said, slipping wearily into a chair. "When I left, Sheriff Brownlee and your daddy and Freeman's daddy were after him."

Wesley walked to the window and looked out in the direction of Black Pool Swamp. "They'll never catch Freeman," he predicted. "Freeman knows that swamp better'n all of them put together. He won't come out until he wants to."

"I don't know, son," Mother said. "Sheriff Brownlee was shootin' his pistol off up in the air and yelling that he'd get the bloodhounds if Freeman didn't come back, and you have to remember Freeman's daddy knows that swamp pretty good, too."

"Not like Freeman," insisted Wesley.

"But the bloodhounds, they'd find him," I said.

"Maybe. Maybe not," Wesley whispered. "Maybe not."

They did not find Freeman that afternoon. At first darkness, my father told us, Sheriff Brownlee stood at the mouth of a logging road leading into Black Pool Swamp and yelled, "Hear me, boy! I'm comin' back! I'm comin' back, boy! And I'm takin' you outa here. Ain't no man, white or nigger, ever got away from me, boy. You better give up." Freeman had not answered Sheriff Brownlee's threats and Brownlee had lost his temper. He emptied his pistol into the ground and screamed that he would return with a truck loaded with deputies carrying shotguns, and he would get bloodhounds trained to chew the legs off escaped criminals.

My father was tired and wet, but he was irritated that Sheriff Brownlee had threatened Freeman. "Man or boy, it don't matter. All that'll do is scare him more, make it harder to get him out."

"What would Morgan do?" asked Mother. Morgan was my father's brother, and he had been sheriff of Eden County for years before retiring to fish the Savannah River.

"He'd go into the swamp and stay until he found the boy," my father said simply.

"By himself?" I asked. "Is that all, Daddy?"

"It's just one boy."

"But Freeman knows that swamp inside out."

"It's a boy against a man, son. Don't ever forget that."

My father did not know Freeman. In Black Pool Swamp, Freeman was not a boy. He was an animal. No man could trap him.

"I don't like it," Mother fussed. "Freeman's all alone in that swamp, and he's got a sheriff firing off his pistol like crazy! That man's no good. He never has been. No wonder there's so much trouble in the county. He's kin to Old Man Alfred Brownlee, and that's the craziest man in Georgia. In fact, Old Man Alfred's first wife was my first cousin on my daddy's side, and she used to say that whole family didn't have enough sense to get out of the rain!"

"Mama, Freeman's all right," Wesley assured her. "Freeman's fine. He's been livin' in that swamp all his life."

"But it's damp out tonight," Mother protested.

"Freeman's dry," Wesley said. "He's got more'n a dozen places to hide where it's dry as bein' at home."

"There's snakes in there," Lynn whispered.

"Freeman raised most of them," Wesley argued. "Heck, Lynn, it ain't the Okefenokee. There ain't no alligators or nothin' like that in there."

"Not what Freeman says," Lynn answered.

"Freeman would say anything about Black Pool Swamp, Lynn, and you know it. There ain't nothin' in there but some rabbits and beaver and squirrels," Wesley replied dryly.

"And snakes," Lynn added.

"Yeah, some snakes."

Wesley knew Freeman well. Freeman had a dreamer's pride in Black Pool Swamp. To Freeman, Black Pool Swamp made the Okefenokee seem like a mudhole. It angered him when people made fun of Black Pool and he had invented outrageous stories to enhance his position as the only real authority on those two hundred acres of dark, forbidding woods. He told of an albino bear, eight feet tall, whose shimmering white fur was streaked with dried blood. He told of bobcats as huge and fierce as Asian tigers. He told of a killer wolf, a twenty-foot rattlesnake, a vicious wild boar with foot-long tusks, and he swore he knew the entrance to a secret underground cave where Indian warriors were buried. Occasionally, Freeman would present a bone from a decayed cow and tell us it was the remains of a careless human who refused his warnings about the dangers of Black Pool, or the Great

Okeenoonoo, as he called the swamp. Okeenoonoo, Freeman claimed, was an ancient Cherokee Indian word meaning Woods of Death.

The WPA had drained Black Pool Swamp in the mid-thirties and the signature of woeful, frightened men who had only their muscles and the promise of Franklin Delano Roosevelt to believe in, was still carved in crisscrossing drain ditches that found the banks of Beaverjam Creek. The ditches had become covered in a death mask of honeysuckle vines and swamp grass, drooping and rising out of the depressions where WPA men had shoveled for WPA wages. Industrious beavers had whittled stick dams out of small hardwoods, and had laced the dams together near the creek. The dams had again clogged Black Pool Swamp and there were acres of barely moving surface water seeping over the rims of WPA ditches, covered in a death mask of honeysuckle vines and swamp grass.

To those who feared the woods, Black Pool Swamp was imposing and, in its way, evil. To Freeman and those of us who lived south of Banner's Crossing, Black Pool was an endless wonder, a huge playground to be discovered with each eager excursion. We had hacked off fox grape vines to swing, yodeling Tarzan yells in the soprano voices of boys. We knew which ridges of heaped-up dirt to walk in the watery bottomland. We had learned to cross back and forth over Beaverjam Creek, balancing on the trunks of fallen trees that had washed out of the banks of the creek in sudden flooding. We knew where to find the dens of red fox, where the giant canecutter rabbits played, where catfish or eel could be caught by grappling, and where the remains of several whiskey stills belonging to Freeman's daddy could be located. Once, Wesley and I had even discovered one of Freeman's man-made caves. It was a shallow hole running into the side of a steep hill overgrown with mountain laurel. Freeman had found a land flaw, a curious wash-out scooping into the hill, and he had carefully sculptured his cave out of hard clay and mountain laurel roots. It was a magnificent hiding place, a quiet, cool fortress protected from wind and rain by a natural upper lip that curled over the opening. It was not a large cave, but Freeman had obviously spent long, dreamy hours there. Wesley found some *Grit* newspapers and a cache of cured rabbit tobacco, and there was evidence that Freeman had experimented with building a small cooking fire. We did not tell Freeman about our discovery, but we began to respect his stories of caves and hiding places in the Great Okeenoonoo.

We ate supper in silence, listening for some new off-sound among the voices of Black Pool Swamp. Perhaps Freeman would speak to us in one of his animal tongues, and we would understand. He would tell us where he was, what he needed, how he felt.

An owl celebrated its confusion of sleep and rest and Wesley lifted his face toward the sound, straining to recognize Freeman's playful imitation. The owl called again and Wesley relaxed. Unlike Laron Crook, Wesley knew the difference between Freeman and a bird. The owl was real, and would cry again and again, until Wesley slipped away and tied knots in the four corners of his bedsheet and then the owl would stop crying and bury its head underneath its wings. I did not know why owls obeyed Wesley's strong superstition, but they always did and we would silently marvel at this great power Wesley had. It was a spell not even Freeman could explain, though he declared that an owl, like the vampire, was Satan's creature and tying knots in bedsheets strangled owls much in the same manner as flashing a cross in the face of a vampire stifled the gruesome urge for human blood. "It's all the same," Freeman had told us. "For every evil spell, there's a good one. Ol' Wesley just accidentally discovered one about owls."

We were half listening to a radio comedy show when Dover arrived with Freeman's parents.

"Go to the kitchen," Mother told us, "and be quiet."

The grownups sat in the living room and talked in voices we could hear only as distortions. Occasionally, the low, grave tones of the men would be countered by the painful choking cough of Rachel Boyd. She had tuberculosis and her lungs had shriveled into small tender sores that bled a sickening red mucus when she could not control her coughing. Her illness had isolated Freeman, who could not wholly accept the wheezing, emaciated woman as his mother. To Freeman, his mother was someone vigorous, someone who had been warm to touch, whose skin had been flushed red with the vitality of Irish blood. He still loved this once-upon-a-time mother, this weakened substitute, but he was quietly horrified by the coolness of her gray coloring and the nauseating mucus odor of her breath. He had watched her suffer her incredible pain, watched as she lay motionless in bed fighting to conquer the spasms that were squeezing her lungs, and he had heard her mumbled, bewildered prayers for relief, incoherent prayers of half-promises and a beggar's pleading. Freeman had listened to the women of Emery speak of ". . . poor Rachel Boyd," and he knew what they meant: his mother had a terminal illness. In a vision that had eased into his dreams many times, Freeman knew she would die in early life, her lungs drowning in their own phlegm. Her lungs would die first and then the spillway of her throat would die, and then her brain and then her heart. Her heart would die last, wanting to live against terrible, predictable odds. Her heart would die of suffocation, pumping frantically, unreasonably, until it could no longer pump.

Freeman's vision of his mother's fate had been transferred to us, not by description, but by some mystic union we shared, and as we listened to Rachel Boyd choking in our home, I believed she longed for death, wished for death with selfish yearning.

"Louise, you hear her?" I asked, whispering.

Louise nodded. She moved to the side table where Mother kept drinking water in an enamel bucket, and she poured a dipper of water into a clean glass. "I better take this in there," she said. "She'll be needin' it."

Louise put the glass of water on a mahogany serving tray that Amy had given Mother for Christmas, and then carried it into the living room. Louise was the oldest daughter still living at home and she understood her responsibilities; she was part girl and part woman, part sister and part mother, and she had a gift for separating the roles.

"Is she dyin'?" asked Lynn when Louise returned.

"Hush," commanded Louise. "She might hear."

We sat and listened. We could hear the men talking and I knew Dover had become angry. His voice was tense and high-pitched, and I thought he must have been pacing because his voice changed positions through the sheetrock wall. Occasionally, Dover would pause and there would be a deeper bass reply from my father or Freeman's father.

"Dover's all worked up, ain't he?" I asked Wesley.

"Yeah," Wesley replied.

"Wonder why he's so mad?" Lynn whispered.

"Sssssssssssh," Wesley said suddenly, whirling in his chair. Outside, Short Leg and Bullet barked. Wesley moved to the back door and opened it.

"What's the matter?" Louise asked.

"Sssssssssssh!"

Wesley stepped onto the back porch. He looked into the heavy, blank darkness. He whistled sharply and Short Leg and Bullet stopped barking.

"What's the matter?" Louise repeated. "You hear somethin'?"

"Freeman," Wesley said quietly. "It's Freeman."

At first I did not hear it. There was nothing but a low

wind and the brushing sound of wet leaves against wet leaves.

"I don't hear nothin'," I said.

"Listen," Wesley warned.

And then I heard it: a shrill, long whistle folding into the wind, riding an invisible sound wave and carrying the eerie message that Freeman was safe.

"It is!" I exclaimed. "That's Freeman!"

"It ain't nothing but the wind," Louise argued. "Ain't nobody can whistle like that."

"He's got a cane flute," Wesley explained. "That's his cane flute."

The flute whistle floated in again, clear and strong. Wesley stepped outside and returned the call of the whippoorwill. There was a long silence and then a whippoorwill replied from somewhere in Black Pool Swamp.

"Maybe he knows his mama and daddy's over here," Lynn said.

"He knows," Wesley replied. "We better tell them."

We followed Wesley into the living room and Wesley told of Freeman's cane-flute signal. Rachel Boyd wept quietly, burying her face in a large handkerchief. Dover asked Wesley if he was sure the whistle had been Freeman and Wesley said, "Yes, I'm sure."

"I reckon it's so," Dover agreed. "Freeman used to keep that cane stick with him all the time."

Odell Boyd nodded and sucked on a hand-rolled Prince Albert cigarette. "The boy's got them things everywhere," he said. "I showed him how to cut one out, oh, couple of years ago. It's Freeman, I reckon."

"You know where he is, son?" my father asked Wesley.

"No, sir. He could be anywhere. Freeman's got lots of places in the swamp."

"That's the truth," added Dover. "Lots of places."

"Places we ain't never seen, Daddy," I explained.

"He knows more about them woods then anybody," Odell Boyd muttered. "More'n me, even."

"Wesley said he'd be fine down in the woods, Rachel," Mother said quickly. "You said that, didn't you, Wesley?" Mother's voice betrayed her. She was thinking of Freeman being Wesley or me.

Wesley hesitated. He looked at Mother and then at Rachel Boyd. "You ain't got to worry about Freeman, Mrs. Boyd," he said softly. "He'll be out in a couple of days, soon as he gets some time to think about it."

Rachel Boyd did not answer. She closed her sunken eyes and struggled with a convulsion trembling in her throat.

"Me'n Colin'll go down in the morning and see if we can find him," Wesley continued. "Maybe he won't run from us."

"Good idea, Wesley," Dover said. "He's close to you boys, and that's for sure. Maybe I'll take off from the REA crew and go with you. Reckon it'll be too wet to do much work, anyhow."

"But the sheriff's comin' back with his deputies, ain't he?" Lynn asked. "They'll be all over the place and . . ."

My father's gaze stopped Lynn in midsentence. "They'll start up by Rakestraw's Bridge," he corrected. "It'll take all day to get down here."

"Well, they'll bring in bloodhounds and I guarantee it," Dover said gravely.

My father walked to the living room window and looked out into the gray-black sheet of fog. "They been to your place, Odell?" he asked.

Odell Boyd shook his head. "Not directly. They's been a sheriff's car over that way. Saw it as we was leavin'. Reckon they must be expecting Freeman to come home."

"Freeman ain't about to do that," Dover declared. "Shoot, that boy's got better sense than that. They sure don't do him credit, they think that."

"They'll be watching," my father replied. "They'll be wanting somethin' of Freeman's to get the scent if they bring in hounds."

The room suddenly became quiet. Funeral quiet. No one moved. I could see gaunt, restless bloodhounds straining against their leashes, gouging clean, sharp furrows out of the ground with their claws, yelping at the scent of Freeman lingering in an old shirt or jacket. I could hear the primitive Ho's and Yo's of the bloodhound master urging his trained killer dogs to sniff out the unseen vapor trail of Freeman's escape, and I had a grotesque vision of Freeman cowering in the arm of a high limb on a water oak as triumphant men circled their fourteen-year-old prey and laughed at his fear of drooling, hungry dogs with white, flashing teeth.

Odell Boyd flipped open the lid of his tobacco tin. "Maybe them dogs couldn't find no scent if we'd scrub all the boy's clothes," he said.

"Makes no difference," Dover answered. "They'd just take the whole pack of 'em in where Freeman's bed is and they'd get it. Don't make no difference, Odell."

"Reckon that's the truth," Odell Boyd mumbled, licking his cigarette into a roll.

"Like I said a while ago, there ain't much a man can do in a case like this, Odell. Ain't much at all," Dover counseled.

"Reckon that's the truth."

"Best thing to do is post bond for the boy and get Old Man Hixon to take a settlement. I reckon he'd talk about it. Anyway, I ain't so sure he believes Dupree anymore'n I do," Dover declared.

"He sure didn't sound that way this afternoon," argued Mother. "You'd have thought Freeman robbed Fort Knox, the way he was carryin' on."

"Yes'm. He sure sounds that way sometimes," agreed Dover. "I seen him lots of times, mad like that. He gets over it, though."

Rachel Boyd moved forward in her chair and reached for Mother's hand. Her body heaved with a deep gurgling in her lungs.

"He's my boy," she said hoarsely, sadly. "He ain't done nothin' like stealin'. He wouldn't do that." She turned to Wesley. "Wesley, he wouldn't do that, would he? You know him. He wouldn't do that."

Wesley stepped forward and handed Rachel Boyd the glass of water from the mahogany tray. "No'm," he said gently. "Freeman wouldn't do nothin' like that. There's a truth to it. It'll come out."

"It will, won't it?" Freeman's mother whispered. "Pray God there's a truth and it'll be told. It ain't Freeman. I know it ain't." She searched Wesley's face for its magic.

"Yes'm," Wesley said.

"It'll be like the boys said, Rachel," Mother added softly.

Odell Boyd cupped the thin cigarette in his hand and stared at the burning tip. "I'll see Hixon. First thing in the mornin'. Maybe I can work it off."

Dover stood. "Best I take y'all on home," he suggested. "Maybe me'n the boys can get us a early start in the mornin'."

Wesley tugged me from sleep before dawn, motioning silence. Garry still breathed his warm, even rhythm of dreams. We dressed quickly in the umbrella of orange kerosene light in the middle room, and I could smell the spice of morning coffee and oatmeal from the kitchen.

"Now, I mean it," Mother instructed as we ate. "Both of you stay together and don't go driftin' away from Dover. I don't trust boys bein' out in the woods this early."

Mother worried about us. She did not consider that we had often been in the woods before dawn, checking rabbit boxes. But this was a particular day, with a particular mission, and she sensed an unseen danger. She filled our bowls a second time with bubbling oatmeal and spooned rich butter on top. "Eat it up," she said firmly. "It's stopped raining, but it'll be chilly by the creek."

Wesley poured a second cup of coffee. "Does Daddy think Freeman stole that money, Mama?"

"I guess not. Your daddy's had his own trouble with Hixon. Two or three times, he's tried to double-charge your daddy for fertilizer."

"I remember," Wesley said.

The white light of morning stretched its fingers over the rim of Black Pool Swamp and froze the horizon with its dull, aluminum color. Dover's truck stuttered to a halt outside and we heard several voices.

"Dover's got people with him," I said.

"Why?" asked Mother. "He didn't say anything about bringing anybody with him."

Wesley and I went outside. Dover was removing a cardboard box from the cab of his truck. Alvin and R. J. and Otis stood sleepily, moving their balance from foot to foot, yawning, stretching. They said listless hellos. Otis leaned against the back fender and stuck his hands in his pockets.

"Why's everybody here, Dover?" asked Wesley.

"Because, ol' buddy, I have figured out what we're gonna do to keep Freeman outa the strong right hand of the law! Yessir, got the plan when I was feedin' Bark last night, so I stopped by and got the boys this mornin'."

"What're you talkin' about, Dover? There ain't nothin' we can do," I said. "Nothin' except look for Freeman."

"Sure there is," Dover exclaimed. "Absolutely. Now, me and you and Wesley and the boys here know there ain't nobody gonna find Freeman in that ol' swamp if Freeman don't want them to find him. Ain't that right?"

"Well, yeah, I guess. Wesley?"

Wesley nodded.

"Exceptin' for one thing," Dover added. "One thing, and one thing only." Dover was becoming excited.

We waited for him to continue. He looked at Wesley and motioned slightly with his hands, begging Wesley to ask about the one thing that would trap Freeman. Wesley did not respond. Dover turned to R. J. and Alvin. Alvin blinked and yawned.

"One thing," Dover repeated. "Ain't y'all got any idea? What's the Sheriff plannin' on doin'?"

"Bringing in deputies," I answered eagerly.

Dover was disgusted. "Shoot, ain't no deputies gonna find Freeman. What else?"

"Bloodhounds," Alvin said, suddenly awake. "Gonna bring in bloodhounds. That's what they was sayin' at the store last night."

Dover snapped his fingers and slapped his thigh. "You got it, Alvin. You have put your finger slap-dab on it, boy! Bloodhounds!"

Dover carried the cardboard box to the tailgate of his truck. He pulled open the folded-in top and pulled out a handful of wadded shirts and pants.

"What's that?" asked Wesley. "Whose clothes you got, Dover?"

"Freeman's, Wesley. These are Freeman's clothes. His mama gave 'em to me early this morning. Them bloodhounds want to smell Freeman, well, by granny, they're gonna smell Freeman!"

Wesley picked up a shirt and examined it. "All right, Dover. You gonna tell us what it is you got in mind?"

"Well, Wes, every one of us is gonna take one of these pieces of Freeman's clothes and we're gonna drag them through Black Pool Swamp, goin' in all different directions. That way, when them bloodhounds get in there, they'll be goin' crazy, trying to find which smell to follow."

Dover made his announcement like a politician at a chicken barbecue. His plan was remarkable. It was a plan that would have baffled Sherlock Holmes, and Dover was drunk with the giddiness of his brilliance. He turned slowly on one heel, prying into each of our faces, begging our awed approvals. A wide, open-mouthed smile covered his face like a half-moon and there were very small sounds of "Yeah? Yeah? Yeah?" clicking on his tongue.

"Damn, Dover!" exclaimed Alvin. "I ain't believing it. You make that up? All by yourself?"

"I did. I sure did, Alvin. Well, almost by myself," Dover answered proudly. "I heard this radio show where Sam Spade or Mr. Keene, Tracer of Lost Persons, or Boston Blackie, or somebody, stopped a crook from killin' somebody by doing almost the same thing! And, boys, if it can work for Sam Spade, it can work for us!"

Wesley smiled, nodded, separated Freeman's clothes. "It's a good idea, Dover. I ain't sure it's something we can do, but it's one good idea."

"What'd you mean, we can't do it?!"

"Daddy may not like it," answered Wesley. "Maybe it's against the law."

"Against the law? What's against the law, Wes? Sam Spade done it! It ain't against the law to go draggin' clothes in the woods. Alvin, you ever hear it was against the law to drag some old clothes in the woods?"

Alvin grinned. "Not me, Dover."

"I ain't talking about that," Wesley said quietly. "I'm talking about interferin' with a lawman's duty, or something like that."

"Wesley, you beat all, you know that?" argued Dover. "We're talkin' about Freeman. Freeman! If you was in there in place of him, he'd be doin' the same thing, and more. Ain't no telling what Freeman would do! Dammit—and I'm apologizin' for saying that— but you can be some kind of stubborn, Wes! You ain't right all the time, you know!"

Wesley did not answer. R. J. spat through the slit of his front teeth. Alvin picked up a rock and threw it at a fence post, hitting it dead center. Dover kicked at the ground and pulled at his pants.

"All right," Dover finally said. "I'll go ask your daddy. He says it's all right, you and Colin can come along. Don't make no difference what he says about me'n the others. We're gonna do it, and we ain't afraid to take the chance."

Dover had leveled Wesley and Wesley knew it. "Aw, that's all right," Wesley said. "Ain't no need to ask Daddy. We'll help out." There was a right and wrong to the matter, but Wesley was not certain right and wrong was important. Helping Freeman was part of it, and belonging to Dover's inspired production of a radio drama was part of it. Wesley knew his leadership had limits. He knew there was a difference between leading and demanding, even if he had reason for making demands. There was a thing, a rare click, in Wesley; it tempered his logic, balanced it with impulse, and as predictable as he seemed, no one ever knew what Wesley would do.

"Now, that's talkin'!" exclaimed Dover. "That's the way I like to hear you talk, Wes! All right, let's do it this way!"

Dover squatted and brushed a fan-shaped design in the white sand of the front yard. He drew a series of loops, circles, and lines with his finger. At the bottom of the fan, he scrawled the letter N. "That stands for North," he announced proudly. "I learned to do that in the Army." At the top of the fan, he lettered an S.

"That's South, ain't it?" Alvin asked.

"You got it, Alvin. That's South. S for South."

"Put you a W on the right, Dover," Otis said, cocking his head to study the design.

"The W goes on the left, Otis. W for West. E goes on the right. E for East," Dover corrected.

"Yeah . . ."

Dover studied his lettering. "You got it, boys? This here's Beaverjam Creek. That there's Rakestraw Road." He made wavy lines with his finger.

"Dover, you got the S and N upside down," R. J. said.

"What'd you mean, R. J.?"

"North's that way, and South's that way, according to the creek."

Dover looked again at his map. He stood and walked on the other side, peering at his design like a hawk after a rabbit. Then he looked around him, settling on the sun with its red yoke rupturing and running into the trees. "Yeah, you're right, R. J."

"What'd you need N and S for anyhow?" asked Otis. "That don't mean nothin'. We know the swamp."

"I guess you're right, Otis. Just thought I'd like to teach you boys somethin'," Dover explained timidly. "Anyway, this is it: R. J., you take off and go over toward the Goldmine Road; Otis, you skirt around that upper beaver dam and follow the old creek bed; Alvin, you stay on the high ground, up where we hunted them doves last year; Wes, you'n Colin go right down the middle of the swamp, since y'all live here and know them low places better'n any of us, and I'm gonna go over toward Tanner's Branch."

"Me'n Wes don't have to go together, Dover," I volunteered. "He can go one way and I can go the other."

"You stay with Wes," ordered Dover. "And I mean it. Anythin' happen to you and your daddy'll skin my hide. I ain't about to get your mama and daddy on my back."

"But . . ."

"You stay with me," Wesley said firmly.

"Aw . . ."

Dover erased his map with his shoe. "Now, we all are gonna start up there near Rakestraw Road, down below the bridge. All you gotta do is drag them clothes along behind you. When you get to some place where ain't nothin' but snakes and lizards can get in, take them clothes and stuff 'em inside of your shirt, and backtrack a little ways, then cut off to one side. That way, it ain't gonna do nothin' but confuse them ol' dogs."

"Why's that, Dover?" asked Otis. It was easy to baffle Otis.

"Hell, *I* can smell Freeman in them clothes," declared Dover. "I swear that boy puts off a stink. When them bloodhounds start sniffin' out Freeman, they ain't gonna smell nothin' but Freeman."

Dover issued articles of Freeman's clothing and Wesley went into the house to tell Mother we were leaving. He returned with a paper sack.

"Mama fixed some food for Freeman, in case we find him," Wesley explained. "I reckon she thinks he's starving."

"Your mama's a good woman, Wes, and that's the truth," Dover said. "I guess Freeman knows how to take care of himself, but if we don't find him, just leave it somewheres. Freeman'll find it. You better believe he'll know where we are, even if we don't know where he is."

Dover drove his truck over a logging road that had become spotted with broom sage—a blown, forgotten highway. He stopped a quarter of a mile away from Rakestraw Bridge.

"All right, boys, y'all get started," Dover instructed. "I'm gonna drive the truck back out to the road and I'll circle back and pick up here."

"It's gettin' late," Alvin noted. "You ain't gonna have time before they turn loose them hounds."

"Shoot, we got plenty of time, Alvin. You ain't never seen a bunch of sheriff's deputies at work, have you?" Dover said.

"No, I ain't," Alvin admitted.

"Well, first thing they gonna do is build a fire up there where they park their cars and trucks, and don't ask me why. They's always building fires, no matter how hot it is. Then they got to wait for ol' Jim Ed Felton to bring his hounds, and Jim Ed'll have to stop two or three times on the way to show off them dogs at country stores. Don't ask me about that, either. That's ol' Jim Ed. Loves to show off them dogs. Even when he gets up there where the sheriff's waitin', he'll spend a hour talkin' about which dog tracks best, which one howls loudest, which one's in heat. Hell, it'll take a couple of hours before they get ready to start."

Dover had truly impressed us with his knowledge. There were times when we did not respect the fact he was a man and we were boys, that he knew things we had never thought of.

Wesley and I slipped and stumbled down a steep hill leading to the upper spill of Black Pool Swamp. It was a part of the swamp we did not know well, because it was outside our boundaries, north of the imaginary north line that protected us, isolated us from threat and danger. We had hunted there with Freeman, and once each year we crossed through that damp, mossy seepage to a lush cane growth on Little Tanner's Branch, and we cut a summer's supply of fishing canes. But there was an unusual quiet to this part of the swamp, as though some untold horror had left its presence and that presence overwhelmed everyone and everything invading its influence.

Wesley had a pair of Freeman's work pants and I carried the food Mother had packed in a paper sack. I walked ahead of Wesley, watching for suckholes, soft pools of sand and water that pockmarked the swamp. We decided to edge close to those pools, knowing the dogs would plunge stubbornly into the middle of the mire and be slowed by the laborsome work of clawing their way to firm ground. If we could trick them into four or five suckholes, we would then lead them straight up the steepest hill we could find, then down again, and up again, then back into the swamp.

We quickly discovered three suckholes and Wesley made certain the scent of Freeman's work pants coated the ground. A huge pond of backed-up water we had never before seen forced us to the bank of a hill.

"Must be some new beaver dams," Wesley guessed. "They been chewin' on every tree in here."

We walked silently along the rim of the pond, where the heavy perfume of tiny blossoms from tiny flowering plants lingered like sweet breath. A rain crow fussed at our intrusion. Huge black gums and water oaks and ash and beech had been nibbled down and the bark stripped clean. At the base of the trees, there were flat, neatly circled chips.

"What'd they strip the bark for?" I asked Wesley.

"I ain't sure," he admitted. "Maybe it's the sap they're after. Maybe that's what they eat. Maybe they use it to plug up their dams, like tar, or somethin'. I heard Halls Barton say they stripped the bark off to cure the logs. Maybe that's it."

We walked the shoreline of the water bank until we found the dam, a majestic heap of sticks and logs jammed into the runway of the branch. There was a long, curving wing on both sides of the branch, a fort-like pile of limbs built to nudge the water into select run-arounds in a slow, seeping fashion.

"Be some good fishin' there," observed Wesley. "We'll have to remember it. Don't guess nobody knows it's here. Not even Freeman."

"Sure he knows," I said. "Freeman's been all through here."

"He'd have told us about this. It's a lots better dam than them behind the house. Naw, Freeman don't know about it."

We had lingered too long and Wesley increased our pace until we crossed back inside our boundaries, and we were easy about where we were and where we were going. As we moved along, Wesley thought of a way to further confuse the bloodhounds. He took Freeman's pants and rubbed them up the trunks of several trees, as far as he could reach, then he would stick the pants in his jacket and broad-jump away from the base of the tree. Fifty feet away from the tree, he would begin dragging the pants again.

"That'll make 'em think they got Freeman treed," Wesley said proudly. "Might even bring the sheriff and his deputies in tryin' to find him. They'll be goin' crazy."

"Ain't they gonna smell us, Wesley?"

"Sure, but it ain't us they're supposed to smell. It's Freeman, and Dover was right about one thing—these pants stink enough. I bet Freeman had been wearin' them a week or longer."

Nearer to the center of Black Pool Swamp, where we played, Wesley began to call softly for Freeman, but there was no answer.

"Do an owl," I urged. "Maybe he'll answer an owl."

"Owls call at night. Don't you know nothin'?"

"What about a bobwhite?"

"Well, he might answer."

Wesley did a bobwhite. We waited. He whistled again. Nothing.

"Freeman," I called out. "Freeman!"

Wesley turned his head slowly, like a bird listening to the wind. "He ain't gonna say nothin'," he mumbled.

Freeman did not answer, but I could feel him, sense his presence. He was near, watching us.

"He's there, ain't he, Wesley?" I whispered.

"Maybe."

"Ain't no maybe about it. He's sneakin' around and you know it."

"We ain't got time to find out. We gotta get back to the house."

"Let me drag the pants a little bit, Wesley," I begged. "You been draggin' all the way."

"All right, but make sure they stay on the ground.

I'm goin' on down to the sand bar to see if Otis has crossed the creek yet. You come on down there."

Wesley left quickly, disappearing into the woods. I turned Freeman's pants inside out and carefully pulled them after me. Not even Wesley had thought of turning the pants inside out, and I was pleased with the brilliance of my idea: if bloodhounds could smell Freeman on the outside of his pants, they would go slobbering crazy when they picked up a whiff of this fresh odor.

I decided not to follow Wesley's path. If the bloodhounds had become accustomed to our scents, going separate directions would have to divide the pack and we would then contend the bloodhounds were worthless, because they could not tell one scent from another.

Dragging Freeman's pants through the woods was the first important, man-type thing I had ever done, and I began to feel the oppressive responsibility of a newer, higher calling. I could see men sitting around service stations talking about the daring and, yes, the genius, of my woodmanship. Dragging pants was a man's job, they would say, a man's art, and I had, at twelve, advanced all recognized knowledge of the subject by turning the pants inside out. And they would talk—probably in exaggerations—of how the fresh, powerful scent of Freeman had been sniffed off oak leaves by a wild dog covered with bloodsucking ticks and driven insane with rabies, and how that dog had begun stalking me, slithering along on its belly like a bobcat, until it found me, off guard and unawares. They would lower their voices when they retold the part about the dog's charge, leaping through the air toward my twelve-year-old back, and how I had turned, Freeman's pants in one hand and a jagged walking stick in the other, and how I had had time to do only one thing—fall away and jab the walking stick into the throat of the diving dog. And after the telling, the men would sit quiet in their service stations and nod. Their telling and sitting and nodding would make a legend of my helping Freeman, and I would protest. Any man—man, that is—would have done the same thing.

I found a walking stick, with the suggestion of a point, and then circled the hill where, when we were younger, we had spent exuberant hours on torn-apart cardboard boxes, sledding down a carpet of pine needles. It had been a childish time, a time when there was no difference between black and white and our babyhood friends included the children of Negro sharecroppers. In the days of our sledding, we had been totally free of the distinction of Our Side and the Highway 17 Gang. We did not know there was a difference between us and anyone. We did not know, because we did not care. The days were too filled with adventure, too crowded with pleasures of running, physically running, after the quicksilver of seasons. The running had kept us joyously alive, had reminded us of our realness and quickened our imaginations of what it was like to be a spinning member of a spinning universe.

I passed a fox den that was unusually deep, burrowed beneath a surface root of a black gum tree, and an inspiring bit of trickery exploded in my mind. I pulled Freeman's pants over the opening of the fox den, generously rubbing the ground with Freeman's scent. I wrapped the pants around my walking stick and carefully shoved them deep into the den, scrubbing them against the walls of that dark, dry hiding place. I then walked away in giant steps, holding Freeman's pants above my head on the stick. If Jim Ed Felton's bloodhounds could still tell up from down, they would turn into whimpering fools at the fox hole. And if Jim Ed found them there, braying at a hole in the ground, he would kick their butts and sell them to the highest bidder.

There was no reason to drag Freeman's pants any longer. There was a certain justice to leaving Freeman in a fox den. Freeman would love that touch, I thought. Freeman would have done exactly the same thing.

"Colin, what in hell's name you doin', boy?!"

I did not expect Freeman's voice. It struck me like a great weight, broke my knees, and crushed the breath out of me. My heart erupted like a volcano, careened off my ribs, and lodged somewhere underneath my left armpit. I sank to the ground, and Freeman was over me like a cloud, catching me before I fell forward.

"Hey! What's the matter, boy? You all right?"

I tried to motion for Freeman to catch the stick in my hand, the one holding his pants, but he did not understand and the stick fell away.

"C'mon, boy! Damn! You ain't gonna die on me, are you? God Almighty, boy. C'mon."

Freeman slapped me twice across the face and suddenly the fear rushed out of my brain and my heart began to ease back into my chest cavity.

"Yeah, yeah, Freeman, I'm all right," I mumbled, sitting down and breathing deep. "Damn. You have to scare me to death?"

Freeman smiled, smiled his King-of-Black-Pool-Swamp, Chief-of-the-Great-Okeenoonoo smile. "Shoot, boy! I gotta be careful. You know that."

"You could've whistled, or somethin'."

"Yeah. Guess I could've. Where'd Wes go?"

"Down to the sand—hey, how'd you know Wesley was with me?"

"Shoot, I been watchin' you for a hour. What'd y'all doin', anyway? You look like a bunch of fools draggin' a pair of pants through the woods. Even seen Alvin and Otis doin' the same thing. Y'all crazy?"

I explained Dover's scheme and Freeman radiated. He loved the plan and he loved the attention.

"Damned if that ain't the end-all," he said happily. "Yessir, that is about the finest piece of thinkin' ol' Dover has ever done, or ever will do. Hard to believe he's got that much sense."

"He said he got the notion from a radio show. Sam Spade or somebody."

"Sam Spade? Well, by granny, it ought to work. Sam Spade, huh? I didn't hear that one. Did you? You hear it?"

"Naw. Hey, Freeman, what'd you think about pokin' them pants of yours in that fox hole?" I asked.

"Son, that is pure genius. Yessir. Pure genius.

Couldn't've thought of anythin' better myself. Guess I messed it up, trampin' all around here, but that's some kind of thinkin'. I'm proud of you. Yessir, I am, and that's a fact."

Freeman's compliment was highly flattering, but his mood changed quickly and he became strangely tense.

"What'd you gonna do, Freeman?" I asked. "Sheriff and his deputies are gonna be all over the place."

Freeman picked up a stick and started chewing on it. "Well, I ain't too sure. I ain't goin' to no jail, and that's the truth. Not for somethin' I ain't done."

"You didn't steal that twenty dollars, did you, Freeman?"

"Steal it? Shoot, I never even saw it! If I was goin' to steal something, it'd sure as Satan be more'n twenty dollars. You know I got more sense than that."

"They'll catch up to you, Freeman. Sooner or later."

"They ain't never gonna catch me, and you know it. C'mon, let's go find Wesley."

We moved quickly through the woods, across a net of drain ditches covered with surface water, and followed the bank of Beaverjam Creek. Freeman moved like an animal, completely noiseless and graceful. Watching him slip like some wind creature through the trees, I realized it was impossible to tell he had been there. Perhaps bloodhounds would siphon off the steps he had taken, but no man could follow the evidence of Freeman's movements. I had never before believed his stories about melting into the woods and becoming part of them; now I did, and I remembered other exhibitions of his skill. Once, when Wesley and I had camped with Freeman, I saw him snap the head of a cottonmouth moccasin in a move so blinding it frightened me. "I could do that ten times out of ten," he bragged. Now, following him, I knew he had not lied. Freeman became an ethereal extension of himself in Black Pool Swamp. In Black Pool—in the Great Okeenoonoo—Freeman was free, free from any of the pitiful suspicions we had when he told his tales.

Wesley was sitting, half-hidden, beside a water oak twisted and knotted in some eternal pain. He was not surprised to see Freeman.

"Here," Wesley said, handing Freeman the paper sack of food Mother had prepared for him. "Mama's worried you're starvin' in here."

Freeman devoured the sandwiches and baked sweet potato.

"Damn, that's good!" Freeman declared, swallowing the last sandwich. "Boys, y'all have got one good mama, and I'd swear to it on a stack of Bibles as high as my head."

"Talkin' about mamas, you got one that's scared to death," Wesley said.

Freeman's face was furrowed and he seemed extremely tired. "Yeah, I know it. Figured she must be pretty upset when she and Daddy come over to your place last night. She all right? She—she any sicker?"

"She's worried, Freeman. You got to expect that," answered Wesley. "You her only child and you're runnin' around in here like some fool, hiding from the law. You know you can't do that." Wesley was irritated.

"Well, Wesley, I reckon that's something you can't know about. I reckon that's something that me and only me has to answer," Freeman said slowly.

"Freeman, you're breaking the law by runnin'. It's plain and simple."

"Dammit, Wes! Don't start throwin' no preachin' at me! Law? What law? I get arrested and throwed in jail for somethin' I ain't done, and you call that law? I didn't steal no twenty dollars. I ain't stole nothin'! Nothin'!"

Wesley knew he had pushed Freeman. "All right, Freeman, let's look at the thing, piece by piece. You say you didn't steal Hixon's money? Well, why was it in your shirt pocket?"

"How'm I supposed to know? I ain't got the slightest notion. I reckon Dupree done it when I took my shirt off and hung it up on the back door of the store. Don't know any other time it could've happened."

"O.K.," Wesley continued. "Why didn't you tell that to the Sheriff?"

"Tell him! Dammit, I told him a hundred times. Maybe a thousand. He just kept sayin' to shut up or he'd smack me shut. Said he was gonna throw me in jail and bury the key. Goda'mighty, Wes, I ain't goin' to no jail."

"If you ain't goin' to jail, how you think you can make it in here?" I asked.

"I'll make it, Colin. Don't need to fret about that. I got ways. Lots of ways."

"Freeman, you may hide out here and not get caught. I don't know," Wesley said. "But they'll be after you until this thing's over. You oughta let the Sheriff take you, and my daddy'll make sure you don't spend one night behind bars. He'll make bond, and I know it. Besides, Daddy's got lots of people he knows over in Edenville. He don't like Brownlee one bit, and he ain't about to let nothin' happen to you."

Freeman was obviously affected by Wesley's assurances. "I reckon you're right, Wes. Your daddy's a good man, and I know he's got some pull over at the courthouse. But—but, Wesley, I can't do it. I just can't, and that's that."

I knew Wesley would argue. I knew he would think of some reason for Freeman to surrender, some reason that Freeman could not deny.

"What'd you want us to do, Freeman?" Wesley asked.

Freeman looked at Wesley, then at me. We were both surprised. Wesley had not protested. He had accepted Freeman's position.

"I been thinkin' about that," Freeman replied eagerly. "Three things, Wes. Three things."

Wesley nodded. "What are they?"

Freeman moved closer to Wesley. "First thing is to get to Dupree. Find out why he stuck that twenty dollars in my pocket."

"You sure it was Dupree?" I asked.

"Had to be. I been thinkin' about it. You know Dupree swore he'd square up with me for what I said to him that day at school. Well, I just made all that up, right there on the spot, but there must've been somethin' that went on down there on that farm. Anyhow, he never forgot it. Every chance he's had this summer, he's denied it."

"What made you say anythin' about him on his granddaddy's farm, Freeman?"

"Well, Wes, it just popped in my head, that's all," Freeman explained. "I'd heard one of his granddaddy's hands tellin' about a bull chasing Dupree out of the pasture, and that was the only thing I could think of when Dupree was lippin' off to Colin."

"It ain't gonna be easy," Wesley said. "We'll try. What else?"

"I'm gonna be needin' some food from time to time. Whenever you and the others can get somethin' together, put it in a sack and leave it somewhere."

"Where?" I asked. "Ain't no way we can tell where you gonna be."

"I tell you what. The REA's gonna be cuttin' through near here," Freeman answered. "Leave it where they quit cuttin' every day. I'll find it."

"That's two things. What else, Freeman?" Wesley pressed.

"Don't know if you can do it, Wes. Maybe I'd better take care of it myself."

"What?"

"My mama. She—she ought to know I'm all right. I'd go over there, except I know there's been a sheriff's car around, and it might get Mama and Daddy in trouble."

"I'll try."

Freeman was quiet. He stared at the ground. "I'd appreciate that, Wesley. I sure would."

Wesley unwrapped Freeman's pants from my walking stick. "You really think you can hide from the law, Freeman?"

"In here, I can."

"What about them bloodhounds?" I asked.

"Shoot, y'all got 'em messed up. Anyway, they ain't got a chance followin' me in the water, and there's where I aim to be the rest of the day."

"What if somethin' happens? What if you get a snake bite, or somethin'? Here, you want these?" Wesley offered Freeman his dirty pants.

"Naw, y'all keep 'em. Don't be worryin' about me, Wes. If I get snakebit, I'll yell."

Wesley looked at Freeman as though he would never again see him. "Take care, buddy."

"Yeah."

"Take care, Freeman," I said.

"You, too. Good thinkin' on them pants, ol' buddy."

"Yeah."

"See you, Freeman," Wesley muttered.

"I'll whistle some night," Freeman replied, grinning. He turned quickly and slipped away into the woods. He did not make a sound leaving.

"He's spooky, ain't he?" I said.

"Yeah."

11

It was noon by the sun. The sun had burned away the fog pockets of morning and dried the upper crust of plowed fields, leaving a powdery film of dust. It was hot. Wesley and I hooked our jackets over our shoulders as we crossed through a pasture where we had found dozens of Indian arrowheads around a rock bed of hard, white flint. After a rain, hot in the sun, you could smell white flint.

"I bet the sun'll burn the scent we put down," I complained.

"Doubt it," Wesley said. "May make it ripe."

We were damp from the undergrowth of Black Pool Swamp and tired from miles of wandering. Wesley walked slowly, his head down, struggling with the quarrel of how he would reply to the inevitable question: "Did you find Freeman?"

"No," I answered for Wesley, who turned his back to Mother and cringed at my lie. "No, Wesley didn't, Mama."

I had only half lied; Freeman had found us, or me.

"What happened to the food I gave you?" asked Mother.

"Uh—we left it, hopin' Freeman would find it," I quickly answered. "Could've been he was watchin' us all the time."

Mother sighed. She could see Freeman, alone and trembling, eating soggy sandwiches and a cold sweet potato. "C'mon, I've fixed some lunch," she said.

Lynn wanted to know where we had been, what we had done. "Dover came back about an hour ago," she told us. "Daddy went with him over to where the Sheriff is."

"Did Mama say anythin' about us not bein' with

him?" Wesley asked.

"Nothin' I heard," Lynn replied. "Garry took off to the branch, sayin' he was lookin' for Freeman, and Mama had to go find him."

Wesley and I ate lunch and changed clothes. Otis and Alvin and R. J. drove up in Dover's truck as we were leaving the house.

"Where y'all been?" Alvin asked. "Dover's been worried."

"Ain't easy goin' through that swamp," Wesley complained. "Y'all had a picnic trampin' through the woods. They turn the dogs loose?"

"Turn 'em loose? Shoot, they ain't even there," R. J. said, giggling. "Dover was right. Ol' Jim Ed Felton must be talkin' to everybody between here'n Edenville. You oughta see Brownlee. He's havin' a fit."

"He got his deputies out lookin' for Freeman?" I asked.

"Naw," Alvin laughed. "Them fools is sittin' around a fire, just like Dover said. Hotter'n four hundred hells out here and them fools has got a fire goin'. Y'all see any signs of Freeman?"

"Uh—naw," I said. "Nothin'." Wesley and I had agreed not to tell anyone of our encounter with Freeman, and I knew he had not changed his decision. His greatest test was Mother, and he had not told her.

"Well, c'mon," Alvin said, "let's get on over there."

Wesley and I jumped into the back of Dover's truck and Alvin geared it forward, jerking and spinning. "Hold on, boys! Here we go!" he yelled.

Alvin drove Dover's truck like a madman until he topped the hill above Rakestraw Bridge and then slowed to a crawl. The two tornadoes of dust curling off the back tires rushed up and swallowed the truck in a red cloud, and Otis said Alvin was crazy if he thought Dover wouldn't know he had been speeding. "Dover'll have Alvin shinin' this thing from bumper to bumper," he predicted, stuttering with the drumming of washboard ruts in the road.

A few hundred yards from Rakestraw Bridge, Alvin eased the truck over a caved-in culvert wedged in a shallow ditch beside the road. Some forgotten chain gang paying the wages of premeditated evil had long ago planted the culvert and packed it tight with top soil from Carey Carter's pasture, and Carey Carter used the culvert as a bridge to work the richest bottomland in Eden County.

"Hit the tootfeed, Alvin!" R. J. urged. "Spin a wheel!"

Dover's truck cried as Alvin slipped the gear from second to low, scraping steel nerves.

"Dover heard that!" Otis shouted.

"Shuttup!" Alvin snapped, braking to a stop. Dover's truck had a mechanical temper that only Dover could handle.

"Gun it," R. J. suggested. "Feed it some gas, Alvin."

Alvin tapped the accelerator and the truck eased forward, rolling over a work road of bermuda grass, past a stand of sassafras trees and into a clearing near the creek. Sheriff Brownlee and his deputies had established their base of operations in the clearing and there were several cars and trucks parked in an orderly line. A small fire burned needlessly beneath the cool shade of a stunted oak, and two deputies were sitting against the trunk of the tree fanning themselves with their Eden County Sheriff's Department hats.

Dover was waiting for Alvin to park the truck.

"Great Goda'mighty!" Dover exclaimed. "You get caught in a dust storm, or somethin'? Look at that, Alvin." He wiped his finger along the fender and held it up for Alvin's inspection. Dover loved his truck.

"Uh—got caught behind the mailman up yonder on the ridge," Alvin lied apologetically. "He was boilin' up the dust, Dover. Anyhow, I'll help you shine 'er up later."

"Well, all right," Dover muttered, rubbing the dust off his Captain Marvel lightning bolt on the driver's door.

"Where's Daddy?" I asked.

"Down yonder at the edge of the creek, talkin' to Odell," Dover said. "Hey, what took y'all so long, Wes?"

"Draggin' through that swamp ain't easy," Wesley replied. "We come back by the house to get somethin' to eat and change clothes."

"Yeah," acknowledged Dover. "See any sign of Freeman?"

Otis interrupted before Wesley could answer. "They didn't see nothin'. Told you, Dover. Told you Freeman ain't about to show his face."

Dover led us away from the truck and away from the clearing, where the deputies rested. He wanted to talk and he did not want to be overheard.

"All right," Dover said as we squatted in the shade of a pine. "I ain't sure this is gonna be what we thought it was. Them deputies don't give a damn about runnin' around in that swamp, and Brownlee wouldn't care if he hadn't made such a show of things yesterday." He looked at Wesley. "Your daddy's already offered bond, Wes, and Brownlee's a little scared not to settle on it. He's comin' up for re-election and he knows your daddy could cost him a lot of votes over here. But he's got them hounds comin' somewhere and he's madder'n a settin' hen since they ain't here. He left a little while ago to find Jim Ed."

"Guess maybe they'll call off the dogs, Dover?" R. J. asked.

Dover shook his head slowly. "No. That ain't likely. Brownlee's in too deep to do that. He'll run 'em. But it ain't gonna help him much if what we've done works like I think it will. They'll just go whacky, that's all. Go off somewhere, scratching their tails, and Brownlee'll have to believe Jim Ed's dogs are worthless."

"Freeman'll still have to go over to the courthouse and be charged, won't he?" Wesley said, thinking aloud. "They couldn't do it no other way, unless Mr. Hixon dropped the charges."

"Guess that's right, Wesley," Dover agreed. "And it'd be kind of hard to get Freeman to do that, even if we could find him."

I wanted to tell Dover that Freeman had already rejected that idea, but I couldn't. Wesley began to braid a pine needle. He stared at his fingers and his forehead was furrowed with the strain of thinking.

A half hour later, Sheriff Dwight Brownlee roared into the clearing and jumped out of his car, kicking the door closed with his heel. We followed Dover into the clearing.

". . . What he said," Brownlee was complaining to his deputies. "Said he'd been down to Blakley Creek Bridge all mornin'. That damn fool ain't got as much sense as them hounds! I told him Rakestraw Bridge. Goda'mighty! Blakley Creek's down in Elbert County. Ain't even the same damn county!"

Brownlee was furious. His huge red face was splotched with anger. Sweat coated his tan shirt under the armpits and down his spine. His pants were covered knee-high in beggar's-lice, where he had wandered earlier in the edge of Black Pool Swamp, waiting for Jim Ed Felton.

"He comin'?" asked one of the deputies, throwing a handful of sticks on the dying fire.

"Right behind me," Brownlee answered, spitting. "He better be. He ain't, and his bloodhound-rentin' days are over and done."

Jim Ed Felton arrived a few minutes later, driving a Ford pickup with its hood tied down by bailing wire. He had built a complex of removable hog-wire cages on the truck body, three cages to each side, and in each cage Jim Ed had a bloodhound.

Jim Ed Felton was in his fifties. He was slightly hunchbacked and he walked with a limp that gave him the appearance of hopscotching as he followed after his dogs. He wore bib overalls and a plaid flannel shirt. His overalls were stuffed in lace-up, calf-high boots. He had a holstered .38 pistol strapped around his waist by a narrow belt which fit above his lumpy stomach. On his head, he wore a baseball cap stained by sweat and oil. Jim Ed Felton was a sideshow.

"Where in hell's name you been?" demanded Brownlee as Jim Ed began to open his cages and drag sleeping dogs to their feet.

"Had to stop over at Goldmine and gas up," Jim Ed explained. "I done run near a tank tryin' to find y'all."

"Well, by God, you have wasted enough time and that's the truth," complained Brownlee. "That boy could be in Madison County by now!"

Jim Ed laughed as he yanked at one of his dogs. "C'mon, Bell, stand up, you no-good hound. Shoot, it don't make no difference where he's took off to, ol' Bell'll find him, won't you, ol' girl?"

Bell was Jim Ed's favorite dog. She was so old she needed a wheelchair. Her tan and black coat was decorated with scars of other chases in other, younger years. There must have been five yards of wrinkled skin on her face. She looked asleep even when she stood. Jim Ed pulled at her leash and Bell moved one paw. "C'mon, ol' girl! Wake up," he urged. "You gonna fall flat on your face, you crazy hound."

Brownlee was stunned. "Goda'mighty! You ain't expectin' to run that ol' leftover, I hope!"

"I am," Jim Ed said emphatically. "Ain't a dog in ten states got a nose like Bell. Takes her a mite to get it goin', but she's the best."

"Hell, Jim Ed, she can't move! Look at that. Damn dog's fallin'!"

Bell fell on her side and Jim Ed squatted to pet her. Bell rested her head on her master's arm and closed her eyes.

"Let me tell you somethin', Sheriff," Jim Ed warned. "Bell don't run, none of 'em run. That's my way and that's the dogs' way. Now whether you believe it or not, Bell could trail a grasshopper fart for fifty miles."

Brownlee kicked at the ground and cursed. "Well, get 'em on it! I ain't spendin' the rest of my life after no boy!"

One of the deputies handed Jim Ed two shirts and a pair of shorts belonging to Freeman. Jim Ed went from dog to dog, rubbing their noses with the garments and giving them a pep talk. "Take a whiff . . . Yeah . . . Yeah . . . Good boy . . . Smell that stink . . . Smell it, boy . . ."

The dogs began to stir, straining restlessly against their chain leashes.

"Now, we gonna get 'im," Jim Ed chanted. "Yo, boy! HO, BOY! C'MON, BOY! YO, BELL! YO, BELL, YO!"

Bell raised her ancient head and the loose skin tumbled from her forehead to her jowls. She pushed up on her front legs and a deep, short bay cracked in her throat.

"Attay, girl, Bell! Yo, Bell! Yo!"

Bell struggled to stand on her back feet. She answered Jim Ed: "A-ruuuuuuuuuuuuuuuuuuuuuuuu-uuuh!"

"YO, BELL, YO!"

The other dogs pranced and whimpered and began to sniff the ground. Bell stretched her front legs and the joints in her shoulders popped.

"Yo, Bell! Yo!" The spirit of the chase was rising in Jim Ed. "C'mon, Blue! Ho, Red! Ho, Sue!"

Jim Ed started dragging his dogs across the clearing into the edge of the swamp. Brownlee chased him in short, skipping steps.

"Where you goin'?" Brownlee yelled.

"After that there convict," Jim Ed answered, hopscotching after his dogs.

"He ain't no convict, dammit, Jim Ed! He's a boy."

"After that there boy, then."

"You want my deputies?"

"What for?!"

"Chasin' them hounds, that's what for."

"Don't need 'em. Ol' Bell'll get the scent and the dogs'll follow her."

"What'd you want us to do?"

"Nothin'," Jim Ed called as he crossed a gully. "You hear me shoot twice with my pistol, you come runnin'!"

"Don't you go shootin' at that boy, Jim Ed!"

"I ain't. Yo, Bell! Yo!"

Jim Ed and his dogs vanished into the swamp, a crashing, rushing mob of justice trumpeting its mission in a concert of yo-ing and chesty baying.

We stood and listened. Dover was tense. He leaned against the cab of his truck, his head down, and chewed on a twig. If Jim Ed's dogs did not split and chase the trails we had planted, Dover was thinking, Freeman could be in grave trouble. Dover did not know, as Wesley and I did, that Freeman was miles away and had probably spent the afternoon wading in Beaverjam Creek. Freeman may have been in some danger, but he would not panic and if Jim Ed's dogs did find him, it would be because he had relaxed and made a mistake.

"That's ol' Bell," one of the deputies said, as a long, mournful howl rose up from the swamp. "Yessir, ol' Bell's got the scent."

Dover walked to the edge of the oak shade. "Maybe that's a rabbit they hollerin' about," he suggested.

"Rabbit? You don't know nothin' about blood-hounds, I reckon," the deputy replied. "Ol' Bell wouldn't give a rabbit the time of day, if she's on the scent."

Dover's face screwed tight in wrinkles. "She that good?"

The howl reached a higher octave: "A-ruuuuuur-rrrrrrrrrrrh!"

"She's that good, mister, and that's God's truth. I was on a chase with Jim Ed few years back, when I was workin' down in Elbert County, and ol' Bell tracked Asa Miller's oldest boy right down the middle of Elberton on a Saturday afternoon. They wrote that up in some dog magazine."

"Well, Asa's boy must've been layin' down one hel-luva stink," Brownlee argued. "That hound can't hardly walk. Ain't no way she can track."

"This your first time with Jim Ed, ain't it, Sheriff?"

the deputy asked. "I reckon you must've been using Wilbur Sims' pack."

"Yeah. Too bad Wilbur died. Them was good dogs," Brownlee answered.

"Well, you'll see what I mean about Jim Ed," the deputy promised.

Bell howled and was echoed by Blue and Red and Sue and the others. Jim Ed's voice was an excited shriek above the low baying of his dogs.

"She's got it!" the deputy yelled. "Yessir! Go get 'em, Bell!"

Odell Boyd fumbled with his tobacco tin of Prince Albert. His small eyes were red. He turned and walked away toward the creek, the fearful sound of a dog pack hungry after his son thundering in his mind.

For a horrible moment, I thought Dover's plan had failed. The dogs were moving together, following a single slim path, fighting for the lead. Then, suddenly, the dogs separated, and we could hear Jim Ed screaming for them to bunch and follow Bell.

"What's happenin'?" Brownlee asked his deputy.

"They split. Goin' different ways."

"Split? He had 'em leashed."

"He takes them off when they get hold of the scent."

"What'd they split for?"

"Don't know," the deputy answered, fanning his face. "Maybe the boy walked in circles."

The dogs were delirious, each coveting a different trail and baying for the rest of the pack to follow. They sounded like children quarreling over the lordship of a game. Jim Ed's voice was now shrill and angry, a distant cursing maniac threatening to kick in the skull of every dog in north Georgia.

Dover smiled. Otis snickered and hid his face in his hands. Alvin and R. J. laughed aloud, and Wesley said, "I didn't know bloodhounds would split like that."

"Well, son," the deputy began, "can't never tell about dogs of no kind, but I'll lay you odds ol' Bell ain't off the true scent. Yessir, that ol' hound don't need them others."

Odell Boyd walked back from the creek. He was a changed man. He whispered something to my father and my father nodded. Then my father stepped close behind Dover and said, "You got more sense than I thought you had."

Dover grinned and drummed his fingers on the hood of his truck. "Me'n Sam Spade oughta be partners," he declared.

My father walked away with Odell Boyd and I asked Dover, "Does my daddy know what we did?"

"Sure, he knows. Odell told him this mornin'."

"And he ain't mad?"

"Colin, you don't give your daddy credit, boy. No, he ain't mad. He thought it was a good plan; didn't think it'd work, but he liked the idea."

We settled in the shade of the oak and listened to the confusion of bloodhounds chasing the phantom of Freeman's scent. In an hour, the dogs were miles apart and hopelessly bewildered.

My father had walked home, permitting Wesley and me the privilege of staying until Jim Ed Felton returned, and our presence annoyed the Sheriff. He slouched against the oak, scowling, and he waited for the two telltale pistol shots from Jim Ed.

At sundown, Laron Crook arrived, walking up from the road. One hand was wrapped in gauze and he carried his Bible in the other. His Boy Scout canteen was strapped over his shoulder.

"Sheriff," warned Dover, "that man comin' up yonder is a preacher of sorts. Reckon we better watch our language."

"I ain't gonna cuss unless he starts to preachin', and then I'm gonna be the damnest, ravin' madman you ever saw. What's his name?"

"Laron Crook. Him and his daddy run a mule farm."

"Crook?" Brownlee repeated, checking his memory for the name. "That the same Crook from down in Bio? Same ol' loon who got took at ol' Preacher Bytheway's revival?"

"That's him," Dover said.

"Same man that goes around baptizin' dogs?"

"One and the same, Sheriff. One and the same."

Brownlee breathed deeply and sighed. "I ain't believin' this day. Well, I'm goin' off in the swamp to look for Jim Ed. If that ol' fool's around when I get back, I'm liable to kick his butt."

"Don't worry, Sheriff, I'll take care of him," Dover said. "I know how to handle Laron."

"You better. And tell him I'm already baptized. He throws any water on me and I'll put a size ten in his tail!" Brownlee left for the swamp, stepping great strides.

Laron walked up and pushed his straw hat up on his forehead. His eyes were glassy. "Praise the Lord!" he declared.

"Praise the Lord!" Dover responded. "C'mon, Brother Laron. Sit a spell."

"Bless you, Brother Dover. How's Bark?"

"Bark's fine, Laron. Just fine," Dover answered. "What happened to your hand there?"

"One of God's creatures bit it. You know creatures don't know nothin' about not bitin' the hand that's feedin' it."

"That old mule ain't learned yet, huh?"

Laron clucked sympathetically. "Time, Brother Dover. Time. It takes time and patience to calm God's creatures."

"You know about Freeman?" asked Alvin.

"I do," Laron answered, turning to Odell Boyd. "I been prayin' hard for his soul, Brother Odell. And for you, and Sister Rachel."

"I'm appreciatin' it," Odell Boyd said solemnly. "I do, Preacher. I sure do."

Odell Boyd and the two deputies moved away from the fire and out of the reach of Laron's influence. Laron's reputation had become well known.

Dover told Laron about the bloodhounds and Jim Ed, and about the accusation by Dupree that Freeman had slipped the twenty dollars from the counter in Hixon's General Store. Laron listened and nodded, twitching in holy pain as Dover flavored the story with details of how Freeman was alone and hungry and frightened.

"Praise the Lord!" Laron thundered at the conclusion of the story. He caught Wesley by the arm and closed his arms. "O Good God in heaven," he prayed, "listen to these poor, sinnin' servants—say amen, Wesley . . ." Wesley mumbled amen and Laron continued. "Just as you took care of ol' Daniel in the lion's cage, well, take care of Freeman in Black Pool Swamp. Amen! And just as you fished ol' Jonah outa the briny deep and the whale's throat, we want you to pluck ol' Freeman outa the quicksand of trouble . . ."

Otis giggled and Dover covered it with an amen that had a driving finality.

"That's good prayin', Laron," Dover said quickly. "Ain't that right, Wes?"

Wesley cleared his throat and nodded agreement.

"Thank you, brothers. I been practicin' hard and it makes me feel good to know my prayin' is bein' heard by folks as well as the Lord God Almighty Jehovah," Laron declared.

"Well, them's upliftin' words," Dover assured.

Laron hugged his Bible and began to sway in his squatting position, clucking in his throat, trying mightily for a visitation of the Holy Tongues.

It was well into darkness when Brownlee returned from the swamp, his pants covered with cockleburs and beggar's lice, and stained pokeberry purple. He mumbled something about Jim Ed coming in with his dogs and started to curse fate when he realized Laron was sitting near the fire. "Uh, sorry, Preacher," he said. "It's been a long day."

Laron blessed Brownlee with forgiveness and asked

if the dogs had found Freeman.

"They didn't find nothin', Preacher. Not even a rat's turd. Them dogs went in a dozen different directions. Jim Ed's been roundin' 'em up for a couple of hours."

"Dogs is strange creatures," Laron empathized. "Ain't no way to figure 'em. Mighty strange."

"I can't understand it," Brownlee said. "That ol' Bell Jim Ed was braggin' about got stuck in some fox hole few miles down and wouldn't leave it for nothin'." He scanned the woods. Lightning bugs blinked pinpoints of light against the deepening blackness.

Laron amened and announced that God had selected him to be a missionary to animals. Dogs digging in fox holes was like man digging in sin, according to Laron. He began a fascinating parable about a mule team. Mules were either pullers or pushers, Laron explained, and you had to be careful not to match two pullers or two pushers. "Takes one of each," he said. "That way there's a balance. The pullers don't kill themselves and the pushers don't go to sleep on you. Same with men. Takes all different kinds, don't it, Sheriff?"

"Well, yeah, I reckon you're right, Preacher," admitted Brownlee. "I don't know much about mules, but—hey, yonder comes the dogs!"

Jim Ed had his six dogs on leashes, yanking and kicking and cursing the whimpering, bewildered animals. Laron was seized with a holy calling; he tried a Laying On of Hands on the bloodhounds and Red bit him on the leg. Jim Ed threatened to kick Laron ". . . in the ass . . ." if he interfered again, and Brownlee warned

Jim Ed about using abusive language in the presence of children and preachers. Laron began praying in a gasping frenzy and Jim Ed called him a ". . . slobberin' sonofabitch . . ." Brownlee pushed Jim Ed against his truck and vowed to arrest him if he didn't behave. Otis began petting Blue and Blue began yapping. Suddenly, we were surrounded by dogs, sniffing, braying, leaping.

"Goda'mighty!" exclaimed Dover. "Get outa here, boys!"

"Wait a minute!" ordered Brownlee. "What them dogs goin' crazy for?"

Jim Ed leaped into the middle of his dogs. "They got the scent, that's why! They got the scent they been chasin' all day!"

Bell was at my feet, head lifted, howling. "Aur-rrrrrrrrrrrrh!"

"What'd you talkin' about, Jim Ed? These boys ain't been nowhere but right here," Brownlee said. "Right here!"

"I don't care where they been, my dogs know what they smell and they smell them boys."

Dover raised his hands to calm the storm. "Wait a minute. Wait a minute. There's got to be some sense in this."

"Start talkin'," Brownlee commanded.

"Well, now, there might be a lot of truth in what Jim Ed's sayin'," Dover began. "Fact is, me'n the boys has been out in the woods."

"Doin' what?" Jim Ed demanded.

"Doin' what? Well—uh—we was checkin' out rabbit paths for settin' rabbit boxes. Just messing around.

Shoot, these boys are all over them woods, and you know it, Sheriff! They live around here."

"That don't explain nothin'," declared Jim Ed. "Lookin' rabbit paths? This time of year? Ain't no fool gonna believe that."

Laron began mumbling. He yelled, "Help me, Jesus!" and began mumbling again.

Dover began to play with the cottonseed in his ears. He was angry. "Who says when you can or can't check out rabbit paths? We was lookin' which way the REA was comin' and just started checkin' paths, and that's that! Anyhow, what's them dogs doin' barkin' up our tracks? It's Freeman they supposed to be after."

Jim Ed lowered his voice. "I'll tell you why, Mister. Dogs trail what scent's on the ground. And I know exactly what y'all done. Y'all got some of that boy's clothes and drug them along the ground, that's what! Hell, I seen that trick a dozen times! Keeps the dogs confused, makes 'em wonder what they supposed to be doin'. Well, by God, you ain't gettin' away with it!"

"BLESS THESE POOR, BARKIN' DOGS!" Laron shouted, flinging his arms in the air.

"Jim Ed, you better watch that mouth or I'm gonna throw you under the jail!" Brownlee hissed. "Don't go givin' me no such line like that! You tryin' to get me to pay you for a nothin' day, and I ain't fallin' for it, buddy! I reckon I've seen a trick or two in my time, too! Wilbur Sims told me there was nothin' blood-hounds everywhere."

Jim Ed exploded. "You heard him say they was out there!"

"And it makes sense to me," Brownlee answered. "Makes a lot of sense. These boys live around here. They bound to spend time in the woods."

"Well, you think what you want to, by God! I'm charging for me'n my dogs and you'll pay, or I'll see you in court or hell, one or the other!"

"Don't push me, Jim Ed! Them ol' hounds ain't worth a fart in a windstorm and you know it," growled Brownlee. He whirled and yelled to his deputies, "Get them dogs in them cages, now! Right now!"

Dover motioned us to his truck, grabbing Laron by the arm as Laron struggled to unscrew the top of his Boy Scout canteen. "C'mon, Brother Laron, we'll give you a lift," he whispered. "C'mon, Odell."

"In time, Brother Dover. In time," answered Laron. "I'm about to do some baptizin'."

Dover pulled on Laron and began to drag and guide him to his truck. Laron was jerking in his shoulders and water was sloshing from the canteen. He began to babble incoherently, as Dover and Alvin lifted him over the tailgate.

"Amen! Brother Laron! Amen!" Dover chanted. "Ain't that right, boys?"

"Amen," answered Otis.

"Amen," echoed R. J.

"Lord, Lord, forgive them!" Laron shouted, flinging water.

We drove away as Sheriff Brownlee and Jim Ed Felton began to shove one another. Laron was spraying the barking, following dogs with water, admitting their souls to God's glory. Dover was laughing uncontrollably as we crossed the caved-in culvert and pulled onto the dirt road. "They ain't never gonna find Freeman," he predicted. "Never! Them dogs is so mixed up they don't know doodley-squat about Freeman! Y'all just keep quiet if anybody asks you anythin'. Tell 'em you're too little to answer questions to the law."

12

Freeman Boyd's escape became an emotional Dare-You line dividing Emery, a Dare-You line overlapping the gray concrete of Highway 17. The split was between Good and Bad, Right and Wrong, Yes and No, Guilt and Innocence.

Freeman's crime—alleged crime—was incidental. Anger was not applied to the deed itself, but to the attitudes toward that deed. If it had been Dupree who was accused of stealing twenty dollars, or two thousand dollars, it would have been ballyhooed as a mistake in bookkeeping, and Dupree would have been crowned a martyr, exultant in his experience.

Because it was Freeman, and Freeman was of the Other Class ("Not like everyone else" was the phrase), the accusation became a drama of class distinction. It was an argument of ugliness and anyone with grit willingly took sides.

To those of us who watched it from that inquisitive perspective of less than five feet, five inches, younger than fifteen years, it was the fight at Emery Junior High School, the Georgia Power Company versus the

Rural Electrification Administration, Our Side versus the Highway 17 Gang.

But the adults had lost the dynamics of their imaginations.

Two days after Freeman escaped into Black Pool Swamp, there had been three fights over the matter. Freeman's defenders went 3-0, partly because the insult to them was great and partly because they were considerably meaner in a conflict of honor.

Yet, in the frenzy of Freeman's supposed crime—the serious debate of serious men and women in serious disagreement—a curious effect developed: Freeman, the person, was ignored; Freeman, the symbol, became a competition of words said and words not heard.

In the debate of Freeman, the debaters completely obscured concern of finding him. There seemed a general agreement that Freeman would be found, or would surrender (probably surrender) and that would be that. No one talked of rescue. Rescue would intrude on the polity of argument.

Indeed, politics made an appearance in many forms. Sheriff Brownlee, embroiled in re-election gibberish, realized the folly of insulting an entire community by pursuing the fugitive Freeman Boyd, a minor; it would be wiser to remain clear of internal conflicts. In politics, not being seen is often as important as kissing babies.

Thus, it happened that Homer Dove, a deputy for twenty years, was assigned the duty of finding Freeman. Homer Dove was recognized by Eden

County citizens as the laziest man in the western world, and Homer disagreed only mildly; it wasn't laziness, he explained, it was patience. In that regard, Homer was the South's leading Southerner. He lived by the motto: Be Not the First By Which the New Is Tried, Nor Yet the Last to Lay the Old Aside.

Homer began his search for Freeman by sleeping all day in his patrol car, parked in the shade of young sweet gums near Black Pool Swamp.

And there was the politics of persuasion, of threat and boycott. Dover was especially intrigued with the power of the people. He addressed a passionate plea in Freeman's behalf to members of the REA right-of-way crew. Do anything, Dover said. Take up a collection to pay Freeman's bond. Shoot Georgia Power Company transformers with rat shot .22 bullets. Boycott A. G. Hixon's General Store. Dover was inspired, and inspiring. He reminded his coworkers that they were fond of Freeman (the men had no thought about Freeman one way or the other, but they agreed there was no reason to dislike him), and he delivered a wonderfully poetic description of what the REA meant to unfortunates like Freeman. "It gives poor folk a chance," intoned Dover. "Makes 'em feel like somebody, and, boys, that's what they're seein' when they see all this work goin' on."

The men did not weep, for weeping would have been unseemly, but it was easy to tell they were emotional. One of them, a giant of a man with a goiter stuck in his throat, volunteered not to patronize Hixon's General Store until Freeman was cleared of all charges and had received a public apology, and the other men yeah-ed his decision. That vow lasted until afternoon and then it melted in the salty heat of a blistering sun, when the vision of Coca-Cola, bottles slippery with ice, drove the crew to panic. "To hell with it," one of them said. "We'll take up a collection."

And most damning was the private politics—the trickery of the mind: I must do something to help Freeman, but I won't object if it serves me as well. Politics of illusion.

I was guiltiest of all in being lured by private politics. I was seized with an idea of aiding Freeman by the clever deceit of appealing to Megan's confidence; if she knew anything about a setup instigated by Dupree, I believed I could pry the secret from her sealed lips. It was, by all appearances, a noble proposal. Yet, I knew there were two problems: how to see Megan and not be seen at that seeing, and, second, how to concentrate on my mission. Megan was an influence I could not trust; I knew I would have to be cold and demanding, and I knew I would have to think only of Freeman—*Freeman, Freeman, Freeman.*

Coincidence solved my first dilemma. Megan and her mother came to our farm to buy apples from my father's abundant orchard, and my father made me go with Megan to gather them. I fussed, dramatically, as Lynn giggled, but I obeyed. "Be quick, now," Megan's mother said as she drove away. "I'll be back soon. And make sure there's no worm holes."

I did not speak to Megan until we were well into the orchard and concealed from view by distance and the low limbs of trees bowing with fruit. "Megan," I began, "I wanta ask you somethin'." She smiled and said, "Yes?" Suddenly my purpose collapsed. Pale green eyes, hair as blond as a full moon. "Yes?" she repeated softly. "Uh—nothin'," I mumbled. "Just—just—ah, wondered what's been happenin' this summer." She talked of the summer, of girlish things. She made me inspect the apples she picked. She asked if I had spent time drawing (I had not). She wanted to know if Wesley and Lynn and I planned to attend the Emery Methodist Church Youth Fellowship hot dog roast and hayride (we did). Her presence and her questions assaulted my nerves. I tried, I earnestly tried to remember Freeman. Once I even shut my eyes and squeezed his face into focus on the silver membrane of my mind, but Megan touched my arm for attention ("Is this a worm hole?") and Freeman disappeared into a pit of gray quicksand.

But the thing that endorsed the selfishness of all the political moods and incentives was Freeman himself.

Freeman was performing his dreams. He had escaped and no one could find him in the Great Okeenoonoo. He was a defying spirit in the best of defying postures, and he could not resist teasing us. Each night, Freeman confirmed his safety and the pleasure of his adventure by playing messages for Wesley and me—messages of lyrical lightness in cane-flute code.

During those first uneasy nights, the messages occurred almost precisely at nine-thirty. Wesley, faithful in his promise, would tell Rachel Boyd of

Freeman's night tune, and Rachel Boyd would smile her appreciation. To Odell Boyd, the evidence of Freeman's survival was more than comfort; it was also a braggart's claim of beating the odds, and everyone in Emery quickly learned of Freeman's evening concert.

On the fourth night after his escape, three cars crammed with thrill seekers (Mother called them thrill seekers), arrived in our yard at nine-fifteen. They were there to hear Freeman and Freeman did not disappoint them. He played a broken song, a wounded lamentation of high, piercing notes, and the crowd answered in a chorus of dog calls and bird imitations. Freeman loved it. He replied with a musical ditty that must have been suggestive; all the men laughed and slapped their thighs and said, "That's ol' Freeman!" And they were right. It was Freeman being Freeman, a boy reveling in secrets only men understood; men and Freeman. They left and forgot their worry of Freeman's plight. "That's ol' Freeman," they repeated the next day. "Ol' Freeman's fine." And then they began again the fiery dispute over class distinction.

"By God, Freeman proves it! They's a difference between folks in Emery, all right! They's people lookin' down on other people! Maybe it's electricity, like they say. Maybe that's it."

Each night my mother prepared sandwiches and packed them in a paper sack for Freeman, and Wesley and I would carry the food to the end of the day's cutting by the REA crew. We would leave the food and return home immediately. At nine-thirty, almost precisely, Freeman would whistle his appreciation. I was certain Wesley had confessed to our parents about seeing Freeman on that first day of search, because there was never any question about the sandwiches, but I did not ask for the truth. Wesley could be everlasting when explaining truth, and I never fully comprehended his views of such important topics.

On Saturday following Freeman's Monday escape, Laron Crook announced he would conduct an afternoon prayer meeting at Sosbee's Spring and enlist heaven's forces to aid Freeman. It was an earnest offer, and we elected to attend—particularly since the novelty of Laron's conversion had ebbed and adults avoided him as a fanatic who did not have the good sense to know when and when not to be religious. It was our duty to attend, we reasoned. Laron was especially fond of Freeman. Too, Laron was leaving on Sunday to join Preacher Bytheway in a campaign near Augusta; Preacher Bytheway had had problems matching his success in Emery and was in desperate need of a worthy witness, one whose confessions would be unforgettable.

We attended, obediently. Alvin predicted that Freeman would appear himself, if he knew what was happening. "Freeman would give a week's pay to see this," Alvin said.

It was a lively, but abbreviated session. Laron prayed and practiced his Laying On of Hands, and was into a few words of Speaking in Tongues when he slipped and tumbled head-first into Sosbee's Spring. He told us a stick jumped up from the ground and tripped him, and that it was an omen he would have to ponder as he changed clothes. We wished him good fortune in Augusta and he promised to bring us all souvenirs if he could find something appropriate at the Greyhound Bus Station.

After Laron left, we tried to plot some way to help Freeman, but we knew our planning was useless. Freeman would have to help himself.

"Well, I hope y'all can do something," Jack said. "There ain't nothin' more I can do. Mama told me to stay clear of it, all of it. If she knew I was here, she'd take a stick to me."

"Why?" asked Wesley.

"Shoot, Wes, I don't know. All the fussin' that's goin' on, I guess. Mama said she didn't want none of us around it and we had to stay at home."

"Yeah, well, that's all right, Jack," counseled Alvin. "I know how that is. My mama used to make me stay home all the time, too. She'll get over it. Anyhow, Freeman's all right. He'll stay in that ol' swamp and keep playin' that cane flute until somethin's done about provin' he's innocent."

"Yeah."

"Yeah."

"Yeah."

We all knew Alvin was right. Freeman was stubborn. And Freeman was having more fun than he had ever had in his life.

That night, Freeman did not play his cane flute. There was no message. Wesley and I walked below the barn and whistled, but Freeman did not answer.

"Wonder where he is," I said. "Why ain't he answerin', Wesley?"

Wesley frowned. "I don't know," he replied quietly. "I don't know."

Doom.

I did not know what doom really meant, or why it sounded and looked so uncompromising as a word. Doom rhymed with tomb. When printed, doom had two round, closed white eyes, resting everlastingly between a D-for-death and an M-for-mortuary. Sometimes the Negroes we knew lamented the ". . . passin' over" of a loved one by saying he, or she, had been visited by The Doom, and The Doom was even more final than doom as a single word. There was another character to doom: it could be felt, physically felt, as rain can be felt miles away and hours before it finally arrives. Feeling doom, as we learned in the beautiful folk language of Negroes who knew the truth of it, began with a single unexpected oddity—a redbird out of season, hail out of cloudless skies, dogs cowering under the house, a pine tree releasing its needles in a single night. There were dozens of signs, if you knew how to read them, knew the quaint mysteries of their ethereal beginnings. Yet, even if you did read them, you were helpless against the Unknown of doom. You simply stopped what you were doing and waited, waited for a warm breath followed by a chilling breath (always on the face), and then you knew it was finished and you had only to discover where doom, or The Doom, had visited. Afterward, you talked about it, and said: "I knew it would happen. I could feel it."

Freeman had not signaled. He had not answered the pleading of our own calls, first as whistles and then as yelling. As we stood and waited, Wesley and I both realized the swamp had become suddenly unfriendly, dark as ink. We heard a rolling sigh in the top limbs of the tallest trees, and then we heard nothing. Nothing. Not even katydids or frogs or owls.

Wesley called in a half-voice, "Freeman!"

His half-voice half-echoed once.

"Wesley," I begged, "let's go home!"

Doom. What we had been told was incredibly accurate. This was the first sign, the oddity. A premonition of Freeman trapped in the glue of a giant spider web, dangling and trying to cry out but unable to find sound in his body, raced through my mind, and just as quickly I heard the gentle voice of my sister Ruth as she told again of Mother's premonition of Thomas. Ruth, too, had felt the warm breath of doom that day; she, too, had said, "I knew something had happened. I could feel it."

Doom. Wesley warned me not to say anything about Freeman. "Mama'll just worry," he explained. "Maybe Freeman sneaked off to go see his folks. Maybe that's it."

Mother did not ask us if we had heard Freeman's whistle. It was expected that we had had our boyish, adventuresome exchange and Freeman had retreated to wherever he rested in Black Pool Swamp. Wesley positioned himself in the middle room, near my father and beside the corner window, and pretended to listen to a radio comedy show.

The comedy ended, its laughter pushed away by a music bridge, and a baritone news announcement of the world's events, and my father switched the radio off. We did not care very much about the world's events. The world was a place we heard about in baritone-and-static descriptions.

"How far's the REA crew, son?" my father asked Wesley.

"Almost out of the woods, down near the branch. Won't be long before they get to Beaverjam Creek," answered Wesley.

"They'll be stringin' wire before we know it," my father said.

"Yessir," Wesley mumbled.

A strange cat with fur like pressed black velvet leaped onto the windowsill and stared inside. He arched his back and rubbed against the glass pane, then dropped silently out of sight. And I remembered: "A cat's a bad sign, for sure," Willie Lee Maxwell had told us after his mother died. "I knowed somethin' was bad wrong when this here cat followed me all day long. Didn't make no sound at all. Never took them cat's eyes off'n me all day. Knowed it was somethin', and that night when I was lyin' in bed, I was woke by the hot breathin' of The Doom, hot as fever . . ."

"Sure quiet out," Mother said from the kitchen. "Must be gettin' ready to rain."

No, Mama, I thought. It won't rain. The quiet means doom, Mama. Tonight, Mama, someone (Wesley, me?) will feel a shadowy warm breeze, and then a chilling breeze, and it will be over. Freeman will be eternally trapped in The Doom.

"Better go to bed, boys," suggested Mother. "Church tomorrow."

Wesley stared at the windowsill as though the cat would return. He answered, "Yes'm."

On Sunday morning, in the wedge between night and day, Wesley and I slipped away to see if Freeman had taken the sandwiches Mother had prepared and we had left at the end of the REA cutting. The paper sack was still there, still on the last stump of the last tree to fall. Wesley opened the sack and scattered the sandwiches for birds. He stood for a moment and searched the swamp, then he turned and walked briskly away, toward home.

"You gonna tell Daddy, Wesley?"

"No, not now."

"Why not?"

"Maybe Freeman went home."

"Maybe he didn't."

"We'll go by his house on the way to church. His mama'll tell us."

"What if he didn't?"

"If he didn't—I don't know."

Rachel Boyd stood behind the screen door, her arms folded against her breasts. The screen, stretched and loose from being pushed, distorted her, froze her in the tiny squares of wire meshing. The tuberculosis that had rotted her lungs had also pulled her eyes deep into their sockets and there were times when she appeared completely blind; this was one of those times.

"No, Wesley," she said. "Freeman's not been here. Why'd you ask? He's all right, ain't he?"

"Uh—yes'm, he's fine. We ain't seen him, but Freeman's takin' care of himself," Wesley muttered.

Rachel Boyd stepped closer to the screen door. Her eyes were black, swollen by blue lines sweeping in a quarter moon over her cheeks. "Why'd you think Freeman would come here, Wesley?" she repeated.

"Uh—nothin'. I thought, well, maybe he'd be needin' a change of clothes."

"I left some things on the line couple of nights ago, and I reckon he got 'em. They was gone the next mornin'."

"Yes'm."

"Don't know why he didn't just come on up and see me. He knows it'd make me feel a lot better to see him."

"Yes'm," agreed Wesley. "Maybe he thought it'd get you in some kind of trouble, helping him out. There's some kind of law, I think . . ."

"Don't make no difference, Wesley. He's my boy," Rachel Boyd said quietly. "He's my boy."

"Yes'm."

"Try to find him, boys. Tell him to come see his mama."

"Yes'm," I replied.

"Sometimes children don't understand how hard it is . . ." She gasped for breath and suppressed a gurgling in her lungs.

"Yes'm," Wesley said. "We'll try, Mrs. Boyd. We'll spend time this afternoon, doin' some looking. Uh, reckon we'd better be goin' on to church."

Rachel Boyd nodded, holding her throat with her hand. She swallowed and said, "Wish you boys would say somethin' for Freeman. At church."

"Sure will, Mrs. Boyd," I replied. "Mama said the same thing."

Emery Methodist Church meant much to us. It was the coolest of buildings, and I imagined it was inhabited by a congregation of invisible angels who billowed against the ceiling of the sanctuary, like balloons slipped away from the fingers of children. The angels were quieter than eternity when people were in the church, but their breathing was detectable in its frost coolness and you knew—knew without being told— that you were in the presence of holiness.

In the past year, I had been swayed by the church and had spent many hours contemplating the merits of being sprinkled into membership. It would require extraordinary discipline to forsake numerous preoccupations that were offensive to the church, but pleasant to body and mind; yet, I admired the safeguard of knowing Jesus could forgive me in the batting of an eye, and, in 1947, with the rumor of terrible bombs, there was serious speculation that every living creature on Earth could perish exactly that fast—in the batting of an eye.

Unquestionably, baptism had its advantages.

But it wasn't the angels, or the gambler's toss-up on

baptism, that most impressed me in subdued hours at Emery Methodist Church: it was Rev. Neil Eldridge.

He was an old man now. Emery Methodist Church would be his last appointment in a lifetime of appointments, and he would retire. He would no longer obey the three-year pulse beat of God's call to carton-and-box belongings and move to another white, clapboard church in another white, clapboard setting of farm families. Moving had been his habit, his expectation, his instinct. He had not studied great theologies in a seminary, and God, or the Bishop, had never called him to a great church. But his voice had numbed even the most scholarly and decorated churchmen, and he was often summoned to Atlanta to deliver prayers of especial meaning. His was a voice able to penetrate the latched, inner iron gate of Hell, even in whisper; a voice able to coax sinners writhing in damnation up from Fire and Brimstone, up through the narrow slit of brilliant light that was heaven. It was a voice that entered the *whole* body—was there, imploding, before the listener knew he had been filled with sound.

He was majestic in his oldness, his white-hair, blue-eyes oldness, but he was very slow in movement and often now he lost the continuity of what he was saying or thinking. It was sad to see him in those moments. Majestic old man, slightly broken in the shoulders, seized by forgetfulness, absently scanning the Bible opened before him, searching for God's presence cowering behind the lettering of familiar verses, and knowing his sermon of then—the sermon he intended—had become cluttered with thousands of older sermons. Waiting, waiting, waiting, waiting—perfectly still—for some miraculous transfusion of the plasma of youth and vigor; waiting, and not understanding the embarrassing lapses that fell on him in midsentence like a stroke, clotting his mind and silencing his stories of the vulnerability of Jesus. He was quite certain Jesus' vulnerability—the assailable Jesus—was the catalyst of God's greatness; else, how would the triumphant Jesus—the invulnerable God-man—be clearly understood by congregations who knew more of injury than of conquering? Once in a sermon, he had even spoken in an admirable way of the crucifix of the Catholic church. He had his own philosophy of that venerable symbol: it was God's screech of pain, performed in the agonized stretch of Jesus' punctured hands, in the spike pounded into and through Jesus' feet, in the spear rip of Jesus' abdominal wall, in the nest of thorns shoved onto Jesus' head. The Trinity—God the Father, God the Son, and God the Holy Ghost—was frozen in that scene, frozen in the heartstroke of time wedged between the plaintive Hebrew of St. Matthew ("Eli, Eli, la ma sa-bach-tha-ni?") and the simple, whispery ghost-giving in the King James English of St. John ("It is finished."). It was a noble scene, Rev. Neil Eldridge believed, a scene to be studied and remembered, and a scene made worthy by the assurance of the Empty Cross—". . . *our* symbol," he proudly proclaimed.

Rev. Eldridge knew of his congregation's split over the matter of Freeman Boyd. He could look from his pulpit and place the quarrelers—those who believed in Freeman's innocence were on the right, and those who believed him guilty as charged were on the left. Rev. Eldridge's congregation was split by an ax and the wound was a red carpet that divided the pews from the altar to the back of the church.

He did not speak of Freeman, not by name. He selected the story of Cain and Abel as his sermon topic, and he preached with such remembered vitality he seemed wholly different. His mind was rapid and sure, his presence strong as hypnotism, and his voice—his voice was thunder far away, rolling, rolling, rolling, entering the mind and blood and muscles and nerves. He abandoned his pulpit and stood with his head back and his eyes fixed on the ceiling of the sanctuary, where invisible angels praised him with the frost coolness of their breath.

He spoke a parable of brothers and forgiveness, and he challenged each member to read and remember the church motto hanging over the piano:

> I am only one,
> I cannot do everything,
> But I can do something.
> And what I can do,
> By the grace of God,
> I ought to do.

He closed the service with the first and last verses of "Just as I Am," and a benediction that left every man, woman, and child limp with unworthiness. It was a benediction inscribed on the flint of our souls, a masterful solicitation of God's wonderfulness and His power to heal the wounds of strife.

Outside, after services, there were mumbled, awkward apologies for misbehavior, and a few people whispered hope that Freeman would be found and the entire, ugly affair would be concluded as a dreadful mistake.

Dupree was there, standing sheepishly to one side and trying not to be affected by the influence of:

"Preacher's right. Fightin' among ourselves is wrong, bad wrong."

"What I said last week, well, I didn't mean nothin'. Y'all know I didn't mean nothin', I hope."

"My fault as much as yours . . ."

"I reckon I started it . . ."

"This is too good a community to be tore apart by arguin'."

"Yeah . . ."

Dupree did not know how to accept this, people humbling themselves before other people. He edged away from the crowd, slipped away like a thief who has considered every risk except divine intervention. He looked queasy and ill.

Wesley saw him, read him, knew what Dupree was thinking. "C'mon," he whispered to me.

We trapped Dupree beside the tall concrete steps. "Good sermon," Wesley said. "Good sermon the preacher had."

Dupree turned his blushing face and spat into the shrubbery.

"Yeah, I sure thought the preacher was right in everything he said," continued Wesley.

Dupree dropped his head and jammed his hands into his pockets.

"Uh—I don't know exactly how to say this, Dupree, but I guess I'm apologizin' for all the bad feeling we've had between us," Wesley added, offering his hand to Dupree.

Dupree was surprised. He ignored Wesley's hand and tried to push past us, but I stepped in his path.

"Don't see why we can't be friends, Dupree," Wesley said. "What's happened is behind us."

"I pick my friends," answered Dupree arrogantly.

Wesley stared at Dupree and Dupree did a half-turn away from us.

"Well, I can understand that, Dupree. I surely can," Wesley admitted.

"Ain't nothin' the preacher said makes me think no different," Dupree snapped. "Nothin'. It ain't me that's been buddy-buddy with a thief; it's y'all. You ain't about to find a Hixon foolin' around with no Boyd. But I guess you Wynns don't care."

Anger leaped into Wesley's face, then vanished, and he said, "I guess that's right. I always did think Freeman went out of his way to aggravate you."

"What're you talkin' about?!" I demanded. I thought Wesley had gone crazy. If Dupree ever wanted to make one of us crawl, Wesley was crawling.

Wesley did not answer me. He inched closer to Dupree. "I want you to know I never did believe what Freeman said about you and that night on your granddaddy's farm," he whispered.

The blood left Dupree's face in a flash flood of embarrassment. He began breathing in short, uneven gasps.

"Nope. Never did believe it. And I want you to know I didn't," Wesley continued. "Besides, if it did happen, we all got to learn to forgive one another. That's what it says in the Bible."

Dupree was weak. He swayed into the concrete steps.

"I don't know what you're talkin' about," Dupree protested. "Ain't nothin' ever happened on my grand-daddy's farm. Nothin'! Where Freeman Boyd got that idea, I don't know. But I'm tellin' you, I'm sick to death of hearin' about it. I mean it."

"Well, you know Freeman," Wesley sighed. "That boy's a wonder."

"That boy's crazy as a drunk nigger."

Wesley pinched off the leaf of a boxwood. "Now that might be right. That may be the truth. Nothin' happened, huh? Nothin' at all?"

Dupree stared hard into Wesley's face. He pushed between us and walked away.

Dupree did not stay for Sunday school. He crossed Emery Road to the railroad track and turned toward his home.

The Sunday school lesson was about the Prodigal Son.

In the afternoon, Wesley and I wandered through Black Pool Swamp, searching and calling for

Freeman. He did not answer and we could find no evidence of where he had been.

Finally, Wesley agreed to investigate the one cave we knew about.

"He'll just have to get mad about us knowin'," Wesley reasoned. "If he's hidin', then we ought to know why."

"We already know he's hidin'," I argued. "That ain't no secret."

"Well, not from us, he ain't. He knows if we were goin' to tell on him, we'd already have done it."

"Yeah, I guess you're right."

The cave was deep in the swamp and we had to cross through a fort of blackberry briars before the woods fell off in a sharp drop to its watery bottomland. Halfway across the strip of blackberry briars, we heard voices and Wesley signaled for me to squat down out of sight. The voices were distant and we could not understand what was being said.

"Willie Lee and Baptist," Wesley whispered, motioning with his hand in the direction of the swamp.

The voices were moving, skirting the edge of the woods and traveling away from us. They were too far for their words to hold shape, and we did not know what they were saying, but I knew by their heavy tones that Willie Lee and Baptist were serious, and I felt uneasy about eavesdropping on these two men who had spent hours with us in the happy, restful play of fishing.

We waited until the voices disappeared and then we waited another ten minutes, not moving.

When we were certain they were not returning, we slipped quietly into the woods.

"Wonder what Willie Lee and Baptist was doin' out here?" I asked.

"Who knows? Maybe fishin' down by the beaver dam."

"They didn't sound like they was fishin'."

"How'd you know what they sound like when we ain't around 'em?" Wesley replied sharply. "They're always cutting up with us, but that's just the way colored people are around white people. You'd be surprised how they are when they're all alone, just talkin' to one another."

"Willie Lee ain't different. I know Willie Lee ain't."

"Willie Lee may be the most different of them all, Colin. Shoot, where's your sense? He's the strongest one man around here and he's colored; that makes him different."

"What's different about them?"

Wesley paused and pushed away a cobweb stretched in a lacy bridgework between two sassafras trees. "You know, sometimes I wonder about you. You know that? Bein' colored ain't easy. How'd you like to have Dupree give you the 'nigger' treatment? Or buy stuff at the back door of Hixon's store? You think about that, and then you'll see how they feel."

We picked the tiny spears of blackberry briars from our clothes, then dropped into the swamp and headed for Freeman's cave. Ten minutes later, we were there, stepping silently across beds of moss that grew like a royal carpet leading to a royal throne.

For a moment, Wesley stood frozen, staring up at the covered mouth of the cave head-high above him. He seemed to be listening for a heartbeat, a faint warning that Freeman was there and did not want to be found. Then he called, barely in a whisper, "Freeman?"

There was no answer. Wesley stepped closer. I followed, touching him. "Freeman? You there?" I called.

No answer. Wesley pulled quickly up the slight incline and pushed away the doorway of brush leading into the cave, and crawled inside. "C'mon," he said.

Freeman was not in the cave, but he had been there. We could feel his presence, as though the heat of his body had coated the hard clay walls. Just enough light slipped in under the lip of the opening to prove Freeman had spent his hiding there. There were dead coals of a fire, a mattress of pine needles, squashed-out rabbit tobacco cigarettes, and wadded wax paper from the sandwiches Mother had prepared.

"Wonder how long he's been gone?" I asked, rolling over on Freeman's pine-needle bed.

Wesley was on his knees, studying the cave. He touched the dead embers. "Don't know," he decided. "Don't think he's been here today."

Wesley crawled on his knees to one side of the cave, where Freeman had dug out a shelf for his *Grit* newspapers and rabbit tobacco. There were two paper sacks rolled into bundles and shoved back on the dirt ledge. Wesley picked up one of the paper sacks.

"What's that?" I asked.

"Don't know."

Wesley rolled nearer to the opening, in the light, and

gently squeezed the bundle. "Feels like clothes."

"Well, see," I urged. "Freeman won't care."

Wesley did not like this invasion of privacy, but he had a commitment: he must find Freeman, or at least learn if he was safe. "Well, I guess," he mumbled. He peeled open the sack and shook its contents onto the ground. It was a pair of pants, rolled into a tight wad.

"Just his pants," Wesley said. "Guess he changed when he got them clothes off his mama's clothesline."

I picked up the pants and unrolled them. There was a long tear on the thigh of the right leg.

"Wait a minute," ordered Wesley. "What's that?"

He slipped nearer to the light and pushed the pants down into the cave's opening. He mumbled something I did not hear.

"What?" I demanded.

"Blood. That's blood on his pants," answered Wesley, his voice suddenly tense and worried. "Blood all over that leg. Lots of blood."

A quick, warm breeze whipped over my face. Wesley looked at me. He was holding his breath. The pupils of his eyes widened. "Wes?" I whispered, "did you feel that?"

Wesley moved instinctively away from the opening of the cave. "It ain't nothin'," he answered, trying to regain his courage. "Nothin'. Just your imagination."

"No, it ain't," I said. "No, it ain't. You felt it, and you can't say you didn't. You saw that cat last night, too, Wesley. You saw it, and you was thinkin' the same thing I was thinkin'. Willie Lee told us about cats."

"Maybe we did feel somethin', but maybe it was

just the wind."

"I know it was the wind! Wind of The Doom!"

"Shuttup!"

"Let's go home, Wesley," I pleaded.

"We ain't goin' nowhere until we look this place over good. Get that other sack up there."

"You get it. I ain't touchin' nothin'!"

Wesley turned in disgust and knee-crawled to the shelf. "I should've left you at the house. You get scared at the drop of a hat, you know that?"

The other paper sack was far back on the ledge. Wesley pulled it out and opened it. He rolled to his left and shook out Freeman's shirt in the light. The shirt was caked with dried blood, brown-red and sickening.

"Goda'mighty!" Wesley sighed. "Oh, my God!"

"Somethin's happened, Wes! Somethin' bad! Freeman's dead, ain't he?!"

"No, he ain't dead!" Wesley said, tugging at my arm. "C'mon, let's take these things to Daddy."

"What if somebody's out there?" I resisted. "What if somebody's out there waitin' to kill us, Wesley? Waitin' to cut our throats!" I was becoming hysterical.

"Ain't nobody out there! Nobody! Now, c'mon. . . ."

Wesley broke the sentence in half. He looked toward the opening of the cave, and then looked at me. His face was ashen.

And then I felt it: a cool, kissing breeze, stroking my face with invisible, icy fingers.

"That's what the boys said and that's what they found, Odell. Don't know what it means, but I thought you'd better be told."

Odell Boyd listened in silence to my father. He was sitting on a sack of fertilizer in his barn, holding a cigarette with long, dead ash hanging stubbornly to the burning stub. He looked old and lost. His face was sunken from sleepless nights, and the gray of his hair and second-day beard was a gray of burden and hopelessness that had been suppressed by false good times as a dealer in premium corn whiskey. Odell Boyd had never learned to protest his reputation as a community fool and a harmless jester. Sadly, he had accepted that reputation as his calling and he had learned to glow in the backslapping, good-timing moments of recognition when he would be called on to perform his sorry comedies. Freeman was not like his father; Freeman had learned early to fight, and his determined individualism had won respect. Freeman refused to suffer in private and pretend in public that nothing bothered him; he refused to do stunts for a laugh and a "Ain't he somethin'?" pedestal. Freeman understood that kind of damnation. He had lived with it all his life.

"I appreciate y'all comin' to tell me," Odell Boyd said slowly. "You reckon the boy's hurt bad?"

"He could be," my father said. "That's a lot of blood on his clothes. My boys should've said somethin' about him not playing his flute last night, Odell.

Maybe we could've been out already, lookin'."

"Yessir," Wesley said. "We should've said some-thin', Mr. Boyd."

"That's all right, boys," answered Odell Boyd. "Y'all been mighty good to Freeman."

My father began to pace, thinking. He said, "Was there anything else, boys? Anything about where that cave is? Anything at all?"

I remembered Willie Lee and Baptist. "Yeah, Daddy," I said. "We . . ."

Wesley interrupted. "The Pretlows live down that way. Maybe they saw somethin'."

"Wesley," I said. "What about . . . ?"

"You know the Pretlows, Daddy."

"Wesley . . ." I repeated. "What about . . . ?"

"Yeah, son. I know them," answered my father.

Wesley glared at me and I knew he meant for me to be quiet.

Odell Boyd fumbled with his tobacco tin. "They's mean, them Pretlows. Freeman never had much to do with that bunch."

"Me'n Colin can roam around this afternoon and early tonight. Maybe we can run across Freeman, or where he's been," Wesley said, ignoring me.

My father agreed. "Odell, I guess we can stop around at some houses this afternoon and get some people out by in the morning."

"Get Dover," advised Wesley. "He'll be glad to help out."

Wesley and I left to cross the swamp from Odell

Boyd's house. We walked, not talking, until we were well into the woods, then Wesley stopped and sat on a cushion of needles.

"Look," he said, "I knew what you was wantin' to tell Daddy, about Willie Lee and Baptist, but that might've got 'em in trouble."

"But, we heard . . ."

"I know what we heard. Now, think about it a minute. If Willie Lee and Baptist are mixed up in them bloody clothes, it can't mean but two things: either they did somethin' to Freeman or they helped him out."

"They ain't done nothin' to Freeman," I protested.

"Well, I don't believe that either. So, that leaves helpin' him, if they're mixed up in it at all."

"Wesley, I know that," I said. "I ain't that dumb. And it seems to me Daddy ought to know it, too."

Wesley picked up a pine needle and began to braid it. "All right, so we tell Daddy about it," he reasoned. "What's gonna happen? Daddy and Mr. Boyd's gonna go straight to Willie Lee and ask him, and what's Willie Lee gonna do?"

It was a good question. "I don't know," I mumbled.

"Well, he'd just stand there like he was deaf and dumb and not say the first thing, that's what."

"Why?"

"Willie Lee ain't about to get involved in somethin' that may get the law on him."

"That don't make sense, Wesley. Heck, if he ain't done nothin' but help."

"It's what Willie Lee thinks. After what happened to

July last year, he won't say a word."

"Who?"

"July. Lives over in the Bio community. He's Willie Lee's cousin. They caught him last year for all that stealin' and for tryin' to set up a shotgun trap for some man."

I did not remember anyone named July and I had never heard of a shotgun trap.

Wesley explained. "July had it rigged to go off when the man opened his front door. Would've killed him for sure."

"Did it?"

"What?"

"Kill him?"

"No, it didn't kill him," Wesley answered, puzzled because I had to ask such ridiculous questions. "He came in the back door just as July was goin' out a window."

"He was lucky."

"Luck didn't have all that much to do with it. The man never used his front door, but July didn't know that. I reckon he thought all white people use front doors and all colored people use back doors."

I was fascinated by the story, and I could understand why Willie Lee would be silent. The law believed in Bad Blood as readily as it believed in fact, and the law would not hesitate to point out that Bad Blood flowed in cousins as well as brothers and sisters.

"What're we gonna do?" I asked.

Wesley tossed the braided pine needle aside and began to work on another. Finally he answered,

"We're gonna stay around here, just wandering around, until sundown. Then we'll slip up to Willie Lee's house and see if we can see anythin'."

"What if Willie Lee takes a shot at us?"

"We'll yell out, that's what. Willie Lee ain't about to go shootin' at us."

The plan seemed workable. There would be enough cover, behind trees and Willie Lee's barn, to hide, and if we could coax Willie Lee's dog, Big Boy, to us, we would have no fret of warning. Big Boy knew us as well as he knew Willie Lee's own children.

Willie Lee lived with his wife, Little Annie, and their children in a tenant farm house owned by Hugh Shivers. The house had once been a sharecropper's place and a white family named Pennefeather had lived there, portioning out their meager living in an unwritten agreement with Hugh Shivers. But the land became anemic and had been planted in pine seedlings. The Pennefeathers moved to another share-cropper's house and another unwritten agreement, and Willie Lee moved into the Shivers' Place (tenant houses were always called someone's Place). Since he did not farm, Willie Lee paid rent and did occasional odd jobs for the Shivers family.

Wesley and I loved Willie Lee's home. It was open and warm and there was always the gaiety of small, brown babies, wallowing in play and in aggravation. Little Annie kept the red-sand yard swept clean of leaves and chicken droppings with her dogwood-brush brooms, and she had decorated the windows of the house with hand-me-down curtains that she had dyed bright red. Often, after fishing with Willie Lee and Baptist, we would return to the house and parch peanuts or eat well-cooled watermelon, and listen in wonder to the musical tales and arguments of those strangely funny brothers.

We wandered aimlessly, talking, deciding that Freeman was not badly hurt, or he would have stayed in his cave. We were sure Willie Lee and Baptist had aided him and we were convinced that we would find Freeman that night, at Willie Lee's house.

By late afternoon, we were below our home, and Wesley decided to tell Mother we would be out at night. Mother fretted. If something had happened to Freeman, if someone had caught him and sliced him out of meanness, then that same someone could surprise us. "We won't go far," Wesley promised. "We won't even go in the swamp." Mother reluctantly agreed. She knew Wesley would not break his promise.

We did not need to go into the swamp. Willie Lee's house was across Beaverjam Creek. It was near the swamp, but not in it.

The moon was at quarter, a suspended cradle rocking gracefully in a garden of stars. It was bright enough for light, dark enough for hiding. We did not use the flashlight Mother had insisted we carry. We did not need it. Wesley and I knew the road to Willie Lee's by memory, by step-count, and by feel.

Wesley decided to circle Willie Lee's house, to slip through his pasture and approach from behind the barn. "It'll take a little longer," he judged, "but if Big Boy starts barkin', Willie Lee may think its nothin' more'n a fox, or something."

Big Boy did bark. Once. We stopped and froze. We were in the pasture, very near the barn.

Wesley whistled softly and we heard Big Boy thumping across the yard, wagging his tail and panting. He slipped under the barbed wire fence and trotted toward us, whining his dog's hello. "Good boy," Wesley whispered, patting Big Boy and hugging him close. "Good boy. C'mon, now, keep quiet."

We slipped noiselessly to the dark side of the barn, behind the house. Wesley had plotted beautifully. From the corner of the barn, we could see directly into the kitchen window of the house.

Willie Lee was stripped to his waist. In the shadowy orange of a kerosene lamp, his blackness deepened and his muscles expanded. Willie Lee was a statue of black marble, hard and noble. He moved across the room and lifted a small, laughing child from below the windowsill. The child was naked and curled his tiny, baby legs underneath as Willie Lee held him in one giant palm. Then he reached below the window sill with his free hand and lifted another laughing, naked baby into the air. He held them both up, like two toys. Even from our distance, we could see the uncontrolled laughter spilling out of bright baby eyes.

"Freeman ain't there," I whispered.

"Maybe not," answered Wesley. "Shhhhhhhhhh."

Little Annie appeared, framed in the window. She was carrying something in her hand. Willie Lee dropped one of the babies onto her shoulder and she shuddered in put-on anger. Willie Lee laughed heartily enough to be heard across the yard. He gathered his two children to his shoulders, like small, weightless bundles, and walked out of the window frame.

Suddenly, the house seemed soundless and diminutive. Willie Lee's hugeness had been replaced in the kitchen by the delicate frailty of Little Annie, who circled the kitchen table, gathering dishes.

"Wesley, he ain't there."

Wesley did not answer. He studied the yard, estimating the distance between the barn and the house. "Maybe we can get closer," he whispered. "If Big Boy don't start goin' crazy."

"Willie Lee could shoot us before we know what happened," I argued. "Wesley, I don't care the first thing about bein' shot."

"Hush! Let's wait a minute."

Little Annie moved in and out of the window frame. We could see her wood stove through the window, a wood stove almost identical to my mother's, with top warmers that had white enamel doors. Little Annie opened one of the doors and slipped a plate of leftovers into the warmer. Then she disappeared through a door leading to their bedroom, leaving the kitchen empty.

We waited, two lumps pinned to the dark pine slats of Willie Lee's barn. The merriment of night began in Black Pool Swamp. Millions of insects declared their insect existence, caroling for recognition and losing all recognition because their voices were larger than their bodies. The sweet perfume of honeysuckle and fern and wild, unnamed swamp flowers expired like smoke from the cooling day-furnace of the bottomlands and floated in a gas ribbon, face-high, across the yard. Big Boy sprawled before us, at the corner of the barn, resting his head on his out-stretched front paws, watching us with his brown, play-expectant eyes. Big Boy thought we were retarded, standing there, two lumps pinned to the dark pine slats.

Wesley slipped to his knees and crawled forward. I prepared to follow him, but I saw Willie Lee entering the kitchen and I pushed back into the wall.

"Wesley!" I called.

"I see him," replied Wesley.

Big Boy whimpered and barked. Willie Lee moved to the kitchen window and looked out, his great body snuffing the light. Big Boy barked again.

"Shhhhhhhhhhhhhh! C'mon, Big Boy!" Wesley pleaded.

Big Boy thought Wesley wanted to play. He barked again and jumped around in a circle.

"Quiet, Big Boy! Quiet!"

I looked again toward the house. Willie Lee was no longer at the window. I heard a door open.

"Big Boy! What's goin' on? Hey, Big Boy!" Willie Lee called boldly.

I pulled at Wesley's shirt. "That's Willie Lee, Wesley! Let's get outta here!"

"Shuttup," Wesley retorted.

"But, Wesley . . ."

"Hey, Big Boy! What'd you see, fella?! Somethin'

there, Big Boy?!"

Willie Lee was approaching from across the yard, moving cautiously like a soldier stalking a machine gun nest in a World War II movie.

"Wesley," I whispered.

"Shuttup."

"Hey, Big Boy," called Willie Lee.

Big Boy was confused by his master and by Wesley's frantic motions to keep him quiet. The barking became louder.

"Ain't but one thing to do," Wesley whispered. He stepped out from behind the barn and into the dim light of the quarter moon. "Hey, Willie Lee!" he called.

I slipped to the edge of the barn, still in cover of darkness. Willie Lee was in the middle of the yard, his body coiled in a half-crouch, his giant's arms poised before him.

"Willie Lee! It's me! Wesley!"

"Who is?" demanded Willie Lee.

"Me! Wesley Wynn! Me and Colin are out here!"

Willie Lee did not move. His face was disfigured by a savage wildness. His fingers were curled like steel hooks, his feet spread and firmly staked. His chest heaved. In that moment, Willie Lee could have killed us, or anyone. It was the first time I had ever seen a black man ready to fight.

"Hey, Willie Lee! C'mon! It ain't nobody but me and Colin," Wesley called. I could hear his body weaken in his voice.

"C'mon out," Willie Lee growled. "Out here where's I can see you."

There was no groveling in his command, no sound of inferiority, no apology, nothing passive or submissive. Willie Lee—*that* Willie Lee—was someone we had never known, a power unimaginable.

"We're comin'," Wesley announced meekly. "C'mon, Colin."

I stepped quickly beside Wesley and we walked forward two steps. Wesley caught my arm and held tightly to it. I could feel fright in the desperation of his grasp, yet I was comforted by his touch. We stood very still, staring at Willie Lee. Big Boy jumped around us, barking gleefully.

Slowly, the animal in Willie Lee calmed. His chest relaxed, then his legs, then his arms and fingers. But he did not smile.

Willie Lee said, very deliberately, "Wesley, if you ever come up to my house after dark, you come up by the road and knock on my door. You hear me?" His voice was a weapon, cutting us.

"Uh—yessir," answered Wesley.

Willie Lee turned his face to me. "You understand, Colin?"

"Uh—yessir."

"You could get killed sneakin' into a man's yard," Willie Lee added. "Easy killed. Now, what y'all doin' out here beside my barn?" His voice was calmer, but he was still direct and in command.

"We—we come lookin' for Freeman," Wesley told him.

"Freeman ain't here," answered Willie Lee, quickly, bluntly.

There was a pause. Night poured between us and Willie Lee like a waterfall. Wesley kneeled to play with Big Boy, who panted for attention.

Wesley spoke evenly, quietly. "But you've seen him, Willie Lee. You've seen him, ain't you?"

"Why'd you say that?"

"Because me and Colin heard you and Baptist in the swamp earlier."

Willie Lee stood erect. His head turned slowly to his left, but his eyes did not leave us. He spoke hesitantly. "Me? Me and Baptist? No. No. Must've been somebody else."

Wesley did not look up from Big Boy. "It was you, Willie Lee. You and Baptist. That's why me and Colin come over tonight. To ask you. Nobody knows about you and Baptist, nobody but me and Colin. If we'd of told, there'd be an army over here, and you know it."

Something clicked in the darkness to our right. Wesley and I froze. We knew the sound: the hammer of a gun snapping into place.

"Put it down," Willie Lee ordered.

We looked into the midnight pit, the canopied blackness of a chinaberry tree with massive limbs. Baptist stepped from the heart of the pit, lowering the shotgun he held in trembling hands.

"Wesley?" I muttered. "Wes . . ."

Willie Lee interrupted. "He ain't gonna hurt you, Colin." Then he laughed easily. "You know Baptist ain't gonna hurt you! Put that gun down, Baptist!"

Baptist eased the hammer back into its safety position. He thumbed the barrel lock and the breech broke, snapping a .12-gauge shell into the air. Baptist caught the shell like snatching a fly out of the air. He clucked his tongue, winked, and smiled, exposing a bannister of yellowing teeth. "Oh, Lord, no, I ain't gonna hurt them boys," he said. "Not my fishing buddies! We thought y'all was a booger man sneakin' around here."

It was incredible. Baptist changed personalities in thirty seconds—from a man who could have blown us apart, to a smiling, jesting caricature who had often amused us with his foolishness and half-wit ramblings about the Soldier Ghost.

"Didn't see me, did you?!" Baptist clowned, stepping in and out of the midnight pit, exaggerating a shuffle dance step.

"Sure didn't," Wesley said solemnly.

"Sometimes I don't make as much noise as a shadow," Baptist bragged. "Sometimes I'm so quiet I scare myself. Yessir, one of these nights I'm gonna catch me a ghost!"

"Yeah, and someday I'm gonna make me a million dollars," Willie Lee replied dryly. "C'mon in the house, boys. We'll talk."

Wesley had exercised a mild bluff with Willie Lee, but it was enough. Willie Lee knew it would be senseless to deny that he and Baptist had, indeed, been in the swamp, though it did not occur to him to press Wesley for stronger evidence.

Freeman had been at Willie Lee's house, earlier that day. But now he was gone, and Willie Lee swore he did not know why he left, or where he went.

"He come here hurt, cut bad on his leg," Willie Lee explained. "Lost a lot of blood, and Little Annie patched him up some. Then he told me and Baptist about this cave of his down in the swamp and talked us into goin' back down there and hidin' his bloody clothes. When we come back, he was gone. Little Annie said she couldn't stop him."

"We found them clothes," Wesley confessed. "That's why we got worried."

"You know about that cave?" Baptist asked, amazed.

"We found it a long time ago," I explained. "But we never said nothin' to Freeman about it."

"That's boy's somethin'," Baptist mumbled. "Crazy, that's what."

"Where'd he get a change of clothes?" I wanted to know, forgetting what Rachel Boyd had told us about the theft from her clothesline.

"Sneaked them off his mama's line, couple of nights ago, is what he told us," answered Willie Lee. "Said he didn't want to cause his mama any grief by seein' her."

We sat quietly for a moment, all of us shaking our heads as though we were bewildered in unison, and awed in unison.

"That boy's somethin'," Baptist said again. "Crazy."

"You guess he'll be all right?" Wesley asked Willie Lee.

"He was cut bad, Wesley. Bad. And weak. He was awful weak."

"How'd he do it?" I asked.

"Said his knife slipped when he was whittlin' some

pine shavin's for a fire," Willie Lee replied. "Just plain slipped."

"We took them clothes to Daddy and he took them to Odell Boyd," Wesley said. "They've been around gettin' people together. We'll look the swamp tomorrow."

Willie Lee stopped his slow rocking. "You didn't tell about me and Baptist? You didn't say nothin', did you?"

"Nothin'," Wesley assured him. "And we ain't goin' to."

"I appreciate that," Willie Lee said quietly.

"Me, too," Baptist added.

"Maybe we can find him quick," I said.

"I hope so."

"Me, too," Baptist added.

"We'll look around here," Willie Lee suggested.

"If you see him, just knock him over the head and get him over to the house if he won't come no other way," advised Wesley.

"That's what it's liable to take," Baptist said. "That boy's somethin'. Crazy."

Baptist left with us, pledging to protect us from the evils of night, at least as far as the turn-off to his house.

As we walked, Baptist began to talk. Alone, away from Willie Lee, he was different. Serious. Profound in the way people who do not mean to be profound, are.

"You boys know why Freeman up and took off?" he said—not as a question, but as a prelude to a statement. "Well, it was because of what folks would've been sayin' if they'd of found Freeman over there to Willie Lee's house."

"What'd you mean, Baptist?" I asked.

"Well, now, Colin, you think about it. If they'd of found Freeman, all them folks that don't like him would've been teasin' him about bein' a nigger-lover, and them that does like him would've been wonderin' why he took up at a colored house, and that would've made 'em think they'd been wrong about Freeman all the time.

"And—" Baptist paused to breathe and hammer the night with his fist "—it would've been worser for Willie Lee. They'd of called him a white-trash lover . . ."

"Who would?" I demanded. I could not believe anyone would dare Willie Lee's anger by senseless remarks. Besides, Freeman was not white trash, and Willie Lee was not a nigger; Willie Lee was colored.

"Who would? Lord, child, don't you know nothin'? Everybody! White and colored both. Everybody!"

Even Wesley was amazed by the interpretation Baptist had applied to Freeman's disappearance.

"That don't make sense, Baptist," Wesley argued. "People ain't that way."

Baptist was horrified. He could not believe Wesley was so misinformed. He stopped in the middle of the road and began to sway from side to side, mumbling to himself. Finally, he said, "Boys, Baptist has got to teach you two white chillun somethin', and teach it right now. Sit down. Sit down, right here."

"In the middle of the road?" I said. "Here?"

"In the road," Baptist emphasized. "Slap-dab in the middle of it."

And we sat. In the middle of the road. In a close circle.

"It's like this," Baptist counseled in a voice that had told many stories in the hush of night. "Now, you boys is smart. God knows you smart! Brains on top of brains, I reckon. But there's one thing you ain't learned about, and that's people's meanness. Mean? People are me-e-e-e-ean, boys! Bad mean! You ain't never seen it, I reckon. Ain't many folks gonna cross your daddy to show you they got meanness in 'em, and that's why, but I'm tellin' you, I've seen meanness runnin' outta people like blood outta a stuck pig! So has Willie Lee. So has Freeman. That's what makes him different from you boys. Freeman knows about meanness. And you know somethin', boys? If . . ." Baptist paused. "I better not say that," he added.

"Say what?" Wesley prodded. "Say what, Baptist?"

"Nothin'." He was sullen.

"Baptist, you better say it, because it ain't fair to start somethin' and not finish it."

"All right," Baptist whispered. "But you made me. You remember that."

"We'll remember," I replied eagerly.

"Well, I know y'all and Freeman is big buddies. Freeman done said it a lot; he likes y'all better'n anybody. But—and this is what I didn't wantta say . . ."

"Say it!" urged Wesley.

"But if it come down to a choice between takin' up

for Willie Lee or y'all in sayin' that Willie Lee had helped him out, well, Freeman would take up for Willie Lee."

We did not answer Baptist. We couldn't. We had never thought of a dilemma so complex, so threatening, so unsolvable.

"You made me say it," pleaded Baptist, breaking the silence. "You made me."

Wesley shook his head and his mind snapped into focus. "Shoot, Baptist, I can see that. Any fool can see that. Ain't that right, Colin?"

"Yea," I said, and the more I thought of it, I was certain Baptist was correct.

We left Baptist at the turn-off to his house, and we walked silently in the red wheel tracks of the clay road, walked in red wheel tracks packed and shining in the quarter moon.

As we neared our home, I said to Wesley, "I never heard a colored man say 'nigger-lover' before. Why'd he do that?"

"Oh—that don't mean nothin'. It's just somethin' people say," Wesley answered.

"Sounds nasty, don't it?"

"Yeah," Wesley replied heavily.

"Wesley?"

"Yeah."

"You gonna tell Mama about Willie Lee and Baptist?"

"No. I promised."

"Ain't that like lyin'?" I asked.

"I guess. Maybe. I don't know."

Mother asked: "Did you see any sign of Freeman?"

"No'm," answered Wesley. He looked at me.

"No'm," I repeated.

"Well, they'll be a good many people lookin' tomorrow," she assured us. "They'll find him, boys. They'll find him. The Sheriff's even coming."

14

By early morning, Monday, there were more than forty men and boys gathered in our yard. My father and Odell Boyd had delivered the message of Freeman's bloody clothes and the message had spread from home to home with amazing swiftness.

"Freeman Boyd's been hurt. Meet at the Wynns' house."

"Freeman Boyd's been hurt . . ."

"Freeman Boyd's been . . ."

"Freeman Boyd's . . ."

"Freeman . . ."

"Meet at the Wynns' house . . ."

It was one of the marvels of Emery that important events were shared, alertly and with full impact. It was as though the incident of discovering Freeman's bloody clothes pricked some microscopic cell and the entire body responded instantaneously, along all the nerve cords and nerve endings, where farmhouses clustered like fingers at the turnarounds of dirt roads.

The message had lapped into itself, in many tellings, and it had been understood. The men and boys appeared in trucks and cars, or walking, and they waited to be told what they should do. Most of them were there because that is where they should be, because they were needed. They talked in low voices and their faces were set in the frowning mask of tragedy. They knew—knew beyond doubt—that Freeman had been critically injured, or Freeman had been kidnapped, or Freeman was dead. And as the stories were delivered from person to person, words heaped upon words, thoughts splintered into half-thoughts and quarter-thoughts, the stories became passions of anger and accusation.

"I heared it was nigger doin'. More'n likely them Pretlows."

"More'n likely."

"Odell oughta take him a double-barrel and scatter him some niggers. That'd do it! Pin one of the black devils up against a barn with a two-by-four and you'd hear some talkin', I reckon!"

Wesley and I listened, astonished. Baptist had been right. If we had told about Willie Lee, there would have been a mob storming his house. There were men in that crowd who were there because of the bloody clothes. Bloody clothes. Blood. It was the blood, not Freeman, they wanted to find.

"Wesley," I whispered when we were alone, "what if they go by Willie Lee's house?"

"Freeman ain't there," Wesley answered. "Now, you shuttup. Just shuttup."

"But . . ."

"Shuttup! They're afraid of Willie Lee, anyhow. Not

a man out here would face him, not even if they had a shotgun in their hands."

The image of Willie Lee standing, leaning to fight, his hands poised to kill us, materialized in my mind. One shotgun would not make a dent in his body, not a dent.

Sheriff Dwight Brownlee and Deputy Homer Dove huddled with my father and Odell Boyd and Dover. Dover had a plan for covering Black Pool Swamp.

"We'll break up in two groups," he announced. "One followin' one way and the other followin' another. Now, they's two branches goin' into Beaverjam Creek from around here. We'll be coverin' most of the bottomland if we'll follow them two branches. Now, best thing to do is fan out on both sides of them branches and don't leave nothin' to question." Dover paused, not certain if he should say what he wanted to say. He made his decision: "Men, there's one other thing, and this may sound a little bit crazy, but this ain't just a boy we're lookin' for; this here boy don't want to be found and he knows more about bein' in them woods than the whole lot of us put together. I guarantee you, he can hide places that gnats can't fit in. So, keep a good eye."

The searchers separated into two groups and with eager exchanges of confidence, marched away to begin their determined mission of finding Freeman Boyd—marched away with a brisk step for their pace and a firm jaw for their commitment. They would be keen-eyed and constant, and would not waste the intimacy of an occasion that had yanked them, abruptly, from their routine and presented them with a profound duty. It was the mood of men going to war, convinced their enemy would be vanquished before the call to supper, and how good it would be to sit in later days and tell the Why and How of their service to a noble quest.

"Good luck!"

"Hope we find him first!"

"Holler if y'all see anythin'!"

"Don't worry, Odell, we'll turn them woods upside down!"

"Hey! Betcha we make the creek first!"

"All right, you boys! Don't go gettin' lost!"

We watched as Sheriff Brownlee and his group followed my father and Odell Boyd into the new ground leading toward Beaverjam Creek, then we turned in the opposite direction and followed Dover's military stride through our pasture. Dover had wanted the boys of Our Side in his party. He knew we understood more about Black Pool Swamp than any man there, with the exception of Odell Boyd, and Dover was obsessed with the thought of his group—his Number One Team—finding Freeman.

The branch we would trail sliced through the bed of our pasture in a wide, deep furrow. When he lived at home, before college, my brother Hodges constructed magnificent dirt-and-plank dams across the trough of the branch and we swam daily at sunset to wash away field dirt. The dam was always in the same location, just above the barbed wire fence separating our pasture from Black Pool Swamp. Below the dam, the branch narrowed and slithered into the swamp, and that was our starting point, our ". . . jump-off place," as Dover appointed it.

There were twenty-four people in the group and Dover divided us, twelve and twelve, to scout both sides of the branch. "Spread out," he instructed. "We ought to cover more'n a hundred feet on both sides. When we get to the bottomlands, we'll let the boys go through there. They know them ridges better'n the rest of us."

We began our search in energy. Two hours later, when the sun was at noon and you could see heat rising in its wavy, liquid veil, we stopped for rest. The men were red-faced, their brown workshirts stained chocolate by perspiration. A few had been thoughtful enough to purchase cans of sardines, or Vienna sausage, and peanut butter crackers, and they shared their meager lunches, drowning the food with branch water. My mother had given each of the boys of Our Side a sizable sweet potato she had baked earlier, and we ate gladly.

"It's hotter'n four hundred hells in here," one of the men observed. "I ain't seen a snake doctor flyin' anywhere, it's so hot. Reckon we'd better slow it down, Dover, or some of us'll be stayin' around for the buzzards."

Dover dipped his handkerchief in the branch and squeezed water over his neck. He closed his brown eye and squinted toward the sun with his blue. "Yeah," he said. "We ain't far from the bottomlands. Maybe we'd best let the boys go on ahead and look there, and we'll tag on along the branch. It narrows down around here, anyhow."

"The beavers got some dams a little piece on down," Otis added. "That's when you can't do nothin' but walk the hills."

Dover nodded. "Right. Wesley, reckon y'all can cover them bottoms?"

"Yeah, Dover. We'll get 'em."

"Well, we'll be pretty close behind. Y'all find anything, give a yell."

We left the men at rest. Wesley, Alvin, and I moved down the east side of the branch. R. J., Paul, and Otis followed the opposite bank. The beaver ponds pushed us to the hills, forcing us to trail in a widening parallel, like the raised arms of a capital Y, and then we dropped off into the watery bottomlands of Black Pool Swamp.

"I been thinkin' about them bottoms," Alvin said solemnly. "Even thought about 'em yesterday, pitchin' against that bunch of college smart alecks from Athens, and that was before I knew Freeman was hurt. I'm tellin' you, Wesley, if there's any place that a man could hide a body, this is it. I mean, slap forever!"

Alvin had good reason for his apprehension. The drain ditches were there, grave-deep, covered with a death mask of swamp grass and vines. If someone had killed Freeman, it would have been easy to dispose of his body in the ditches, where the mire swallowed objects like some giant glob.

"What'd you think, Wes?" asked Alvin.

"I doubt it," answered Wesley. "We'll look 'em."

"What made you think about them ditches yesterday, Alvin?" I wanted to know. "I mean, when you was pitchin'."

Alvin laughed nervously. "I don't know," he admitted. "I was just throwin' away, and all of a sudden, I got this here funny feelin' about Freeman. Just happened."

Wesley looked at me. His eyes widened. He swallowed hard. "C'mon," he said.

It took an hour to walk the ditches, with Alvin peering cautiously into fresh depressions where beaver had crashed in playful games of hide-and-seek, or whatever games beaver played in lost hours of enjoying the murky kingdom they had created. In the middle of the bottomland, we met R.J. and Otis and Paul.

"See anythin'?" asked Alvin.

"Nothin'," replied R.J. "Nothin' but some duck feathers. I reckon there must be a lot of fox around here."

"Must be," Alvin acknowledged. "We seen feathers on this side, too. And rabbit droppin's. Canecutters, by the size of em."

We left the bottomland and walked along the bank toward Dover and the other searchers.

"Where you think we oughta be looking, Wes?" asked Paul as we walked.

"Don't know," answered Wesley. Then he added, "I ain't got the slightest idea." Wesley was discouraged and puzzled.

"Me neither," I said. No one ever asked my opinion, because I was too young and too small to have an opinion, but occasionally I volunteered a few remarks to remind myself that I belonged.

Paul laughed. "Colin, where'd you go and hide if you was in here?"

"That's easy," I told him. "I'd go climb up my tree."

"Now, that's dumb," Paul replied. "Who'd go hidin' in a tree?"

Wesley stopped abruptly and wheeled to Paul. "Hey, wait a minute," he exclaimed. "That ain't so dumb! That's the one place we ain't even thought about lookin'."

"Yea, that's right," Otis said. And then, "What're you talkin' about, Wes?"

"Freeman's tree. He's got this tree. Must be the biggest beech in Black Pool Swamp, and it's hollowed out up in the trunk. Got a hole running from top to halfway down. Freeman said it'd been struck by lightnin' dead in the center, and he dug it out and drilled him some drain holes in the trunk. Even fixed him a kind of roof over it. You can't even tell it's there unless you climb it."

Alvin was skeptical. "Aw, shoot, Wesley, Freeman ain't gonna be hidin' in no tree."

"Maybe not," Wesley argued, "but it's the one place we know about that we ain't checked. C'mon. It ain't all that far."

Freeman's tree was not a tree as other trees are trees; it was a monument. He had taken Wesley and me to its location a few times, but he warned us against ever going there without him. A man's tree, according to Freeman, should never be trespassed. A tree was put on Earth by God for one man and one man only, and it was simply a matter of man and tree meeting at the proper time. "It's a feelin'," Freeman had described. "There ain't no system to it at all. You just walk up to a tree someday and there it'll be and there you'll be and you'll know. Then you just take out your knife and carve your initials in the bark, and that does it. From then on out, that tree belongs to you, son, and it don't make no difference whose land it's on."

We had obeyed Freeman's instructions about staying clear of his tree. There had been times, in fact, when Wesley and I walked in circles, skirting the area, just to avoid casting eyes on the F.B. proudly sliced in the bark—F.B. that had healed into a scar and turned dark in age and weather. It was Freeman's tree. It even had Freeman's pride.

But we had been impressed by Freeman's advice and had spent days begging that Unseen Presence to fall over us as we walked the woods, innocent and receptive. Eventually Wesley decided such a discovery had to be a private quest, and that it had to be totally unexpected. He was right. One day, during my probation because of my association with Megan, I was wandering in the edge of the swamp and Something made me stop and look up. There, waiting patiently, was My Tree.

My Tree was a sycamore. It was not as majestic as Freeman's beech. It did not have limbs elbowing anemic pines and water oaks out of its stretch; there was nothing intimidating about My Tree, nothing bold and absolute. My Tree was straight and thin. It had bark that was young and smooth, a gray-white bark with flecks the color of ink. My Tree had a childish look, a woefulness that seemed almost apologetic, and it appeared clownish wearing a squirrel's nest at an awkward tilt in a limb flopping too far from its trunk. But I loved that tree, loved it from the first accident of looking up and seeing it and wondering why I never before knew it was there. I took my pocket knife and carved C.W. in the bark, high up, boring in the periods with the small blade. My Tree. I knew that someday it would be as complete as other trees I had read, where legends of childhood were carved in a code language of initials. Who loved Who. Which year When. Hearts and Arrows. Puckered lips. Poems. Yes, poems. Two days after discovering My Tree, I gouged out a three-word poem: Eyes of Green.

We followed Wesley in a single file over the spine of a hill that Freeman had named Hog Mountain. As a mountain, it was an insult. As a hill, it was peculiarly out of place in Black Pool Swamp. At the bottom of the slope, there was a small branch—a half-branch— fed from an underground spring. We found the animal path of the half-branch and trailed upstream until we reached a clearing. Freeman's tree was a hundred yards across the clearing, at the base of a separate gathering of hills.

"That's it," announced Wesley, pausing to scan

the clearing.

"Where?" asked Alvin.

"Over yonder, Alvin," I said, turning him in the direction of the tree. "That big beech tree across the clearin'."

From a hundred yards Freeman's tree looked like a fighter, wild and daring. It seemed to recognize our presence. A wind we could not feel swam through a pond of leaves in the top limbs of the beech, and the limbs waved a greeting to us.

"Damn! That's a big'un, all right," Paul muttered.

"Just like ol' Freeman, ain't it?" R. J. said. "Yessir, the biggest, meanest-lookin' tree in here and ol' Freeman's got claim to it."

The limbs waved again, but not in greeting. Now it was a warning, a mute's signal to leave. Something, some nerve at the base of my skull, began to tighten. I whispered, "Wesley, Freeman ain't there. Let's go."

"What's the matter?" Wesley asked, annoyed.

"He's right," Paul replied. "Let's go. I ain't too crazy about what's here."

Paul had sensed it, the gesture, the silent caution that pushed against us. I looked at R. J. and Otis. Bravery seeped from their faces as they stared at the tree, hypnotized.

"Maybe it's best we go get Dover," suggested Alvin.

"Why?" asked Wesley. "It ain't nothin'. Just imagination. Shoot, Alvin, you're the oldest one of us. What're you scared for?"

Alvin was not convinced. "It ain't fair to Dover," he protested. "I ain't scared, Wes. It's just that Dover'll think we ain't tellin' him everything."

"Well, I'm goin' over there," Wesley announced in a loud voice. "Y'all can come with me, or y'all can stay right here. I don't care."

Wesley stepped into the clearing and began to cross toward the tree. Alvin followed. Then R. J. and Otis and Paul. I did not want to go, but I did not want to stay behind, alone. "Wait a minute!" I yelled. "Wesley! You better wait, or I'll tell Mama!"

Wesley stopped. He was angry. "Well, c'mon, if you're goin'!" I raced to him, beside him, close to him, our arms touching as we walked.

The clearing was a courtyard for Freeman's King Beech. Visitors were announced by the trumpets of crickets and sparrows. Wildflowers waved like banners. Near the tree, in a slight curving terrace, two lines of scrub ash bowed in eternal servitude, their curtsying limbs bent toward the ground.

We stopped fifteen yards away from the tree.

"See anythin'?" whispered Otis.

"Nothin'," answered Paul, also whispering.

"Wesley?"

"Nothin', Otis. Nothin'. Ain't no need to be afraid."

"What's that, Wesley?"

"What's what? You don't shut up, Paul, you're gonna scare Colin to death!"

"That, dammit! That!"

"What?"

"Hangin' there! On that limb!"

"I don't see nothin'!"

Paul took two steps closer to the tree and cupped his

hand over his eyes. "Damn!" he said. "There!" He pointed to a limb of the tree.

We saw it at one time, in the exact, precise moment, as though our eyes were one with one vision seeing one thing.

Three snakes. Three snakes grotesquely slaughtered, their skins peeled away at half-body, peeled back to their tails, with the skins looped over the limb and tied in a bow like a ribbon. The exposed flesh of the snakes from half-body to their tails had bulged and ruptured in the heat and had soured to a deep purple color. The heads of the snakes had been smashed into a pulp of bone and muscle and the half-body still covered with skin had dried to a brittle grayish brown.

The stench gagged us. Gnats swirled around each snake, like hundreds of tiny vultures.

"Goda'mighty!" R. J. gasped. His face paled. He clutched his throat with both hands and turned away.

"It's the Snake Spell!" whispered Otis.

"God . . ." Alvin mumbled. "Goda'mighty!"

The Snake Spell. Yes. It had to be. Three half-skinned snakes hanging from a limb. The Snake Spell. Voodoo. Dark, secret, African magic.

"Wesley . . . ?"

"Shuttup, Colin. I see it."

The Snake Spell. They had told us of the Snake Spell when we were babies, each of us. It was a spell of ultimate horror to keep restless boys quiet and obedient. ("You behave, or that old witch woman's liable to put the Snake Spell on you! Then you'll see! Then you'll be sorry!")

"Let's go find Daddy, Wesley . . ."

"Wait a minute. Don't go thinkin' about them stories," snapped Wesley.

Stories?

The Snake Spell was more than stories. It was real. People said so, so it was. It was real.

People said it had been used against one of the Pretlows, a child-beater, and he had fallen dead in the snap of a finger.

People said it had been used to cripple Hugh Shivers' father after he had spit on an old black man for sport, when the old black man refused to hambone.

People said it had been used to produce boils and warts on the bodies of dozens of hard, selfish rich people who delighted in mistreating poor blacks and whites.

The Snake Spell was real.

People said so.

"Wesley, maybe we ain't close enough to get hit by it," whimpered Paul. "Let's back off, easylike."

Wesley was irritated by Paul's trembling. "Paul, I ain't done nothin' to be afraid of," he said, convincing himself. "Now, you can walk or run or do whatever you want to, but I'm stayin' here. Anyway, maybe it's meant for helpin' somebody. Maybe Freeman. If there's a place where somebody made a fire, that means it's a helping spell."

"I never heard tell of that," Paul begged.

It was true. The Snake Spell could be for Good or Evil. People said so. It depended on secret incantations and secret gestures, and the presence of a ritual fire. If the spell was intended for Good, there would be a ritual fire. Always, always, the Good spell demanded a ritual fire. The fire produced ashes and ashes were used to rub on whoever needed help, and that person magically acquired the power of the wood that had been burned.

Wesley moved away from us, cautiously. He circled under the snakes, dangling like chopped fox-grape vines. A few feet from the trunk of the tree, he stopped. "It's here," he called quietly.

We were suddenly released from the paralysis of fear. We moved quickly, in a lump, to Wesley. On the ground was a ring of rocks, carefully stacked. The inside of the rocks was charred. Three small pyramids of ashes were formed in the exact center of where the fire had been.

We were very still, commanded to be still by a phantom force that seemed centered in the three small pyramids of ashes.

"I thought that old witch woman was dead," Otis whispered.

"No," Wesley answered softly. "No, Granny Woman ain't dead. But she didn't do this. She's too old to be walkin' around in the woods. That woman's more'n a hundred."

"Who done it, Wesley?"

"I don't know, Otis. Maybe Freeman. Maybe he's just bein' Freeman and trying to scare us, or something."

Alvin squatted and pushed in the peak of one of the pyramids. "This ain't been used," he observed. "Whoever set it up didn't get no chance to use it. Maybe they'll be comin' back."

"Maybe," Wesley said.

"I'll bet that's right," R. J. added.

Alvin carefully rebuilt the pyramid, pinching the top and smoothing the sides. "We better tell about this," he advised.

"No," answered Wesley. "No, let's keep it quiet right now, Alvin. For a time, at least."

"Why?"

"Everybody knows the Snake Spell comes from Granny Woman," explained Wesley. "Everybody. If we told about findin' this, half those men out kickin' around this swamp would go stormin' over to Granny Woman's house and cause all kinds of trouble."

"Yeah, I reckon that's right," R. J. agreed.

"But if Freeman put up this spell, he'll be comin' back," Wesley continued. "And it'd be a lot better if we could find him here, than havin' people go crazy trying to get answers outa Granny Woman."

Wesley was remembering Willie Lee and Baptist, and his promise not to involve them. He also knew every black in Emery would be committed to Granny Woman's defense if anyone threatened her.

"All right," Otis said, "what're we sayin'?"

Wesley looked at the snakes, then at Alvin. "What'd you think, Alvin?"

"Seems to me we ought to camp out somewhere close by and take turns watchin' for Freeman," Alvin suggested. "If he's comin' back, it won't be before night."

"That's good," agreed Wesley. "Anybody else got any ideas?"

No one spoke.

"That's that," announced Alvin. "We can say we're goin' to Wind's Mill in case Freeman shows up there."

"Better take Dover with us," Paul suggested. "Havin' him along will make it easier to get out."

"Yeah," R. J. said. "Wes, we tell Dover about this?"

"Yeah," answered Wesley. "Paul's right. We need Dover. But let's don't tell anybody else."

"We better take a vow," counseled Otis.

Paul agreed. "Yeah, we need a vow."

"C'mon, Paul, there ain't no reason for that!"

"Wesley, we always take a vow."

"Yeah," argued R. J. "Ain't that right, Alvin?"

"Don't make no difference to me one way or the other," Alvin answered, meticulously perfecting the top of the pyramid of ashes. "I ain't superstitious."

"Let's swear," I said, pulling at Wesley's arm.

"Well, all right, get it done with!" replied Wesley.

Above our heads were three half-skinned snakes. A ritual fire, with ritual ashes was at our feet.

We crossed our hearts and hoped to die.

15

It did not seem reasonable that Freeman would mock the Snake Spell. He believed more firmly than any of us in the ancient heritage of Granny Woman Jordan. But Freeman did not think of her as an ". . . old witch woman." She had The Power, and The Power was

277

more than witchery.

Granny Woman Jordan had been a slave girl in the Civil War. In the battle of Kennesaw Mountain, she had suffered shell shock and when she again woke to reality, she discovered she was in an orphans' home in Charleston, caring for wiggling white babies. The proprietor of the orphanage referred to her as ". . . a perfect granny woman," and that is why she adopted the name. In those years when her body was commanded to sleep-walk and sleep-work and sleep-live by another shadowy person, Granny Woman misplaced fragments of her past; her real name was one of those fragments.

Wesley and I knew many tales of Granny Woman because we were privileged to hear them from Annie. Annie was one of twenty children born to Granny Woman, and she was the mother of Little Annie, Willie Lee's wife. When I was very small, Annie—My Annie—worked with my mother during weeks of canning and harvesting. Annie had a special regard for me; I was her Child Baby, and I quickly fell in love with that wonderful black woman who smiled a wrinkled, missing-tooth smile and whose eyes carried a star burning in the dark, liquid heavens of her pupils. My Annie had the longest, shiniest, softest black fingers in the entire world and she knew how to bend and shape them in dozens of caricatures for playing animal shadows on the wall. My Annie cooked cakes for me. Chocolate marble cakes. She would say, "Oh, my Child Baby! He wants a cake. What color cake you want, Child Baby?" And I would answer, "Cake the color of you, Annie." Mother tried often to discourage Annie from indulging me with chocolate marble cakes, but Annie ignored her. Once, in desperation, Mother hid the sugar and Annie walked two miles to Hixon's General Store, where she charged five pounds to my father's account. "That baby's *my* baby, too," declared Annie. "He wants cake, Annie's gonna cook him cakes!"

I was very spoiled by My Annie.

My memories of Annie were baby memories, though my mother visited her often and Annie made an annual pilgrimage to spend an entire day with Mother. On those days (always with an air of holiday), Annie would embrace me with laughter and tell again an old story of the day I became angry and, in temper, ran away from home, only to return at sundown, declaring I would give my family one last chance before seeking a better residence. But I did remember the Snake Spell, first told by my mother and repeated with marvelous dramatics by My Annie. And I remembered specks and flashes of Annie's gleaming face as she spoke in a trembling voice about voodoo, and I had believed Granny Woman was blessed with knowing secrets no one else knew, secrets that reached back, back, back, forever back, back to Africa and a tribe of godlike magicians, fierce and mighty and proud.

In the late thirties, Granny Woman had become a character in harmless stories, a myth. During World War II, she emerged as a symbol of hope, an emissary between the Unknown and the Frightened. There were stories of sorrowful white women applying to Granny

Woman for supernatural assistance. Their husbands, or sons, were missing in action. They had prayed, yes, but God, through the U.S. Army, had not answered their petitions and they had surrendered to this last possibility, this mystery of Granny Woman Jordan. For a time, Granny Woman accepted them, offered audience, and read for them messages of terrible truths. But it was not truth the women wanted; they wanted pain-killing fantasies, cool breezes of assurance. And Granny Woman stopped seeing them, refused to hear their squalling hysterics. She was very old, nearing one hundred years, and she became more and more an unseen person. After the war, she disappeared into the back bedroom of Annie's home, into a room that squeezed over her like a womb, and she curled into the fetal position on a feather mattress. To my knowledge, she was seen by only three white people during those years of solitude: Tommy Holcomb, the debit man, who saw her by accident, and Wesley and me.

On Granny Woman's one-hundredth birthday in 1946 (her age was estimated; she was, perhaps, even older), Mother had dispatched Wesley and me to Annie's, bearing a gift of a hand-knitted shawl. The occasion was most memorable.

Annie and her husband, Claude Miles, lived in a small house, a toy house with unpainted clapboards darkened by exposure and years. The roof had overlapping wood shingles, and the shingles had been patched in mole dots of tin cans hammered flat and covered with tar. A front porch, broken and limp on one corner, extended the length of the house. The damaged front porch made the house suffer, piteously suffer, like a man who has the half-face of a stroke. There were two front windows peering out from the lid of the porch. The windows were small, weak eyes, diseased by the cataracts of old screens turned brown and bubbled inward. The front screen door had lost its bottom hinge and hung like a scab on a healing sore. Wads of dead grass lodged in the porch planking. Islands of broom sage grew tall in the white sand ocean of the unkempt front yard.

Behind the house the skeleton of a large barn leaned awkwardly, tilting forward on one corner like some great stubby-winged bird wanting to fly. Rot-black hay—grass and grain stems not fit to eat—was shoved against the barn door. Corrugated tin flapped on the roof—metal feathers on the great stubby-winged bird. A well shelter, between the barn and house, had a broken back from a fallen limb that had been cut and rolled away. Mulberry bushes and chinaberry trees grew in drawfed clusters at the back of the house. A fig bush, the only tended tree in the yard, grew alone in the edge of the pasture.

"Don't nobody keep this place up," I whispered to Wesley as we entered the yard on Granny Woman's one-hundredth birthday.

"They're all too old," he said simply.

The hand-knitted shawl and the remembrance of Granny Woman deeply affected Annie. She decided to introduce us—her Child Baby and his brother—to Granny Woman.

"Go down yonder and dig me up some red dirt," Annie instructed, "whiles I tell Granny Woman somebody's comin'."

We did not know why she wanted the red dirt, but we did as we were told. Annie took the red dirt and some starch cubes and wrapped them in wax paper.

"Give these to Granny Woman," she told me.

"Why, Annie?"

"Granny Woman loves them things. Rather eat them things than table food," explained Annie.

"She eats red dirt?" I inquired, astonished.

"Red dirt's good for you, Child Baby."

We followed Annie into Granny Woman's room. It was a half-size room with a half-size window. The window was covered with burlap sacks, sealing the light except for a straight, dusty, arrow-beam crossing over a bed and plunging into a table beside the top of the bed. The table was draped with a delicate lace cloth. A kerosene lamp was in the middle of the table, on a chipped plate, and a rocker was beside the bed. The back of the rocker was also dressed in the delicate lace cloth.

Granny Woman was in the bed. She was older than any living creature I had ever seen. Her skin was drawn and parched and appeared coated with paraffin. Her lips were pale brown and cracked. Her sunken eyes were black caves. Her hair was thin, white, lifeless, a curled thread braided in rows across her skull. Her mouth opened and closed, opened and closed, like the mouth of a lizard licking the air.

Annie slipped a pinch of red dirt into Granny

Woman's opening and closing mouth and Granny Woman nodded childishly.

Annie began to talk to Granny Woman in a shrill shout, waving her arms in exaggerated gestures, arranging her words like ABC blocks, to be somehow seen as well as heard. I wondered if Annie had become addicted to those hand signs through years of caring for her mother.

We were introduced, but Granny Woman did not know we were there. Annie broke a starch cube in half and slipped it into Granny Woman's mouth and Granny Woman lay back into her pillow, sucking on the starch. She seemed asleep in her mountain of pillows, lapsed into dream space, and I remembered what my mother had said about old people running away in memory, and how their minds lost control, confusing time and people and place. I wondered if Granny Woman had hurled herself, in one tremendous leap, across time, back to the Civil War, back to a day of killing when, in one breath, she had exhaled slavery and inhaled the poison of being sentenced to years of mindless wandering, years when she knew nothing, felt nothing, remembered nothing.

The white, chalky starch drooled from Granny Woman's lips as she flew aimlessly about in her astral escape, swirling in worlds of half-images.

Annie led us away, outside.

We had not talked of seeing Granny Woman because Annie had pledged us to silence. She did not want curious spectators with carnival expectations spilling into her yard. Granny Woman was not a sideshow.

Granny Woman was old and wanted to be alone. Let people think of her as a witch, ". . . a conjurin' woman," and let them believe she could hex them and make them vanish from the face of Earth if they violated her privilege of age.

It had been that experience Wesley recalled when he saw the three half-skinned snakes. The Granny Woman we had seen was incapable of casting spells, even if she did have The Power.

Someone else had staged the props of the Snake Spell.

It could have been Freeman; Freeman knew what was required, but he also respected the solemnity of those rites. It could have been Annie, but Annie was also old and Annie vigorously denied inheriting any of Granny Woman's gifts. It could have been Little Annie, who often behaved in a quietly removed and pensive manner, as though she anticipated experiences before they occurred. And, it could have been Willie Lee, warning Wesley and me to keep our promise— Willie Lee knowing we would, eventually, remember Freeman's tree.

But it could not have been Baptist. Baptist was more afraid of snakes than of the distinct, and oppressive, possibility of meeting the Soldier Ghost face to face. If the Soldier Ghost had a face.

Dover was weakened by our news of the Snake Spell. He had never been so impressed with any news, he said, and he proposed the theory that Granny Woman had called on the spirit world and the spirit world had lifted her, bodily, and transported her to Freeman's tree, where she performed the Snake Spell on stroke of midnight. Dover was an absolute believer in ". . . things greater than our thinkin'." He had learned that much in his palm-reading course, he said.

"It may be Freeman's doin'," Dover admitted, "but I doubt it, boys. Older you get, the more you learn how to recognize things for what they are. That old woman's got The Power, and there ain't no doubt of it. I could curl your toenails with some of the stories I know."

"It ain't gonna hurt, keeping watch on that tree," R. J. said.

"No, it ain't," Dover answered matter-of-factly. "It ain't bad thinkin', boys. I don't mean that. I just got my doubts, that's all."

"We can say we're goin' down to Wind's Mill," Alvin again proposed. "That way, ain't nobody gonna worry."

"That's good thinkin', too," Dover said. "But we'd have to be up and back early. The search starts again tomorrow. Sheriff said we'd keep it up until we found somethin'."

We returned to Black Pool Swamp in pre-night, in that time when day's light is a thin sheet of ice, hurriedly melting.

Dover cautioned us that we were not camping; we were on a mission, and the tiniest nerves in our bodies would have to be alert.

"No fires, no talking," Dover said. "We'll take turns sleepin' and watchin'. Freeman's sneaky."

There were seven of us, including Dover, and the odd number confused the watch order.

"Ought to be two at a time," insisted Alvin.

"Yeah, but that leaves us one short, or one too many, dependin' on how you look at it," observed Dover. He thought for a moment. "Tell you what, I'll be awake anyhow, so let's just take the six of y'all and draw straws."

Otis argued that Dover could not stay awake all night. Dover dismissed Otis with an indignant stare and broke six pine needles into various lengths—two short, two long, and two between short and long. We drew for watch, short to long. Otis and R. J. had the first turn, Alvin and I were second, and Wesley and Paul were last.

We selected a sentinel's position on a ridge thirty yards away from Freeman's beech tree. It was an obstructed position because of the undergrowth of dwarfish swamp bushes, but it had two advantages: we were above Freeman's tree, and we were on a mat of pine needles; pine needles did not crackle when you moved.

"All right," whispered Dover. "I don't want nobody sayin' nothin' for the rest of the night. If you see anythin', shake the rest of us."

"Dover?"

"What is it, Paul?"

"What if we have to pee?"

"Lordamercy, Paul!"

"Well?"

"Well, pee."

"Where?"

"Where? What'd I care? Anywhere! In your pants! Now, shuttup!"

"Paul?"

"Yeah, Alvin?"

"Don't pee on no oak leaves."

"Why?"

Alvin snickered, controlled himself. "It'll sound worse'n a cow pissin' on a flat rock."

A single bar of laughter rose in harmony from the chorus of hidden, night-covered bodies.

"Shuttup!" commanded Dover, spitting the word.

Silence. Night. Nerves on ready. I thought: nothing will escape me; I have lived these terrible moments before. I remembered the Japs and how they had tried to slither like worms through our net of death, and how we had pressed our ears to the ground and plotted their creepy movements with the radar of our hearing.

I pressed my ear to the ground. Nothing. Perhaps the cooling of Earth. Nothing more.

I could hear only the breathing, the minor note of breathing, lungs stroking unevenly, lapsing into an involuntary syncopation of laborsome rhythm. The breathing. And night. Everywhere night.

Freeman's tree was shapeless in that early darkness. It was a blob. A shapeless blob shoved into other shapeless blobs, flat and deeper than deep pits that are bottomless in the eye of imagination. It would be the best time of the night for Freeman to slip unnoticed past our blind spying, and return to his rites of supernatural medication—if, indeed, the rites were for Freeman.

And then the light began. At first, barely there. Light like dew from the tilted spoon of the quarter moon; light from the spears of stars, hurled millions of miles and pinging off the waxy shields of leaves; light of foxfire, sprinkled haphazardly in phosphorescent dots over the carpet of Black Pool Swamp, glowing in never-blinking eyes.

The light pulled Freeman's tree up from the blob, lifted it like a fighter rising from the lap of his ring corner, his body shimmering in the reflection of his might, and behind the rising figure of Freeman's tree, smaller trees thrust outstretched but untouching fingers, throwing the fighter forward.

Then we could see plainly the tree, bold in its reach and spread. Dover had not seen the Snake Spell and we tried to tell him, by mouthing, the location of the snakes, but Dover did not understand and mouthed back, "Where?" Wesley motioned for him and Dover edged forward on his elbows and stared down the barrel of Wesley's finger. When he saw the snakes, his eyes widened in astonishment.

"Lordamercy!" Dover exclaimed in a loud whisper.

The chorus rose again: "Shhhhhhhhhhhhhhhhhh-hhhh!"

Dover slipped back to his position and stared at the tree. He was mesmerized.

Otis nudged me out of sleep and dreams and leaned to

whisper in my ear.

"I'm sleepy," he complained. "You and Alvin take it."

"O.K.," I replied in my smallest voice. "What time is it?"

"Ain't no tellin'. Dover's got the watch in his pocket."

"Where's he?"

"Asleep," sighed Otis. "Been asleep for a half hour."

"See anythin'?"

"Nothin'. Oh, yeah. R. J. thought he saw a scorpion. Better keep lookin'."

"Yeah."

I rolled out of the quilt and Otis wiggled into my place. He stretched once, and his body slowly contracted into the curl of a comma. He was asleep in five minutes.

Alvin signaled that he was awake and on duty. He pointed one of his long, skinny fingers toward Dover and laughed soundlessly, mocking Dover's grand determination to stay awake the entire night. Paul began to snore easily and I jabbed him with my foot. He rolled on his side and the snoring stopped.

Freeman's tree also slumbered. Its massive limbs drooped and the crown of its growth was limp and folded. Occasionally, the wind would whirl under and up, lifting the leaves lazily, and the tree seemed to shudder, as though flipping away an insect.

Below us, in the swamp, a beaver slapped its paddle tail against the water and the sound cracked like a bullet zinging off a rock. Dover snapped out of his sleep.

"What's that?" he whispered, breaking his own commandment.

"Beaver," Alvin said softly.

"Uh—see anythin'?" asked Dover.

"Naw," answered Alvin.

Dover looked at me. I shook my head.

Dover yawned, stretched, checked the motionless bodies of Wesley and R. J. and Otis and Paul. He pulled his watch from his pocket. "One-thirty," he whispered. "Y'all keep it till three."

"You gonna stay awake?" asked Alvin.

"Of course I am!" Dover hissed. "I been awake!"

Alvin smiled and winked at me. "Oh . . ." he said.

Dover did not sleep. He rested one eye at a time. The blue eye and then the brown eye. He looked strange, demented, one eye closed as easily as other people close both eyes.

At three o'clock, we woke Wesley and Paul, and Alvin and I tried to sleep, but we could not. We were awake. We stared at the stars and plagued Dover by mimicking his eye trick. The seriousness of our mission weakened in that game—until Wesley heard me giggle and kicked me sharply.

"Quit it!" he warned.

"That's what I say," added Dover.

At five o'clock, the sky began to pale into a gray and the stars began to withdraw, washed out by the antiseptic warning of day.

Dover stood and stretched and nudged Otis and R. J.

with his foot. "C'mon, boys, let's get up," he said in his normal voice. "We got to get up and get back to the truck, so's we can be back at the Wynns' by six."

We were only a mile from our house, but Dover had parked his truck near Rakestraw Bridge and that was a two-mile hike. Dover did not want anyone to know we were not at Wind's Mill; he could not explain why he had camped in Black Pool Swamp, watching a tree.

R. J. rubbed his eyes and yawned. "Anythin' happen?" he asked.

"Nothin'," Paul answered. "Nothin'."

"Them snakes still there?" Otis wanted to know.

"Yeah," Dover said lazily.

Otis stood and kicked the circulation back into his cramped legs. He stared at Freeman's tree. "Where?" he asked.

"Where, what?" Alvin replied, rolling up his quilt.

"Where's the snakes?"

"On the limb."

"Where on the limb?"

"Can't you see nothin', Otis?" snapped Wesley.

"You show me, Wesley. By granny, I must be blind."

Wesley walked to him and looked at the tree. His mouth opened slowly. He took two steps down the hill. "Dover," he said.

"Yeah, Wes?"

"They ain't there."

"What ain't?"

"The snakes."

The snakes were gone. Vanished. We ran and stumbled down the hill, toward the tree. Dover had a flashlight and beamed it on the limb.

"I'll be damned!" Dover exclaimed, looking up at the limb. "What happened?"

"Let me have the flashlight," Wesley said. "Here, Dover."

"What . . . ?"

"Here! Just shine it here."

Dover turned the beam toward the ground, toward the ritual fire. The three pyramids of ash had disappeared, completely. It was as though they had never existed.

"Goda'mighty!" R. J. whimpered.

"What happened?" I begged. "Wesley . . . ?"

"I don't know," Wesley admitted, his voice quivering.

"Boys, let's get—get out—of here," advised Dover.

"Damn right!" Alvin added. "Damn right! And fast!"

"Where's Paul?" asked Dover. "Paul?"

Paul did not answer.

"Paul!"

"Gu—Gu—Gu—Gu . . ." Paul stuttered. He was leaning against the trunk of the tree, his voice paralyzed.

"What's the matter?" Dover demanded. "What you sayin'?"

Paul's head bobbed with effort. "Gu—Gu—God—Goda'mighty!"

"C'mon!" commanded Dover, grabbing Paul. "Let's go!"

We did not speak again until we had emerged from the woods and into Harley Vandiver's pasture. There we stopped to roll and tie the bedding we had been dragging, and in the thinning darkness I could see that we were all sweating profusely.

"Didn't nobody see nothin'?" asked Dover, wiping his face with his sleeve. "Nothin' at all?"

We mumbled negative answers.

"I'm swearin' I can't believe it. I just can't," continued Dover. "We was lookin' at that tree every minute and didn't see nothin'. I tell you, boys, that's the work of that old woman. Mark me, that's it!"

"Maybe we just didn't see what happened," argued Wesley.

Dover cocked his head and looked at Wesley with an astonished expression. "Now, that's just what I been sayin', ain't it, Wesley? No, we ain't seen nothin'. Nothin' at all. You can't expect to see nothin' that witches do."

"That's not what I mean, Dover."

"Well? What're you sayin', Wesley?"

"I mean, maybe we just couldn't see. There's lots of sticks and vines and things like that down there, and we was a long way off. Maybe we looked so hard, we just got confused at what we was seeing."

Alvin disagreed. "Wesley, you mean you think them snakes never was there?"

"No," Wesley said. "They were there. They were

there when we got there, but that don't mean that a possum didn't crawl out on that limb and pull 'em off. A possum will eat anythin', I hear."

"What about them ashes? What about them?" R. J. demanded.

"They could've blown away in the wind," answered Wesley.

"Wesley," Dover said, speaking slowly, "you and me and everybody here knows that didn't no possum drag away them snakes. You and me and everybody here knows that the Snake Spell don't work unless them snakes is cut down and buried. Even when it's meant for good. Now, what you say, well, that ain't the answer. Maybe we won't never know what the answer is, but me and you and everybody here knows that ain't it."

"Yeah, I guess you're right," admitted Wesley. "But we still better not say anything."

Dover nodded. "I ain't arguin' that. There's bound to be some people wantin' to blame everythin' on that old woman. When it's light, we'll go on back down there and look around. Maybe we can find somethin'."

We did not have to return to Freeman's tree, or to Black Pool Swamp, to find Freeman.

As we drove into the yard of our home, we saw a crowd of men gathered around the barn. My mother's Ford was parked near the barn door and two men were inside the car, packing the back seat with quilts and pillows. The other men watched, quietly.

Lynn met Dover's truck and said in a loud, but

funeral whisper, "They found Freeman, Wesley! Found him down in the barn. He's passed out."

"When?" asked Dover, excited.

"This morning. Daddy found him when he went to feed the mules. Mama's been down there tryin' to put a gauze bandage on his leg. Louise said it was full of pus and infected and might have to be cut off!"

"Good Lord!" exclaimed Dover. "They better get him to a doctor."

"That's what they're fixin' up the car for," explained Lynn. Her voice trembled. "Louise said Freeman looked about dead, Wesley. She said he looked awful."

Dover parked his truck beneath a pecan tree and we sprinted for the barn. Halls Barton stopped us.

"Don't go in there, boys," Halls said sternly. "That barn's full of people now. They'll be bringin' him out in a minute."

We huddled and waited.

"How bad's he hurt, Halls?" asked Dover.

"Bad" was the answer, and the word fell like a sentence of death. "He must of lost all his blood, way it looks. Mrs. Wynn's tryin' to clean him up."

"Is Odell in there?"

"He's inside. He's pretty tore up," Halls Barton said.

We waited. Inside the barn, men moved about on the heavy flooring, and we could hear murmuring. Then the men began to spill out of the door, waving their arms, pushing away a crowd that had already stepped aside. Mother and Louise came out, with bandages and bottles of medicine and a wash basin in their hands. Mother was crying.

And then Odell Boyd came out, cradling Freeman in his arms like a baby.

Odell Boyd's eyes were red dots. Fear masked his face. His lips quivered and the left side of his face twitched. We rushed forward to see Freeman.

Freeman looked dead. His face was ashen. Ashen. Ashes. Freeman's face was coated with ashes.

"It was Freeman," whispered Dover, stunned. "It was Freeman who done it."

Wesley reached and touched Freeman's arm. He said, very quietly, "Freeman?"

Freeman opened his eyes. They were dry—filmed in a dry, dull membrane. He tried to smile, but the smile fell in an avalanche from his cheeks. He opened his mouth, closed it.

"The car's ready, Odell," someone said. "Let's get him to the doctor."

Odell Boyd surrendered Freeman to the waiting hands of men in my mother's Ford. They eased him gently to the quilts, holding his leg tenderly.

"Put a pillow under that leg," dictated Mother, and one of the men obeyed her.

"He's ready, Mrs. Wynn."

"Fine," replied Mother. "We'll take him to Royston. Somebody better go get Rachel, but don't tell her he's bad hurt. Just that he's been found."

"We'll do that, Mrs. Wynn," volunteered Dover. "C'mon, boys, let's get to the truck!"

My father called, "Don't get in the way, boys!"

"We won't," I promised.

We raced to Dover's truck. Garry was sitting at the

296

steering wheel, pretending to drive.

"C'mon, Garry, get out," ordered Wesley.

"I'm goin'!" Garry protested.

"No, you ain't! Now get out. Louise," called Wesley.

Louise promised Garry he could carry the towel used to clean Freeman's leg, and Garry left, appeased.

As we rode toward the Boyds' home, Dover began to pat out the road's rhythm by slapping his hand on the dashboard. "I don't know how he done it, but ol' Freeman plain made fools outa us, and that's all there is to it," he observed. "Yessir, Freeman may be half dead, but he ain't changed one iota."

Rachel Boyd was confused by Dover's news that Freeman had been found. Her mind locked in a mild trance and she asked for her husband.

"Odell's with Freeman," Dover gently told her. "You come with us, Rachel, and we'll be takin' you to the hospital."

"But Odell just left a little while ago," she protested. "He was goin' to be first for the search party."

"Yes'm," replied Dover. "Well, that's where he was when Mr. Wynn found Freeman. He was right there with him."

"Oh . . ." Rachel Boyd said, and then she said nothing else. She walked out of her house and slipped into Dover's truck. She did not hear our subdued hellos and she did not answer. She stared out of the truck window as Dover drove—stared at the landscape jerking away in the opposite direction.

At the hospital, Rachel Boyd embraced my mother

in the lobby, clinging, begging for Mother's com-
forting to pass to her. I was very moved by that
embrace. Two mothers. One had buried a son; the
other was suspended by uncertainty, and both understood yearnings that are contained only in the womb.
"He'll be fine," counseled Mother. "Come on. I'll wait
with you."

Mother led Rachel Boyd into the waiting room, with
its gathering of nervous, silent people. Odell Boyd was
sitting beside an ashstand, holding an unlighted cigarette. He stood and looked at his wife, but he did not
speak. He sat again and began to roll the cigarette in
his hand, staring past the cigarette, staring into the hospital floor, into nothingness. Rachel Boyd and Mother
sat opposite him, and Mother repeated, "I'll wait with
you, Rachel."

And they waited. In silence. Holding hands.

It was not the first time Freeman's parents had been
in the hospital, sitting, waiting, afraid to move.
Freeman had almost died when he was seven. He had
had a ruptured appendix and suffered unbearably until
Old Doctor (we called him that; his name was Dr. Tutt
Hill) cut him open and cleaned him out. Old Doctor
was indelicate in his report of the operation. He said,
"It was like drainin' a septic tank." That remark was
repeated over the years by every person in Emery, and
was considered extremely humorous.

Freeman had bragged excessively about his bravery
in facing death. He wore his scar like a medal and anytime his one-upmanship was challenged, he would rip

up his shirttail and point triumphantly to the evidence of his ordeal. "Death," he had advised us, "will put you to thinkin'. I know. I've faced it. Twice. I was about to die anyhow, and then Old Doctor took his knife to me. Shoot, it takes a man to face Old Doctor's knife." But Freeman's finest description of his operation was of the experience of gagging on ether. "I thought I was fallin' into the longest, darkest, never-endin' tunnel in the world," he said. "I kept tryin' to pull that thing off my nose, but I didn't have the strength to move. And I just kept fallin' and fallin' and fallin'. I thought I was fallin' into another world."

One thing happened that Freeman did not talk about. When he left the hospital, he carried with him a foot-tall chalk statue of a rabbit. The statue was a gift from the nurses, and he was deeply affected by their caring; he was seven years old and he had never received a baby's present. My mother said Freeman had cried in front of the nurses, and that he held his chalk rabbit until he arrived home. There, he placed his gift on the mantel of the living room fireplace and it was never moved.

The uncertainty ended in an hour. Old Doctor stepped into the waiting room and stood, kneading his lower back with both hands. His eyes narrowed into a scowl as he noticed us—Freeman's friends—clustered in one corner. Old Doctor delighted in scaring us. "I need me some blood from these boys," he growled. "Boys' blood ain't easy to find these days and I got me a mule that needs a transfusion."

We knew Freeman was all right.

Mother stood and smiled. "Take them all, Old Doctor—if you can save a good mule." Then she asked, "Freeman's not in danger, is he?"

"Danger, hell! Ain't nothin' wrong with that boy!" thundered Old Doctor. "Odell, you must be feeding him alligator meat. Toughest damn hide I ever tried to sew up. Goda'mighty! You could use him to wrap up baseballs!"

Rachel Boyd tried to stand, but couldn't. She began to sob quietly, and Old Doctor walked over to her and knelt.

"Rachel," he said softly, "you just don't worry. Freeman's fine. Another day and he'd have had gangrene, but he's fine. Lost some blood and I had to do some fancy sewing, but he'll be braggin' about that scar for years."

Rachel Boyd reached for Old Doctor's hand and squeezed it. She nodded her gratitude and tried to swallow her tears.

"C'mon, Rachel," Old Doctor ordered as he stood. "You need a good get-well, perk-up shot!" Then Old Doctor turned to us and crushed us with a stare so powerful it forced us to step back into the wall. "By God!" he roared. "Next time I start cuttin' on a boy, I'm goin' after the whole damn lot of you! I'm gonna cut off legs and arms and swap them around like I'm playin' checkers. I'm gonna get me a crosscut saw and a blind drunk to help pull, and I'm gonna do the damnest cuttin' any man has ever done!"

With that, Old Doctor whirled on his heel and

crashed through the waiting room door. "C'mon, Rachel," he ordered, and Rachel Boyd followed him.

We were frozen to the wall. I could hear the adults snickering. And I could smell the antiseptic scrub-soap Old Doctor had used after his delicate artistry on Freeman.

"Old Doctor—he's something, ain't he?" said Dover, laughing easily.

Odell Boyd lit his cigarette. "That's the truth," he agreed. "That man comes near bein' a saint."

"I knew Freeman would be all right if we could get him to Old Doctor," added Mother. "I just knew it. There's nothing to worry about now, Odell."

"Yes'm. I'm sure grateful."

"You and Rachel stay up here as long as you want," continued Mother, easing into command. "Dover can bring you home." She looked at Dover. "Dover?" He nodded. "Now, I'll go on with the boys and take care of getting the ladies over to make supper for you and Rachel, Odell."

"That's sure thoughtful," Odell Boyd said. "I expect Rachel'll be wore out; she ain't slept much."

Mother was now in full charge and everyone recognized her authority. "Well, don't worry about a thing. Not a thing. We'll take care of it."

The Women's Society of Christian Service of Emery Methodist Church had a unique charity called the Bread and Butter Committee. It was so named because members of that appointment moved with astonishing speed and humanity to provide food, cleaning, and general household conduct whenever someone in the community needed assistance.

As Chairwoman of Desserts for the Bread and Butter Committee, Mother hurriedly prepared four huge pans of peach cobbler, and she agreed to drive Wesley and me to Emery on her way to the Boyds.

"Can we go see Freeman tonight, Mama?" I asked.

"No! I can't be driving all over, day and night."

"What if Dover goes? Can we go with him?" I pleaded.

"Well, I'll have to think about that."

Mother said yes in marvelously playful ways.

As we neared Emery, we saw Alvin and Paul walking along the road.

"We'll get out and walk the rest of the way," Wesley said.

"Where y'all goin'?" I asked Alvin as Mother drove away.

"Down to Allgood's," replied Alvin sleepily. "We was up at Hixon's, but ain't nobody there. Halls Barton came by on his tractor and said everybody was down at Allgood's."

"Why's everybody there?" Wesley wanted to know.

"Aw, Old Man Hixon sort of run everybody off from his place," Alvin explained. "Said he was gettin' a shipment of stuff in and he couldn't have people millin' about. But that was just his excuse. He didn't want nobody talkin' to Dupree."

"Was Dupree there?" I asked.

"Yeah. Hidin' behind the nail bin, stackin' tenpenny nails," Paul said.

We walked lazily along the road, throwing gravel and talking. We were still bewildered about the snakes. We knew Freeman had cut them down and had rubbed the ashes over his face, but we could not determine when he did it.

"Had to be in the last watch," declared Alvin. "Didn't happen when me'n Colin was watchin'."

"Well, I guess that's right," Wesley concurred. "But I was lookin' all the time and I didn't see nothin'."

"Me, neither," Paul said.

"Maybe Freeman didn't have nothin' to do with it," I suggested. "Maybe he got some ashes from somewhere else."

"Naw."

"Naw."

"Naw."

"Well, maybe," I protested.

"Anyway, we ain't supposed to say nothin' about it until we can talk to Freeman," cautioned Wesley. "Everybody's got to remember that."

Paul was shocked that Wesley would question the integrity of his friends. "We vowed on the Big Gully Oath, Wesley!"

Wesley did not answer. He had seen a lot of heart-crossing and hoping-to-die ceremonies, but he knew our weakness for dramatic flair. All of us had committed treason, and none had died. Wesley and Alvin—because Alvin was older—understood the difference between the heat of promise and promise, itself.

Ferris Allgood was genuinely enjoying the company

303

of increased traffic at his store, but he was not actively promoting business. He was sitting in one of the two cane-bottom chairs on the front porch of his store, leaning against a windowsill and laughing happily at the tales of men who had waded around Black Pool Swamp in search of Freeman.

Ferris recognized us as we approached. "Hey, boys, c'mon! Pull up a handful of dirt and have a seat," he called. "Y'all want anythin', just go get it and leave the money on the counter. Got some near-freezin' Dr. Peppers."

Ferris Allgood did not care if everyone in Emery cheated him; he ran a store for companionship, not for profit.

For an hour we listened to absurd speculations on Freeman's escape, Freeman's woodmanship, Freeman's injury ("You reckon it *was* a bullet from the Sheriff's gun?"), Freeman's innocence and/or guilt, and Freeman's chances with the law.

"Well, I was there," declared Capes Pilgrim, "and I'm sayin' there ain't no judge in hell and half of Georgia gonna find that boy guilty—not if they can keep Freeman lookin' like he was when they took him outa that barn. Lordamercy! They'd be so much pity, you could shovel it with a seed scoop!"

"He was drained, and that's the truth," Billy Dean Millford added. "His face was gray as last night's ashes. Didn't have a drop of blood in it."

Alvin nudged Wesley and Wesley quickly interrupted.

"Mama said they had to give Freeman two pints of

blood," Wesley said, and the men turned their faces to him.

"That so?" mumbled Capes Pilgrim. "I ain't heard that. Anybody else hear anythin' about Freeman gettin' blood?"

"Yeah," said Ferris. "Yeah. Sure. They give him blood. Dover come by for a few minutes after he took Odell and Rachel home, and he said they give Freeman blood. But I thought he said two quarts, instead of two pints."

"Goda'mighty, Ferris! He'd be deader'n a stuck pig if they had to give him two quarts!" someone exclaimed, and an argument began concerning the amount of blood in the body and how many pints were in a quart.

Wesley had turned the conversation. He knew every man at Allgood's General Store had heard of the Snake Spell and Granny Woman Jordan. He did not want to give them time to think of Freeman's powdered face and begin the simple deduction that would lead them to the Snake Spell.

"Uh—what'd you think will happen to Freeman now, Mr. Allgood?" Alvin inquired.

"Hard to say, Alvin. Hard to say. I guess that's up to the Sheriff."

"Ben? You know more about them things than any of us. What'd you think?" Billy Dean Millford asked, speaking to Ben Alford.

"Yeah," someone added. "Ben, you ought to know."

Ben Alford lived on Little Emery Road. He had a vegetable farm and a new Buick Silver Streak he called Beowulf. Ben named all his cars and tractors. He had been to college and he said he'd learned the names from studying history and world literature. Ben Alford was an unusually smart man.

"Well," Ben began. "This is what I think: It's—it's hard to say."

"That's right," Ferris agreed. "That's what I say."

"But, on the other hand . . ."

"Go on, Ben," Ferris urged.

"On the other hand, it might mean somethin' if we could let the law know how we feel about this case— as a community, I mean."

"That's a good idea, Ben," Capes Pilgrim said. "But—but how'd we do that?"

"Take up a petition. That might do it," Ben replied.

The men became serious. "Explain that," one of them requested.

"It's simple. We write out a thing sayin' we believe there's been a mistake somewhere, and we're all of a mind that they just ought to drop the matter. Then we get as many people as we can to sign it, and we carry it to the Sheriff."

Ben Alford was declared a genius. He was also appointed to write the necessary plea and have several copies printed. The copies would be circulated by everyone at Allgood's General Store, including the ". . . young folk," as Capes Pilgrim ordained us.

That night we visited Freeman. Everyone except Alvin. Alvin, Dover speculated, was with Delores. "He's been a little tense," Dover said. "I told him to meet me at Hixon's if he wanted to come, and he didn't show up. I guess ol' Alvin's growin' up, all right."

The reunion with Freeman was joyful—converging, slapping, punching, speaking in an unintelligible tongue. It was the same joy as a home run, or a no-hitter, or two points at the buzzer, and there was a reason for it: it permitted us to later invent our own truth and remembrance of the occasion. If you are polite and patient and intent on hearing every syllable of what others are saying, there is nothing to invent; you are not only bound *to* reality, you are bound *by* it.

Freeman was wedged into a mound of pillows, lapping the cream of attention. He pulled himself into a sitting position, offering complaints of excruciating pain. "Uh, uh, damn!" he muttered. He wanted to contrast his deed with his physical disability, and he had a right. It was amazing that Freeman had rationed his strength and skill with such discipline.

We told Freeman of the petition Ben Alford was writing and Freeman was humbled by the news. "Tell Mr. Alford I'm grateful," he said. "That might help out. I ain't got no idea what's happenin'. Sheriff told Daddy he'd wait to make up his mind what to do. It ain't the money botherin' the Sheriff, it's my gettin' away from him."

"I can see that," admitted Dover. "He's got election comin' up and it'd look bad no matter what he does. He lets you go and people'll say he was took by a boy; he takes you in, and they'll say he was showin' off."

There were many questions about Freeman's days as

a fugitive—what he did, where he hid (Wesley told him of knowing about the cave; Freeman was shocked), how he had injured himself (his knife slipped, as Willie Lee had reported to Wesley and me), and, finally, R. J. asked, "How'd you get them snakes down outta that tree with us looking?"

"Yeah, how'd you do that, Freeman?" Otis urged.

"Well, all you got to do is think about it," explained Freeman. "I knew y'all was there when you come up, makin' all that racket, so I just crawled on off and went to sleep myself. I was pretty tired and weak by then, but I'd come across the Snake Spell earlier in the day and I knew it was a sign, so I thought I'd go back later, after dark, and cut down them snakes and coat myself with them ashes . . ."

"Wait a minute, Freeman," interrupted Dover. "You say you found that spell? You didn't make it?"

"Goda'mighty, Dover! You crazy! I ain't about to go doin' nothin' like that."

Dover closed his brown eye and slowly nodded his head. "I knew it. Told you, boys. Told you it was that old woman."

"Well, I don't know who it was," admitted Freeman, "and I don't give a care. It was there, on my tree, and I ain't about to question it."

"How'd you get them snakes down, Freeman?" pressed Otis.

"I sneaked down to the tree a little before y'all started standin' up, and from where I was I could see y'all better'n y'all could see me," Freeman continued. "I was low enough to get them ashes rubbed on me—

you know, I swear that works!—and then I just waited. Soon as I saw Dover stand up and stretch, I jumped up and yanked them snakes down. I didn't have to cut 'em; they just popped loose."

"That means you was still around there when we run down," suggested Paul.

"Still there!" Freeman laughed incredulously. "Lordamercy! I thought Colin was gonna step on me! I was just under a bush."

"Well, what happened then?" I asked.

"When y'all left, I buried them snakes and was goin' over toward the Big Gully to rest and try to figure out what to do, when I split open that cut and I thought I was gonna bleed to death. That's when I went and got in your daddy's barn. I figured I might see one of y'all and get bandaged up. I don't remember nothin' else."

It was, even in Freeman's telling, a sensible story. But he had deliberately omitted one fact, and Dover recognized it. "I don't understand one thing," Dover said. "When you was found, you had a bandage wrapped around your leg. Where'd you get that?"

Freeman dropped his eyes. And then he lied. "Well, I don't want nobody saying nothin' about this, but I broke into a colored house and picked up some stuff. Some of these days, I'll go back and leave some money."

And Dover believed Freeman's tale.

"Just one thing," Freeman said as we were leaving. "Don't nobody say nothin' about that Snake Spell. People'll think we're crazy."

We pledged our silence.

"Tell Alvin they whacked off my leg," Freeman kidded. "That'll make him sorry he didn't come to visit."

"He'll be around," Dover promised. "I reckon Alvin's busy."

"Yeah," Freeman said, grinning.

17

Ben Alford's petition read:

> To Whom It May Concern: We, the undersigned, in all good intention and being of sound judgment, do solicit, petition, and beg fair consideration of justice in the incident of Freeman Boyd, minor, vs. A. G. Hixon, in the matter of an alleged theft in the amount of $20.00 (twenty dollars) by said Freeman Boyd from the premises of Hixon's General Store. We entreat the following: (1) that said incident and alleged theft be dismissed on grounds of hearsay and circumstantial evidence, and, further, that it is a misunderstanding of such far-reaching consequences, that it has created community strife; and (2), that all parties, accused and injured, resolve all past and present differences in the gentlemanly manner of a handshake. This petition has been prepared by the hand of Ben Alford, A.B.

And Ben was the first to sign. In bold lettering. With many curls and waves.

There were ten copies of the petition. Five were distributed among adult volunteers and five were given to

Wesley to distribute among Freeman's friends.

Dover had returned to work with the REA right-of-way crew, but he permitted Alvin to borrow his truck and we spent a full day contacting all the farm families who lived south and west of Banner's Crossing.

The following morning, we invaded Emery.

"All right, we'll divide up," ordered Wesley. "We can walk these houses. Now, it may be that most people have already signed, and it may be that some people won't sign at all, but that don't matter. Don't push it. A lot of people are obligated to Mr. Hixon, and they won't want their names on anythin'."

I was assigned the houses along Little Emery Road, and across Highway 17. Megan's house was across Highway 17.

"You're bound to love that," kidded Alvin. "Maybe her mama ain't home and you can get in some time."

"Leave him alone, Alvin," warned Wesley.

"Naw, Wesley, I don't care," I said. "Alvin's forgot that Delores lives over there, too."

Alvin's face narrowed. "You little poot, you knock on her trailer and you'll be missin' a fistful of fingers! I'll talk Delores into signin'!"

"Just thought I'd save you the trouble," I crowed. "Yeah, Alvin, I'd be happy to help out, ol' buddy."

"Colin, you wouldn't know what to do with Delores if you got her," Alvin hissed.

And he was right.

The Little Emery Road was a quarter-mile, single-lane dirt road, running from Hixon's General Store along the Southern Railroad track to Prather's

Crossing on Prather's Road. Once Little Emery Road had gone beyond the crossing and had carried travelers on the Elberton-Royston route. Highway 17 changed that. Little Emery Road was amputated, and its only traffic was those people who lived on that quarter-mile stretch—Wade and Margret Simmons, the Holcombs, and Ben Alford.

Megan's home was on a hill across Highway 17 and the railroad track. I could see it clearly and I wondered if, by the rhythm of chance, Megan would see me on Little Emery Road, alone. Perhaps she was watching from the screened front porch. Perhaps. It could happen. If she was watching, if she did see me, she would walk outside. I slowed my pace. It would be tragic to be one step too fast, one step out of view. I stopped, picked up a rock, and threw it at the railroad track. The rock pinged on the steel rail. Megan did not appear. I thought of what Alvin had said. Megan would be surprised to discover me at her front door, delivering a petition. I wondered if her mother would be at home.

I missed Megan.

A dog barked in front of Ben Alford's yard, near Prather's Crossing, and I saw Sonny crossing Highway 17. I knew he had not seen me and I decided to hide behind a hedge of diseased boxwood planted along the road between the Simmons' and the Holcombs' houses. I did not know why I wanted to hide, but I did. I wondered why Megan had not seen me.

In a few minutes, Sonny appeared, walking a rail. He did not know I was watching and he was playing Hero by balancing on the rail and jabbing the air with an imaginary broadsword, like Sinbad the Sailor. His mouth was flapping in soundless hisses and dares, and he feigned a minor wound—a needle prick in the arm that he bravely suffered while killing a half-dozen fools with one sweep of his gleaming sword. Another half-dozen attackers rushed him from behind and Sonny raced along the rail in quick little Chinese steps, fighting for balance; if he fell into the moat below, he would be chewed to bits by a three-headed sea monster that had not been fed in a month. Sonny turned on the rail, swished once, twice, ducked a swipe, took a second wound in the left thigh, moaned, gasped for breath, swayed on the narrow bridge above the famished sea monster, almost fell, did fall (one foot quickly down, then up again; Sonny cheated at everything, even his games). He grabbed valiantly for an invisible bridge support, kicked one killer in the groin and, whipping his hunting knife out of his belt, flicked it straight through the heart of his last enemy. Bleeding from the arm and leg, breathing deeply, thanking God with slow, serious, soundless mouthing, Sonny Haynes stood victorious on the slender steel rail—two hundred feet in the air. He spat triumphantly and defiantly into the moat and the three-headed sea monster slithered away below the cinders and crossties.

I stepped into the road and yelled, "Hey, Sonny."

Sonny fell from the rail and tripped backward, bouncing on his tail.

"Hey, Sonny, you all right?"

Sonny's face was crimson. Sinbad the Sailor had

never fallen flat on his tail. He tried to avoid my eyes. "Yeah, yeah," he mumbled. "You give me a scare, that's all."

"Well, you give me a scare, too. Shoot, I was just walkin' up through the field there and I didn't see you."

Sonny stood and tenderly brushed away cinders from the seat of his pants. "Whatcha doin', anyhow?" he asked.

"Taking this petition around. You heard about this petition?"

Sonny noticed the paper in my hand and frowned. "Yeah," he said. "I heard about it."

"You signed one yet?"

"Naw. I ain't signing nothin' that'll let Freeman Boyd off from what he done," Sonny snorted.

"Lots of folks already signed," I said.

"Lots of folks is crazy, too."

"You really see him take that money, Sonny?"

"See him? Damn right, I saw him. Me'n Dupree was right there. We saw him, all right!"

I tried to measure Sonny as Wesley would have measured him. "Wesley said you'd have to go to court and swear on a Bible what you saw," I replied. "He said . . ."

Sonny was startled. "Court? I ain't goin' to no court!"

"What Wesley said."

"Where'd he hear a thing like that?" Sonny asked, paling.

"I ain't got no idea, Sonny. You know I don't know what Wesley's talkin' about half the time. Just what he said, that's all."

Sonny had respect for Wesley. He knew Wesley was smarter than any of us, and, if Wesley said something was true, it probably was.

"Dupree didn't say nothin' about that," mumbled Sonny, dropping his face. He kicked a cinder off a crosstie.

I had Sonny measured and I knew it. Wesley would have been proud.

"Well," I said innocently, "it won't make no difference, anyhow. You just say what the truth is, and that's all. Can't nobody do nothin' to you for telling the truth . . ." I paused, as Wesley would have paused, and then I said, "It's lyin' that gets to a judge, I hear."

"Lyin'! What'd you mean, lyin'!" snapped Sonny.

"I don't mean nothin'. I'm just talkin'."

Sonny was nervous. He rubbed a red spot on his elbow. "Yeah, well, I got to go."

"Sure you don't wantta sign this petition?" I asked.

"My—my daddy's already signed one, I think. Mr. Alford come by. I reckon that'll do for the whole family."

"Your daddy signed?"

"Maybe he did, but that don't mean he thinks I'm lyin' about what I saw!"

"Yeah. Well, see you, Sonny," I said.

"Yeah, see you."

Sonny continued in a brisk pace toward Hixon's General Store. I knew he would tell Dupree everything I had said.

Wade and Margret Simmons were not at home, and the

Holcombs had already signed Ben Alford's copy of the petition. I crossed Highway 17 and walked cautiously toward Megan's home. It would not be easy to appear casual, and I knew it. I began to whistle quietly. I kicked at clods of dirt. I pretended I was lost in a dream, and could easily walk past Megan's home without recognizing it. If it worked, Megan would run out of the front door and say, "Colin, what're you doin' over here?"

I approached the house, my head down, reading aloud the words of Ben Alford's petition. Megan did not appear. I stopped and pulled a maypop from a vine growing in the gully. I smashed the maypop hard with my heel. It was rotten inside. I wiped the rot off my heel by scraping my foot across a clump of Johnson grass. I was almost in front of the house and Megan had not appeared. I thought, "Damn!"

I walked quickly to the screen door of the screened-in front porch and knocked. I heard footsteps inside the house. Small footsteps.

"Yes? Who is it?" a voice called.

"Uh—Colin Wynn," I answered weakly.

"Who?"

"Colin Wynn," I repeated.

"Just a minute."

I knew it was Megan's mother.

The front door opened and Megan's mother moved lightly across the porch and opened the screen door.

"Colin!" she said happily. "Come in."

"Yes'm," I replied.

"What can I do for you?" Megan's mother asked as

she motioned me to the swing hanging from a rafter. She sat opposite me in a rocker.

"Uh—I—I'm helpin' pass around this piece of—this petition," I stammered. "It's something Mr. Alford wrote up for Freeman Boyd."

"Oh, yes, Megan told me about that. May I see it?" I handed her the petition.

"By the way, you just missed Megan. She went to play with Marie Arey. She'll be disappointed."

"Yes'm."

I sat in the swing as Megan's mother read the petition. I could not dismiss Megan's face from my mind. This was her house. She lived here. Her presence was everywhere, an ethereal reminder of every secret thought I had ever had. I tried to swing and the chain squealed in pain: Aghhhhhhhhhhhhhhhhhhhh! Megan's mother looked up from her reading and smiled. I stopped swinging and folded my hands across my lap.

Megan resembled her mother. Except for her hair. Megan had blond hair; Megan's mother had dark hair. Hodges, my brother, had once said you had to look at a girl's mother to know what the girl would look like when she got older. He had also said that parents of girls never liked the boys their daughters liked.

I wanted to leave.

"Uh—maybe you don't want to sign it," I said hastily.

"Oh, no. I think it's a good idea," Megan's mother replied warmly. "Shows community spirit. Do you have a pencil?"

"Yes'm." I gave her a pencil and she signed in the same sweeping cursive motion Megan used when she wrote.

"Thank you," I said.

"That's all right," she replied. "I'm sure sorry Megan was away. She's fond of you."

I could feel my face tightening with redness. "Uh—yes'm."

"You come again, and play."

"Uh—yes'm."

As I walked away, I made a vow, a cross-my-heart vow: I would never again get within a mile of Megan's home. Nothing was worth such agony.

Ben Alford's petition had impact. Sheriff Dwight Brownlee received it in the presence of Happy Colquitt, photographer and editor of *The Eden County Garden.*

Happy Colquitt published a front-page picture of Sheriff Brownlee holding ten copies of the petition, and beneath the picture was an editorial which became a mild endorsement of the Sheriff's re-election chances. One of the paragraphs in the editorial read:

It is this writer's opinion that Sheriff Dwight Brownlee acted wisely in accepting the petition by Ben Alford of the Emery Community, regarding an alleged incident between a minor and A. G. Hixon's General Store. The incident, of course, is subject to legal settlement in due process of law, but it is encouraging to note that a community has the gumption to stand up for one of its own, and that the county sheriff is sympathetic to such unity.

The editorial further noted that Sheriff Brownlee had conferred with Judge Foster Harris and that Judge Harris was pondering the ". . . weight of the documents." My father explained the expression had nothing to do with pounds, but was a poetic legal term suggesting ". . . the scales of justice."

Judge Harris pondered for a week. One of the men who worked with Dover on the REA right-of-way crew, and boarded at a house in Edenville, said he had heard a rumor from Hilda Benson, who was a librarian, that Judge Harris had pondered himself into a state of frustration. If he allowed the petition to have influence in any legal action, Judge Harris would be petitioned out of business; if he ignored the petition, he would catch hell seven ways to Sunday.

The man on the REA right-of-way crew told us that he had told Hilda to tell Judge Harris about Freeman's bravery in Black Pool Swamp. "That ought to make some difference," the man said solemnly. "I hear tell that anybody in that swamp is in danger of losin' his life. I hear tell the real name of that swamp is the Great Okeenoonoo, and it means Woods of Death, or somethin' like that."

Later, Dover explained the man's ignorance. "He ain't from around here, and when Freeman first found that out, he took to puttin' the poor fellow on, especially after he told Freeman he was scared of snakes."

While Judge Harris reviewed his predicament, the

citizens of Emery waited and wondered—wondered aloud and in marathon sessions at Allgood's General Store, which had become the Gathering Place.

There was a story from Edenville that Sheriff Brownlee had decided to forget Freeman's escape as an act motivated by fear, and something to be expected of a fourteen-year-old. Freeman said of the decision, "Damn right, it was fear. That fool was about to lock me up and melt the key."

There was also a report that Judge Harris had inquired, on the sly, if A. G. Hixon would simply drop his charges against Freeman. A. G. Hixon refused; he had too much prestige invested in the incident, and though there was speculation that he, too, doubted Dupree's accusation, he was trapped by his commitment.

None of us were certain what actually happened, but early one morning, after he had been released from the hospital, Freeman announced at Allgood's that his father had accepted the services of Jackson Whitmire, attorney at law.

"Jackson Whitmire's takin' my case for a dollar, or something like that," Freeman said, "and I'll guarantee you he ain't worth much more'n that, but watchin' that man at work is pure pleasure, I hear tell. He already told Daddy that if they call in a jury, he'll wave to them, or somethin', and that means whoever's on the jury'll leave and put it up to Judge Harris about what's to be done with me."

Freeman's confusion was understandable. According to my mother, Jackson Whitmire's estimation of the law was, at best, muddled. He had a won-lost record considerably lower than the Atlanta Crackers', who were in fifth place of the Southern, but he did enjoy an unusual reputation as a courtroom performer. Most of Jackson Whitmire's cases ended with hysterical pleading, many tears, and a summation that seldom had anything to do with the case before the court. There was one trial, my mother said, when Jackson Whitmire had been so theatrical the jury actually applauded him, and then ruled against his client.

The Freeman Boyd case would give Jackson Whitmire an opportunity to be a central figure in a celebrated event. Besides, he was confident Freeman would be carried triumphantly from the courtroom on the shoulders of Judge Harris. "I'll get him off," he bragged at Allgood's one afternoon, after interviewing a number of Freeman's friends and supporters. "There ain't gonna be nothin' to it. I'll get him off free as the day he was born."

"Why, that'd make him naked as a jaybird," observed Ferris Allgood.

"Now, that'd be a sight to behold, wouldn't it?" Jackson Whitmire responded. "Freeman, naked as a jaybird, ridin' the shoulders of a judge."

And everyone laughed heartily.

We were encouraged by the boasting, but there was still the nagging uncertainty of Dupree's contention that it was a Hixon against a Boyd. We were not fools; names mattered, and we knew it. Still, it was a new time. It was 1947. The REA was coming, and as the right-of-way crew hacked through the swamp we could hear the warning sound of change—the falling of trees, the singing of crosscut saws, the cadence of sling blades, the echo of the ax. The differences between Our Side and the Highway 17 Gang were diminishing in the evidence of the REA, and we began to realize Wesley had been accurate in his confrontation with Dupree: the only true difference was attitude—what we thought and what they thought. That was all. Yet, names mattered, and we knew it.

"You just can't trust people," admitted Freeman. "Shoot, there ain't no way they can prove I took no money, but you can't never tell. Old Man Hixon's got some pull in this county and that's for sure."

"What's Mr. Whitmire got in mind, Freeman?" asked Wesley.

"I ain't got the first notion," answered Freeman. "He said he had him a plan worked out. Won't say what it is, but he swears it'll never see the light of day in a courtroom. Said he'd been haggling with the Judge. I don't know what it is, but he's cocky as a bantam rooster in a yardful of hen turkeys."

Two days later, we were summoned to the Eden County Courthouse.

"I don't know why they want all you boys," fussed Mother, as she drove us to Edenville. "It just don't seem right."

"Who all's goin' to be there, Mama?" Wesley wanted to know.

"Well, just about everybody you can think of," replied Mother. "You and Colin, and R. J., and Otis, and—Paul, and Dupree, and that little Haynes boy . . ."

"Sonny?" I asked.

"Sonny—yes, that's his name. I don't know why I can't remember that boy's name," Mother said. "I can remember his oldest brother, Whitney, but I can't remember him. Whitney's married to the Desmond girl, who's Gladys Presley's first cousin."

"Yes'm," Wesley said. "Who else, Mama?"

"Who else?"

"Yes'm. Who else'll be at the courthouse?"

"Oh, I don't know. Lots of people. All the parents."

The courthouse was an aged, two-story building of granite blocks with the word JVSTICE chiseled over the main door. (I could never understand why the U in justice was a V.) The building was in the center of Edenville and people referred to the area as Courthouse Square.

Sheriff Brownlee met us at the front door. He wore a starched and pressed new uniform, and his badge gleamed from hard polishing.

"Is everybody here?" Mother asked sharply.

"Yes'm," Sheriff Brownlee answered courteously. "You're the last ones."

"What's this about, Dwight?" demanded Mother.

"Now, Mrs. Wynn, it ain't much. Just a little interview. Judge is tryin' to find out what's happened, so's this thing can be settled."

"Well, I don't know why he wants these boys," snapped Mother. "It's plain that Freeman didn't do anything wrong."

"He just wants to talk, Mrs. Wynn. That's all."

We were led to Judge Harris' office. It was a huge, oppressive room with a high ceiling. In the center of the ceiling, a four-blade fan whirled slowly. The odor of the room was musty, like old clothes.

No one spoke as we entered. Parents were seated along one wall, and their sons were seated together in two rows of chairs placed in front of Judge Harris' desk.

"Boys, y'all can take a seat over there," Sheriff Brownlee whispered. "Mrs. Wynn, if you'd sit over there . . ." He indicated an empty chair and Mother sat beside Angus Waller, R. J.'s father. My father was the only father not present; he had refused to attend, realizing his dissatisfaction with the county law enforcement would make this an upsetting experience.

Dupree and Sonny sat together on the front row, with Freeman and Otis and Paul. Jack and R. J. and Alvin were on the second row, where Wesley and I sat. We exchanged nods, but no one spoke.

We waited for Judge Harris, subdued, anxious. The room was silent, awesomely silent. Dupree popped his knuckles and tried to appear calm, though his hand trembled. Sonny sat back in his chair, his shoulders slumped forward. His face was as white as milk glass. Sonny was frightened. Freeman was amused. He leaned forward in his chair and rolled his pocket knife from hand to hand. A smile was pressed on his face. Alvin and R. J. and Otis and Jack sat perfectly still, uncomfortable, each wondering why he was there and each seriously doubting the advisability of having Freeman as a friend.

A side door opened suddenly and Judge Harris entered his office and walked briskly to a raised swivel chair behind his desk. He was a short man with a head that extended abnormally forward from his neck, giving him an appearance of someone who had spent too many hours leaning over a desk deliberating the fate of others. His face had two terraces of flesh running off the corners of his nose and into his jowls. His eyes were close-set and steady and I knew instantly that he could freeze water with a stare.

Judge Harris did not say Hello, thank you for coming, or It's a nice day. He sat, surveyed the room, and began. "I've been in a meetin' all morning with Jackson Whitmire, who's representin' Freeman Boyd in this matter, and Rayford Callagan, who's representin' A. G. Hixon, and I'm telling you all that it seems to me there's a lot of smoke for such a little fire. Now, I aim to ask some questions and see if we can clear the air a little."

Judge Harris paused, shuffled through some papers on his desk, and continued. "There ain't the first thing about this session today that's one-hundred percent legal, but it seems to me the spirit of the law might best be served by bringing you people together and sayin' straight out what everybody thinks. Things get settled that way that don't do nothin' but bog down when everythin's all legal.

"Now, who's Freeman Boyd?" he asked.

Freeman raised his hand. "Me, Your Honor, sir," he said. Jackson Whitmire had coached Freeman well.

"Who's Dupree Hixon?" Judge Harris asked.

Dupree half stood. "Me—uh—sir."

"That's good enough. Now, the rest of you stand as I call your name."

As our names were sounded, we stood, silently, then sat again. Judge Harris studied us with his never-blinking gaze. He asked our parents to stand and introduce themselves, though he knew each by first name. Judge Harris was remarkably official.

"From what I've been able to piece together," the Judge said, swiveling in his chair, "there's two things here: an alleged theft of twenty dollars, and some old-fashioned disagreements. Whitmire tells me he's got information about a threat Dupree Hixon made against Freeman Boyd, and then along comes Dupree Hixon later on and accuses Freeman Boyd of stealing twenty dollars from his daddy's store. Now, A. G.—" he turned to A. G. Hixon "—I know it ain't the twenty dollars that makes the difference to you; it's the principle of the matter, and I can appreciate that. But if all this comes down to a case of spite and revenge, then you know as well as I do, A. G., that it's a matter for the people involved to settle and has no business whatsoever in a courtroom." Judge Harris studied A. G. Hixon. "Is that right, A. G.?"

"Yessir, that's right," A. G. Hixon replied meekly.

"All right, now let's get to some questions," rumbled Judge Harris. "I want everybody to know why there's no lawyers in this room. This ain't court. It ain't a trial. And I'm not about to have somebody objectin' every minute, and over nothin'. Now . . ." He read something from the paper in front of him. "Now, it seems there's more to this than stealin' money, like I said. Seems like there's been bad feelings going on over there in Emery for some time now, and that's what I want to know about." He paused and looked at Freeman.

"From what I've been able to find out," the Judge continued, "there was a big fight over at the school, and it got out of hand. Says on this piece of paper that Jackson Whitmire gave me, that a little while after that fight, Dupree Hixon made his threat against Freeman Boyd, after Freeman Boyd accused Dupree of questionable behavior. Now, who's goin' to tell me about that?"

No one answered. No one even moved.

"Well, there's no need to be afraid. I ain't sendin' nobody to jail. Anybody can speak up and say whatever he wants to. Dupree Hixon, why don't you tell me about that?"

Dupree struggled to his feet. He looked at his father. A. G. Hixon was nervous.

"Go ahead, son, and just tell it in your own words," urged Judge Harris.

"Well, sir," Dupree began, "I—I never threatened nobody. No sir, I wouldn't do that. That ain't right."

Judge Harris flipped a page of the paper before him. "You didn't say something like, 'I swear to God and Jesus I'll get you, if it's the last thing I ever do!' You didn't say that to Freeman Boyd?"

"Uh—no, sir. I—I can't remember sayin' nothin' like that. I may've got mad. Freeman Boyd's always pickin' on people, makin' people mad."

"Did Freeman Boyd accuse you of doin' something

and you didn't like it?" asked Judge Harris sharply.

Dupree cut his eyes to Freeman. Freeman glared at him.

"He—he's always doin' things like that, sir," answered Dupree. "He's always tryin' to make people mad."

Judge Harris nodded and turned in his chair. "But he didn't say nothin' that would make you wanta pay him back?"

"Uh—no, sir."

"All right, son. Sit down. Freeman Boyd, you tell me about all of this."

Freeman stood, dramatically pulling himself up on the crutch he used, but no longer needed. Jackson Whitmire had not missed a trick.

"You don't have to stand," advised the Judge.

"Yessir," replied Freeman, sitting.

"Now, just tell it in your words."

"Well, sir, Your Honor, sir, it was this way, sir . . ."

"You don't have to say sir all the time."

"Yessir. Well, anyway, Dupree and Sonny and Wayne—Wayne ain't here, sir—and some of them got to kiddin' Colin one day—Colin's the littlest one on Our Side, sir, and he's right here—and they kidded him somethin' bad, and Colin wanted to fight them, but he's too little, so some of us, me and Otis and Paul and R. J. and Alvin—they're sittin' here, sir—well, we just took up for Colin, and . . ."

"I can appreciate wanting to help out a friend," said Judge Harris, "but it don't seem to me that any of this has anythin' to do with the question. Did you, or did you not, accuse Dupree Hixon of somethin', and did Dupree Hixon make a threat against you?" The Judge was irritated.

"Yessir. He sure did. That's what I was gettin' to," replied Freeman.

"Well, get to it. You been around Jackson Whitmire too much, boy."

"Yessir. Well, anyhow, when we started in to helpin' Colin, they got nasty and started callin' him names and things, and I just said something about Dupree down on his granddaddy's farm—I just made it up, sir—and, well, sir, that made Dupree awful mad and he swore he'd see I lived to regret it, and I guess that's what the problem's all about, sir, if you ask me."

Freeman's explanation had bewildered everyone, including Judge Harris. Dover would have loved it, but Dover was working with the REA.

"Well, that's clear as mud, young man," grumbled the Judge. "What'd you think about bein' threatened?"

It was a sensible question, but Freeman regarded it as foolishly unnecessary. He smiled and looked around the room. I knew he was about to laugh aloud.

"Well!" thundered Judge Harris. "What's so funny about that?"

Freeman turned angrily toward the Judge. He met the narrow-eyed gaze and challenged it. There was a long silence as the two combatants struggled.

"Well!" repeated Judge Harris.

"Sir," Freeman said simply, "I been threatened lots of times. What's one more?"

It was an honest answer. Completely honest.

Freeman had never been so honest. And Judge Harris knew it.

"All right, young man," the Judge said quietly.

"Yessir."

No one in the room moved. Rachel Boyd coughed painfully. Freeman looked at his mother, then turned back and began to cross and uncross his fingers. Judge Harris leaned forward. He picked up a pencil and began to drum the eraser on the table. Finally, he said, "Who else was there?"

Otis and Paul and Alvin and R. J. and Jack and Sonny raised their hands. Wesley nudged me. "You was there," he whispered. I raised my hand.

Judge Harris looked at each of us. His eyes stopped on me. "You Colin Wynn?" he asked.

I tried to speak, but nothing happened.

"Tell him yes," whispered Wesley.

"Ye—yessir," I answered softly.

"Is that what happened, what Freeman Boyd said?" asked the Judge.

"Uh—uh—uh . . ."

Wesley nudged me again.

"Ye—yessir."

Judge Harris looked at Otis. "Is that what happened?"

Otis nodded. A girlish "Yessir" squeaked out from his dry throat.

Alvin and Paul and R. J. and Jack all confirmed Dupree's threat, and Judge Harris turned his deadly stare to Sonny. "Is that what happened?" he asked again.

Sonny was paralyzed. He was deaf and dumb. His head was cocked to one side and he could not move it. The Judge repeated his question. Sonny looked pleadingly to Dupree, then back to Wesley. He was remembering what I had said that day on the railroad track.

"Well?" Judge Harris asked curtly.

"Ye—ye—yes—yessir," stammered Sonny.

Judge Harris glared at Dupree. His face inched forward, unlocking from his neck. "That's enough of that," he said evenly. "Now, did you see Freeman Boyd take twenty dollars from your daddy's store and put it in his shirt pocket, young man?"

Dupree nodded hesitantly.

"You did, for sure?"

Dupree nodded again.

"Why would he go and leave somethin' he'd stolen in a shirt pocket?" pried Judge Harris. "That don't make much sense, if you ask me."

Dupree was barely audible. "I—I don't—don't know, sir."

Judge Harris shifted his gaze to Sonny. "Did you see him take that twenty dollars, young man?"

Sonny's eyes were watering. He tried to look away, to avoid the question.

"I'm waiting," said Judge Harris in a surprisingly gentle voice. "Just tell me the truth, son, that's what we're after. The truth, and that's all. Did you see him?"

There was a long, terrible pause, an eternity of quietness. The fan above our heads made a low fluttering sound as it churned the air.

Sonny's head was down. It was a posture of defeat.

"No, sir," Sonny answered in a hushed, breaking voice. "No—no, sir. Du—Dupree said—said he—he did. I was—was up in the front of—of the store."

"That's all we need, son," the Judge said quietly. "If that's the truth, that's all we need."

A. G. Hixon stood abruptly. "Foster," he said to Judge Harris, "let me ask my boy."

Judge Harris nodded. "Go ahead, A. G." He leaned back in his chair and laced his fingers.

A. G. Hixon walked to Dupree and put his hand on Dupree's shoulder. "Son, I ain't mad. I just want the truth, and I want it now. Right now. You tell me the truth and everythin' will be all right. Now, these people are our neighbors and our friends. They won't hold nothin' against you. These boys won't hold nothin' against you. You tell me, and I'll believe what you say. But, son, if you ever do anythin' right, do it now. Tell me the truth."

Dupree could not look at his father. He crossed his arms, uncrossed them. He buried his face in his hands and began to sob.

"You made it all up, didn't you, son?" asked A. G. Hixon in a sad voice.

Dupree nodded his head slowly and cried openly.

"It's all right, son. It's all right," his father said, stroking Dupree's neck. "It's over and that's what matters."

"Dupree made me say it, Mr. Hixon," whimpered Sonny. "He made me." Sonny searched the audience for his father.

"I know, Sonny. I know," counseled A. G. Hixon.

"You were just trying to help out a friend."

"Are you satisfied about what happened, A. G.?" asked Judge Harris.

"I'm satisfied, Foster. I'll take care of it, and I'm sorry about this. Sorry about all of it. I apologize to Freeman and everybody here. This whole thing just got out of hand. The boy's sorry, too, and I know it."

"Well, I'm dismissing this meetin' and I hope it's been a good lesson for everybody here," the Judge announced. "It just goes to show you what can happen when good people let little things get in the way. And I hope you boys understand that there's more'n enough arguin' going on—people fighting and killing. If you ever have to fight—and you will soon enough—make sure it ain't among yourselves. Never any call to fight your own kind. Now, all you boys get up and shake hands."

It was an imperial order, and we obeyed. We shook hands with everyone, even Sonny and Dupree.

Otis whispered, "You mean Sonny's my own kind?"

"Shuttup, Otis," commanded Alvin.

And it was over. The matter of Freeman Boyd, alleged thief, was over.

That night my father said, "Boys, remember what happened today. Remember it."

18

No one ever knew all the facts of the Freeman Boyd case.

But no one cared to know.

It was best to leave some things unanswered. If there was an excuse for speculation, even the tiniest excuse, the story would last, and lasting, to the people of Emery, was more important than the fact that it had even happened.

Freeman and Wesley and I made an oath (no, an agreement) never to tell of Willie Lee and Baptist and what they had done. We could not betray them, even to praise them. Willie Lee and Baptist were our friends. We would not be half brave with them.

There were several versions of Dupree's behavior on his grandfather's farm, though Dupree continued to protest his innocence. The story I enjoyed, the one I believed, had Dupree luring a girl named April, one of his cousins, into his grandfather's barn one night. The girl followed Dupree, pretending interest. In the barn, she stripped Dupree of his pants and threw them into a mule stable with a wild mule, and then she left Dupree in the hay. Dupree was covered with mites before he mustered the courage to slip, half-nude, into his grand-father's house.

And there was the argument, appropriately con-ducted at night, about the Snake Spell and who had effected it in Freeman's behalf. None of us told anyone of what we had seen, and what had happened; we knew no one would believe us, and we would be accused of inventing fantasies. Oddly, though, we never learned the truth of the Snake Spell. Freeman reluctantly continued to deny performing the ritual. Dover was certain it was Granny Woman, in collusion with the spirit world. Otis thought it was a visiting witch. Alvin believed it was Wesley, because Wesley had insisted we search Freeman's tree. I believed it was Little Annie. Little Annie had liquid brown eyes and I could not forget an afternoon when Willie Lee told Wesley and me—in a casual way—that Little Annie had the gift of going into the woods and feeding wild animals from her hands.

But even if we had confessed everything, it would have been accepted only as the blithering of young boys with absurd notions, for in the days following Dupree's tearful admission of guilt, two truths developed concerning Freeman Boyd—the True Truth and the Truth of Distortion.

People preferred the Truth of Distortion.

The Truth of Distortion had a peculiar influence on adults, and was woefully naïve. In its telling: A Thing happened to a Boy and that Boy, being boyish, ran away, got into trouble, and required the unified effort of able men doing an able duty. The Truth of Distortion failed to recognize the threat of The Doom, the intervention of the spirits, the genius of Freeman's dominance in Black Pool Swamp, or any of the other realities that were clearly evident, except to adults.

There was Dover, of course, and Dover was an adult, but Dover had had the good sense to resist adulthood. He was not ridiculous, as people said; he simply was not willing to accept becoming a man under terms of surrender. Dover did not separate Yesterday, Today, and Tomorrow. He was all of Yesterday, all of Today, all of Tomorrow, bits and pieces of all he had been, all he was, all he would ever be. Dover knew the True Truth of Freeman (except for the part about Willie Lee and Baptist), but he refused to compromise his childhood-manhood freedom by arguing the point. Let the players of the Truth of Distortion strut their worth. It puffed them up to take the credit, and, for a time, relieved the oppression of their surrender. Dover knew we didn't care. He knew we looked upon it as humorous raving. One afternoon, he even said it: "They's got more heroes in Emery than they had at the Alamo. Shoot, boys, we ain't got time to think about it. They's too much goin' on, goin' on everywhere you look."

And he was right.

On Saturday night, Emery Methodist Church had its annual hayride and hot dog roast at Wind's Mill. Megan was there. She nudged her hot dog near me on her clothes-hanger spit and managed to touch me several times—accidentally, of course—as the heat of the fire forced her to silly wiggling. And when our Sunday school teacher decided to teach us the Virginia Reel, or one of those awkward, stumbling dances, Megan managed to be my partner. The giggling was sickening.

A baseball scout from the Atlanta Crackers appeared at Harrison baseball field on Sunday to check the feats of Alvin. William Pruitte had mailed weekly reports to the Crackers, with aggravating little notes, such as "Any team in fifth place in the Southern needs help." The scout could not believe what he saw. He wanted to sign Alvin on the spot, but Alvin did not tarry after the game to discuss the offer: he had pitched a no-hitter.

There was the gleeful night when an old dream was partly realized, a night of ambush against a group of older boys from Royston, who had begun raiding my father's apple orchard under the mask of darkness. They rode in an open jeep, lights off, and talked about the ". . . dumb country hicks . . ." who were too stupid to know what was happening. They had no idea we were hiding all those nights, watching and listening.

And they had no idea we were waiting, on that night of ambush, with stout flips and pockets filled with green chinaberries. We caught them totally unawares in a crossfire. They yelped and screamed and drove into a ditch. But they never returned to raid our orchard and we secretly regretted it. We had devoted hours to strategy and we became expert in hit and run, hit and run, like boy guerrillas defending our honor and, yes, our boundaries. We were very sure boundaries, even invisible boundaries, were meant to keep us in, and we were just as sure those same boundaries were meant to keep outsiders out.

There was too much happening, happening everywhere we looked.

And nothing was as magnificent as the REA. The REA was coming. Let the players of the Truth of Distortion strut their worth. Let them be puffed up by their illusions of heroics. The REA was coming. Any fool knew the REA was more important than anything that had ever—ever—happened.

19

They had been there with their tripods and telescopes and their pantomime of "Left!" or "Right!" or "There!" and they had amazed us with the stubborn accuracy of their line, straight as a ruler's edge. Straight from there to there. Another angle. There to there. Straight. Electricity must run in straight lines, I thought at the time. And then the right-of-way crew, swinging their axes and sling blades, pulling their crosscuts, following those straight lines, there to there, there to there, working in inches. The men of the right-of-way crew had become faces and voices we knew and we had followed them as boys followed famous baseball players in large cities. They had tolerated us, answered our questions, fooled us into helping them drag limbs and brush. We served them with peaches and watermelons—watermelons with warm, dripping hearts popped. But they had sliced through the woods leading from Emery, and they had crossed Black Pool Swamp and Beaverjam Creek during the time we spent searching for Freeman, and now they were gone, met by another right-of-way crew cutting from the opposite direction, like some east-and-west railroad track fusing together in a dot on a map.

Now other men arrived, men with huge post hole diggers, men with muscles, men uttering "Uhhhhhhh-hhhh!" with each thrust into the ground. They were brooding, introverted men, as though the physical torment of digging was an assignment of madness. They were like convicts who worked the road gangs. Always another road, another hole to dig, and the sense of Never Ending closed over them like a coffin. They did not talk with us, and we shriveled under the hardness of their stern faces.

One morning a tractor trailer, pulling a flatbed loaded with long creosoted black pine poles, appeared above our house, near the old Civil War cemetery, and we knew the REA was not a fake. Men may play cruel games by surveying and cutting and digging holes, but men would not waste long creosoted black pine poles on a hoax.

And, so, we watched the REA arrive. Poles being hoisted and packed and guy-wired. Great rolls of shining wire, like spun thread, pulled and stretched and attached by strong-faced linemen, perched godlike on limbless creosoted black pine poles. In each of the linemen, I saw Thomas, remembered Thomas, believed Thomas could be touched. I wanted him to speak to me, to speak from the top of his godlike perch, but there was never any sound when the man on the creosoted black pine pole became Thomas. There was only his face and smile and eyes with This Morning's Sun burning blue.

The REA arrived in my father's labor. Days of pipe-cutting, with steel shavings from the pipe cutter falling into silver curls on the floor of the barn. And the afternoon of uncrating bathroom fixtures—slick, white enamel instruments of Belonging, with small brown envelopes of guarantees, brightly printed and scripted like a diploma, promising promises of luxury and durability.

The REA arrived with a heavy-set electrician, binding our house with his crisscross of wires, boring holes in our walls, popping the metal slugs out of receptacles (I collected those slugs and gave them to Garry and told him they were nickels), dropping light cords from the exact center of rooms, and, finally, in an act that was both theatrical and remarkably honest, he fitted each light switch and receptacle with a metal covering, and then he left. We could not avoid staring at those metal coverings; behind them a million-trillion Zs would pile up, spinning wildly, their sharp edges buzzing like a finishing saw.

The REA arrived in the wind, whistling and dancing through the shining, pull-and-stretched-and-attached wires. We would sit in late evenings in the pine tree windbreak that pinched off at one end of skinny oaks in the new ground, and listen to the wind get its roaring charge at the hill. The wires had been tied off in that section as though someone had tuned them for a violin. If you closed your eyes and listened, you could hear the wind playing its solo concert against the wires, a concert of funeral and eerie and distant moods.

School began, the session after cotton blooms had curled into brown cocoons and were being nudged off their pedestals by tiny bolls bulging with the white fabric. We always had that school session, that awkward Between Session of waiting for the full opening of the boll. During the wait, we attended school. When the bolls opened, school closed, and we began the slow, boll-by-boll, stalk-by-stalk, row-by-row picking of the cotton, backs bending, drawn to one side by a guano sack strapped to our shoulders. To boys who could hear the voices of creeks and understood the impatient temper of the sun calling them to play, the Between School Session was a cruel apprenticeship to the Preparation for Life. There was no real holiday: we worked in school while waiting for the cotton, and then we worked the cotton while school waited for us.

But this session, Indian summer of 1947, was different. Alvin and Lynn and a few others had graduated from the ninth grade and were attending Royston High School. We missed them, especially Alvin, but we had all moved up—"progressed up" according to the progress reports we had received in spring—and we were learning the size and contents of new books (old books with new hands opening them). There was a new teacher, pretty, young, a girl out of college who had an astonishing chest. ("She's got patriotic and Jello tits," declared Otis, his eyes agog. "They snap to attention when she's standin' and they jiggle when she walks.") She also made the mistake of sitting too often on the edge of her desk and allowing her dress to ride up above her knees. Otis and Paul immediately became attentive students after years of lackluster scholastic pursuit. And there were two new basketball goals, with new backboards, that William Pruitte had helped Wade Simmons build. With that evidence of confidence, we, the players, dedicated our athletic futures to a vigorous effort to master the fundamentals and ". . . go all the way." That meant the Eden County Tournament, played in Edenville High School's gymnasium. We had been there before, in the same tournament. Drew a bye in the first round and were slaughtered in the second. We lost to New Hope in that game because we did not have ". . . finesse," as William called it. We knew how to toe-heel-toe-kick, but we did not know a great deal about the game as an organized competition. We had been seduced by thoughts of rah-rah-rah-ism, and by the promise of a Hershey's candy bar before games and an orange stuffed with confectionery sugar at half-time. But this required a willingness to be organized, and that was a problem. Organization demanded painful adjustments and too often imposed bewildering restrictions. Playing the Standing Guard, for example—the guard who never crossed center line and dedicated his share of glory to defense. Dear God! There was time enough to be a Standing Guard! Most of the adults we knew were Standing Guards.

And always there was the REA—the REA running in angles of ruler-edge straightness from Emery and into Black Pool Swamp, south of Banner's Crossing. The line was there, during that Between School Session. A few more days of tinkering. A hookup to this house, or that house. A few more transformers to be placed. The inspection by the inspectors. A few more days and the REA would serve us a sacred communion, a very special blessing.

We—Our Side—tried to be humble. Humility makes the man, Wesley declared, and he gave humility one of his finer efforts: he spent hours at school with Dupree, attempting to prove forgiveness. But we all realized humility had met its match, if not its master, in REA pride. Jack observed it was like the Christians and the lions: the Christians believed and meant well, but the lions didn't know from Adam what was happening, and didn't care as long as the catering continued.

It was a far-fetched comparison, but there was a tidbit of fairness in the view. We had Christian intention (Wesley ensured that), but we also had a lion's hunger. As the days passed, and we waited, the lion in us began to devour the Christian.

We were not uppity. We were smug. We posed. We dribbled casual hints about *our* new appliances being more modern than *their* old appliances. We volunteered to host Boy Scout meetings and, if anyone cared, a group of us were planning a hayride and a night yard dance, to be held in one of *our* yards and lighted by one of *our* outside spotlights. That is, maybe we'll have a yard dance. Ho-hum, there's so much to plan. Can't tell what we'll think of. I heard tell Betty Tully has a new electric record player. Hey, didja know Jack Crider's thinkin' about entering the 4-H Club countywide contest on experiments in electricity?

Megan did not like the smug me, the lion at feast. At recess one day, she said, "Well, you sure changed! If you had any notion what you sound like, you'd take another look at yourself!"

"I ain't changed," I countered. "What makes you think that?"

"The way you act, all stuck-up."

"Stuck-up? Who's stuck-up?"

"You are."

"Megan, that ain't fair."

"Fair or not, it's true! It's true, all right."

"You sayin' you don't like me? That it? You gone back to likin' Dupree? That it?"

She was furious. "You're not worth liking. I don't know why I liked you in the first place."

"It's Dupree, ain't it?!"

She exploded. "No! NO! No, it ain't! It's—it's you!"

"Me?"

"You!"

I did not know how to handle this temper. No person in the entire world had ever confused me as much as Megan, not even Wesley.

"Megan . . ."

"What is it?" she said sharply.

"Uh—nothin'."

"What is it?"

"I was just—ah—wonderin' . . ."

"What?"

"Uh—would you—uh—let me have a—ah—picture of you?"

Her eyes softened. "A picture?"

"Yeah."

"You really want one?"

"Yeah. I guess."

"Can I have one of you?" she asked.

"You'd probably just throw it away."

"No," she said quickly. "No, I won't. I'll keep it . . ."

"Well, I guess . . ."

"Will you keep mine?"

"Uh—sure. If you don't tell nobody."

"I won't."

"Megan?"

"Yes?"

"Uh—this year, when we go to the basketball games, will you—ah—sit with me on the bus?"

She smiled. Asking a girl to sit with you on the bus was first question in a three-question series. Will You Go Steady? was the second question, and Will You Marry Me? was the third question.

"Uh—huh," she answered.

The commitment began to crush me. "Well, you don't have to, if you don't want to," I said.

"I want to."

"Maybe we'd just better see how things turn out."

"You taking it back?" she asked.

"Me? Naw. Just can't tell how things might work out."

"All right."

"You still mad at me?"

"About what?"

"Bein' stuck-up."

"Oh, I didn't mean that. You're not bad stuck-up."

The recess bell clanged. Megan smiled and walked away. Oh, God, I thought, what have I done?

It didn't matter what I had done. Nothing could be

stopped. Too much was happening.

The announcement was printed, front page, in *The Eden County Garden*. The headline was:

NEW POWER LINES TO BE TURNED ON

The REA had completed its spiderwebbing and its hookups. On a given date, at a given hour, the main switch, off somewhere beyond our imaginations, would be pushed, or pulled, in a ceremony featuring speakers and officials and a ribbon-cutting (there was always a ribbon-cutting), and electricity would leap along the messenger lines to flood our homes.

We invited Freeman to join us in the middle room of our home to celebrate the announced date and the announced hour. Wesley had been right about the Boyds' not getting electricity; they were too far off the line.

There were five of the twelve children still living at home that day—Louise, Lynn, Wesley, me, and Garry. When the hour arrived, whoever did whatever he was supposed to do, wherever it was, and the 100-watt bulb dimmed, then burst with light. No one said anything. We stood about, leaning against the walls and looking. Mother sighed. Lynn, standing beside the wall switch, flipped it to OFF. The room called back its gray shadows. She snapped the switch to ON and the shadows raced away into hiding, disappearing in the brightness. She snapped the switch from ON to OFF, OFF to ON, again and again. The shadows seeped in and out of the walls with the suddenness of magic. Finally,

Garry tugged at Louise, who was his particular sister-mother, his protector and comforter, and said, "Lynn better quit doin' that. She's goin' burn out all the batteries."

Burn out all the batteries.

There are no batteries. No batteries, Garry. The only batteries we need are for flashlights.

Thomas would be happy. He would strut around the room and explain everything. He would laugh and tell Mother he had a special surprise for her, and he would hand her a colorfully wrapped present, with paper ribbons blooming into a flower, something electric, something to be plugged into an outlet and something to make her world wonderful.

"Well, you ought to make a speech," Mother urged my father.

"It's bright," my father said. "Maybe we don't need that much bulb."

EPILOGUE

We are easily deceived.

The REA changed our lives.

The REA made us more comfortable.

The REA also destroyed us.

Destroyed something—some intangible security people have always enjoyed in isolation.

The world came into our house on those shining, singing wires. The world came in, intruding and changing, commanding us to obey its hypnotic lure. The world came in like a torrent, pouring out of every motor and gadget and instant, fumeless light, and it changed us.

One night games of racing with Bullet and Short Leg through Black Pool Swamp stopped. We stayed inside and developed pretensions about the sophistication of having electricity. We became the Highway 17 Gang, or the Our Side Gang. We tried—it was madness we tried so hard—but we could not consume the spectacle of electricity. It was always too much, and not enough. It drove its Z-ing beams between us, drove us from huddling, stopped our asking and answering, weakened our dreams. Electricity was sudden. We were not.

There were nights, in the first months, when we could hear Freeman whistling deep in the bowels of Black Pool Swamp, a lonely, mournful whistle, and Bullet and Short Leg would howl at him. Once or twice, Wesley and I walked down to the barn and returned his call, but Freeman never answered. He knew. He knew we had, without intention, betrayed him, and the fight at Emery Junior High School had been a waste of time.

On those nights, without wanting to, we lost Freeman Boyd, and losing him was one of the ways the REA destroyed us.

No one was surprised when Megan began to sit with me on the back seat of the school bus, to and from basketball games. The differences between Our Side and the Highway 17 Gang no longer existed, having been healed by the drug only Wesley knew—psychology. I did not care what people said about huddling in the dark corner of a school bus, and Megan did not care. We held hands, a jacket or sweater over our arms, as though hiding our hands would hide our caring. Megan's hand was warm and I memorized its touch forever. She was very gentle. I carved her initials on my tree, above my own, and told her about it. She smiled happily.

We were inseparable, Megan and I. In high school, we began dating ("Oh, there's a couple now. Megan and Colin. Going steady. You wait. You just wait.") and Megan's hands began to coax me away from my boundaries, my boundaries of north and south, east and west. There was an exhilaration in her hands, an exhilaration in the yearning to touch her, to be touched, to not touch and talk quietly about the little gods of curiosity haunting our thoughts. There was storm and calm in our embracing.

I gave her a floating opal necklace on a Christmas. The man in the jewelry store smooth-talked me into buying a chain that was too short, fitting tight on Megan's neck. "I'll exchange it," I said. "No," she answered. "I want it." The opal rested in the pool of her throat.

Our song—*our* song—was "Till Then."

I think we both knew there was something delicate and fragile between us.

It was not flirtation.

I told her that I loved her, and she returned the words. We knew it was not flirtation.

For years we balanced one another, two people with a delicate and fragile sharing. Then we grew into other personalities (I do not know how, or why) and the balance no longer existed. One night, on the annual hayride sponsored by Emery Methodist Church, the hayride to Wind's Mill, I told Megan I wanted to date someone else. She buried her face in my chest. Her body tightened against mine, and the moisture of her breathing savagely attacked my equilibrium. I tried to retreat, to retreat back into my circle of isolation and protection, my boundaries of north and south, east and west, my boundaries of Black Pool Swamp and Rakestraw Road. Megan held fiercely to my hand.

Years later, I visited Megan three days before she was married. I presented her with a book of poems, a book I had helped compose. They were college poems and poor excuses of the Great Emotion, but I had nothing else to offer. We sat in her living room and talked uneasily about earlier days of perfect harmony and laughing, racing moods. ("Do you remember . . . ?" "Of course, I do; you were nervous . . ." "And you said . . .") We had coffee and cake. She was wearing the floating opal necklace I had given her; the opal rested in the pool of her throat. She wanted me to see her wedding dress. It was white and lacy and belonged to a woman I no longer knew. Then, as if by signal, we both became silent. There was nothing more to say. She walked with me to my car.

"All of this confuses me, Megan," I told her. "I feel so far away, in a place I have never known." And then I said, "If you ever need me, find me." And I meant it.

Her face was tucked. She nodded. I lifted her chin

with my fingers. There were tears in her eyes. Pale green eyes.

She put her hand on my face and pushed the hair back off my forehead, an easy habit recalled from easy times.

"Oh, I bought you so much candy . . ." she whispered.

"Yes . . ."

She leaned forward and kissed me. Gently, she kissed me. Then she walked away.

It was one of the rare, clean, precious moments of my living, and it ended the Emery years. Wesley, Freeman, Otis, Paul, R. J., Alvin, Dover, Willie Lee, Baptist, Dupree, Sonny, Wayne, Annie, Granny Woman, Shirley Weems, the fight, the REA, church, Emery Junior High School, the hayride—all of it ended there, there with Megan. Ended with a finality that made me shudder.

From that day, everything was different.

And there are times, so often, when I long to adopt Alvin's old habit and walk backward—quietly, shyly, as Alvin walked.

On the Big Gully Oath, I would try it. Cross my heart and hope to die.

But I know what Wesley would say: "The problem with walking backward, is that you see only where you've been."

Center Point Publishing
600 Brooks Road ● PO Box 1
Thorndike ME 04986-0001 USA

(207) 568-3717

US & Canada:
1 800 929-9108